What a Wonderful World This Could Be

Praise for Lee Zacharias

Lee Zacharias is one of those profoundly rare writers, a natural. Her voice is one you can trust, and her characters are real, moving, and come from the experience of someone who knows what trouble human beings get themselves into.

—Craig Nova, author of *The Good Son*

Across the Great Lake

Across the Great Lake is one of the most intensely written and beautifully conceived novels to come my way in many a season. Seldom have I read a story with so much life on the page. I will be thinking about these characters for a long time.

—Steve Yarbrough, author of *The Unmade World*

An astonishing novel of high intelligence and moral rigor. Lee Zacharias is a master. Like Harper Lee and Marilynne Robinson, Zacharias reminds us of the lasting powers of childhood.

—Elaine Neil Orr, author of *Swimming Between Worlds*

At Random

In this superb novel, one tragic moment entangles a seemingly good marriage in a web of guilt, suspicion, and fear. Lee Zacharias eschews both cynicism and sentimentality to do justice to the human heart's complexities. *At Random* is wise, sublime, and unforgettable.

—Ron Rash, author of *Serena*

A spellbinding beginning. A frank examination of the legal system in America. A fascinating introduction to Montagnard culture. And a steely-eyed and heartrending account of marriage in which both parties are complex and whole. This is a novel of accomplishment and polish that deserves to be on every Best Books of the Year list. I simply could not put it down.

—Kelly Cherry, author of *We Can Still Be Friends*

Lessons

Lee Zacharias is both witty and wise. *Lessons* is a lively and engaging story, full of the conflicts and humor, the feelings and events, of life as it is lived here and now.

—Annie Dillard, author of *Pilgrim at Tinker Creek* and *Holy the Firm*

Wonderfully readable, engrossing … a novel of intelligence and vitality, humor and richness … great storytelling.

—*Publishers Weekly*

Helping Muriel Make It Through the Night

Lee Zacharias is a sassy, tough, natural writer. Her stories are bold announcements of her presence as a woman, a visionary, and a force in American literature.

—William Harrison, author of *Lessons in Paradise*

Lee Zacharias has a keen eye, an excellent ear, and when she wants to, a very sharp tongue … *Helping Muriel Make It Through the Night* introduces a talented and dedicated writer who has, clearly, already arrived and can stand on her own with the best in the business.

—George Garrett, author of *Death of the Fox*

What a Wonderful World This Could Be

Lee Zacharias

Lake Dallas, Texas

FIRST EDITION

What a Wonderful World This Could Be is a work of fiction. Names, char-acters, places, and incidents either are the products of the author's imag-ination or are used fictitiously. Any resemblance to actual events, locales, businesses, companies, or persons, living or dead, is entirely coincidental.

Requests for permission to reprint any portion of this book should be sent to: Permissions
Madville Publishing
P.O. Box 358
Lake Dallas, TX 75065

Author Photograph: Michael Gaspeny
Cover Design: Jacqueline Davis
Cover Art: a vintage camera by apartment, and a brickwall backdrop by AVN Photolab. Both images are licensed through Shutterstock.

ISBN: 978-1-948692-50-2 paperback; 978-1-956440-21-8 hardcover; 978-1-948692-51-9 ebook
Library of Congress Control Number: 2020941260

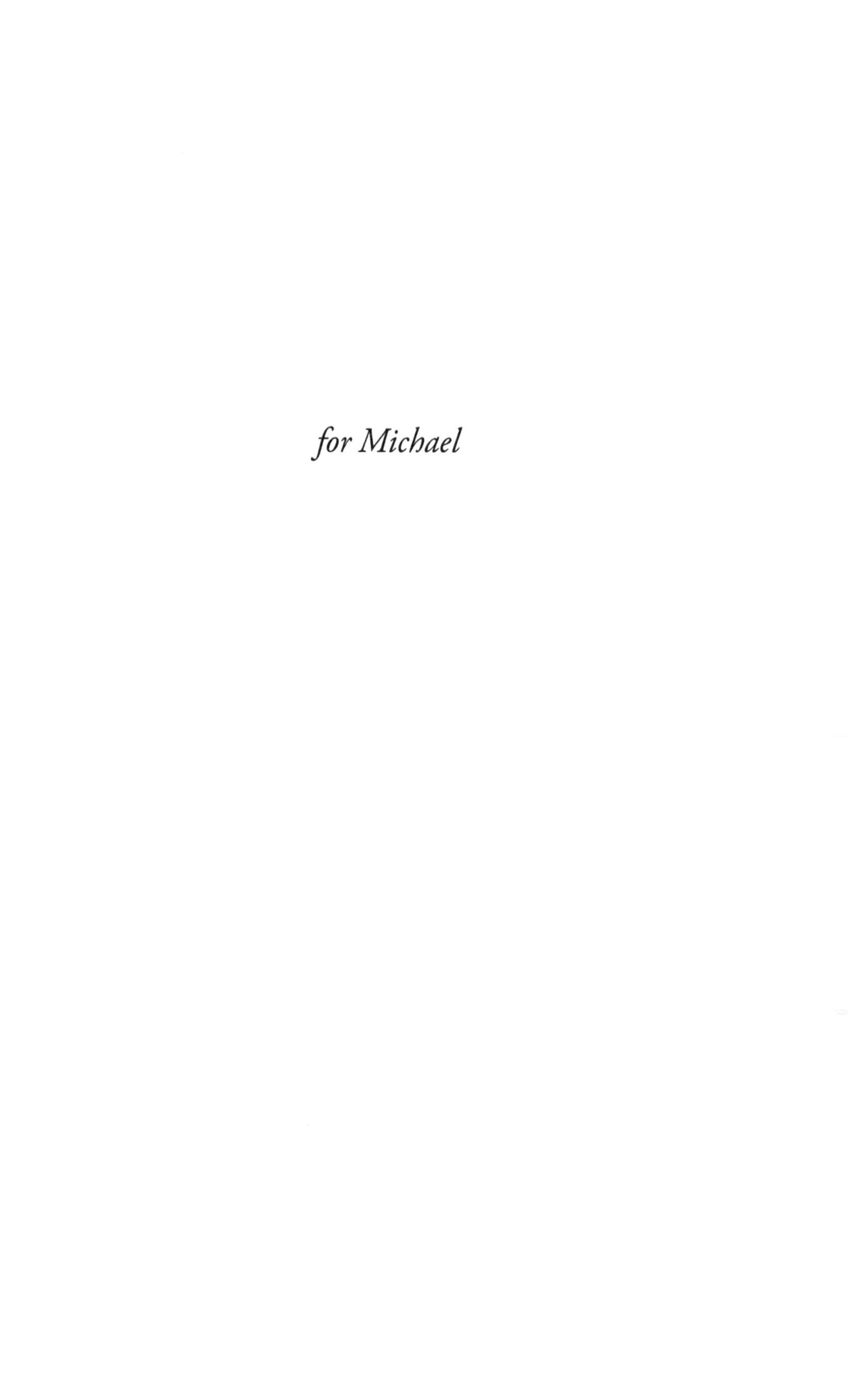

for Michael

In some old magazine or newspaper, I recollect a story, told as truth of a man ... who absented himself for a long time, from his wife.

—*Nathaniel Hawthorne,* "Wakefield"

"Wake up, Penelope ... Odysseus has returned."

—*Homer,* The Odyssey

"My oh my, what a surprise,"

—*William Kennedy,* Ironweed

Chapter 1

March 2, 1982

But why would she be in the student darkroom? Alex has her own enlarger, and at the university there's a lab reserved for faculty. Why would she be printing in the big room where the kids drip fixer across the floor no matter how many times she tells them to drain their prints and please use trays, where a radio is always tuned to the top 40, belching and repeating like a drunk reciting a bad joke?

She can't get the plot of this ridiculous daydream right. She tussles with the implausibility on length forty-one, shallow end to deep, her arms drawing wishbones in the cyan-colored water, hands pausing for a moment like commas at her sides. In the next lane someone is churning up on her. She can feel the water rocking and veers to avoid him, bumping her hand against the side of the YMCA pool. Her goggles are leaking; chlorine sears her eyes. Speedo surges by, chin resting on a red kickboard. He spends hours warming up. When he swims he concentrates. When she swims she diffuses.

Every morning she ticks off thirty-six laps, which she counts in lengths because lengths have destination, but laps are only circles. Speedo—she doesn't know his name—thinks about his time, she fantasizes, maybe the other swimmers plan the perfect crime, make grocery lists, or do their taxes. Probably every one of them scores the perfect comeback in a word war, those disputes that rankle in the mind an hour after the clerk is nasty or the letter from the irate parent arrives with its pointed little list of *cc's*. Civilization hangs by the thread of the mental tongue-lashing.

How else to pass the time?

The black tile cross is moving toward her, and she turns to push off the wall again, but really she's in the darkroom now, the student darkroom—because that's where she wants to be. She's making test strips with her back to Ross, her student, the one with the shy smile and loose walk that suggests some ease in his body the reclusive smile does not predict. He has talent, but so do a lot of students. It's genius that is rare, talent just common enough to be cruel. She noticed him first for his face, for the deep color that always looks as if it has just sprung to his cheeks, for the beautiful smile so slow to break, the elusive eyes and elegant nose. She would like to photograph him.

At an enlarger across the room he is timing exposures.

They meet at the developer like archetypes at a well, their prints swimming toward each other in the huge communal tray. Individually they agitate and watch the second hand. She bends to see her image bloom. Instead his reflection, tinted amber by the safelight, ripples by and as she looks up to check the clock again, lifting her print with rubber-tipped tongs, re-forms on her retina. They spend the next ten seconds at the stop bath. In the fixer his hand brushes hers, lighting up her body like a shock, or like the little bliss of recognition in a song coming to its chorus. She is the inventor of this fantasy; she has choices, and as she kicks off the wall, plunging deep enough to soar beyond the diving board, she chooses that his hand touch hers again. When she lifts her face to breathe, he smears it with kisses. Their prints will bleach away before they remember to put them in the washer.

Or—

She stands to adjust her goggles and glides into forty-three, the best length of her mile, although she does not understand why it should always be on this one that her rhythm finds the ocean, that the tedium of counting should take her to this luminescence that must be something like the intuited enlightenment of Zen. She has never been a mystic, and yet there is that moment when she feels the arc of her own movement perfectly concentric to the earth's slow rotation, feels herself pulled by its core of energy. No need to dream away the boredom then—her strokes are as compelling and effortless as dreams. When Speedo spurts by, she scarcely notes his passing, although on other laps his wake can leave her feeling swamped and helpless as a rowboat in a storm.

Once she tried to explain length forty-three to Steve Kendrick, her oldest friend, fumbling with her words because she was afraid that it would sound like so much hocus-pocus he would laugh and recommend she take up chanting. "Oh sure," he said as if such harmony were as everyday as breakfast. "I used to feel like that sometimes playing basketball." "Basketball?" Alex scoffed, dubious of any inner peace to be found in a gym smelling of sweat, farts, and moldy sneakers. When did he play basketball? "Basketball," Kendrick repeated firmly and smiled. "You're looking good these days, Alex."

It's the swimming. Her waistline has appeared.

It was there a year and a half ago, but wasn't quite so flashy. Then a bad cough turned into pneumonia. For a month she lay in bed, certain she was dying. She tried to feel tragic: her life cut short, to die in the last bloom of youth and never have lumbago, arteriosclerosis, or glaucoma! That might not be enough to make everyone weep, but it was the only life she had, and if she didn't feel tragic about it, who would? Instead she felt tired. When she went back to the darkroom, she became dizzy breathing the chemicals. Standing at the sink, she had to clutch its rolled edge to keep from collapsing. When she thought about her life, she decided there was too little light, not enough air, too much time spent in the dark trying to record the radiance, not enough motion. She bought a warm-up suit and a pair of Nikes and pulled a ligament on her first half-mile. She took up swimming.

Speedo is doing the butterfly now, wrapping himself in veils of bubbles, sending the water slapping against the trough. She removes her goggles to begin the backstroke, aligning herself with the beam above. Although the rest of her mile will be pleasant—she never really strains and so she never tires—her daily communion with the cadence of the earth is over. As curiously as it comes, it always goes around length forty-four or forty-five. One day she would like just to swim and not to measure. The first ten lengths are hardest, but, even on her bad days (too much wine the night before, a sulfuric burning behind her nose that might be the first sign of a virus, goggles that leak so badly she cannot do the crawl), when she gets to eleven she knows she could go at least eleven hundred. She imagines how night would fall, a slow dimming in the windows where derelicts peer through the fog, twilight leaching across the roofs where she has watched the summer sunshine thin and harden into winter. When the view goes black and the lifeguards all go home, overheads switched out behind them, she is still pacing the pool in the chill gray sheen the moon casts upon her cupped fingers, dipping her shriveled face in and out of the black water.

The only problem is it's boring, and so she brings Ross with her, not because she wants him (she would never take up with a student) but because she needs someone, anyone, to make the laps go by. All the same, she is dreadfully embarrassed when she meets his class to critique prints. "Ross?" she asks, making a point not to avoid him, but he lowers his eyes and whispers, his voice shivering inside her ear like a moist web of breath. "The whites need more detail," another student advises the one whose picture is push-pinned to the wall. Alex smiles. The student who's spoken has the makings of a fine printer but nothing to print. She has yet to figure out what she wants to photograph.

Like Alex now, though Alex has a file of old negatives to reprint until the tones take on the patina of heirloom silver, a way to kid herself she hasn't lost her eye. Still, she identifies with them, in a way, the students who would like to be Diane Arbus (always Arbus) but can't find any giants or Mexican dwarfs. Winos are freaks to them. They wear sixty-dollar sneakers to photograph the bums in Monroe Park and cannot get their own wide eyes out of the picture.

You are the subject of your photographs, she tells her students. You *act* upon the object. They take this as a license—they're all for self-expression, and at their age it probably doesn't hurt them to confuse that with self-indulgence. Sooner or later their cameras will teach them what they need to know, that the only truly good photographs come of neither the world out there nor the world within but of the unique balance.

Photography is about *light*, she has to remind them.

She's lost count. Sixty? Sixty-two? Sixty, she decides. Her flutter kick raising curtains of water, eyes fixed on the ceiling as her arms spiral, she thinks of Ross. Junior? Senior? A kid. Because a *kid* is harmless. Anyone else might ask her out.

When her hand connects with someone's foot, Alex rescues her goggles and resumes the breaststroke. Speedo has left. In his lane a man with a round white belly is flailing toward the wall, trunks fluttering at his hairless thighs. It seems obscene to know the secret naps and folds of strangers' bodies, to spread her legs into a kick as a man she's never met swims up behind her.

What she ought to do is get it together, meet someone, go to a party, stay all night. One of these days she will.

One more time she adjusts her goggles, rubbing her thumb inside the lenses to clear the steam. The pool is beginning to crowd with lunch-hour swimmers. Her mouth is dry. Chlorine. All day her skin gives off a scent like bleach. If she had a lover, he would be aroused every time he did the laundry.

Alex twists and pushes off the wall again. She spends her last lap in the darkroom with Ross, and when his safelight shorts out, she climbs on the counter to fix it, wiggling the bulb in its socket until the light spangles down her spine. She is still buzzing with the shock when she turns to jump down and Ross raises his arms to catch her. In slow motion he raises his arms. The safelight showers them with sparks. And the radio plays a fanfare.

As soon as she hoists herself from the pool, she heads for the shower. She's running doubly late—leaky goggles, the unexpected wait for a lane—but if she skips lunch she'll have time for a minute in the sauna. After class she needs to run by the International Safeway, having promised to cook dinner for Kendrick. She never bothers for herself, and then she worries that she'll die clogged like a drain with Lean Cuisine and Chicken McNuggets. The Safeway should have trout, which would be nice with coconut rice or fennel au gratin.

At the front of the locker room, the director of the health club is watching a game show on TV. The lockers rattle with the sad hysteria of housewives desperate to win a set of Samsonite or a year's supply of pork and beans. Alex flips through the magazines. Already she can feel oxygen imploding in her blood. Water dripping from her hair forms a blister on the ragged cover she retrieves from the bottom of the pile as with a sudden hush the noon news begins.

There is something about the voice of a newscaster that always commands attention, for a moment anyway. In that voice even the date seems imperative. Any date. Today's. She is still standing before the television, wrapped in a thin wet towel, blood a blind white heat in her veins, when a face she once knew as well as her own, *his* face, the face she hasn't seen for eleven years, flashes on the screen and the newscaster goes mute. She sees his lips move, but for some reason she can't hear what he is saying. Then the sound comes roaring back.

> In Washington today former civil rights and antiwar activist Ted Neal was shot after turning himself over to the FBI. Neal, who disappeared in 1971 while under investigation for a series of bombings, was speaking to reporters outside the Hoover Building when the unidentified assailant opened fire.

Afterwards, more clearly than the film clip, she remembers the stricken face of the health club director as she says, without expression, "That's my husband," and slowly turns to walk back to the sauna.

Afterwards.

Afterwards, in the parking lot, she cannot remember where she left her car. Everything seems strange, as if it is all something she has seen before but can't quite place. The light hurts her eyes, like sand. And when she finds her car—but there are missing sequences in this action, as if a film has been badly cut and spliced, but she must have found it, she is in it, there are her keys, the crack in the dashboard, though she can't remember backing up, only the jolt and flat, sickening crash of metal on metal, a sound as abrupt and irrevocable as gunfire, and fixed for a moment in her rearview mirror the tinted blue mound of windshield frozen over the face of the other driver, who leaps from the mirror into the sunlight that is still dazed and gritty all around her, bellowing, "Omigod, omigod! Lady, do you realize this is a brand new Mercedes that just left the showroom, omigod, lady, what have you done?"

And that's when she cried.

Chapter 2

1960

She had a father. Five years later the notion still seemed marvelous; his appearances still surprised her. Alex hadn't met him until she was ten, when his third novel, *Katie Blue*, hit number one on the best-seller list and her mother sued him. He turned up at the door of their house in Limestone one night, a trim but thickset man whose gorgeous face was already beginning to puff and darken with drink, and when her mother appeared behind Alex in the foyer, he tipped an imaginary hat and nodded. "Just thought I'd see for myself what the bastard looks like. Come on," he said to Alex. "I'll take you to the movies."

Alex liked the Towne Art Cinema, one of those shabby little college town theaters with free coffee in the lobby, where by the time she was thirteen she was sneaking to see the work of Antonioni, Bergman, Fellini, and Buñuel with college boys who hated subtitles but had heard that girls who hung out at the Towne Art believed in free love. When her father asked why they didn't take their silly groping and smooching to the Paramount like normal kids, Alex squeezed his hand and gave him a naughty smile. "Because John Wayne might spank me if he saw."

Her father preferred circus pictures and the banter of Rock Hudson and Doris Day. She liked to drag him to the Towne Art to hear him complain, "Oh Christ, it's not a movie, it's a *film*." He was in love with popular culture, and his house in Los Angeles—Lost Angeles he pronounced it—was a monument to bad taste, from the fiberglass fountain awhirl with colored lights to the matadors painted on black velvet. On the lawn he had installed a flock of pink plastic flamingoes, just as her mother had strewn her former boyfriend's gigantic metal abstractions across the yard of their Midwestern home. Most of the sculptures were rusting, and no one bothered to trim the grass that went to seed around their bases.

The Towne Art was her special place. She had begun her first period in a pair of white toreador pants she wore to *The Cranes Are Flying*. In the ladies' room, where bedraggled black velvet curtains filled in for doors, another professor's daughter gave her a tampon; afterwards they swiped the curtain, which Alex wore home as a sarong. A week later her father was her date. "Do you think there's more to life?" she whispered, grinning, as she settled beside him with a box of popcorn to watch Chukrai's *Ballad of a Soldier*.

He kept his eyes on the screen. "People who become preoccupied with themselves at an early age miss out on much of what life has to offer," he advised. "Watch the film."

"It's sentimental." She tucked a greasy hand in his.

"You'll appreciate the value of sentiment when you get older," he promised.

"How's Mariana?" she asked with a gleeful giggle.

"Nancy," her father said morosely. Mariana was last year's wife.

The truth was her mother didn't care what she did, but it was wonderful to have her father for an ally. She had the handsomest father of any of her friends, and he was famous. He knew how to get to her mother, who, for whatever reason, still bore him a silent, pinched-white anger, when Alex had never been able to penetrate the indifference that was the constant of her mother's attitude towards her. There were advantages to her situation. No one ever asked if she had her homework done, her room picked up, or where she'd been. The girls she knew disappointed their parents daily.

So she had no fear of getting caught, even though many of the Towne Art patrons were her mother's colleagues, art professors and students who seemed to wear their sandals and pallor like badges of the trade. With her friends she picked up the fraternity boys, unmistakable in their button-down shirts, and after the closing credits the girls disappeared in a conspiracy of hiccups and mirth, leaving behind only their outrageous pseudonyms: Andrea Doria, Polly Ethyl, Ida Claire. The boys came to pick up bohemian girls—bohos Alex and company called them, and all the way home she and her friends whooped with delight over the lines with which the boys tried to elicit their views on premarital sex. "I told him I didn't think it was wrong as long as you did it with your eyes closed," Alex squealed, "and he watched the whole movie with his eyes closed. He *licked* my neck!" They fell to the sidewalk in seizures of laughter. "The Boho and Bozo Show" they called it.

A movie here, a dinner there. Her father's wives had no need for an illegitimate stepdaughter who'd been left to run wild. He never wrote; he didn't call. When she accused him, he scowled and said, "People who drink shouldn't use the telephone or mail letters."

The summer she turned fifteen she made him take her to see *La Dolce Vita*. Afterwards they had dinner at Minelli's, where a hot wind from the ventilator swept across the parking lot as they opened their car doors. Although the red-checked tablecloths were never clean, candles dripping rainbow wax down the straw skirts of Ruffino bottles were the hallmark of sophisticated dining in a town where the only other place to eat after eight was Hoot's Drive-in Bar-B-Q. At Minelli's her father would let her have wine.

He stumbled on his way to the table. He had spent much of *La Dolce Vita* in the men's room with his flask, but he always kept himself tidy. They were celebrating, as she saw it. Though he hadn't told her, *Katie Blue* was finally going to be made into a movie. She had overheard her mother talking to a lawyer.

Her father opened the menu and sniffed. "Don't order anything with sauce."

"I'll have veal scallopini with *lots* of tomatoes," Alex responded.

The knotty pine bar was almost empty, but a chime of silverware and conversation drifted in from other rooms. The waiter brought chianti, and in exaggerated Italian Alex read the label out loud. The glasses were too small, and the waiter had to pour them to the rim.

Her father raised his. "To *la dolce vita*. The veal will have rancid garlic, and you'll get the sauce on your white dress."

"I will not." Alex sipped, a little too fast.

"Take it easy," her father advised. "Your mother'll run my balls through the wringer if I bring you home drunk."

"Are you kidding?" Her mother wouldn't notice. She settled back against her seat. "Anyway I've never been drunk."

"Neither had I at your age." His eyes looked glazed. A faint crust of soap had dried in the silver-tipped nubs of his sideburn. "How old are you again?"

"Fifteen," she said in a voice loud with pique. "And you forgot my birthday."

"I take it back," he said, adding, "I'll have Nancy pick something out." He nodded toward the man at the bar. "Philosophy?"

She didn't want a present from *Nancy*.

Her father smoothed a twenty-dollar bill between his fingers and laid it in the ring of yellow light on the tablecloth. Alex glanced at the stool where a young man sat drinking beer from a frosted mug. He was a slender man with mildly good looks of a pale, academic sort: rimless glasses, a bad haircut, and a way of sucking on a pipe that seemed to be intended as profound. The bones in his face were delicate as birdbones. Ninety degrees outside, and he was wearing a wool jacket. "What a twerp," she said. Too tweedy for art, too mannered for science, too shabby for business. "English."

"What about history?" If there was anything her father hated more than an artist, it was an academic. He was a broken record on the subject. Alex felt irritable. She'd outgrown this game, just as she'd outgrown the Boho and Bozo Show. If he wasn't going to tell her about his movie, then she was in a bad mood.

"I don't know why you have to be so paranoid," she said. "For your information, my mother doesn't care what either of us do. I don't think she thinks about you at all."

"Well, her lawyer thinks about me all the time." Her father seemed to sink into gloom, then snapped himself up and poured another glass of wine. "Comparative literature. Reads Dostoevsky without the help of Constance Garnett. *Sprechens Sie Deutsch. Parley vus francais. Habla cocker spaniel.* Or wait, I've got it. School of Letters."

"He doesn't look smart enough," Alex said, annoyed.

"Aren't you nice?"

"And I wish you would not mention in front of me how much money my mother is trying to get out of you on my behalf. *That* isn't nice." In her emphasis wine sloshed from her glass. She meant to be severe with him, but her voice was petulant. "Why don't you just give her the money, and I wouldn't have to be so embarrassed? Sometimes I think you don't love me at all."

"Wrong," her father said coolly. "Your mother doesn't love you. I love you very much." Alex sulked. "I've offered her money. Believe me, that's not what she wants. Not really." Her father's voice had softened; he looked contrite. "History?" he wheedled.

"Some parents," Alex said and forgave him, because it couldn't be helped, she knew. "You guessed that already. For God's sake, Daddy, look at his jacket. Goodwill. One hundred percent herringbone in July. He teaches freshman comp and writes poetry on the side."

"Poetry utterly without merit."

"Sentimental," she agreed.

Her father smiled. "Sophomoric. Completely lacking in both music and concrete detail. Very good," he conceded. "What are you going to do with the trophy?"

Alex cheered up and mugged at the candle, clasping her hands before her chest in a discreet mockery of the victor's sign. Inspired, she tucked the twenty dollar bill into the neckline of her sundress. Then, while her father poured himself the last of the chianti, she crossed her eyes at the white spaghetti straps and gently squeezed her breasts between her arms to see if she could make cleavage. When she looked up, the poet was watching her in the mirror. She blushed and took another quick sip from her glass. The wine made a warm place inside her, but gooseflesh rose along her arms.

"Who do you think is going to win the Democratic nomination?" her father asked.

"I don't know." A waiter came through the room with an empty tray, and, as the kitchen door pushed open, she heard a faint snatch of a ball game from a radio inside. "Who's running?"

Her father gave her an elaborate look of scorn as he signaled the waiter for more wine. "Ah youth. It's so comforting to know the future is in their hands."

The poet was coming toward them. Alex looked over her shoulder, but the table behind them was empty. Something slipped inside her stomach. He had overheard them. He had overheard *her*. She wanted to die.

"Are they really going to make a movie out of *Katie Blue*?" she blurted, fastening her gaze on her father.

The man stopped. His feet seemed to stammer, he looked down at them as if they'd done something unbecoming, and his color rose. "Sorry," he mumbled, because the movement had caught her attention. He hadn't overheard them after all; he had simply mistaken her father's summons for more wine.

"Join us," her father called without turning his head, and made an open gesture with his palm. "Have a drink. Where the hell is our waiter?" Two waiters flanked the kitchen door, but neither was theirs, and both were as impassive as museum guards. The poet looked as if he would back away but didn't. Her father pumped the empty bottle up and down in the air. "Well, for God's sake, man, are you or aren't you going to sit down?"

He sat, with the unhappy expression of one who leaves a party at two after announcing his departure at ten. Having misread her father's gesture for the waiter, who was at last bearing a fresh bottle toward them, he was stuck. Alex was touched. She imagined his childhood as a long fidget at his parents' dinner table while the other boys played outside. And now her father would advise him to give up poetry. He didn't know what he was in for. Her father was just drunk enough to confide that she had called him a skinny twerp who didn't look smart enough to be in the School of Letters.

She smiled at him. "Don't believe a word my father says," she heard herself say. "He's always telling stories, in fact, he writes best-sellers." She was sorry on two counts. "Your father," the poet echoed, eyes widening in an obligatory *gee-whiz* that made him look foolish, just when she'd decided that he didn't look like such a twerp after all. And her father was furious.

"I believe that our friend is unlikely to be familiar with the TV dinners our culture so vulgarly gobbles as best-sellers. Heroic couplets, is it, or do you dine on terza rima?"

But Steve Kendrick wasn't a poet; he was a photographer. He had taken a job teaching at Wallace University in the fall.

"You mean like journalism?" Alex asked.

"Art," he said, and her heart sank. Her mother taught in the Art Department at Wallace. "Don't," she warned as her father began, and to her surprise he dropped it.

"I thought you looked familiar," Steve Kendrick said. "What have you written?"

Her father drummed his fingers on the table. "*Katie Blue*," Alex said. "It's going to be made into a movie."

"What's it about?"

"The story of a slut." Her father's smile was sardonic.

"Who's going to play Katie?" Alex demanded, suddenly giddy, unmindful of Steve Kendrick, who was patting his pocket for the pipe he had left on the bar, mumbling something about looking for the movie, excusing himself to get his beer. "Are they paying you lots and lots of money? Can I come watch when they shoot? You could introduce me to Paul Newman."

"Written by a whore. I thought you didn't like *movies*."

"You have to get the waiter to do it," Alex said impatiently to Kendrick, who had annoyed her attention by rising but failing to depart. "It's against the state law to move your own drink. Some state, huh?" Her voice took a whiny edge as she turned back toward her father. "I didn't mean it about the money. I'm just excited, that's all."

"I thought you only got excited about depression in black and white."

Alex looked down. There was a purple stain on the bodice of her dress. Chianti. It would never come out.

"Alienation. The meaninglessness of modern life. Excuse me, existence. Now *that*'s what I call meaning."

Alex tossed her head. "Don't be a bore," she said. "Anyway, I liked *Nights of Cabiria* better. *La Strada* was the best, but that wasn't depressing, it was just sad." She thought of the strong man sobbing for love, too late. "Will you ask? About me watching them shoot?"

"No."

She turned to Kendrick. Her father didn't bring out her best, though what that was she wasn't sure. Something waiting, like a secret. "What kind of pictures do you take?"

"Well," he began, but her father interrupted.

"Never ask an artist that. If you want to know, ask a critic. Union rules."

The candle made a golden teardrop in each lens of Kendrick's glasses. Alex couldn't see his eyes, but she thought his smile looked weak.

The waiter brought her scallopini. "Don't pay any attention to my father. He's just pissed off because we went to the movies and I wanted to see *La Dolce Vita* instead of *Psycho* like a normal girl." She raised her fork.

Kendrick laughed.

"What I hate about these *auteurs*," her father said, giving the word a twist that made it sound more pretentious than foreign, "is the way they think life has been given to them as their own personal subject, then sit around with their fingers up their asses and expect the rest of us poor slobs to adore them for telling us how profoundly of shit it smells."

This time the corners of Kendrick's eyes crinkled into lines when he smiled.

Alex persisted. "Because normal girls would rather watch people get stabbed than bored."

"I can't ask," her father said quietly. "I'm not writing the screenplay, and even if I were ..."

"Where's your dinner?" Alex narrowed her eyes at him. "You better eat. Here." She slid her plate across the table. "It's not that bad, honest."

"... they don't let writers within a mile of the set." The tablecloth had bunched beneath her plate, which he ignored. "And I've never met Paul Newman."

"Well, that's okay." She held her wineglass to her eyes and squinted to make things pretty. "You didn't tell me what kind of pictures you take," she said to Kendrick.

Kendrick was twirling his pipe in his hand. "You know your daughter would make a good model. She has very natural moves."

"My daughter is beautiful."

Alex flopped her hand back and forth to be funny and gave them a dopey smile. "Do you take pictures of naked women?"

"Of course he does," her father said. "But Mr. Kendrick is an artist, and artists don't believe in naked women. They think when you take your clothes off you're nude." His breathing had begun to require the noise of effort, and small vines of blood seemed to have sprouted and tangled below the skin of his cheeks, though they must have been there all along.

"Isn't my father nice?" she said. "Actually he's drunk, but he can be almost as much fun when he's sober."

"Don't be a brat," her father said.

The flame that rose to her face surprised her.

"Maybe you'd pose for me?" Steve Kendrick's voice was low. He was looking at her. "I don't mean nude."

"She can pose naked if she wants," her father said, "but I won't have her posing nude." He held his empty glass up and fumbled at the bottle. "Now my wifey's another story. Since we live in L.A. she figures she's a natural for the movies. Marvelous tits and absolutely no talent. Not even on the couch. So of course she needs her illusions to get by."

Alex stood so quickly she knocked over her glass. "Pay the bill," she ordered. Simultaneously, as if each eye took in a separate scene, she saw Kendrick right her glass and her father pull his flask from the lining of his jacket. "Give that to me. You're too drunk to drive."

"I'll be glad to chauffeur." Kendrick pressed the fallen twenty-dollar bill into her palm. "You dropped this," he said.

Chapter 3

1960

When the phone rang Alex was sprawled in a lawn chair on the deck, reading *Wuthering Heights*. Weeks later she would find the novel where she left it, rutted and swollen with rain. It was a muggy day, and she fanned her hair up from her neck as she lifted the receiver. The sky had turned overcast, or she might have gone to the pool. Not that she enjoyed the pool—it was crowded, the water tepid, the cement slimy with tissues and oil. Every stroke risked collision, and her best friend, Jo Ann Yellen, yakked all afternoon about the boys who splashed them and shoved them under and showed off with impossible dives. The boys seemed unbearably stupid to Alex. All the same, the pool was someplace to go, and Alex preferred it to the new shopping center, where Jo could loiter for hours, gushing over clothes. Last summer Alex had relished these diversions; this summer she felt disconnected. Her mother had spent the month of June in Japan. All winter she and Jo had planned their delinquency. They would have Alex's house to themselves: they would invite boys; they would raid her mother's liquor cabinet; they would play "Jailhouse Rock" at 3 a.m. But when the time came Alex felt indifferent. And now her mother was back; her father had been and gone. There was nothing to look forward to but the sweltering humidity of July and August and Jo's daily phone calls until school began.

Except it wasn't Jo. She had promised, Steve Kendrick said, to consider posing for him, and he wondered if she had made up her mind.

"I guess so." She hadn't promised anything that she could recall. She was a little disconcerted. After he'd dropped her off, there was no telling what her father might have said. "Well maybe, I mean."

"Tomorrow would be good, but if you have plans any time would be fine." He rushed his words, and Alex couldn't tell if his tone was distracted or offhand. "An hour ought to do it." Looping the phone cord, she frowned at the offending familiarity of the kitchen. She had dripped honey on the counter at lunchtime, and the formica was strung with ants. "You can call me back if you need to ask your mother, or I'll be glad to talk to her. I'm strictly legit, I promise. Always pay my bills and leave a forwarding address."

"She's not home." Alex's voice was flat. Without knowing he had decided for her. "Besides, I can do what I want, she doesn't care."

"Are you sure?"

What did he think! She didn't answer, and after a while he said, "How about tomorrow then?"

"Okay."

"I'll pick you up at ten o'clock. Or is that too early?"

He had a habit, she noticed, of beginning with the definite and ending with the tentative. It struck her funny. She didn't know many people so eager to compromise. "You don't have to pick me up. I can ride over on my bike."

"Great." He gave her the address. "If the light's good, there's an old house in the country I've been wanting to shoot. Bring your swimsuit and we can cool off at the quarries." His voice dropped off. "If that would be okay with your mother."

"She's not home," Alex insisted.

"When she gets home," Kendrick said, then added, "Didn't your mother ever tell you not to let strangers know you're home alone?"

"My mother never told me anything." Alex hung up slightly dazed. She had never been to the quarries, where drunken townies drove rusty Chevrolets off cliffs and shot beer bottles off the rocks. Stonies, the children of the Wallace faculty called them, as if their parents' tenure were a tour of duty and they had come to live on base in a foreign land. In fact they would have felt more at home in the places where their parents took Fulbrights, for they knew German and French and might learn Serbo-Croatian. They had no desire to master the nasal twang that set them giggling at the clerks in the Lerner Shop, who inquired "Kin I help ya?" in tired, hopeless voices, flashing their bad teeth, as high school girls with fourteen-carat virgin pins and mouths full of orthodontia picked through the merchandise just killing time.

The apathy that had recently overcome her in what she now saw as the mere tasks of a teenaged rebellion lifted. Sneaking cigarettes and liquor, picking up boys and making out: that was fine for Jo Yellen; her parents objected. But what was the point for Alex? Humming, she wet a rag and wiped the ants off the counter.

But the next day threatened rain, and Kendrick decided to shoot in his studio, which was also his bedroom, or would have been his bedroom if he had not put his bed in the living room. Everything in his apartment was backwards, the front door opening into a mattress, the refrigerator in the hallway, a bathroom three times the size of his cramped kitchen. His studio wasn't at all the glamorous stage-set she imagined, just a room filled with junk and papered with an old-lady print of pink cabbage roses.

"Anyway, the porch is nice," she said when she finished her tour. She didn't mean to be rude, but wouldn't it be just as rude to forge a compliment that anyone would recognize as false? You might tell someone who was average looking that he was handsome, but you would never tell anyone who was deformed. "I thought photographers had darkrooms."

Kendrick seemed amused. "It's in the basement."

To begin he had her pose on a stepladder against a backdrop of seamless paper. It took a long time, and she wasn't sure how to hold her mouth or where to put her hands; the lights were hot; she had a lump in her throat she couldn't swallow. The knot in her bathing suit strap dug into her neck. It would show, of course. Disgusted, she looked down, at the bright spandex flowers blooming through her thin white blouse. But he'd told her to bring her suit. Surely he didn't think she would change in the woods, leaving her underwear in a pile for him to see and bugs to crawl inside of. Or maybe he did. He was probably a little bit cracked—why else would he want to take her picture? She stole a glance at him, head stuck beneath a black cloth to adjust the big wooden box camera. He looked so ridiculous she giggled. "Good," he said.

Though he kept up a conversation—had her father gotten back

to the West Coast, was July always so sticky?—he scarcely seemed to listen while he fussed with the lights and fooled with the bellows, and talking to someone who wasn't listening made her feel stupid, and feeling stupid when it wasn't her fault made her feel cross.

When he was done he hunched over the top of a bookcase, writing, then held out a pale blue check.

"What's that?" She stared at his scratchy handwriting.

"A dollar-fifty an hour okay with you? I can give you cash if you prefer, but this way I have a receipt."

She crumpled the check into her shorts pocket. It made it seem like a babysitting job. She thought of the fathers who drove her home while she hunched over her books in the front seat, hoping they didn't expect to have a conversation.

"Are you hungry? I can make a tuna sandwich."

"Okay." She watched him crouch before the refrigerator. She was nearly as tall as he was, but something male in the prominent cords of vein along his forearms and swirl of hairs at his wrist bone made her feel self-conscious.

While he made the sandwiches, she explored the living room, lifting the lid of his humidor and sniffing Cherry Blend. It smelled woodsy, sweet and substantial, suffused with the merry spirit of a Christmas card. "Are these yours?" she called as she examined the photographs hanging on the walls. Some were landscapes; it was hard to say what others were, though one was a nude whose head had been cut off and whose body was burnished with light in a way that made it seem metallic. They were black and white, but it seemed to her they had something more in common, a mystery or dignity that seemed to derive from their overwhelming silence, as if in the act of being stilled their subjects had been cut from the rest of the moving world.

They ate on the porch. "Sorry there's no lettuce." A pearl of mayonnaise clung to the corner of his mouth.

"I like your pictures," she said, seated on the railing.

"Maybe I'll hang one of you." He must have dabbed the spot off while she blinked. There was a shadow at his throat where the collar of his work shirt opened. "Do that again," he said as she lifted her hair to fan her neck, and in confusion she dropped it. "So," he said after a minute, "what did you think of *La Dolce Vita*?"

No one had ever asked her such a question.

"You know, your dad's not that far off on Antonioni—there's a man enchanted with ennui. And sometimes I get the feeling that Bergman must tell strangers at bus stops what he dreamed last night, but Fellini's got a heart, though I'm not sure you'd know it from *La Dolce Vita*."

"I *love* Fellini."

"*Nights of Cabiria*, *La Strada*," he remembered.

"Did you ever see this movie called *The Bicycle Thief*?"

"Rosselini. You know Fellini assisted him on *Open City*?"

Across the street an Indian woman was sweeping her steps while two dark-skinned children in sunsuits filled a sandpail with dirt. "*The Bicycle Thief* was sad," she said.

He kept looking at her with his eyes half-crinkled behind his rimless glasses. "Yes. It was."

"Did you ever read this story by Nathaniel Hawthorne?" she asked abruptly. "It's called 'The Minister's Black Veil.' We read it in English last year."

"The guy who writes about witches?"

"That's 'Young Goodman Brown,'" she said. "We read that in *junior* high. Anyway, this minister always wears a black veil, he won't let anyone see his face, not even the girl he's supposed to marry, so she chickens out, and when he dies they bury him in it, and even after his body's all rotted away and stuff the veil's still there. Pretty creepy, huh?" She finished her sandwich and fanned her hair up again. She had a headache she was so hot.

"You mean they dug him up?"

"No." She frowned. "I don't think so."

"How else would they know the veil was still there?"

"Well, the story just says so." Alex looked at him impatiently. "Don't you read books?"

He smiled and rocked back in his chair. "Mostly I read photography journals and movie reviews."

"I read books. I don't have anything better to do." She paused, trying to remember what she meant to say. "Anyway, that's what you reminded me of when you were using that black cloth."

"Before or after he died?"

Her mouth pinched. She hated to be teased.

Kendrick dropped his feet to the floor. "Would you like some cookies?"

"No thank you." She finished her iced tea and picked up her plate again. "Thank you for the sandwich."

"Thank *you* for the sitting." He followed her to the kitchen where she put her plate and glass in the sink.

"You're welcome." He lounged against the refrigerator in the hallway, blocking the door as they watched a roach disappear beneath the baseboard. "Did you know you have bugs? You can get spray for those, you know."

"Not those. They're special developer-fed roaches—they drink Dektol and it makes them grow up big and strong." She stared at him blankly. "And when they get to be the size I want I feed them stop bath."

"Oh." Her voice was flat.

His eyes widened slightly with surprise. "I was kidding."

"It's just hot," she said and brushed by him.

"Don't you want to see your pictures? You can give them to your boyfriend."

She turned around. "I don't have a boyfriend."

He didn't blink. "Your mom and dad then. I'll develop these tonight and make some prints tomorrow. Come by Wednesday if you want." He walked her to the door. "Still looks like rain. Why don't I put your bicycle in the back of the wagon and drive you home?"

She wasn't mad. Why, she wasn't sure, but she didn't want him to see her house. "It won't rain," she said.

She went back on Wednesday morning. The sky had cleared, although by two o'clock it would be a milk-white haze, and the heat would only grow more oppressive as the sky turned the color of a cloudy glass.

"Going swimming?" he asked, and her face warmed as she glanced down at the flowers splashing through her pale pink blouse. She had worn her suit again in case he still wanted to go to the quarries.

He hadn't known Limestone had a pool. "I'll have to check it out," he said as he handed her a big brown envelope. "Voilà."

She laid the packet between them on the porch rail. "You wouldn't like it. The pool, I mean. The kids act pretty dopey."

He had a way of almost but not quite smiling. "I see. I'd feel out of place in this temple of youth—considering I'm so old."

He was teasing her again. "That's not what I meant," she said coolly, although it was. Only kids used the pool, kids and an irrelevance of young mothers, who gathered around the kiddie pool with their diaper bags and floats. She didn't want him to see her dunked or gabbing with Jo Ann. "It's crowded is all. You can't really swim."

He opened the envelope.

"Oh!" she cried out, startled by her own image, which surveyed her gravely from the top of the pile. It had the same compelling dignity that impressed her in the photographs on his wall.

As he shuffled through the prints, he seemed pleased, almost proud, showing them off as if she should admire them as *pictures*, as if they had nothing to do with her, and after a minute she began to see them that way too, as if the girl were someone she didn't know, someone mysterious and strange and—she drew a breath—irreproachable with beauty. They were wonderful, softly lit, even solemn, though she did wish that the strap of her bathing suit wasn't jutting so conspicuously from her collar. Steve Kendrick seemed to have a knack for catching her just before she offered her say-cheese smile or waiting until it tired, so that the girl in the photographs looked sad, and the sadness seemed lovely and deep, though Alex knew perfectly well that all she'd been thinking about at the time was the crummy weather.

"This one," he said, picking up the print she thought he'd goofed. She had reached her hand up to push her hair back, the hand was blurred, and her eyes were cast downward. But, after he pointed it out, she thought it was interesting. Different. There was something arresting in the inattention of the eyes, as if something had been stolen from her and she hadn't yet missed it. She liked it. He was right, it was the best one.

"I'm going to blow these up 16 x 20. They want that bigger format." He returned them to the envelope and replaced it on the railing. "That's the glory of 8 x 10. You can go wall-size without a speck of grain."

She hadn't the faintest idea what he was talking about. "Well, I think they're very nice," she said, because she thought she should say something.

"Would you like some iced tea?" While he went inside to get it, a sudden breeze blew the envelope into the bushes, and she had to squeeze behind them to retrieve it.

Kendrick brought the tea and a plate of cookies. She set the glass on the railing; then, afraid that it might tip, rested it on her thigh, where it left a ring of dirty water. There was a towel in the basket of her bike, but she didn't want to go get it. Kendrick was standing beside her, his elbow straining against his blue sleeve as he lifted his glass to his mouth. She wiped at the water with the heel of her hand and was careful not to touch the envelope with the pictures. Her arm itched where the bushes had scratched it.

"I'd like to photograph you in natural light. Do you think your mother would mind if you sat again?"

"She doesn't care. She's an artist. She does this weaving stuff." *Christ, you're the only artist I know whose work sheds. Why don't you just get a dog and retire,* her father had said. "Otherwise she couldn't get tenure. The painters are all men."

"You mean your mother teaches art?" Kendrick seemed to have trouble taking this in.

Of course that's what she meant.

"High school?"

"She's at Wallace."

"Why didn't you tell me?" Why was she supposed to tell him? She'd only met him last week. "That's my department," he said.

"So?"

"I wish I had talked with her."

"She doesn't care what I do."

Kendrick gave her a close look. "How old are you?"

"I told you, she doesn't care. Anyway thank you for taking my picture. Nobody ever did that before."

"Are you kidding?"

"Well, except school," she said.

"No baby pictures? First steps? Lost tooth?"

She shrugged.

"Hey, you forgot your pictures," he called as she started down the steps. "Almost your only pictures," he added when she turned, but then he studied her for what seemed a long time before he held them out.

"Would you like to know how to print?" he asked. She would, and so he invited her to come back tomorrow. And then he shook her hand. For a moment she stared at his extended palm thinking what a weird thing to do. Then she transferred the pictures to her left hand. As she was pedaling away, she swabbed her right hand on her shorts. It was the same one she had used to wipe up the dirty water.

Her mother was busy. Inspired by her trip to Japan, she was working on a piece titled "Hiroshima" that would combine woven silk with bits of burnt paper and melted plastic. Alex could hear the blender screeching in the downstairs rec room where her mother was mixing up a sludge that became the paper. When she quit for the day, each day, it was late, past supper, and she looked at Alex with eyes that widened and went blank, as if she was not quite sure what Alex was doing there. Then she disappeared into the bathroom, scenting the soggy air she left behind with bath salts, changed into something pretty, and went out for the night. She would be home sometime after Alex went to bed; she was always at work with the blender by the time Alex rose. For lunch her mother drank V-8; if she ate dinner, she got something out. When Alex was hungry she rode her bike to the IGA in the mauve dusk.

Alex did not mention to her mother that she had met the new assistant professor, and she filed the prints Kendrick gave her in a drawer with her socks. She was sorry she had mentioned posing to Jo Yellen, who wanted to see the results and wondered if he could be persuaded to take her portrait too. Jo did not have a particular boyfriend at the moment, but it never hurt to have a picture handy for exchange in case something developed. "Developed," she repeated and poked Alex in the ribs. "Get it?" Now that she had braces she kept her mouth closed when she laughed, and the sound came out, huh-huh-huh, through her nose.

"I get it," Alex sighed.

She began to ride her bike each day to Kendrick's apartment on East Maple, where the scaling frame bungalows had been subdivided into units rented by foreign students and groups of undergraduate men. Mailboxes sprouted around the doors, and on Saturdays the porches were littered with beer cans, the air spiced with a mixture of ginger, anise, saffron, and curry from the student melting pot. It was the shabbiness that made the street exotic. There were no sidewalks in her own suburban neighborhood; she seldom ran into the neighbors; even her own mother she seemed to encounter by chance. On East Maple Street Mrs. Ramirez waved as Alex pedaled by, while Mrs. Chandra skittered inside from sweeping her steps as fast as she could move in her sari, and the boys next door, who were already assembled on the porch drinking Old Milwaukee by eleven, yelped, "Ooieeee! Wish I could have me a piece of that pie!" and bayed after her like dogs at the moon.

She stopped going to the pool every day. When she did go, Jo Yellen complained she was stuck up. *Stuck up* was Jo's favorite word. Six months before her face had broken out, and now that she had both braces and zits she believed everyone else had airs. "You'll lose your tan," she warned, basting herself with a mixture of baby oil and iodine. "And redheads have such pasty skin. If you want my opinion …" But Alex didn't. She had no opinions herself, and she considered that the world would be a better place if no one else had any either. "I didn't mean it," she said, because Jo looked so genuinely hurt. "I just don't feel like talking today, you know?"

"You *never* feel like talking." Jo gave her new bubble hairdo a pat and scraped her bathing suit down her breasts to expose small quarter moons of white. "Ever since you had your picture taken by that photographer. Personally …"

Something clamped Alex's ankle, and before she could shake free the side of the pool struck her in the shoulder, she felt a cold shock of water, her breath leaked and stung. Jo was shrieking. Alex could hear her even before she surfaced, coughing, blinking the water and sharp sunlight from her eyes. Kevin McCrory grinned as he lunged toward her.

Almost absently she sidestepped, climbed the ladder, and moved her towel back to dry cement. Jo had stopped screaming and turned around to stare. Alex frowned. She felt as if she had missed something, like a joke.

"What's the matter with you?"

"Nothing."

"Boy, are you ever turning into a drip." Jo rolled her eyes and shook her head as Alex spread her wet hair across her back to dry. "I mean, if Kevin pulls you in it means he likes you. The least you could do is show we like him back."

Kevin McCrory had pulled her in. That was what had happened, Kevin had pulled her in. It was not the sort of event Alex would have thought so hard to follow, but there was something wrong with her, some connection that had broken, something inside her spinning loose. Her head felt fizzy. She couldn't seem to comprehend the simplest details of her life.

"What a zombie." Jo wrinkled up her face. "Let's get some French fries."

"You go. I'm not hungry."

"I can't. By *myself*." But at last Jo wiggled off, and after a minute Alex heard her screech, "No! Don't, please, no, Kevin, I hate you, don't!" Alex smiled. Really Jo was so funny sometimes she was cute.

Chapter 4

1982

It is the second death that is the cruelest, the child pulled from the lake only to slip on the stones and plummet, to perish in some other needless way. Reprieved once from the world of shadow, a young man should take care. His loved ones will not easily give up the miracle.

But she is not a widow, not even yet, though she has served for eleven years. That much she knows from the news, which she watches at lunchtime, at dinnertime, at bedtime, listening to the radio on the hour every hour between. Too late to meet her class, she hovers in the darkroom, waiting out the static and top tunes. A few of her students are printing; she sees Ross only when he passes so close she starts. "I thought you were sick," he says, and the eyes she turns on him are wide with alarm. "I've been meaning to ask you—a friend of mine is having some people for dinner on Sunday, will you come?" She reaches a hand back to clutch at the counter. "I don't know your friends," she blurts and flees to the room outside, where Kendrick is waiting.

"Outside," he says and lays an arm around her shoulder to guide her past the two students who gawk from behind the drier. "Do you want to go to D.C.?"

"No," she whispers. She can't remember what they say on the way to his farmhouse. He fixes her a drink; in the freezer he finds two dinners, and they eat without mentioning Ted Neal, though they sit on the sofa in front of Dan Rather. "Cognac," he offers, but the bottle stands with an unbroken seal all the four hours while they wait for the eleven o'clock news. "He won't die," she says once, so tonelessly not even she can tell if it is a lament or a prayer. "You don't have to do this," he answers, but they keep silent vigil until the late news segues to sports. Ted Neal is at a Washington hospital in critical condition.

"You should call," Kendrick suggests, but she doesn't answer, and still neither of them move for the stairs. Pity has melted over his features, and she can't bear to see their familiar landscape re-formed.

Slowly, in an emptied-out voice, she says, "When I met Ted I thought what I wanted was to be a better person." She looks up. "So here I am, bitter."

"Would you like me to?"

On the upstairs landing where he keeps his cluttered desk, a makeshift office between the large bedroom where he sleeps and the small one where she will sleep, they pause. She's reluctant to part with the day, for tomorrow will be the day after, and she will rise already stumbling into the shape of her sorrow. "I would tell you what I feel if I knew," she says. "I don't want him to die." It's too simple. She can't imagine the rest of her life if he lives.

She wakes before dawn and watches the light come. Listens: a chatter of birds, the abrupt blare of a clock radio, and the muffled squeak and sibilance of Kendrick's rising. His socks whisper on the stairs, but what's the point of tiptoes, she won't go back to sleep, the bed's crowded with dolor. She meets him in the kitchen.

"Up already?" She can tell he's not sure if her energy is a good or bad sign. "No news," he says gently. She cracks eggs into a frying pan. "I was going to call the hospital before you woke up."

"Too late now," she says, and his face folds. "I broke the yolks. You'll have to have scrambled." She pitches the shells into the garbage with a peevish lash of her hand. At the table she repents. "They never give out information about patients over the phone."

The call comes after nine. "His mother," Kendrick mouths and motions her upstairs, where she sits at his desk, hand trembling toward the receiver, which releases Justine's sob like a gush of water. "Lexie," her mother-in-law whimpers, and Alex's hand begins to shake so violently she has trouble holding the phone. "I'm sorry, I'm so sorry," Alex murmurs. "Justine, I'm sorry, I can't hear you, could you speak up?" It's monstrous, but she has to know what *critical* means.

"It's terrible … we don't … in surgery for hours …" Alex strains for the syllables. Something about anesthesia. A coma. He hasn't come out.

Dimly she hears the dishwasher throbbing downstairs. She is staring at a wall penciled with phone numbers, a calendar caught on a nail like a kite above its ragged tail of business cards. The desktop is a chaos of pink vouchers. Perhaps one should take such a call in the woods, on a carpet of bluets and emerald mosses; there she might understand what senses a man in a coma foregoes. Or was his last waking too only habit? She cannot make his face flash before her eyes, only this windy clutter of everyday commerce. "I'm sorry," she whispers, but the words have the wrong size in her mouth. She is one of the stricken; she should gnash her teeth and wail. But she doesn't know what else to say to his mother.

"He's on a ventilator." Justine's voice chokes again. "How do they know, less than twenty-four hours later how can they tell he'll never wake up?" When does a faithful wife know, waiting dinner, that her husband will never come home? Her senses seem disembodied, Justine's whimper far away in her ear, at the end of a long tunnel her vision. Justine's message falls into the dead eye of a storm, the terrible calm of her heart. It is practiced at not beating. She takes the news as if she has always known it, there in the comatose muscle where she used to think passion resides. "They say he won't be the same if he survives. How can they say that? How do they know? It's not even twenty-four hours."

"Is Jeannie with you?"

There is a long pause. "Jeannie's in Washington." Another pause, filled with the crackle of another conversation on the line. "The bottom line," someone keeps saying. "We haven't seen her." Downstairs the dishwasher hesitates and thrums into a new cycle. "Jeannie's joined the Sikhs. I know what you're thinking, but it's not like the Moonies or those nuts in Guyana. They run a restaurant in Dupont Circle. Most of them are from very good homes."

For an instant Alex sees Justine: bare feet with bright red toenails tucked on a fancy white iron chair, lips as thick with carmine as her nails. "Welcome to our family," she says with a breezy wave as Alex and Ted climb the steep steps from the drive.

It was the first time Ted brought her home, and she'd been nervous, a nineteen-year-old fiancée, bastard daughter who'd already married one man and lived with another, surely not the bride his parents had in mind. He hadn't warned her, and as she cleared the last step the spectacular charm of the scene struck her like knowledge. White petunias and red geraniums in bloom in the urns, a cascade of ivy over the brick wall, from the garden a perfume of roses, and overhead the oaks, stirring a lace of shadows. It was so lovely it took her breath, and she knew then that nothing she had done made any difference: she was only one of the legions of girls not good enough to marry rich sons.

"It's a disciplined life," Justine says, and with a sharp twist of pain Alex comes back to the phone. Jeannie, they are talking about Ted's sister, Jeannie. She's in shock; she can't concentrate; she can't seem to comprehend. "Maybe it will be good for her."

She had wanted them to like her, Alex remembers sadly. A year of wading through Marx, Marcuse, and Mills, watered down through the Port Huron Statement, and still she had wanted them to like her.

"She's getting married again. A boy from the ashram. They live in separate—dorm rooms, I guess you'd call them—and meet once a month for intercourse."

"It sounds great," Alex says weakly. *Jesus Christ.* Alex had been a bridesmaid at Jeanne's first wedding. For a moment Alex sees her own bridesmaids: Lizzie, still nursing Tice and three months pregnant with Lucy, in a pale blue dress with all the darts straining, and Stacy, looking as if she'd rather overthrow a government than stand up at a wedding, hitching up her gown for the march, and hissing back over her shoulder, "I hope you know this is decadent."

Alex has eaten in the restaurant near Dupont Circle; she has photographed the Sikhs on the neighborhood streets. Maybe she's even photographed Jeannie in her tunic and white turban. Years ago she used to imagine that one day she would simply see Ted on a street somewhere, look up from her camera and there he would be, as if nothing had happened. It was *possible.* Anything had seemed possible then.

"We could have grandchildren yet," Justine says.

It's a rebuke. Or feels like one. She should hang up, but this is his mother.

"Well, I don't know what she's thinking. If only Ted—he was always such a good one for giving advice, even when he was a little boy he was always a leader. Sometimes I think Jeannie would have, well, found herself if he hadn't disappeared. But this is her special time. We have to be happy for her."

A leader—the class president and good Scout, a son any mother could be proud of, and even when they didn't agree, his parents had to admire the courage of his convictions. His mother loved him, and all the years he was gone it never occurred to her to wonder anything but *where.* Alex shouldn't be so angry. She had loved him too.

"First Jeannie, now Ted." Justine's voice fails again; there is only the faint sound of anguish melting into the long distance lines. *Welcome to our family.* Something tears loose inside Alex, she feels a rush of pain so dizzying that she flings an arm out and rears back in her chair. Then she is stripped of her moorings, standing again on a terrace stippled with light, all of them gathered before her mind's eye in the impossible grace of an irretrievable moment, and loss blinds her with a hot mist of tears.

"... was it something I did? Lexie, he's been seeing other women."

Of course he would have seen other women, of course he would, of course. "Ted." The word falls from her mouth, stupid. Her breath comes in shudders and ragged gulps.

"*Dad*," Justine says impatiently. "He wants a divorce."

Please, Alex thinks as she lays her head on a sheaf of pink papers and weeps. She's *impaled* on the conversation.

"Are you there? I know it's not the time to tell you my troubles, but I wanted to prepare you in case you notice anything. Tell me the truth, did you ever notice anything? Lexie? What time is your flight?"

Alex stiffens and sits up. They mean for her to come. It is not an unreasonable expectation. The other conversation still echoes in the receiver. The bottom line, the bottom line. "Justine," she says dully, "I can't."

"What do you mean? *My god.*" Running her finger around the rim of the mouthpiece, Alex brings away a cold tear. "I can understand that you might feel bitter, but if you saw him …"

If she saw him … As in every day of her life? For how many years? When she thought any day might be the day, *hoped*, when all she had to do was close her eyes to see him that first time on the subway again. She was grateful when the image finally wore itself out, grateful to be without hope, because without hope it was done.

And then Cathy Wilkerson turned herself in.

Ten years underground. Five since the fall of Saigon, when many of the Weather fugitives came home, when in spite of everything Alex thought she still wanted him. A decade since Cathy's Weatherpals blew up her father's Greenwich Village townhouse and she and Kathy Boudin stumbled from the rubble into the Underground, leaving three of their dead behind. Justine had phoned that day too, ecstatic with the news that smote Alex like the blinding white light of an explosion, and she understood that more than anything on earth she feared he would come back too.

And now Kathy Boudin has turned up, caught robbing a Brinks truck and charged with murder. There's no end to it. "It's too late. I can't see him," she says.

"No one blames you." Justine's voice is cold with reproach. "You've been lonely, you have another life now. This man—they gave me his number at the school …"

"He's my department head," Alex says.

"You've moved on. But …"

"I have no life. I have work." Her voice is colder than it should be. Once she and Ted planned to have children. Once they nearly did. And when that once was over forever, work is what she chose.

"Ted needs you." But Alex can't—or does she mean won't?—and they must argue the verbs till Justine gives in. "I'll keep you posted. Or don't you care? At least will you pray for him then?"

"Of course." *Brain damage.* Is she supposed to pray that he will die? When they hang up, she splashes her face with cold water at the sink. Kendrick is waiting downstairs.

"Is it bad?"

She nods.

"Dead?"

She shakes her head.

"I'm so sorry," he tells her.

She had forgotten the most staggering thing about grief—that the acts it inhabits are so ordinary. It will have to learn again how to live inside the routine of her needs, and she's boggled by the way the blind beast must try to fit itself to those meager gestures, to eat, sleep, go to the grocery, pay the bills, raging and twisting those deeds into sorrows until it can teach itself the limits of the life which contains it, shrivels, becomes a small thing you can hold in your hand. She makes herself meet classes, endures the calls from Justine, all those progress reports with no progress. "He'd be better off dead," Justine sobs. "I know it's wrong, but I wish they'd just pull the plug. For God's sake, why can't you forgive him, why won't you come?" And still she refuses, as if to see him might be to forgive him, to let him slip off, excused. And then he really would be dead.

The woman who shot him is in custody. Her son is an MIA. Missing in action. Alex makes herself spell the words out: *never use acryonyms* ... And once she thought it was just the little comings and goings of love that could break your heart. She was an American; there was no such thing as revolution or war or famine. What did she know, a teenager reading romantic novels? What did he know, a teenager reading *Das Kapital*?

When Ross asks her to dinner again she accepts, because she feels helpless. Who is she to hand out excuses? As if her will could make a difference. "Don't answer the phone," Kendrick says, "I'll tell his mother you're out," but why bother to refuse phone calls when you can't refuse disaster? Kendrick makes her feel helpless: she needs him right now. She's been staying in the guest room at his house in the county since the story broke. He's the one person who's never deserted her. First a phone call, then a visit after Ted disappeared. And later, when she showed him her photographs, almost shyly, her documentaries of New York, Crow Hill, and the Movement, he got her a show and then a publisher, and then it was school, encouraging her, practically ordering her to go, when she was still so lethargic she had trouble leaving the warm, numb place she had worn in her bed. Maybe he knew he would eventually offer her a job. He's let her play the faithful widow, though she knows how strongly he's disapproved, just as now he disapproves of the cranky apathy she passes for mourning. For her sake, he's with them: she should see Ted, howl it out, and be done. "So I've wasted the best years of my life," she snaps. She can't seem honestly to thank him; he's so necessary he makes her cross. If she is the faithful wife, what does that make him? At least she has a husband. Where is his wife or lover?

When she tells him she is going out, he brightens. "Have a good time," he says heartily. He is happy to see her trying. Or maybe he's just happy to be off the hook for a night. It's only a student dinner, she tells him, but he says it again: "Have a good time."

Ross's directions take her across the Lee Bridge to the scraggly hem of the city's south side. The loop of red and white cabins in need of new paint has the configuration of a wagon train under attack, though it more nearly resembles a tourist court. Toys are scattered over the common grass lot. Though she's seen—lived in—far more dilapidated places, she feels a tug of pity. In the gloomy dusk, the settlement has the forlorn look of occupants who have found themselves stranded.

"I'm glad you came," Ross says as he opens the door. The guests are already assembled in the cramped living room. One she recognizes from the Art Building, Lorraine. "This is Alex," he announces, but Alex will have to pick up the conversation to guess the names of the others, a boy in a Kafka T-shirt who might be Lorraine's date or with the sloe-eyed girl on the long, sagging brown sofa beside a couple who have the insular look of serious students married too young. The wine she hands Ross is meant as a gift, but he leads her to the refrigerator and hands her a glass. From the end of the sofa, where the couple slide over to give her a seat, she can see bunkbeds in the bedroom, with two children dressed in pajamas crawling in and out, giggling and squabbling. Their mother, Marjean, is Ross's friend. Her clear, buoyant voice rises and falls from the bedroom in the cadence of story, and Alex feels something catch in her throat, something that has to do with the small, serviceable rooms, with the domesticity in which they have gathered, that transports her to the little house she fixed up in Limestone all those ages ago, before her history began. A lost sentiment, a road not taken.

When Marjean turns out the bedroom light to join them, she sits on the arm of Ross's chair and says, "Whew," brushing her short brown hair back from her forehead with a careless sweep of her hand. She is not pretty, short, nearly dumpy in her olive jersey and jeans, with wire-framed glasses too colorless for her pale face, but there is something appealing about her, an unaffected grace and good humor. Alex would have expected a girlfriend more like Lorraine, an *artiste* in gauzy cottons, jangly bracelets, and big hoop earrings; or perhaps a petite blonde sorority sweetheart. But Marjean is impressive, chatting easily with her handsome boyfriend's sour friends (or is it Alex's mood? perhaps they are just reticent and solemn) and serving a poorly made dinner off mismatched china, which they hold on their knees, poking at the ground beef, canned corn, and noodles bound in a Campbell's soup sauce. The room reeks of air freshener. Marjean takes in kids for a living (where does she put them?), can have little in common with Lorraine, who is hard at work on a senior project, and yet Marjean draws her out until the girl's hands flutter in the air as she describes the geometry of light that links all her paintings. Alex feels herself close to tears again; Marjean's talent recollects Ted's. When Alex looks for Ross's eye (for what? to signal her ardent approval?), he is watching her with a concentration so searing she drops her fork to her plate with a clatter that pops the children from their room. Marjean rises to shoo them, but nothing will do until Ross bears the girl, Karen, adorably blonde and curly, about the room for kisses. She is two, and her warm cheek is as silky as water. Her brother Billy makes the rounds himself. "Gimme five," he says, but when he reaches Alex his hand locks and he turns to his mother. "Who is *she*?" he asks, and Marjean laughs. "She's Ross's teacher. Isn't she beautiful?" And the evening is ruined.

Yesterday her picture was in the *Times-Dispatch*. A local reporter picking up a local angle—it's a better story than was first expected,

"Weatherman Shot by MIA Mom." On the day Ted stood in front of the FBI Building, he was just another of those underground creatures hatching like locusts. Now he's an editorial, and Alex is obliged to correct headlines: Ted was never with Weather; his heart would go out to the woman who shot him. *Her* heart goes out, it makes her sick, why do they have to hype it as if all history rides on the balance?

"Do you still believe in the Revolution?" the reporter had asked her, pulling at his tie. Years ago she met his type all the time: strangers who seemed to feel they owed her an apology for never having joined the Movement; they were embarrassed to have missed the big party. (What was it Tulip, that girl none of them liked, what was it she had said so spitefully at one of those all-night sessions where they started out to plot a more perfect world and ended up taking potshots at one another? "They make Revolution look like a commercial—buy this and you too can be gorgeous." But she meant Alex. Ted was above her reproach; it was not only for his face that she festered in secret; nor was it for her face, pinched, mousy, that he wouldn't have her. Or had he? Haven't the last eleven years proved she hardly knew him?)

"Goodnight, puddings," Marjean says firmly. When Alex makes her excuses, Ross leaps to walk her out.

"You forgot your wine," he says as soon as they step off the slab stoop, ready to drag her back to retrieve it.

"That's okay, keep it." Once again she is fighting back tears, almost considers confessing, but what can she say? Apparently he does not read the paper. She pulls her jacket close against the chill of the early March evening, more penetrating for the stuffy warmth of the house.

He takes her keys and opens the door of her Toyota. "Thanks for coming."

"Thanks for inviting me."

"Marjean's not a very good cook."

"No, but it's unkind of you to say so" is what she wants to say. Instead she says, "I thought the dinner was fine." They are still standing beside the car, their awkwardness lit up for each other by the small lamp on the ceiling. "Well." The sweet scent of tobacco from the storage sheds nearby chokes the air. On the highway a truck grinds gears.

"I don't live here."

He wants her to know that the children aren't his and Marjean is a part-time lover. She's embarrassed for him. For herself. She knows now why she chose him: his height, the steady cast of his eyes, his somber bearing. Marjean's manner, Ross's looks: it is her eyes that are clouded over with Ted's image. She should have noticed before tonight that the foolish attraction was returned. She slides into the car, refusing to take his meaning. "It's a funny place, all these little cabins. All it needs is a lake."

"She's had a rough time—Billy's got a hole in his heart, and her ex-husband skipped out on the child support. She's a good person."

"I can tell."

His hand still rests on the door. "I wasn't apologizing for her."

"I'm sorry." She puts her face down on the steering wheel. What she means is that she doesn't want to know anything about his life. "I have to go home now."

Chapter 5

1964

The highway that twisted south from Titanville to Limestone was a killer. Every year the legislature postponed action on a four-lane. Every year it tabled a bill to ban the billboards that presided over the landscape like sleazy auctioneers. Nothing had changed, though Alex barely noticed the familiar names flashing by. She was thinking about the afternoon four months ago when she had made love with Ted Neal, whose denim thigh hummed against hers in the steady, sensuous rhythm of the tires. She made love with him, but he was a stranger all the same.

The truck's gears ground up a last hill, and to the left, shimmering in the distance, lay the Wallace campus, crowned by the stadium and carillon. The driver dropped them at the Howard Johnson's on the highway, where Alex ordered coffee and Ted used the pay phone.

"Tired?" he asked as he joined her at the counter, and she swallowed a sudden lump in her throat as she nodded. Her mouth tasted mossy, her clothes reeked, and her hair was as greasy as the truckstop cuisine. For two days they'd been hitching, keeping a running patter of conversation with their drivers. As he talked a lively attention lit his face, vibrant as the pastel vaulting of the vast Midwestern dusk. Seated beside him, she could smell the electricity of his breath as they rode the Illinois lowlands, where the land washed away from the highway like a lost continent. But now, alone with him in the restaurant, she felt shy. A year and three months ago, she had left Limestone for New York. Ten days ago she had moved from New York to Colorado. He had spent the summer in Mississippi with the Freedom volunteers, trying to register black voters. She had meant never to see him again, though all summer while the FBI had searched the state for the bodies of the three missing civil rights workers, she had read the *New York Times*, searching for his name. Now he had come to Colorado to fetch her, and though she could not say why, here she was back in the home town she'd intended to leave forever.

His sister picked them up. Ted hugged her, and they stepped back to look each other over. Jeannie was pretty, with a glossy brown page-boy and her brother's dark gray eyes, dressed in cut-offs that showed off her long, gorgeously tanned legs. She looked as if she had just stepped from the crisp pages of a college yearbook instead of the steamy heat of a record-breaking September afternoon.

"How are you?" he asked. "How are Mom and Dad?"

"Fine." Jeannie giggled. "They got a new basket hound. Leo's favorite spot to go tee-tee is the Heriz in the den, Mom's in a snit, and Daddy's hauling him to obedience classes. Binks was in France all summer—it was so boring in Youngstown I almost died. Anyway, look at you." She hugged him again and adjusted the sunglasses perched atop her head. "You need a new barber, bro."

"This is Alex," he told her, placing a hand on the back of Alex's stool.

Jeannie glanced at her and smiled. "Nice to meet you. Were you in Mississippi?"

"No."

Ted plunked the change for the coffee on the counter as Jeannie said, "Stick with this girl—she's got sense," and Alex added, "It's nice to meet you too."

"Where to?" Jeannie asked as they stepped outside. "Oh god, Teddy," she complained when he rattled off the address of his friends Garth and Lizzie Foushee. "You know Daddy would never admit it, but he and Mom were really worried." Jeannie turned her dark lenses toward Alex. "My brother thinks he can stomp out racial prejudice by learning how to live on twenty-five cents a day. It's his version of share the wealth—share the poverty."

"You should try it," he told her.

"Well, will you call me?" Jeannie asked, her foot tensed on the brake of her white Cutlass in front of a sway-backed house with chipped tarpaper brick siding. Houseplants lined the balustrade in brightly painted coffee cans.

"Promise." Ted was smiling. "I'll invite you to the first demonstration."

Jeannie turned toward Alex again. "I think he'll outgrow it," she said.

Garth opened the door, and a rich aroma drew them inside, where for a moment Alex stood in the dingy light, blind. "Chicken soup," Lizzie laughed, fanning herself in an armchair. "Isn't that a crazy thing to fix in this weather?" She was pregnant, so enormously pregnant that everything else about her, even the halo of fuzzy white-blonde hair, seemed incidental. Garth, who was in the Ph.D. program in Russian history at Wallace, couldn't have been anything but an academic, paunchy, prematurely balding, with black-framed glasses taped around the bow. He was wearing plaid bermuda shorts with sandals and black socks.

"Boy or girl?" Ted asked Lizzie.

She had a laugh that ran through her voice like a silver ribbon. "As long as it's healthy."

"So," Garth said to Ted as soon as the introductions had been accomplished, "baptized by fire. You've got the power of personal witness now."

"How's the mood?" Ted asked as Lizzie hoisted herself from the chair and beckoned Alex to the next room.

"Pretty quiet on the surface, but it's going to heat up. When the Democrats refuse to seat the Freedom delegates the same month the bodies are found, it moves a lot of liberals left. Kids who aren't old enough to vote are already sour on electoral politics."

It was hotter in the bedroom, though the sheet nailed over the window was looped back to let air through a portable screen. "You must be exhausted," Lizzie said. "Alex, right? Would you like to take a shower?" She lowered herself to a squat before a cardboard carton. A mattress nearly filled the room, and the floor was stacked with boxes to make space for the crib rails propped against the wall. "The first thing I always want to do when we get off the road is wash my hair." She held out a towel and a tube of Prell in an easy gesture that seemed to belie the labored balance of her body. "The soup won't be ready for an hour. Take a nap if you want."

"When is your baby due?" Alex asked shyly. She had never known anyone who was pregnant, at least not since high school, where the condition had been as invisible as rumor. She was embarrassed to look, or to look away.

"Tomorrow. Otherwise we would have gone to Mississippi. Were you in Greenwood with Ted?"

"I wasn't in Mississippi." She would have to explain it to everyone she met, and it made her feel deficient, as if she had no past at all. She wondered if Ted had brought other girls to Garth and Lizzie's.

"Ted's a born leader," Lizzie said. "It's good to have him back."

Tomorrow. What could he be thinking of?

When Alex returned to the living room, hair dribbling down the back of her clean white shirt, Lizzie was serving the soup, and Ted was explaining to Garth, "As long as the struggle remains on campus, you won't involve the people. You can't ask a bunch of hillbillies who hate the college to accept some Marxist intellectual as their leader."

"We're not Marxists. We reject totalitarianism."

"You expect them to understand that distinction? To them everything to the left of John Birch is pinko."

"That's why they have to be educated."

Alex sat beside Ted and picked up her spoon. Had he told them he was bringing a girlfriend? (Or was she?) "The soup's great," she said.

That night, for the first time since New York, she and Ted made love on the living room floor. She clung to him in the dark, memorizing his face with her fingers. There was a little flutter in his kiss that wasn't yet familiar. She wanted to tell him that she loved him, but how could she? She barely knew him. She needed to pee, but she didn't want to cut through the bedroom, and she envied him when he rose to go outside. All night she heard the toilet. Pregnant women peed a lot. They got morning sickness. Alex couldn't remember where she'd heard; the lore of womanhood means nothing to girls. She wondered how long they would stay. Surely Lizzie would want them to leave before the baby arrived.

But she woke up happy. She was his girlfriend now.

Lizzie seemed sunny too, humming as she stirred the orange juice, smiling to herself over coffee, singing under her breath as she scrambled eggs. She had a large, ruddy face with a grainy complexion, like a photograph made with high speed film. "Poor Garth," she said to Alex. "He's had a frustrating summer. There's only so much interest men can take in leaky breasts and swollen ankles. It's good for him to talk to Ted."

When the baby came, she wanted to start an integrated childcare cooperative, Lizzie said as she ran a dishpan of hot water. Ed Rayle, the young Episcopal minister, had agreed to donate space at Holy Trinity.

"What are you going to name the baby?" Alex asked as the words of the men's debate drifted out to the kitchen.

"Irene for a girl. We haven't decided for a boy." Lizzie relieved her of a plate and opened a cabinet. The small kitchen bore Lizzie's bright touch, metal cabinets papered in poppy-printed Contact, tomatoes ripening on the windowsill beside a bouquet of wooden spoons. "I like Nicholas. It means 'people's victory'—pretty ironic choice for the last czar, wouldn't you say? Garth won't hear of it, of course. He wants to name the baby for Marcuse, but I'm not naming my son Herbert." She laughed. "Are you going to enroll at Wallace?"

"I hadn't thought about it," Alex admitted.

"You should talk to Ted," Lizzie told her. "Are you with him on this project? He doesn't understand—you can't just walk into a community and make things happen no matter who you are. In Mississippi he had a whole network of organizational support."

He hadn't said anything about a project. What he'd told her was that he wanted to go back to school.

At ten Garth drove Lizzie to the doctor, and Alex stood in the sodden heat of the living room doorway, unnerved. There was a trickle of sweat between her breasts; when she moved in front of the fan, the breeze ruffled the hem of her shorts. In the armchair, Ted tipped his head to regard her for a minute before he crossed the room, his eyes kindling on her face. "I'm glad you followed me."

"We can't stay here," she said. "They're having a baby."

He took her hand, and for a moment she stood caught in the spell of his slate-blue eyes. “Come on.” He nudged her toward the door. “Let’s walk.”

She liked his slightly bowed legs and the strut in his tall, athletic stride. “I’ve never been in this neighborhood,” she confided. The little houses had a sleepy look, as if the occupants might work the night shift. “I went to the University School, and all my friends’ parents taught at Wallace. I guess that’s partly why I didn’t go to college—I felt like I’d already been.”

The sidewalk ran out as they turned uphill behind a grocery with a cash-only sign on the screen door, and the houses thinned, became more ramshackle, lawn ornaments giving way to rusty Kelvinators and stripped cars. A dog curled its lip at them, and Ted tightened his hand around hers. So this was Crow Hill. Alex recognized it from U-School jokes: *What do you call rain on Crow Hill? Running water.* Trash fouled the woods that sloped off to the RCA parking lot glittering through the trees below. “We lived in a neighborhood my dad called Tenure Hollow. My house looked like a dentist’s office; it made my teeth hurt just to walk in the door.”

“What was your dad like?”

“He was an alcoholic.” She paused, twisting her finger in a wisp of hair. “He didn’t take me seriously. I didn’t know he took anything seriously until …”

Ted sailed the stick into the woods. “I *still* want my father to take me seriously. My parents’ house has five bathrooms. I tell them there are people who don’t even have one, and they think I’m going through a phase.”

She stooped to empty a stone from her sandal. “What are your parents like?”

“Rich,” he said. “I went to prep school and learned how to light farts. Maybe I dropped out of college because I felt like I’d already been too. I learned a lot in Mississippi. A hell of a lot more than I would have going to school.” He swept an arm out to take in the tar-paper shacks and parched gardens. “I want to form a collective up here to do community organization.”

So that was his project. She felt the same tingle of excitement that had shivered down her spine at fifteen when she thought Kendrick was going to take her to see the quarries. But this time she had leaped beyond the net of her childhood; this time she would learn the world.

"I don't want to live a sheltered life," he said.

"Me either." The certainty of her voice surprised her. It was the same argument he'd been having with Garth. She understood it now. "Garth and Lizzie want you on campus. There's some kind of group. Lizzie told me. She thinks you should use it to build a base."

"It won't work." He flung a hand out. "*Here?*"

"I think Garth wants you in it because you could lead it and he can't. He doesn't have the glamour."

"It isn't a beauty contest."

She smiled. "No. But I wouldn't have followed him halfway across the country." Was glamour something you could know you lacked, she wondered. Ted had to know he was sexy. "I didn't mean just looks." She couldn't explain; it would sound silly, though what she meant had to do with energy and she didn't think it was superficial at all.

"You don't like him, do you?"

"I don't know him. I like Lizzie."

"With the election coming up Garth thinks the ranks of the left will swell. He's got this vision of a mass movement led by the intelligentsia to reform the system. It could happen, but it's not going to happen as long as they sit on campus, meeting. Do you have any idea how boring those meetings are?"

"Are you a communist?" she asked.

His laughter seemed to roll through the woods as he dabbed at the corner of one eye. "I'm sorry. But you should have seen your face. *She hopes he's not the bloody red menace, but if he is it's too late now.* You are so wonderful."

She supposed she ought to admire his gall. Before she had known so much as his name, he had come to the apartment on West Eighty-eighth Street presuming she would hurl herself into bed, never mind that she had a boyfriend. He had tracked her to Colorado presuming—what?—that she was so daft, that he was so irresistible, that in a single encounter he could have made such an impression she would forsake everything to come back to a hick town she hated and reside in a hovel. Which may have been precisely what she'd done, but he needn't think he had her number, because she wasn't wonderful, she was indignant. "Are you making fun of me?"

"Making fun of you!" He drew a long breath, then fixed his eyes firmly on hers. "I'm not preoccupied with ideology—I think you have to go out there and find out what works. How can you hope to create a new system if you limit yourself to the tools of the old?" The force of his question yielded to a gentler inflection as he laid his hands on her shoulders. "I wanted to tell you back at the house how lovely you are. There is something so completely game and unspoiled about you." He shook his head as if to clear it of a vision. "All summer in Mississippi I kept thinking if I could get *you* to believe in me ..."

She would have told him he was mistaken, she was not the angel of mercy or whatever he'd taken her to be—except she thought that if he believed in her, she might come to be.

They found a bed of dry leaves in the marbled green light of the woods. She thought she had never seen anything so beautiful as the concentration of his features when he quickened inside her. His slate-gray eyes seemed to promise everything that had drawn her to him. "I trust you," she said, and realized it was what she had wanted to tell him last night, when she'd mixed the word up in her head; it was why she had come with him.

"I want to marry you," he said.

She put her finger to his lips, not to rush it. But she carried the promise back with her like a gift, through a landscape more finely textured, more luxuriously hued, as if the world had deepened in their joining.

Lizzie was sitting on the mattress, folding tiny undershirts into a box.

"I don't know why I'm doing this. I've done it a hundred times already," she said hopelessly, pumping her dotted swiss smock up and down on her chest for air as Alex listened to the steadfast purl of Ted's voice in the living room. "The doctor says it's going to be at least another week. I'm so hot. My skin itches, my back hurts, I can't sleep, I might as well live in the bathroom, and he's such a funnyman he tells me, 'You've never been pregnant until you've been nine and a half months pregnant.' *You*—" she patted the great drum of her belly "—are being difficult."

But in the afternoon, as they made the salad, Lizzie suddenly froze. Alarm passed like an apparition over her face, and then the ghostly expression settled, rounding her mouth and whetting her eyes almost as if she were listening for something. "Look down."

Alex reached for a towel. "I'm sorry. I must have splashed when I washed the lettuce."

"I don't think I'm peeing." Lizzie gripped her arm as another drop rolled off her ankle. "Garth!"

The Foushees named the baby Tice. "It doesn't mean a thing as far as I know," Lizzie said, tapping against the nursery window to point out her neonate for Ted and Alex. The babies were all so tiny, with little red faces wrinkled up like raisins. Tice seemed to be mostly undershirt and diaper, sleeping with his rump stuck up and the back of his fuzzy white head toward them. Back in her room, Lizzie opened the teddy bear Ted and Alex had picked out that morning. Her skin seemed illuminated, as if a lamp were burning inside a soft silk shade, and Alex thought that's what it means to be radiant. She felt radiant herself, holding hands with Ted on the elevator down to the lobby. "Do you want to have a baby?" he asked her, and she cut her eyes at him as she laughed. "You're kind of impulsive, aren't you?" It seemed like such a good joke he laughed too.

"You're nothing like I thought you'd be," she confessed, lying in his arms on the living room floor while Garth stayed at the hospital for fathers' hours. "You're funny." Everything was funny. It had happened so naturally that was funny too. They had fallen in love.

They looked for a house on Crow Hill. "It has to be a collective," Ted explained, "because that's the only way to get anything done. But we'll get a big house. I *want* time together. We can have our own room."

"A big house up there? Most of those shacks look like they only have one room." She had walked with him to campus, where he was waiting in line outside the Wallace gym to register for classes. Pigeons moaned among the gargoyles, a low dirge punctuated by spurts of laughter as students attired in madras called greetings back and forth. She couldn't imagine taking classes. After New York the campus seemed unreal with its landscaping, its turrets and gothic gates; the students seemed too young. "I'll find one," he insisted.

She smiled. "I've already agreed." She was thinking. The trust his grandfather had left would cover tuition, but the Crow Hill project needed funds. Now that he was going back to school his father would be happy to support him, but he didn't want his father's money. "He's got this way," Ted complained. "He's very generous, but boy does he let you know it."

"I want to get a job as a photographer," she said now. Why not? She couldn't believe she hadn't thought of it before. If she worked he wouldn't need his father.

They moved to Crow Hill the day before Lizzie and Tice came home. Ted had found a big house, which was a small house, but it would do. The kitchen sink drained into a bucket, an extension cord ran out the window to the refrigerator on the back stoop, and the lid to the toilet tank was missing, but at least it had a toilet.

Together they scrubbed the place down, and Garth helped Ted move the refrigerator off the stoop. They bought a hundred-dollar Chevy and a bulky used Raytheon TV. "We'll want to watch the news," Ted pointed out, adding, "I wouldn't mind catching the World Series." They bought d-CON; they bought Raid. Ted nailed together a bookcase and plotted out the project. Alex splurged on a set of pale blue sheets and looked for a job.

She wound up in the darkroom at Vardys, the TV tuner plant hidden behind an eight-foot chain link fence just south of the Limestone city pool. It was not exactly what she had in mind—factory IDs, cranking the big copy camera back and forth, opaquing negatives, burning plates—but she was glad to be in a darkroom again, breathing the familiar scent of stop bath in the safelight's red glow, which blessed the ordinary shapes of sink and counter with magic. Plus the job got her out of the heat, which continued to break records for September, steeping on the tin roof and tarpaper walls while inside she and Ted tried to make love without touching. Mississippi weather, he called it. The factory was not air-conditioned, but the darkroom was in a corner of the office wing. Punching in, she passed from the sweltering vestibule through an airless corridor into the cool sanctum of the managerial class, mostly clerks and secretaries with skimpy paychecks. It bothered her to sign the loyalty oath, though she had no intention of overthrowing the government of the United States and the question of the union—which even she understood the pledge to be about—was moot to her, since she was technically white collar, by title a clerk, who had to wear dresses to earn her daily ration of cool air.

"Isn't the pledge illegal?" she asked Ted.

"Hell yes. It's intimidation."

He had his own stories about intimidation from Mississippi, which had been the greatest experience of his life. He needed to talk about it, and he couldn't talk about it. He was restless, and in the dark that first night as he listened to her stories about Vardys, he seemed also to be listening to something beyond. It was a habit he'd picked up in Greenwood, listening for accelerating and decelerating cars. Once he told her that in dragging the Pearl River for the civil rights workers the FBI had brought up a corpse without a head and another cut in half. "You could drag any body of water in Mississippi and come up with a Negro. It's just that the FBI never bothered before," he said. He was twenty years old, and already he possessed the authority of a worn-in sadness. But still he said, "One person can make a difference. I have a lot of hope," and hearing him say it, she felt that she did too.

She liked the Vardys personnel. Every day she ate lunch at a table of women from the line who asked if she had a sweetie and wouldn't leave off teasing or telling dirty jokes. They gave Alex hope that she could come to be at ease among her neighbors, for there was no way around it: the neighbors made her edgy. Trying to discover the needs of the community, Ted introduced himself to sullen stares.

"Hot enough to fry spit," a man with a scar across one cheek said. "Y'all figurin to fix the weather?"

"No sir," Ted said. "Although it seems to me that rich people don't have any trouble keeping cool. What we'd like to do is help the community get organized, discover some common concerns and bring them to the attention of the agencies that have the power to do something about them. For instance, I notice you lack a number of basic city services."

"We're doin' all right."

Ted squatted in the dirt just beyond the stoop. "You play softball up here? What do you think is going to happen to the Reds, losing Freddie Hutchinson?"

"Hell of a thing when a man can't die on his own time. Three more weeks they would have had it. Phillies won't make the trip." The man spat. His chin was stained brown with juice. "Y'all don't belong up here, sonny."

Ted turned his head. "Nice old Studie you got there. What do you need to get it running?"

"You seem like a nice fella and this gal's prettier than a speckled puppy. They's folks up here think that means in season. You best get her on down the Hill."

Ted stood. "I'm not a bad shortstop. If you can use an extra player, let me know."

The difference between Ted and her was that he was undaunted by squalor. It was not that she was shocked, not exactly, although in a sense she supposed she would always be shocked by a routine of destitution her childhood had not admitted. But she had spent her initial horror in Manhattan, viewing the city's human dregs through the safe window of her lens. The camera had defined her: she did not sleep in doorways; she was the girl who photographed those who did. Ted was comfortable on Crow Hill; in Mississippi he had lived with Negroes. The profound sympathy she had come to feel for James Chaney, the murdered Negro civil rights volunteer, was, by contrast, an abstraction. And, fixed in the mistrustful scrutiny of Chaney's poor white cousins, she found it difficult to maintain the sentiment's lofty swell.

"Everyone has misgivings," Ted promised. "In Mississippi, "there was a guy on our project who cruised white neighborhoods at night singing freedom songs at the top of his lungs. We were all high on freedom. It never occurred to us that the volunteers who had doubts were the only ones Snick respected."

"Which were you?"

"I loved the action," he said simply. "I didn't cruise white neighborhoods, but I understand the guy who did."

"Did you know that Vardys has plants all over the world?" she asked. Repeating the conversation she'd overheard at work, Alex propped herself on an elbow and frowned. "It says right on the application that it's a small family business."

"Of course. Old man Vardys isn't going to advertise that most of his tuners are manufactured in countries where the peons are paid ten cents an hour." Ted rolled toward the wall. He worked too hard. When he wasn't in class, he was trying to organize the neighborhood to petition the city for sanitation service. He had called a community meeting to which no one came, and the bulletin board he'd posted in the front room didn't even have a notice for free kittens since everyone on the Hill just drowned theirs in the creek.

"Discouraged?" she asked.

"Tired," Ted corrected. "Of course it's discouraging, but I have to expect that. I was thinking about Berkeley."

Of course. It had been all they talked about at dinner. Garth and Lizzie came with Tice. They were elated about the California protest, begun ten days before, when the university denied the students just back from Mississippi permission to set up a table for SNCC and CORE. SLATE, the Berkeley student party, was now demanding a revolution that was to begin with the students presenting a list of impossible demands.

"But why impossible demands?" Alex had argued, embarrassed for Ted as Lizzie opened her blouse to Tice, exposing a fat red nipple. Ted had been very quiet as Garth replied, "Because it's imperative to destroy the illusion of the university as a haven."

"But if the demands are impossible isn't the protest corrupt?" Alex asked.

Garth looked irked. "The system's corrupt. The protest is a symbol."

He misunderstood. She was in sympathy with the protest. Ted had taken it personally, and to her the protest was real.

"Do you think Garth was right?" Alex asked him now, rubbing the side of his skull. She loved the secret Braille of his body. "I don't like the way he looks at me as if I have no right to an opinion. Do you think you should be organizing on campus? Do you think students are going to rise up all over the nation?"

"I think I should be organizing the rest of the collective." He stared at the ceiling. "He's wrong about this: Berkeley will politicize students all right, but the issue will tear the left apart. It's a question of revolution for yourself or revolution for others." He rolled to face her. "He is right about needing a base. Anyway, tell me about Vardys."

"Oh, that." She was embarrassed. "There's nothing more to tell." Instead she told him about the angel-faced axe murderess another woman had pointed out in the cafeteria line. "That place is wild. I'd love to photograph the women."

"Why don't you?"

"I couldn't." She thought of herself in New York again, wearing her Nikon like a nametag that said *voyeur*. To her Vardys was an education, but to them it was a job.

"You haven't taken any pictures," he noticed.

She felt vulnerable, more than she had in New York, even when a big black man yanked her toward him by the camera strap and she'd prayed he wouldn't choke her with it or a gang of boys snatched her camera, twisting her arms until she was astonished that they gave it back. If she took pictures, she would make them even more conspicuous than they already were.

"I don't have a darkroom."

The next day he took her to the camera store to buy a used enlarger.

Chapter 6

1964-1965

Their housemates moved in at the end of their first week on Crow Hill. Nelson and Matt took the other bedroom, and Stacy slept on a couch in the front room until she and Matt got together, then Nelson moved to the couch. Nelson had been involved in the civil rights movement, gone to Washington for the anti-testing march, and come back to organize student volunteers to teach in the Titanville State Prison. Over the years his political activities had caused him to drop a number of classes, and though he had been at Wallace since 1958, he was still thirty credits short of graduation. "I'm the next best thing to a drop-out," he liked to say. "I drop in." Matt, a junior who played guitar for the Holy Trinity folk masses, had a repertoire of Woody Guthrie songs that he sang in a clear, surprisingly strong baritone, for he was almost painfully soft-spoken, pale, lanky, with small blue eyes set in a face still puffed with adolescence. He was a born pacifist with no political background beyond his devotion to folk music. Stacy was a senior, daughter of a Chicago ACLU lawyer and a veteran of the sit-ins that had spread north from Greensboro and Nashville, who was forever asking them to freeze while she crawled around the linoleum after a lost contact. She was still getting used to her lenses and often looked as if she were crying, an impression the stalwart set of her chin defied. Her long straight hair made Alex feel over-coiffed, though her own hair was naturally wavy. It was the total effect: Stacy wore jeans and desert boots, Alex the stacked heels, nylons, and A-line dresses required of office help. With her chunky waist and capable jaw, Stacy looked earnest, muscular, substantial, and Alex was surprised when she moved into bed with sweet, dreamy Matt. She would have bet on Nelson, who affected a flashy beat style with his black beard and beret. Though to Alex his cadaverous white skin and womanish hips were nearly repulsive, his demeanor was as forceful as his deep, booming voice, and Alex wondered why he had taken on the modest project of improving the living conditions on Crow Hill, but his commitments had always been eclectic.

Now the house filled with people, and at the supermarket Alex bought everything in family packs, checking off items on her endless lists. Matt was addicted to Coke, Nelson drank tea, Stacy had to have sunflower seeds and unfiltered apple juice, Ted wouldn't eat white bread, and Matt wouldn't eat whole wheat. Alex thought she got stuck with the cooking too often, but Stacy was a terrible cook who fixed huge pots of muddy-looking lentils no one would eat, and none of the men could cook at all. So she didn't mind, not really. She tossed salads in a dishpan and baked lasagna in double batches served to anyone who came. Garth and Lizzie. Garth's friends. A Negro friend of Ted's named Layton, who provoked a new round of surly stares from their neighbors. Even Ed and Margaret Rayle. Nelson was sleeping with a girl named Peggy, who brought her friends, who brought their friends, everyone knew someone, and they all seemed to show up at dinner. Nelson rolled joints; Peggy brought wine in gallon jugs; Matt played his guitar, and Ted taught them the freedom songs he'd learned that summer; they listened to records and watched vintage movies on the TV that wouldn't hold a steady picture. Long after "The Late Show" went off the air they argued ideology, and Alex went to bed to the drone of reform, the incessant howling of the dogs on Crow Hill, and sometimes the faint puling of Matt and Stacy making love next door. In the mornings when she got up for work, exhausted, she emptied ashtrays and posted a note over the sink: DO THE DISHES SOMEONE.

Stacy was working in the Lyndon Johnson campaign. Nelson teased her and sang out "LBJ part of the way" every time she came in. "That's right," she said. "Johnson with eyes open. I'm not going to be one of you assholes who let Barry Goldwater blow up the world just because Johnson's a liar and a shit."

"The Great Society has been tested at Berkeley, and it flunked," Nelson countered. He wore one of Garth's buttons that said *I am a human being. Do not fold, spindle, or mutilate*, but he planned to vote for Johnson. The rest of them were too young. Ted was disappointed in Johnson's refusal to let the Freedom delegates be seated, but he'd also spent the summer persuading terrified Negroes to trust the ballot. He would certainly vote if he could, and he argued with Garth, whose group, Students for a Democratic Society, had considered urging people to stay home.

"Are you going to vote?" Alex asked Lizzie when she brought Tice up to the house one Saturday in late October. Tice opened his mouth in a goofy, silent laugh as Alex reached over to tickle him and scratched her finger on the "I am a human being" button pinned to his sweater. "Aren't you afraid he'll hurt himself?"

"It's no sharper than a diaper pin," Lizzie said, but she moved the button to the canopy of his stroller. "Garth feels that a large Johnson victory will move him right and defuse the left."

"But what do *you* feel?"

Lizzie laughed. "Well, Alex, Johnson's not going to *lose*. Here's a bottle. If he gets really hungry he might take it." Alex had promised to baby-sit while Lizzie got her hair cut.

When Ted came in they took the baby for a walk. "Alone at last," she quipped, crunching along beside him as he bumped the stroller through the red and gold leaves. Since the others had moved in, they had no time together, though his eyes always sought hers across the room, as if they shared a secret, and at such times they were alone, no matter how many others were there. And Ted was feeling more cheerful now that the collective had formed. The Sanitation Department had agreed to meet. In the meantime he had joined the softball game and was chatting up the players, running bases for a one-legged batter who whacked the ball over the head of the centerfielder. "Those suckers can *play*," he'd said, flinching as Alex applied the iodine. He was after Limestone's Parks Department to schedule the Crow Hill team on next season's city roster, though Stacy raised an eyebrow. "Are you working for a democratic society or practicing for the pros?"

It was the softball game that had given him the idea he presented to Alex now. Matt had access to the mimeo at Holy Trinity. They could start a community newsletter. The game had given Alex an idea too. She wanted to photograph the players. It was too bad she couldn't use the press at Vardys—they could have pictures, she could make halftones and lay it out. As the only member of the house with an 8-to-5 job, she'd begun to feel a bit excluded.

Her own project was to print her New York pictures, though she had to rinse them in the kitchen sink. She didn't care if anyone objected; after all, she did most of the cooking. Ted was impressed, and she used his ID at the Wallace library so that he could see the slums and child laborers from the turn of the century through the eyes of Jacob Riis and Lewis Hine, the Depression caught in the lens of the FSA, the alienation in the midst of American plenty revealed by Robert Frank. It made her happy to be able to show him something he had never seen.

She had also started a story hour on Saturdays, and before long the Hill children were hanging around after school, watching cartoons. She was haunted by their faces, the ragged hair, rotten teeth, and dull, agnostic eyes. You could dress them up in velvet, she thought, but one look at their faces and you'd know that they were poor. "What for?" they said when she asked if she could take their pictures, but they were exuberant subjects: mugging, pinching, poking, giggling, making horns, pulling hair. They gave her exactly the images she wanted.

Stacy disapproved. It was exploitation, a separatist activity. Would Alex be interested in photographing middle-class children? Stacy asked. She was interested in these kids only because they were poor.

"I thought we were all interested in these children because they're poor," Alex pointed out.

"*Some* of us want to help them." Stacy squared her shoulders. Alex was just like the photographers who'd used the Depression to make their own names. What had they done for the destitute? Used them. Ripped them off.

"But I will do something for them. I can teach them photography." There was no point in bringing up the story hour. Reading *The Cat in the Hat* wasn't Stacy's idea of social reform. Alex wished she'd changed into jeans when she got home from work, but she had gone straight to the kitchen to chop vegetables for the pistou, which now filled the house with its soothing, wintry fragrance. It wasn't fair, but as she felt Stacy's eyes narrow on her skirt and stockings, she knew she'd already lost. "'Those photographers brought the plight of the sharecroppers to the attention of the government—they brought it to yours."

"They brought it to the attention of people who buy thirty-dollar books for their coffee tables."

"People need art."

Nelson looked up. "People need justice and economic opportunity." The TV flickered without sound while Matt sat on the floor, quietly strumming his guitar. Ted, who had been crouched before the bookcase, stood. "I think it's a great idea," he said.

"Art's not a luxury," Alex protested. "I used to pose. It changed my life when I learned to use the camera. I could get some cheap cameras and show them how to print."

"I used to pose," Stacy mimicked. "Do you think Alex is feeling insecure? Do you want us to tell you how pretty you are?"

Tears stung Alex's eyes, and Matt, who put down the guitar, looked as if he might cry himself. "Lay off," Ted said.

"This is a collective. Criticism makes us stronger."

"Well, you don't have to be so snotty."

Alex tested her voice. "It would give them something constructive to be involved in, and it would be a way for me to be more involved with the community."

"You could contribute more, that's for sure," Nelson said as he sealed a joint and brushed the crumbs back into his baggie.

"I contribute as much as anybody in this house. Who do you think pays half the rent?" Alex gave Ted an apologetic glance. She didn't mean to throw it in his face. "Not to mention I haven't noticed you doing much cooking or cleaning."

"That's just like a liberal." Stacy took a deep hit off the joint and passed it back to Nelson. "They think they can buy anything. I'm talking about commitment."

"I mean it," Ted said firmly, "lay off." Later he held Alex as she fumed. "We don't have organizational funds. Somebody has to bring in some bucks." He was discovering how much truth there was to what Garth and Lizzie said: it was almost impossible to accomplish anything without an organization. On campus he spent most of his time speaking. She was proud of him. As Wallace's only veteran of Freedom Summer, he'd come back a hero. Girls he'd never met trailed him through the Student Union.

She didn't know whether he spoke to Stacy or not, but a few days later Stacy said, "I think we should set aside a time to meet, not just about strategy, but about problems we have with each other. For instance, I know that when I was still tied up with the election Nelson felt my energies could have been better directed. My contacts drive you crazy. Anything else? Alex?" Alex was still mad about the other night and refused to answer. "Okay. We'll come back to you. Ted?"

"Look, I agree we should talk out our problems. I just don't like to see it ritualized into a weekly bloodletting. We need to discuss strategy more than we need to bitch about somebody leaving the cap off the toothpaste."

"Thank you, Ted. That's very helpful. Matt?"

Alex almost smiled. He looked like a kid who wished the teacher would call on somebody else. He looked like a kid anyway, with his big ears and overgrown hands and feet, his face broken out in bumps, always picking at the guitar or his shirt.

"Oh, come on," she said. "I'm not going to get mad. Just because you don't like something I do doesn't mean you don't like me."

"You hog the bed," Matt whispered.

"What?" Ted said.

"She hogs the bed," Matt repeated loudly, and on the sofa Alex and Ted collapsed with laughter until Matt broke into a daft smile.

"Well, it's a start anyway," Stacy said tartly.

Gradually teenagers had followed their younger siblings to the house, now called the Crow Hill Community and Freedom Center. If the children had come looking for friendship, the teens came looking for a party, and Alex arrived home every day to find fourteen-year-olds drinking their beer and going through their records. "Nigger music," they complained of Leadbelly and Josh White. They didn't much care for Dylan, Guthrie, or Seeger either, but they danced to a few old Elvis and Jerry Lee Lewis albums, leaving muddy footprints on the floor cushions and letting in the stray dog Matt had been feeding on the porch. Alex bought a lock for their bedroom door to protect her enlarger. They had already trashed the TV, but that had been on its last legs anyway.

Stacy objected to a locked room in a house with an open-door policy; Ted thought it was time to talk about the policy. "We've been fooling ourselves if we hoped the parents would follow the kids. To the kids the appeal of the Center is that they haven't."

Alex gazed with distaste at the crumpled beer cans and overflowing ashtrays. The dog nuzzled her hand. She couldn't stand to look at its matted fur and rheumy eyes. "Can we agree not to let this damn dog in? It's not even housebroken."

"It's not a damn dog," Matt said.

"As far as the parents are concerned," Ted went on, "we're running some kind of party house where their kids are going to get into trouble."

Stacy blew her nose. She had caught cold, and her glasses gave her face a froggy look. "Those kids don't need our help to get in trouble."

"They were going to shoot the dog." Matt lay his head against its neck.

"I thought we were looking for trouble," Nelson said. "We're here to help the community, right? And lo and behold, a group of troubled youth on our doorstep seeking counsel."

"I don't see much counseling going on," Ted observed. "As far as the neighbors are concerned, we're harboring troublemakers, which does not exactly endear them to us."

"Ted's right," Alex said. "Some of those boys have already been arrested for theft. They use your bedroom to screw. And I'm almost positive one of the girls is pregnant."

"They hate us anyway," Stacy pointed out. "Face it, they're racists. If you gave them money they'd be pigs. If we have to worry about what they think of us, you might as well throw in the towel."

"I've considered it," Ted said coldly.

Stacy rolled her eyes. "Mr. Community Action. It was raining, so he went home."

"We're discussing the open-door policy."

"So what do you suggest? Let's tell Layton that we sympathize completely with the black struggle, but we just can't have him to dinner, it drives the property values down. Check the kids' IDs at the door. Alex and I can get a room in a convent and you all can go to bed at 8 and join the church choir."

"For starters, we can get rid of the marijuana and alcohol."

"God, you're a prig."

Nelson sealed a joint. "Forget that."

Ted sighed. "Okay. But we keep it down a little, huh? Bedrooms locked, kids out by 7, no drugs or drinking till they're gone. Alex, why don't you try talking with the girl who's in trouble, see if there's anything we can do."

"Like what?" Stacy said. "Lend her a coat hanger?"

In January the governor of Alabama spoke at Wallace, and several campus groups joined in protest. As a veteran of Freedom Summer, Ted was a featured speaker, and Alex called into Vardys sick. Nelson was speaking too. "Nelson always speaks," Stacy confided to Alex with a sly grin as the collective huddled over morning coffee, still web-eyed, their voices furred with sleep. "Wallace can't give a parade without Nelson."

The sky was low and colorless, and gray patches of last week's snow still clung to the wet ground. Stacy shivered in her pea coat as they walked from the parking lot toward Wallace Square; Matt ran ahead and backpedaled in place till they caught up. Alex's teeth were already chattering, but Ted's step was buoyant.

"You'd better hope that racist SOB gives a short speech," Nelson muttered, for the plan was to hold a silent vigil until the auditorium emptied, then march on the president's house.

As they came into the square filled with black faces, Alex spotted Lizzie and Tice. On the other side of the fountain, Peggy was holding up a sign. Ed Rayle stood talking to one of the black marshals. When she crossed her arms before her chest two black hands took hers. She was aware that she would not have paid much attention to the events of the past summer if it hadn't been for Ted. She had no right to the sense of moral superiority that rose inside her as students passing on their way to class hastened their step, heads down, as if the real issue was their embarrassment. Watching them, she felt conspicuous and invisible at the same time. Then the silence filled her, she no longer saw the crowd, only, like a beacon hovering before them, the lamp lit in Mississippi that would shine around the world. Her chest clotted. Something was swelling up inside her, trying to get out. It was her soul, she realized, grown so large it strained her ribs and filled her throat. It seemed to her the most profoundly dignified moment of her life. When the crowd from the auditorium dispersed, a hum passed through the circle, and she joined hers to the single voice. Then, as the last words of "We Shall Overcome" were borne off in the damp air and the protestors broke, she was suddenly aware of the cold again and began to spot familiar faces, Ted and Matt off to the left and over there Lizzie with a dark green toboggan pulled low on her head. They lifted their signs, and Ted fell in step beside her for the march. Under the watchful eye of the campus police, the wall behind the president's patio filled with protestors, perhaps a hundred; several climbed trees to listen to the speeches. "Garth's introducing Ted," Lizzie whispered and leaned to retuck Tice's blankets.

Ted was scheduled in the middle of the program, which began and ended with black leaders. Ed Rayle spoke for the church's condemnation of racism. Nelson boomed out an inflammatory, name-jabbing harangue, and then Garth presented Ted, who vaulted to the makeshift platform. His eyes swept the crowd, and Alex's throat tightened.

"The man who profits from another's poverty lives in a poverty of vision and a poverty of spirit. He who would chain others chains himself. No one of us is free until all of us are free."

It was his voice, but she had never heard it projected before, and it rang in his body like a bell.

"He who holds others in bondage lives in the bondage of fear. He who teaches his children to hate will die hated by his children. And he who thinks that there is no blood on his hands had best look into his heart, for this nation's soul is stirring, and its conscience is gathered here. It is gathered in Mississippi, it is gathered in Alabama, it is gathered in Birmingham, in Montgomery; it is gathered in Greensboro, North Carolina; it is gathered in Nashville, Tennessee."

"Amen," someone behind Alex murmured. "That white boy preaches like a brother."

"The governor of Alabama has spoken. We know what he says. One side of his mouth cries 'Segregation now, segregation tomorrow, segregation forever' while the other side claims he bears no malice toward Negroes. Why, some of his best friends are colored—his cook, his gardener, his chauffeur!" A low laugh buzzed through the crowd.

"*Freedom* now, *freedom* tomorrow, *freedom* forever." A scattered applause began and quickly died as Ted's eyes swept the crowd again. "Herbert Lee, William Moore, Medgar Evers, Louis Allen, Michael Schwerner, Andrew Goodman, James Chaney. Seven men who died for asking that our country honor its principles. I mourn them. There will be more, and I mourn them. But how many hundreds are there whose names we cannot mourn, because they dared not ask us to fulfill our promise, because they dared not say what, in their honor, we proclaim: that the freedom of the rich and the freedom of the poor, the freedom of the powerful and the freedom of the weak, the freedom of the white and the freedom of the black, are one!" He lowered his voice. "George C. Wallace has spoken, and perhaps he has made more converts, perhaps there will be a few more men bent upon evil tonight. But the triumph of evil does not require the deeds of a bad man. Evil needs only the good man who does nothing. Take action." He stretched his hand out and in a whisper sent his last words echoing through the hollow. "Good men."

As the crowd broke into applause, Lizzie squeezed Alex's elbow. "He did good." Alex didn't hear the other speeches. Someone leaped on the platform to lead them in the "Ballad of Herbert Lee," and then Lizzie was rushing off to feed Tice, and Stacy was waving and shouting, "Alex! Over here!" Matt grabbed her hand from behind. "Ted was great," Stacy said. "Do you see Nelson? I'm freezing."

"I'm hungry," Matt said. "Let's go to the College Club for lunch."

"You're always hungry," Stacy said.

"I'll find Ted, and meet you." Alex's skin buzzed. What had she missed, buried in the darkroom at Vardys every day?

Ted broke from the crowd. "Hey," he said to her, and she felt a sudden pang, because he'd been wonderful and he knew it; there was nothing she could add. She squeezed his hand, and he flashed a jubilant grin.

At the door of the College Club they paused until their eyes adjusted to the haze of blue smoke. Dishes clattered and waitresses called out orders inside a roar of conversation that rose toward the high ceiling like an ancient tongue.

"Ted! Alex!" Stacy stood on the seat of the high-backed wooden booth. They squeezed in beside Nelson.

"Hey, baby." Layton paused to slap Ted's hand as his group passed to their table. "Good speech. You been listening to de Lawd."

Nelson chuckled. "De Lawd" was the name the SNCC people called Martin Luther King behind his back. They resented him for the publicity he could garner in a day after they did months of footwork. But Ted admired King's ability to stir large groups of people. He had spent the summer dazzled by the rhetoric of black preachers.

"What have you got against Martin Luther King? Don't you believe in nonviolence?" Matt asked.

"As a strategy. It ain't my religion."

"Hey look, there's Peggy," Stacy called, and Peggy squeezed in beside Matt. "Good speeches, guys."

As they opened their menus Alex looked around. Sixty years of college memorabilia covered the walls. Perhaps thirty-five people had formed the circle at the demonstration, and yet it seemed to her that all humanity had joined. Settling back against the high bench, gazing at the lively faces of her friends across a table scarred with Greek letters and initials of sweethearts long since parted, she sighed with contentment. She was home.

Chapter 7

1982

And so how does it happen that after Tuesday, when Ross slips in and out of her class so inconspicuously he seems, conspicuously, to be avoiding (fine—she would like to avoid him too; maybe he'll drop and that will be the end of an infatuation she sincerely repents)—how can it happen that on Wednesday, checking the darkroom, she should find him printing and walk to his cubicle to stand behind him until the air sharpens with intent and he turns around, without a word packing up his negatives and paper? He's a good student, precise, careful to seal the foil inner pocket. He knows what's going to happen, all right, but he's not sure it's worth forty bucks of paper. Already half of her regrets, while the other half admires his nerve. But half and half make a whole, and that's what she wants, not a fraction of herself leftover to think about Ted Neal.

But midway up the sidewalk of West Avenue she loses purpose. It's a beautiful street. She was lucky to get into one of the last rentals in this row of townhouses painted with pretty pastels or sandblasted down to the red brick and gentrified. It's so well tended and charming that at first she felt as if she only sublet while rich owners trotted the globe. Now, as she sidesteps a tricycle on the walk, even her own footsteps feel like someone else's. She hasn't been home for more than a week, and the woman who drove off to the Y with no more on her mind than remembering to stop off at the Safeway seems a stranger, as impossibly innocent as the girl who stood a little dazed on a brick terrace beside a boy who wore the world's sorrows like honor on his high cheekbones. She doesn't have enough resolve to get through this without conversation. "How late did your guests stay?"

"Not late. Marjean has to get up with the kids."

"I liked your friends," she says, although they are already blanks.

He grabs her wrist and turns it, almost as if he's inspecting for razor stripes or holding her against permission. "You didn't tell me you were married."

So he knows. That's how he understands her. It happens all the time, people in pain and shock cruising for the fuck that will shake the broken hearts right out of their bodies.

"I go to school on Monday, everyone's buzzing. I felt like a fool."

"Maybe you should read the newspaper," she says, and the hollow place where her breath should be lurches. She can't get rid of it, this ache that is like the wind knocked out, a collapsing void inside her lungs.

He lets go. "Why did you come and just sit there?"

"Why didn't I stay home and just sit there? It's been a long time since I've seen him. There's not a whole lot I can do."

"I'm sorry." He means it. "If you want to talk …" She shakes her head. His brow is troubled with sympathy, or maybe he's just not sure that fucking the bereaved is polite.

Her apartment smells of disuse, like a motel room that needs the air-conditioning turned on, where a thousand occupants have left no trace but the brown cigarette scar on the tub. Her plants need water; while she tends them, he busies himself checking out what he can read of her from her possessions. White walls, Turkish rugs, hardwood floors sanded and gleaming with polyurethane. All the oddities she's found at flea markets, and any artist or academic might live here. He could have imagined it if he tried.

"Nice place," he says.

"I was lucky."

"Is this your work?" He's looking at the walls. "I saw your book on the '60s."

For a moment they stand, caught in the arch between living and dining rooms, out of conversation. It's the same awkwardness that kept them beside her Toyota on Sunday night, an ineptitude at the inevitable, or perhaps it's only the predictable. Whatever, they're dignifying it beyond its deserts with their hesitations. She sets the watering can on the dining room table and takes his hand to lead him, but for the strange warmth of his palm against hers, a realtor showing a floor plan. She turns down her quilt, and when she turns back to him, he is already undressed, his lean chest polished with late afternoon light. He springs with the merciless art of a cat, a thin coil of muscle pressing through her flesh to her bones, and though she bends into the embrace she feels assaulted, afraid their ribs will give way and their organs mix themselves up together; when they finish she will have to sort out their lungs, hearts, and stomachs like a jumble of clothes. But the pressure is really just her own resistance, less a struggle of flesh than an unyielding of her spirit. His mouth explores hers with a sensual tremor—Marjean has got herself some lover, who lifts Alex like a dancer, locking their eyes; this is a performance, and he means to bring her house down. Lowers her to the sheet in the same fluid ballet, strips off her shirt and jeans, touching all over her body. She should close her eyes to him and give in, but she's fascinated to watch him work all the frail, curled tendrils of her nerves, his fingers stroking like questions (this? here?). She has to see the quake in her thighs to know she is coming, but her body opens to him in a way she regrets even as she is thinking why not? Eleven years. How many wives would have been so faithful? She can't find the rhythm. When he shudders into the moist nest of her arms, they hold him, relieved, though her skin still shivers and trills. "You're quite the athlete," she says flatly, but he's no novice and knows better than to try sealing his bargains with words. She supposes she's sorry only that now it will be awkward in classes. For all his skill he embarrasses himself with his shyness and lack of humor. It's a mean thing to do, but while he's in the shower she dresses and sneaks out.

He does not show on Thursday, and she scans the class with a small sting of conscience—she hasn't been thinking about him. She won't think about Ted, and so she has been studiously thinking of nothing. (Who would guess what a demanding, full-time job that is?) The class's attention seems soiled. Ross has warned her—the mongers are out. Up and down the hall they whisper.

He turns up at the farmhouse that night. Drooped on the sofa in the robe Kendrick fetched with her things from West Avenue, she's sure it is Ross even before she rises, and she cinches the wide satin sash tighter, bunching the neckline between her fingers at the cleavage. She opens the door, looking beyond him to the streaky sunset, and sighs. No doubt he knows that Kendrick is at school. For something to do she brings him a beer, but he holds it unopened, leather jacket slouching from his shoulders in an easy fit that is too sexy to be unstudied. Neither of them sit down. "You weren't in class today."

"You weren't home when I got out of the shower." He's angry. "Whose apartment was it, anyway? You didn't tell me you live with the head honcho."

"I don't," she says. "I didn't tell you this, I didn't tell you that. What? I skipped a couple of lines on my application?"

"Whoa," he says. "You're pissed."

"What do you expect?" But if he reminded her of Ted and is only himself, is it his fault? And if she is pissed, is it with him? Bad train of thought—she needs to get off before it arrives at its destination, for it isn't entirely Ted or even herself, and she doesn't want to discover that what she's really mad at is just *things*. "We're old friends. I've been staying here since …" Her eyes fill as she moves to the sofa and picks up her tea. "I'm not angry with you. I just can't talk about this."

"You want sex with no questions." It's not quite a statement or a question.

"That was a mistake," she says. He opens the beer, still watching her with a wary, skeptical expression. "Look, can you accept that I am just possibly not in my right mind? I'm sorry. I am angry, but it's nothing you did. I just don't want to get involved."

"You've got a funny way of not getting involved." He sips. The fingers wrapped around the can are slender, like his elegant long nose. He has the slightly punk look of a European patrician. He lacks Ted's breadth, the sturdy weight of his shoulders.

"It was a cowardly thing to sneak out. I apologize."

"I don't want you to be sorry." When she doesn't answer he examines the photographs framed along the wall that opens into the staircase, and she cuts past him to sit on the steps, as if to block him as he glances upward, at the prints ascending to the second floor. Underneath his jacket he wears a thick cotton shirt and baggy pants with complicated pockets. "I found Professor Kendrick's book in the library. *Muse*." He is watching her face; there is more to this story than she's told.

She stares at the floor, hugging her knees. "That was a long time ago. It was Kendrick who taught me how to use the camera and the darkroom. I was sitting for him, so he did me a favor." She looks up. "I was fifteen years old, with a crush on my teacher."

He flushes. "I'm not fifteen."

"Twenty? Twenty-one?"

"Twenty-three. I was in Europe a couple of years."

"And so now you feel old because you're a twenty-three-year-old senior with Paris. But I'm thirty-six, and twenty-three seems very young to me." Ted was only nineteen when he bound her forever with his grave voice; she was eighteen. But she has grown older while he's never changed, twenty-seven when he vanished, twenty-seven all these long years. And when Kendrick was twenty-seven, she was fifteen. What counsel can she give this boy? Except that he will grow older too. In a year he'll bemoan twenty-five as a looming watershed and mark it in a morose funk. In ten years he'll wonder how he ever could have been as young as twenty-five. "Besides, I don't think teachers should sleep with their students."

"You think I screwed you for a grade?" Resentment splotches his face. "If you're so fucking moral what are you doing here while your lunatic husband ..." But he wants to keep her and cannot go on.

"You don't know anything about it. To you he's just a cliché, but when I met him he was a hero."

For a second her ears ring with the discord of the old debates that played from shabby living room to shabby living room that first summer on Crow Hill. Stokely had stolen the blacks and left them the poor—at least that's the way it seemed to them then—all the incredible, disorganized mass of it. Welfare mothers, the homeless, the substandardly housed, students, sharecroppers, migrant workers, the Third World, the laborers who didn't dare vote themselves unions. That was the year when they could strike up a conversation on the corner and come home with a new cause, a neighborhood center, free lunch, better garbage collection. And while their rhetoric rattled against the paper-thin walls, outside, in a landscape of tarpaper shacks, cars on blocks, rusted wringers, the lowly citizens of a crueler kingdom lifted wordless voices in song, the sweet harmony of tree frogs, crickets, cicadas. When they left the poor for the war, they had yet to decide who their constituents were.

"So what happened?"

His words hang in the air. Outside there is a faint stirring toward summer, a sound of things hatching that cannot quite yet be heard. Her voice hollows. "He disappeared. He was wanted for questioning in connection with a bombing." She looks up. "Questioning, that's all. He hated that the Movement turned violent, and if he even knew anything it was against his will. Maybe he did; he heard things. I used to think they'd killed him."

"The government?" He leans against the railing. He's incapable of shock. It's the legacy of Watergate. His generation grew up expecting its government to be corrupt.

She shakes her head. "Oh at first. Maybe. The FBI, the CIA. We thought they were out to get us, and actually they were. Did you ever hear of Wellspring? The commune where they trained the SLA of Patty Hearst fame? Tribal Thumb, the May 19th Coalition, Prairie Fire? This woman, Roseann Guston, tried to leave, and they shot her in the head, *murdered* her, just like the Mississippi rednecks murdered Schwerner and Goodman for betraying their white cause. I saw it happen to others, people I revered for their courage. They had ideals. Peace, justice, and maybe that's vague, but do you hear your president promising anything more specific? It was the hippies who added love and reduced it all to silly slogans."

"So you were a radical?"

It's the question she senses in everyone now: how many buildings did she bomb? She refuses to dignify it with an answer. "And the government didn't want peace and wouldn't have justice. So you start with ideals, you want to save the people, that makes you a prophet, pretty soon you've got an ego instead of a conscience—by God if the country doesn't want saving, you're going to cram it down their throats. You break one law, you march where they told you not to—is that a crime?—and then another, you occupy an office, you burn your draft card, and another and another, and just like the war it escalates, and still the government won't listen. So why shouldn't you bomb buildings, and if you bomb buildings why shouldn't you kill anyone who threatens your noble ideals, except somewhere along the line they got corrupted of course, and you're not prophets anymore, you're just thugs." She raises her eyes to meet his. "But not Ted."

"Only now you know better."

"I don't know what I know. That's the problem." She turns her head away. "They should have killed him and left him a hero."

He sits beside her, but she's not ready to give it over to tokens of comfort yet. "He always did have a genius for timing. When it was time for civil rights, he made his parents think about the discrimination they had always taken for granted. When it was time to put a stop to Vietnam, he made them think about a war that was good for business. He pulled out of civil rights *before* black power. Maybe that was the flaw—he never had a cause that was his own." She sighs. "So now here he is again, with a truly contemporary dilemma: to pull or not to pull the plug. And among all the other things—the grief and the anger and the exhaustion, because I'm *tired*—I resent it. I loved him, and I resent having to wish he were dead."

"You think they should pull the plug then."

"I have wished he was dead, but it's not the same thing. Now that he's alive I can't wish him to die."

"But if he's suffering ..." He livens to the argument, a freshman warming to the thesis statement of a paper he's been assigned. Five reasons to ratify the ERA, one syllogism in favor of euthanasia. But she's the one making speeches.

She straightens, shrugging off his arm. "You wanted to know what I'm doing here. Steve Kendrick has been kinder to me than anyone in my life, I should be talking to him, I don't know why I can't." But they never have talked about Ted; she doesn't know anything about his own brief marriage. They're closer than that; they've learned loneliness and respect private sorrows. "I don't know why I have to be so bitchy to him."

"I don't think you're bitchy." He smiles. "You were pretty nice to me yesterday, until you snuck out."

That. Her mouth tics in annoyance: he still thinks it's about him. "Look. Ross." She takes his hand, streaked with umber across one knuckle. There is a nick in his chin, a dark spot of blood in the small lavender blot of a styptic pencil. "It's nice of you to listen, I mean it. I've probably needed to say these things for a long time, but …" But before she can tell him again that anything he might have considered between them is finished, gravel sprays in the driveway, she drops his hand but reacts too late and stands, a bit breathless, only at the clap of Kendrick's boot on the steps.

"Hi. How was your class?" she asks as, much too late, Ross scrambles to his feet beside her. "This is one of my students, Ross Walker."

"How are you doing?" Kendrick sets a slide tray on a table and crosses the room to shake his hand. She's never noticed before how the light creases beneath his eyes. *He* looks tired.

And Ross looks so guilty someone should laugh. A quick mumble, shake, and he's gone—can't wait to get out. His hand might as well have come away from hers marked.

"Nervous young man," Kendrick remarks.

"He's shy." She is embarrassed to catch herself bunching the neckline of her robe again. "He's one of my students."

"So you said." Kendrick sinks to the sofa. "I've seen him around. Another poor moony-eyed pupil. You do attract them." He is going through the mail on the coffee table. "Have you eaten? Want to get a pizza?"

"You don't?"

"Nope. Haven't had a nibble in years." He tosses the mail aside. "So, did he come to confess or just ask about the assignment?" He jingles the keys in his sport coat pocket. He's the only man she knows who still wears blue work shirts with Harris Tweed jackets. They're not a statement; he's simply never noticed that his clothes have gone out of style.

"I don't feel like getting dressed. It's easier to make clam sauce and pasta."

"Sure?" He follows her into the kitchen, linoleum counters the right height for midgets, the original glass-paned doors still on cupboards sloppy with paint, drawers warped beyond closing, the door to his darkroom sealed with black rubber strips. He's always going to renovate, but then a pipe bursts or another ceiling falls, and he spends all his time just patching the place back together. "Well, I imagine he appreciated the outfit. That robe's a pretty slinky number. To a kid …"

"He's twenty-three," Alex says sharply.

"Sorry. I didn't know you were enchanted. He *is* pretty. I overheard some girls in the elevator—he's got his admirers, and you've got some lusty female students. I was positively blushing by the time we hit first. Whoops." He backs off as she turns from the board where she's mincing garlic. She's afraid they will quarrel, and like a slap in the face she'll snap, "I slept with him." Which would be stupid—if she expects Ross to be discreet, *hopes*, she'd best start by keeping her own secrets. At another time Kendrick might have been happy to hear it, or at least to hear that she was sleeping with someone, but hardly a student, and certainly not now, when he would know how seriously she's failing—it's not exactly a sign that she's getting on with her life, and if she can't talk to him it's for that: he knows her too well for her to think she can test words on him as she stutters her way back to whatever the truth of her heart is. The best audience is always a stranger.

Do you know anything about a person, she wonders, until you've known him twenty-one years? Kendrick's fine blond hair is raddled with silver now, thinner, his face has a little more bulk, the line of his body has slackened, changes so subtle she can't say when they happened. It's not that he looks old, only that for the first time she sees how malleable the flesh is to life's seasons. One knows this and still has to learn it: the slow tick of time is really so fast. Only yesterday she was sitting in a restaurant trying to guess his profession. Only this morning she and Ted were walking to a highway in Colorado.

When the water boils, he adds the linguini. She used to wonder what made him so loyal, but after twenty-one years she knows: he is loyal because it is his nature to be. And what will she know after forty? For it doesn't end with this milestone that's almost a joke—their friendship has reached its majority—even at this moment, in this stasis, it is evolving, and though she cannot imagine how, she cannot imagine that she will ever be without him. If *he* should die? The thought softens her face into a semblance of sorrow.

"Any word about Ted?"

She shakes her head. "Actually it was you I was thinking about."

"Ah."

"You should take better care of yourself. You don't eat right. Pizza—do you know how much fat there is in pepperoni?" She stabs the third clove of garlic and turns back to him. "You're forty-eight. People your age have heart attacks, they get cancer." The words fly from her mouth like small fists. "You need fruits and vegetables. Fiber. You should exercise, watch your cholesterol, get check ups ..." In a second he is beside her, taking the knife from her hand as the hot wave of tears breaks.

"It's okay, Alex, it's okay," a lullaby jarred by a noise that she hears far away in the warm, damp cradle of his shoulder, only the noodles boiling so furiously they rattle the burner.

But it's not done yet, and in the morning nothing is changed. They're out of eggs; the bread is moldy. At McDonald's they drink bitter coffee, and she gazes out over the styrofoam litter with dull eyes. "You should go," he advises.

"Whose side are you on? I've got enough problems." Her voice is too exhausted to flare. "I'd prefer not to take on Brad and Justine's divorce. Every time she calls she asks, and I have to tell her I always thought they were very happily married. I've told her so many times I don't remember what I did think."

"You don't have to see them."

"Of course I do. Justine's holding vigil at the bedside. She's got to sit long enough not to look callous when she goes to court to get the life-support shut off."

He's set his empty cup aside to fold arms on the table, leaning forward with a judge's irritating impartiality. "If you don't want her to, get a lawyer. You're his wife."

"What's the difference?" she says. A small child in the booth behind them is jiggling her seat, and a balloon of nausea rises from her stomach.

"Get his lawyer. The guy probably knows a lot. Where he's been, what he's been doing. You're an experienced gumshoe—this is a lead, right?" She shrugs. "You want to know, don't you?" She shrugs. "Alex, for God's sake, wake up! I know there's client privilege, but he's in a coma, and you're his wife."

"Yeah, you said that."

He sits back. "Are you afraid of what you might find out?" She plays with the plastic salt and pepper shakers, not to meet his eyes. "Cut it out. Spilling salt's bad luck." So? her lifted eyebrow says from where she's hunched over the square white grains. She's being a bitch and should quit it but can't.

"Damnit." He slams the shaker out of reach. "You don't want to know because you're angry. You hate his guts, you don't give a shit where he's been or what he's done—fine, admit it, it's nothing to be ashamed of. But quit wallowing. Get professional help if you need it."

She straightens, ashamed. "I'm sorry," she says in a dead voice. "You've been very good to me, and I know I should thank you. I don't hate him."

"It's a noble thing to save the world, but he didn't quite finish the job, and he put you through hell. You don't have to hate him, but it's also a decent thing to stay home and love your wife. He wasn't an MIA, Alex."

For a stunned second nothing happens. Then she flinches, and a whimper escapes the hand cupped to her mouth.

"What do I have to do to shock you? When are you going to react? Your mother all but abandons you, your father—and you'd rather lock it in a suitcase and drag it around for the rest of your life than get mad. There are some subjects on which you can't have no opinion. It's called repression, and it is every bit as bad for you as pepperoni."

She takes her hand away from her mouth. She hates words like *repression*, hates the "professional help" that use them. Man and his therapist instead of man and his conscience. She hates the way they talk about feelings, as if they are growths to be poked and prodded like tumors. She doesn't need a licensed Ph.D. to tell her she's malignant. She doesn't need him, daring her to get angry, waiting to win the Nobel Prize for discovering the miracle cure: take a little tantrum and call me in the morning.

But he's concerned—for that matter, he's right, but she's right too: it doesn't make any difference.

Kendrick sighs. "The point is he had a choice. You do too."

"Love him or leave him, you mean?" She snatches her hand from the table before he can grab it, but he's not going to let her off light. His eyes are steady. "Something like that."

"There wasn't a warrant, he could have just as easily gone home."

"It was a grandstand act."

"I never renounced him. I never renounced the Movement." But she'd said it herself: "If you're not part of the solution, you're part of the problem." The Underground had denounced her, and she never knew if that was why she couldn't find him or if Ted himself had put the word out. Some of them managed to keep touch with their families. Why didn't he? "The government was *wrong*."

But so had the government of the Movement gone awry. It is hardly a coincidence that, in the fallout, the country has turned so conservative. In 1964 some radicals had hoped Goldwater would win. But none of them planned this backlash, she's sure. In the end, for all the righteousness and rigid party lines, their politics were no more calculated than a dare. It turned out that revolution was fun. And what they had protested was as much the fact of government as its crimes, authority, parents no less than presidents. She had shared their anger but not their archetypal fury.

What is so hard, what is unendurable for her, is not his loss—she lost him a long time ago—but to imagine him all along, waiting. What did he see, nights, in the silver stretch of her body? Or did he just reach in the dark, eyes shining on the vanward masses?

"The government *is* wrong," Kendrick says. He is thinking of El Salvador, where the death squads patrol at this very moment with its blessing. "Do you still believe in the Revolution?" the reporter had asked her. *My god.* "I'm a photographer," she answered. "By definition an observer." Which wasn't the truth, because the eye is never neutral and every picture comments on the heart of the picture-maker.

"Is wrong," she agrees. She gives Kendrick a sad smile. "How does it go? 'If you're twenty and not a liberal, you have no heart, if you're forty and not a conservative, you have no brain.'" Let the platitude sum her, even though something wants to argue that justice is a matter for both. What she has learned from her life is that people rarely speak of freedom without coming to mean power. The angel of destruction plucks at the sleeve of the prophet's rag coat. She will never again trust herself to know the hairsbreadth of grace between God's pointed finger and the angel's mad claw.

"Go see him, Alex. You owe it to yourself."

She sighs. "It was all such a long time ago."

"That's why. See him. Let it go."

But she won't, and in the afternoon she changes her mind and goes looking for Ross.

Chapter 8

1960

Almost every morning Alex biked to Kendrick's apartment. She got used to the camera; she forgot it; sitting became the languid, dreamy way she passed time. He was new to Limestone; she had lived there all her life, and though in her opinion there was nothing to do or see, she was charmed to hear it seen with brand-new eyes. He had grown up in Ontario. When he was in high school, he used to hitch rides to Niagara Falls and take tourists' pictures for a dollar. Later he'd lived in New York, trying to freelance while he worked in the shipyard at Elizabeth. She thought it an incredible coincidence. Her mother had once lived in New York too, in Greenwich Village.

"How old were you when your parents divorced?" Kendrick asked, and, with a defiant tilt of her chin, she informed him that her parents had never married. He nodded. She didn't know what she'd expected him to do—slobber with sympathy, maybe, the way her friends' mothers did, even as they peered at her from behind their fingers and wagged their hateful tongues. She was no different from their daughters, all passing the endless sentence of their humdrum girlhoods. She felt sorry for herself, but that was only because her life was boring.

She was dazzled by his photographs, and he explained to her just how he'd accomplished each one. "The Ansel Adams thing," he'd say and demonstrate his filters. "Harry Callahan. Paul Strand." What he had done, he told her, was to imitate every major photographer in order to become a master of technique. That was his first step, learning. Finding his own vision was second. Of course he'd had it all along, but how could you really know what it was until you had the tools to use it? Then you began the first step, learning, all over again. That was the thrill of it, that cycle, which wasn't, strictly speaking, a cycle at all but something more like a spiral that took you closer to it every time.

Exactly what it was he didn't say. His eyes shone inward while his hands spun him off into the heavens. She was used to artists' talk: she had spent her childhood eavesdropping at her mother's parties. Artists bared their shining souls for the sake of self-enchantment. Only a novice would be touched; only a fool would be awed.

She was touched by his foolishness. She was awed by herself. Because she was his vision, she knew.

He showed her how to process film and print. Once she got over her horror of his basement—the very floor seemed to seep through the soles of her sandals, making her bare toes feel vulnerable and queasy; cobwebs brushed her face and naked arms until she felt tangled in a nasty, living lace of air—once her eyes adjusted to the amber depths of the safelight, she was fascinated to watch the blank white paper arrange its mystery of shadows beneath the sheen of the developer. The reflected glow of their two faces bent above the trays steadied her with wonder. Ascending from the darkroom, she would be as startled by the bright blocks of sunshine projected through the kitchen window as the audience at a slide show by the blinding white last frame. She wanted to be a photographer.

But as she wandered East Maple Street in the afternoons with Kendrick's Pentax, she didn't know what to photograph. She was too shy to snap the very pregnant Mrs. Ramirez or the silky retreat of Mrs. Chandra, whose adorable black-eyed baby peeked over her shoulder and begged remembering; she knew better than to try the alcoholics-in-training gathered on their porch next door. She was delighted when she found the blind man on the square, though the pictures weren't as powerful as she'd hoped. It was the angle, Kendrick said, predictable, too far away. She needed to overcome her timidity, learn to move her eye around. "A blind man." He laughed. "You must have thought you were stealing candy from a baby. Go ahead and get close enough to ask next time."

"You mean *ask* if I can take his picture?"

He handed the prints back with the one he liked best on top. "These are better than you think. You've got an eye."

"I heard you the first time," she sniffed, but later she promised herself *you've got an eye*, repeating it over and over in magisterial intonations. While he printed, she studied his books, hypnotized by the sensuous, singing light in the prints of Edward Weston, the majesty of Ansel Adams, and frank dispassion of Walker Evans, though because she had seen Kendrick's work first theirs seemed derivative.

They drove country roads and snapped pictures of each other. For fun he made a sandwich of two negatives, and they appeared together in a print. He never complained when she showed up uninvited or did his dishes or straightened his shelves. She scolded him about smoking, though he didn't really smoke. He had toyed with taking the habit up, he admitted, to cover the smell of the chemicals on his skin (secretly she liked that faint reminder of the darkroom), and now his mother kept giving him pipes. "That's what I mean," she said. "Twiddling around with an empty pipe looks dumb." And overnight his pipes were gone.

Once she arrived to find a woman asleep beside him—she'd been about to knock on the screen door when she glimpsed the platinum hair spread across his pillow, and she turned to go, but he must have heard her, for he called out her name. She waited on the steps, listening to the fan whirr with a dry heat behind her eyes, a deep flush spreading from her face down to her neck as her breath knotted in her throat. Then the screen door creaked, and he sat beside her. "You're up early today." He was barefoot and shirtless, and she saw how the straight dark blonde hairs on his chest grew in little eddies. "Want some breakfast?" Later she decided it had been a compliment that he didn't act apologetic. The three of them ate on the porch with their feet dangling from the railing. "What should I do about Casey?" his girlfriend kept asking, but Kendrick didn't answer, and after a while she quit. It was all Alex could remember anyone saying. The girl was humming under her breath and swaying her small blonde head when Alex left. His girlfriend was nothing to her. Already he was working on the show that would conclude the first year of his appointment, and though he had not said so, she understood that she would be its muse.

He printed her as she was; he double-exposed, tilted the easel and stretched her features, solarized her shadows into auras; with Kodalith he reduced her to lines. It pleased her that he didn't think he had to make her look pretty. She was pretty, she knew that. What he saw in her was something others never saw. Later she would pose by direction; for now she grimaced and preened and pouted and giggled, leaving the camera to make what it could of her whims. He had fallen in love with her face—large copper eyes fluted with green, the wide mouth as artless and provocative as a fey child's. Later she would not know whether she had fallen in love with the camera or the cameraman.

He was scrupulous not to touch her, leaving her limbs to discover their own arrangement for sittings; when they bumped in the darkroom they sprang quickly apart. In the fall he would be teaching in the same department with her mother. It was not in his best interest to do anything that might be mistaken for a gesture, although he phrased his fear as principles. He had a whole list of reasons why they should not get involved, but since neither of them had suggested that they should, the fact of the list, discreetly put in the third person (*teachers who dated students were ... older men*—he was twenty-seven—*should not ...*), only promised that they would. "You should have a boyfriend. Why don't you have a boyfriend?" he would ask, and she would smile politely, and they would let it go.

In August they drove to the house in the country he'd told her about. The station wagon whipped around a green curve, and there it sat, as if a tornado had dropped it there from Oz. A tall stone beaux-arts chateau in the style of a Second Empire townhouse, with a mansard roof of deep gray slate cut in hexagonal plates like fish scales, a chin of weathered black guttering and in the center a single round window sunk in somber moldings like a heavily rimed eye, it looked exactly as Alex had always imagined the House of Usher, luckless and gloomy in the middle of a bright, buzzing field.

Kendrick wanted to go in.

"Somebody lives there." Alex hung back, but the curtain she noticed in an upstairs window was rotting, and the lawn had long since been choked by wild carrot and goldenrod. They waded through the singing weeds to the cellar door, which gave when Kendrick tapped it. "Hello! Anybody home?" Something skittered on the steps, and a snake flashed an opalescent stripe as it slid into the weeds. She clutched at his sleeve, and he allowed that perhaps they should try the front.

The lock was broken. A thin gray light dusted the central hall, where part of the ceiling lay shattered on the parquet floor, and their own powdery footprints followed them in and out of the empty rooms. In the kitchen even the sink had been ripped from the wall, silhouette sunk into the streaked layers of paint and grime, the linoleum littered with emphatic black droppings. In the stairwell baubles of amber, ruby, and bottle-blue light from the stained glass window seemed to roll past them down the stairs. When they tracked into the bedrooms, Alex held her breath and listened, but the only sounds were the slap-slapping of her rubber flipflops and deeper clap of Kendrick's work boots, and a sudden blaze of light that sent her backwards was only the sun caught in a jagged piece of mirror.

"It's hard to believe somebody hasn't made off with that window," Kendrick observed as they returned to the hall to search for the attic stairs. The stairs twisted upward, tilting crazily as the streets in an Expressionist painting. "Too dark," he admitted as he sent the weak beam of a keyring flashlight into the gloom. In the bathroom she crouched to photograph the cracked toilet bowl while he checked the rooms again, choosing the curtained bedroom for its tattered gauze of light.

He set the case of film holders inside the door and headed back to the car for the camera and tripod, handing her a china flower with a button that said *cold*. "A souvenir."

She slipped it into the pocket of her yellow shorts. "I wonder who lived here."

"Evan Beauman."

"How do you know?"

"Also Mrs. Beauman and all the little Beaumans: Ernest, Clark, Samantha, Roderick, and Clarice. I looked it all up in the county records."

"Roderick. I told you it was the House of Usher. *Clarice*." Alex did a pirouette, but the faucet dragged at her waistband, and she crashed into the wall. She rubbed her arm. "I bet she was spoiled. I bet she ran away when she was sixteen and married some incredibly handsome rogue that nobody approved of."

"Rogue?" He looked amused.

"A gambler," she decided. Darker than her father, with a narrow black moustache and dusky flags of color on his cheeks, but giving off the same high scent of whiskey and cologne. She would have liked to find a family album, but the scavengers who had carted the heirlooms off to auction would have hardly overlooked such treasure.

"Didn't say. Evan founded the Beauman Quarry and built the railroad to move the stone. When he died the house and business passed to Ernest, who left them to his daughter Jane, who's in a nursing home."

"How boring."

He laughed. "Are all girls your age so romantic?"

Stung, Alex watched from the upstairs window as his gait lengthened to descend the shallow hill to the road, where the station wagon sat parked in the shade of a dying oak.

She picked up the broken mirror. Her face was filthy. Half moons of sweat stained her blouse beneath her armpits. It was too short to stay tucked in, and her shorts were smirched where she wiped her hands in the darkroom. At home in her closet there was a blotch of wine on her favorite white dress. Didn't he ever get tired of photographing a sloppy schoolgirl in her stupid rainbow of summer shorts? But he never asked her to wear anything special, and she dressed for the bike ride to his house. He still paid her every time she sat. She kept his checks in the drawer with his photographs and her socks. He should have known a girl her age wouldn't have a bank account.

She glanced out the window again. He was bent over the tailgate, a streak of dirt across the back of his blue shirt, a slice of sunlight on his shoulder. On that morning when he made breakfast, she had watched him bend over the oven for the toast, vertebrae rising beneath his skin; then he had straightened, and the ridge sank into a hollow. When he had turned, flushed with the heat, a sheen of sweat in the scrim of dark blond hair that spread across his chest and narrowed at his stomach, she had turned away, because it seemed, suddenly, as if he had been right, she should have agreed the very first time he called that, yes, she would have to ask her mother.

Two white butterflies tumbled over the field mustard and harebell. The air was drier today, but upstairs it was hot. She fanned her face with her hand. What had the Beauman women done to keep cool? Clarice. Dark-haired, she bet, with coal-black eyes and high color on her cheekbones. Gone without a note at sixteen, eloped with a devastating stranger; dead at seventeen of fever. Or childbirth, for which she would have been too delicate. Or maybe she had been just a big-boned, raw-faced girl who married a slack-jawed farmer and raised six kids and lost her figure and her spirit and died of an unbecoming old age like her niece Jane in a nursing home. Alex would have liked to see a picture.

She unbuttoned her blouse. Underneath was a poorly fitted brassiere of white cotton. She took it off. Then her shorts, the faucet clunking dully on the floor. Her underpants, also cotton, printed with little blue flowers that probably showed through her shorts in good light. Without clothes she felt clean. She was beautiful in the way that the ugliness of Walker Evans' sharecroppers was beautiful for that one eternal moment of their art.

She picked up the jagged mirror again. The edge bit her finger, and she licked a drop of blood gritty with plaster. It broke when she heard his step in the hall and dropped it.

"Seven years bad luck," he observed after a minute, his voice choked with dust, and began the ritual fuss of adjustments that set up his camera. The latches of the film case snapped. She clutched her blouse. His first shot caught her still bunching the blouse in an uncertain fist at her chin, dirty face half turned away, eyes looking back, enormous, wary, wounded. In the silence a faint odor of decay that seemed to linger from the Beaumans mixed with the sharp, dry smell of the crumbled plaster and slightly rank scent of her own skin. "How's your father's movie coming?" he asked finally. For a moment she was speechless with rage. Then she let the blouse fall and lay with her back to him in the web of light.

"Has it been cast yet?"

She closed her eyes. The floor crawled beneath her cheek. She felt his adjustments as a tremor in the floorboards, hard against her hipbone. Her body didn't fit the floor, the way a body doesn't fit a bed when it can't sleep. When she heard the shutter again, she sat up, still facing away, arms resting on the windowsill, chin on her folded hands. Across the field the rails of the track gleamed in the sunlight. The air shimmered with silver and gold.

At his request she stood. Her legs were numb; all the nerve endings prickled, more sharply than the dizziness that swam through her as she turned back to the blind gray darkness of the room, slouching against the wall, rotten curtain bunching on one shoulder. She had to force herself not to flinch.

The minister disappeared beneath the black cloth. When his foot knocked against the tripod, he swore. He had run out of things to say, and it seemed to her that the room had grown so quiet they could hear the dust motes twirling in the air.

After he had exposed all ten sheets of film, he snapped the locks of the aluminum case, folded the tripod, and took off his glasses to skim the sweat from the bridge of his nose. They left mean red marks like parentheses on either side. Alex turned her face back to the window. If he gave her a check she would kill him, she would rip his stupid face open with her nails. "If you can bring the film, we'll only need one trip," he said.

Her clothes felt as if they'd grown spores. Fiercely she buttoned her blouse, snaring her fingers in the holes, refusing to do it over when they came out wrong. She left the faucet on the windowsill, though she would have rather hurled it through the pane.

He was sitting on the tailgate by the time she stepped blinking into the sunlight. "I think the quarry's over there." He pointed to the woods beyond the field. "No doubt the track runs toward it. I could use a dip. How about you?"

They followed the railroad until he picked out a faint path downhill. Alex slapped a daddy longlegs from her arm. "They hit the spring in Ernest's time," he explained and went on about his adventure at the county courthouse, something about a half-deaf clerk in charge of records, Alex wasn't listening, she didn't care. She kept her eyes fixed ahead and willed her field of vision to narrow until the black edges met and closed.

A cold breath rose along her legs as the quarry opened below, rock walls shearing down to a pool of still green water. Kendrick led the way to a shelf just above, scraping back branches, warning her of treacherous roots and rocks. A stone slid underneath her sandal; she grasped at a sapling, and the leaves came off. Wobbling, she kept balance, and he withdrew his offered hand.

"Hey, this is great," he cried. Not waiting for her, he stripped and dove. She caught the white flash of his buttocks.

When he surfaced, he slicked his hair back. His eyes looked weak without his glasses, which lay beside her on the rock. She felt like crushing them, like grinding them beneath her foot and flinging them in.

"It's freezing!" he yelled.

She put her head down on her knees.

"Oh come on in, it's not that cold." His voice echoed off the cliffs. "It feels great." She didn't answer. "Refreshing. What's the matter?" he called, but he didn't reach for her ankle or climb out to coax her in. What he saw in her was safely stored inside the insulated bag, in a portfolio on East Maple Street, in her drawer. What he wanted from her had been taken. It was the record of the light she happened to bend.

She turned her back on him while he dressed, then had to listen to him drip and enthuse all the way back to the car.

"Let's go get a burger," he suggested. "I really feel like sinking my teeth into some meat after that swim. No kidding, I feel just like Tarzan. You don't know what you missed not going in."

A dragonfly hovered beside her, suspended on iridescent pastel wings. The light through the trees turned the leaves translucent. Overhead the sky was a tumble of bright clouds. He held out a milkweed. Their eyes met, and then she looked away.

Always she thought she would remember this moment. What she intended to remember was the color of the light.

Chapter 9

1965

Late in the day after Ted spoke at the Wallace demonstration the personnel manager at Vardys summoned her to his office and informed her that her services would no longer be required. It made her angry. All day he had known he was going to fire her but waited until the lines shut down. He hadn't let her say goodbye to the women.

But in the morning she took the luxury of her leisure and overslept. When she woke Ted was sitting on the floor in his sheepskin jacket. "Let's go for a picnic," he said, unpacking his grocery sack to show her the cheese and and bread and fancy tins.

"I thought you had a class." The bag rattled as he repacked it. "Ted! It's January. The ground's wet." He unfurled her corduroy coat. "It's too cold for a picnic," she laughed.

At Silverstone State Park the tables had been stacked at one end of the pavilion for the season, and they spread their feast on the stone ledge overlooking the lake. Mist blurred the spidery black gnarl of the shoreline, where melting snow had brought water seeping over the end of the wood dock. Ted poured wine in Dixie cups, and settled against a stone pillar, reaching around to clack their cups in toast. "Do you mind having dinner with my sister this weekend? My folks sent her money to take me out. I guess they figured if they sent it to me I'd give it to the poor folk."

His twenty-first birthday was Sunday. After some hesitation Alex had selected a baseball glove; he didn't want things, of course, but she hoped he might like that.

"Of course not." Occasionally Jeannie stopped by Dogpatch, the name she had bestowed upon the Crow Hill project, dangling her car keys and folding her legs beneath her on the sofa as she kept a wry surveillance on the bohemian specters of Nelson and Stacy. "My brother, the little friend of all the world," she called him, but for all their differences, Ted and Jeannie shared a past, and Alex was intrigued by the ironic affection that glimmered through their conversation. Ted's descriptions of his parents were so vague: his father was "a businessman," his mother "an aged-out Junior Leaguer more upset I went to jail than I was beaten." But all Alex learned listening to Jeannie was that the cottage the Neals rented on Cape Cod each year had quirky plumbing, Mom wore funny hats, and Dad ordered "wanton" soup in Chinese restaurants.

"I think we should use the occasion to tell her we're engaged." Seated against him, Alex turned her head back. She had assumed they'd simply go down to the courthouse one day. Engagements meant diamond rings and bridal showers. She hadn't expected he would want anything like that. "The demonstration yesterday—there's never going to be an issue as clear as civil rights again. Not for us."

She inched away. "So you figure what we ought to do about it is get married?"

"If you want to." He stood, then leaned down to pick up a stone and skipped it over the lake. "You're likely to lose more jobs on account of me."

"It was a crummy job. I don't even know why I got fired. I took a sick day and I wasn't sick. Maybe they didn't like my work."

"Maybe. But the FBI keeps files. They find the bodies of the civil rights workers, and blame us for going down there." He faced her. "I don't want to force this on you."

"Nelson and Stacy think getting fired's the best thing I've ever done."

"Screw Nelson and Stacy. You're not marrying them."

But I am, she wanted to say, *I'm marrying everything that comes with you*. She wanted what came with him. "I care about people too. I'm just not political like they are, I don't think about the state night and day."

"You want to take pictures." He poured more wine. "I didn't go to Mississippi to save the Negro—I went to save myself." But to do the one he had to do the other. He was always separating out his motivation, while she saw the impulse and act as one.

"I can't feel that constant swell about causes. Stacy says it's the daily shit that gets you down, but it's not just that. I'm not like you. Something has to make the causes real for me."

"Demonstrations are cathartic. I think we have them for ourselves as much as anyone." He stood. "Civil rights is real all right. But it's over for white people."

"She feels for what she wants to accomplish."

"A just society—that's what I want to accomplish. Ought to be easy, right?" He flashed a smile. "Why do you think Nelson always comes back to Wallace? He could do his work anywhere, but this is where he's known." His eyes darkened. "I don't want to be some campus hero. I want to change the world."

"You were wonderful yesterday."

"I have a talent for speaking." He said it as if he were saying he had gray eyes, a sturdy build, or brown hair. "Sometimes it scares me." He took a few steps toward the lake and turned around. "I don't want to be glib. The blacks thought I was glib. They resented my speaking even more than they resented Nelson. You don't know what it was like in Mississippi. They needed us, but they didn't want us there." He toed a root. "The organizers. The people did want us—they looked up to us because we were white. And there you have it."

Back at the shelter he tore off hunks of French bread, cut wedges of cheese and opened tins, licking the oil from his fingers. They left the crumbs for the squirrels, and in the car she snuggled against him, thinking with almost unbearable happiness of the brimming life stretched out before her.

"What did you want to be when you grew up?" she asked.

"Ordinary." His long dimples opened. "Actually I wanted to be a baseball player. Ordinary is what I was. I didn't set out to be a radical."

She sat up. "How did you get involved in the civil rights movement?"

"Garth. He was my instructor for Western Civ."

"I didn't know Garth was your teacher." So he had been Garth's protégé. She wondered if that was the reason they were on Crow Hill instead of meeting on campus. There were so many things they had neglected to tell each other. She sat up. "So it's official? We're getting married?"

"Yes ma'am."

She gave him a sideways look. "And this is your idea of a proposal?"

"I proposed the first time we ever talked."

"You talked about politics."

"I always talk about politics." He paused. "Why do you think I wanted you to come to Mississippi?"

"But I didn't go."

"So I'm asking again. Will you come now?"

"Okay," she said, settling back against him. "Okay then. Yes I will."

She took a job shelving books in the Wallace library, which gave her a staff ID and the use of the darkroom in the Student Union. Her portraits of the Crow Hill children earned her the right to ask if she might photograph the parents. They thought she was crazy, of course (that edge of suspicion sharpened the pictures), but they were people whose lives had passed for the most part unrecorded, and she suspected that secretly they might rejoice in the immortality the camera offered. Through her lens she looked, really looked at them for the first time, and what she saw touched her even more than the dejected landscape, ragged clothes, and blighted teeth. It was the minute twitch of muscle, the effort of the face in service of the most profoundly self-conscious moment it knows, that eternal fraction of the second when the camera takes aim and the body whispers *fidget* while the mind insists *sit still.*

She bought Polaroids and led the children on a shoot around the Hill. "You got somebody in there?" they asked when she lingered at the edge of a weedy graveyard. "What're we supposed to take pitchers of?" Billy whined. "Ain't nothin anybody'd want a pitcher of up here." She saw what bound Ted to Crow Hill. If there was frustration in failure, there was also the satisfaction of knowing the experience to be genuine. She lived in the real world too.

Was it because they had no time together that they never argued? Ted was always at a meeting or on the phone, though he managed to catch her eye whenver he was in the room. He had a quick temper but was slow to show it; she recognized it only in a slight prickle in the air, an almost imperceptible compression of his jaw, the way his cheekbones seemed to flatten, the bracing at the back of his eyes. For all his geniality, he was less tolerant of people than she was. He lacked her feel for domestic life, the capacity for pleasure in its daily rituals. She was glad they never fought.

Stacy and Matt fought. They broke up, and the collective endured a week of barbed silences, blazing whispers, and pointed third-person remarks. Matt brought a girl from Holy Trinity back to Dogpatch, and Alex sat up with Stacy in the living room as the chords of "Michael Rowed the Boat Ashore" rippled off to whimpers in the bedroom.

"Alleluia! Well, she can have the creep," Stacy snapped.

"How could you?" Alex accused him the next day, and he pouted. "Where else was I supposed to go? Judy lives in a dorm."

The next night Stacy brought home a Negro, and Nelson, who approved in theory but objected to sharing the living room with anyone but Peggy, stomped out. A week later Stacy was back in the bedroom with Matt, Nelson was back on the living room sofa, and the collective heaved a collective sigh of relief.

The house was simply too small for five people.

Never mind that sixteen volunteers had shared a Freedom House not much bigger. It staggered Alex, who had grown up in what seemed like acres of cool, creamy space, to think of the families around them crammed into two and three rooms. In Asia generations shared a single room. Here the roommates stumbled into one another in the bathroom, couldn't have diarrhea or make love without the walls thumping out a report. They had no central heat, and winter settled in their spines like an ache. Yet Alex was content. The very air seemed a rich, dense breath of moods as nourishing and cloying as a greenhouse.

The pace of their lives picked up. Four days after Alex was fired Martin Luther King was arrested in Selma, Alabama, where 250 Negroes were jailed for demanding their voting rights. On the other side of the world the National Liberation Front of South Vietnam attacked Pleiku. Ten days after Alex was fired, Lyndon Johnson ordered American planes to bomb North Vietnam and stepped up the draft. Within days of Johnson's order there was a demonstration on campus. Dogpatch had acquired another TV, and at night they watched the ordeal in Selma on Huntley-Brinkley. A white minister from Boston was beaten to death, and again they were hoisting signs, unfurling banners, joining hands and singing in Wallace Square.

Stacy wanted to go to Selma for the march to Montgomery. "Civil rights is over for whites," Ted kept insisting, but the murders of Jimmy Lee Jackson and Reverend Reeb brought the summer in Mississippi back. The Alabama state police charged into the marchers, hurling tear gas, using firehoses and whips, beating them with a savagery that left Alex shocked. "Jesus Christ," Stacy sobbed. "It looks like a war." "It is a war," Nelson said. Ted turned off the TV. "I'm going," he decided.

They were also going to the antiwar march in Washington. "The war is a symptom. It does not address the fundamental problems in American society," Garth cautioned, though of course he and Lizzie were going. Everyone was going. Ted, who mistrusted single issues, was almost anxious to have the marches over so they could return their attention to the problems on Crow Hill. Nelson was moving toward the mainstream of the antiwar movement, Stacy was kicking around the idea of joining VISTA, and Matt was glum. VISTA had it all over Dogpatch: it was funded; it was organized. It was also run by the government that wouldn't send in troops to protect the Negroes in Alabama but had no problem dispatching them to bomb North Vietnam. Having worked in Johnson's campaign, she felt personally betrayed, and she stormed through the house slamming doors until Ted said, "Stacy, we all hate the war, but I like my eardrums." She burst into tears, and Alex realized that it was as much Matt as VISTA that Stacy couldn't make up her mind about.

They drove all night, loaded down with bedrolls, sandwiches, and cookies. Alex rolled down the windows, letting in the damp night air. There was something deeply sensual about driving at night, in the darkness of the landscape slipping by, in the wan green glow of the dashboard and humming of the tires, in the fatigue that spread like a sweet syrup through their bones. In the backseat Stacy and Matt slept in a heap. In the front seat she and Ted kept cozy silence. She liked that about him, his ability to make silence intimate. On those nights when they retired while the others argued on, she felt a quietude as warm and friendly as sleep.

Nelson was riding with Garth. Ted had talked Lizzie out of bringing Tice. "If he were a little black baby, you wouldn't say a word," she argued, but she'd known she wouldn't be going—she just needed to be assured she was not a coward. The protests at Wallace were not like Selma with its threat of violence. If anything they were too safe; lacking risk, they lacked drama, and Alex could see the impatience for excitement on Ted's face. From the first images on TV, she had moved through her days with a dull anger drumming in her veins. Like everyone else, she wanted to go to the front.

Yet, as they stood in Selma, listening to Martin Luther King—"You will be the people that will light a new chapter in the history books of our nation," he told them—as they moved out in flank, her heart was overcome with peace.

Then they passed over the Pettus Bridge, where the state troopers had laid siege, and even as the girders shook, she felt her heart freeze. The face of the country spread out before her, impersonal as any name they had tried to give it, but for the first time in her experience palpable, as real as the broken pipe beneath her kitchen sink. Bayonets affixed to their rifles, the newly federalized Alabama Guard stood between the marchers and the caravans of cars painted blood-red with epithets. Behind the waving Confederate flags faces contorted with hate. But that was not the face of America; the face of America was the Guard. It had been ordered to protect them, though she had no doubt that its sympathies were with the bigots.

They marched till dusk. The air was colder than she'd expected, and she pulled Ted's wool shirt closer as they waited to board the bus that would take them back to Selma, for only 300 of the 2500 who began the march were permitted to walk the two-lane highway to Montgomery. There was a blister on her heel, and on the bus she bent to unlace her boot. Standing beside the driver with a clipboard, a young Negro in horn-rimmed glasses read instructions. They were to stay off the streets; if they were taunted under no circumstances were they to answer back. "Teague Parker," Ted whispered. "He was at the training camp in Ohio."

"The federal government has made efforts to ensure your safety," Parker announced to hisses and scattered bursts of laughter.

For three nights they bedded down on the floor of a Negro church. It had seemed unwise to bring her camera, but Alex wished she had brought a book. In the kitchen at another church, Negro women were cooking for the marchers; a dozen white volunteers drove shiny new garbage pails of spaghetti and beans out to the camps, but there weren't enough jobs to go around. Rain thrummed on the windowsills as Alex studied the faces of Ted's friends. They had gone to Mississippi to risk their lives; it had not occurred to them that they would come to Selma to be bored.

But Wednesday the mood turned festive. All afternoon the volunteers were driven out to rejoin the march, with all the shouting and honking of a football Saturday at Wallace. In the morning the air crackled with energy. As they strode into Montgomery a sudden downpour washed the mud from their faces and strung bright beads of water through their hair. They reached the capitol in streaks of sunlight, 25,000 strong.

Staring at the drawn blind of the governor's office, she remembered the day he spoke at Wallace. *Freedom now*, Ted had said, and she felt the justice of those words beneath them like a tide. Martin Luther King was speaking again. "How long? How long?" The whole crowd swayed as his voice rose. And then they were clapping and shouting until she felt the earth shudder.

The next morning they heard that one of the white drivers who had ferried marchers back to Selma had been murdered.

A month later, standing in Washington, with the warmth of the sun soaking into her shoulders under a dome of bright blue sky, Alex thought about the murdered white driver. She had a name, Mrs. Viola Liuzzo, and a face, for she had greeted them at the hospitality desk at Brown Chapel. And now she was as dead as the nameless Asian women who had the bad luck to be born in a bug-ridden little country the rest of the world couldn't seem to leave alone.

Alex's earliest notions of war came from the patriotic texts she had read in fourth or fifth grade. In ninth grade Jo Yellen had a crush on a boy who played bass drum for the Limestone High School Marching Band—perhaps she met him at the pool, Alex didn't remember how she and Jo came to be at the muddy football field behind Limestone High. What she remembered was Ricky Clapp, the bass drummer who led the band across the field at half time, poor Ricky Clapp, tumbling head over drum into the endzone, where someone had forgotten to remove the string that marked the goal line chalked earlier that week. How tidily the band had fallen, trombones, tubas, clarinets, all dropping row by row after Ricky. At fourteen, her image of war had been something like that, a series of uniformed lines stepping up to fire and fall dead, until at last a line held, the white flag went up, and everyone shook hands. War had seemed a sport more disciplined than football, which she was unaccustomed to watching and could not follow, those unruly heaps of bodies smeared with mud until she couldn't tell the dark jerseys from the light and had to ask Jo who had the ball, which team was winning. "Who cares?" Jo had sobbed, her eyes red with sorrow for Ricky.

A year ago Alex had never heard of Vietnam, and even now the war she had discovered in Mississippi and Alabama was more real to her than the bombs dropping twelve thousand miles away. Here, on the slope behind the Washington Monument, where as many as had marched into Montgomery were gathered, the air was so sweet with promise that it was possible to believe in renewal. Signs calling for withdrawal floated against the sky as vendors moved through the crowd with buttons. Stretching out on the grass to listen to the speeches, she took off her sandals to pull the warm blades up between her toes. There was no government on earth that could resist the temptation of life such a day offered.

In July Johnson began a massive infusion of ground troops, and Stacy tore up her application for VISTA. Congress dragged its feet on the

Voting Rights Bill amid rumors that the President had made a deal. On Crow Hill the stench of garbage rose from the woods, mingling with the fetid odor of outside toilets. Ted wanted to apply for a grant and recruit volunteers from the Wallace med school to staff a free clinic. "Man, I want to get busted for something bigger than dispensing aspirin without a license," Nelson said. All summer they argued about what they should do while history held its breath and decided what it would do with them. In August Alex married Ted in a double ring ceremony in the limestone Wallace Chapel, and when the minister asked who gave this woman, she answered, "I do."

Chapter 10

1982

It keeps happening. Monday at the Village. This morning in the darkroom. Photography students all seem to be afflicted with synesthesia. Turn off the lights, and they assume no one can hear them. As soon as they close the doors to the film closets they start confessing. Over the years, passing through the photo lab or working in the space set aside for faculty, Alex has overheard everything from drug deals to love's ecstatic moans and tearful pleadings.

"What did you and your boyfriend do this weekend?" one of the girls on the other side of the wall has asked.

"Fought," the other answers. DJ, the girl with the spiked black hair in Alex's 244. "It's something we can do together." They laugh, and in the faculty darkroom Alex smiles. For the first time in weeks she is printing, and even in the reeking cubicle she has a bright, new-penny sense of the fresh near-spring morning sun outside. Her head feels as clear as if she's exercised. She slides her print into the hypo-clear and turns on the light. It's a nude shot of Ross, one hip flecked with light coming through her textured white curtain. Though the print will have to dry down, she's pleased with the image. Flipping off the light, she fits another sheet of paper into the easel. The curtain needs burning in.

"Don't you think Ross has interesting ideas?" Lori Sweet. Alex's hand pauses on the raised frame of the easel. Lori is in Ross's class. "Sometime I'd like to get him off by himself and feed him some wine and talk."

"If I ever got *him* off by himself," DJ says, "you could forget the wine and the talk."

Alex drops the frame, tearing the paper, as the girls yip with laughter. Furiously she yanks the paper safe open. Her face is hot. She doesn't want to print after all.

Monday at the Village she'd been half-listening to a drone of conversation in the booth behind her when someone asked distinctly, "What did Ross say?" and suddenly she was straining to separate the answer from the cacophony of a crowded lunch hour. At least the tall wooden back of the booth saved her the embarrassment of swiveling to see the speaker, but then she had to sit while Kendrick and Dave Sheron from Design gassed over the same old art school business, hoping all the while they would leave before the girls in the next booth did. She couldn't catch the response; the other girls seemed to have hushed, powdery voices, sexy in the same way his is. She was disgusted with herself, but that didn't keep her from wanting a look, and she figured it served her right that by the time Dave checked his watch and said, "I've got to hit it," the waitress was already wiping the girls' table.

As soon as she's packed up her paper, she turns on the light and removes her negative from the enlarger.

When they left the Village the low cloudbank had opened into a thin gray drizzle. She and Kendrick shared her umbrella back to the Pollak Building while Dave ducked across Grace to the shoe repair. At a squeal of brakes Alex turned around. Half a block up Harrison, Dave turned too. His curly gray hair had been black when she was hired. Standing in the rain with his shirt sticking to his belly, he looked like an old man, though he is only a few years older than she is.

"Are you going to Buck's after the opening?" Lori asks. "He got a keg of green beer."

March 17. The B.F.A. Show opens at the Anderson Gallery this afternoon. Fifteen days since Ted was shot.

When she's dumped the trays and rinsed them, Alex looks at her print again and laughs. It's washing. Until this moment she's failed to consider how she's going to dry it.

She can hardly put it through the lab dryer—she might as well post it on her door. On her knees she hunts the cupboards beneath the counter for a blotter, but comes up empty-handed. She could tear it up, but isn't that the way guilty lovers always get caught, the jigsaw of evidence hidden in the trash? The pose is much too genuine for anyone to believe that Ross is just a model. He had fallen asleep.

Friday she moved back to West Avenue, telling Kendrick she felt better. She does feel better. Some of the time. Precisely the amount of time she's spent in bed with Ross, so giddy with sex it feels like an emotion. There is no reason for her to feel guilty—male professors bed their students all the time, and she tells herself that every time Justine calls or she sees Kendrick at school. She was relieved when Dave joined them at the Village Monday. She's been trying to avoid him.

Maybe there's a blotter roll in her office.

In the hall she passes Ross, in a melon-colored sweater that warms his skin a shade and causes a muscle deep inside her crotch to contract.

"Hi," he says.

"Hi." She can't permit herself to turn her head.

There are no blotters in her office or the Department office. "One of your students called," the secretary says. "She's wants to talk to you about her portfolio at four."

"I have a meeting." She forgot and will have to tell Ross, who seems to think that she has obliged her afternoons to him. He has a surly streak, she's discovered. "I'm sorry," she said yesterday, when she met with the Search Committee. "I know how you feel." Which didn't help a bit, not to mention that she doesn't know how he feels. She doesn't want to go to these meetings; she has to, and Ross ought to be smart enough to figure out that anyone would rather make love than discuss a university budget crunch.

"Alex?" Kendrick calls from the inner office.

"Yo," she says.

"Have you got a minute?"

He closes the door behind her and sits at his desk with such a grave face that her stomach swoops and regret chills the flesh along her arms. She's committed moral turpitude. He'll have to fire her, and he won't be lying when he says this hurts him as much as it hurts her. She should have thought of that. She might not owe anything to Ted, but how could she be so heedless of him?

"The deans's put a freeze on hiring."

She's too angry to notice if she feels relieved. "What about the Kemp line? After we've already interviewed?" Disgusted, she drops back in her seat, staring at the fluorescent lights reflected in his glasses.

Kendrick is shuffling class schedules. "Can you meet tomorrow at 3:30?"

"Sure." Another afternoon gone. Ross hasn't said where he spends the nights. She knows where he lives, but she's much too proud to walk by, checking for lights like a lovesick sophomore. She can hardly let him spend the nights with her.

"I'll put a note in your box." His chair creaks as he leans back. "Want to catch dinner after the opening?"

She plies a loose thread at the knee of her jeans. She was counting on time with Ross before. Then, when she saw him across the crowded rooms, both of them still flushed and warm from her bed, she would feel a delicious secret between them. As it is they will quarrel; she'll watch him banter with his friends and feel instead the mistake. He won't come to West Avenue after. He'll be going on to celebrate. For all she knows his family will be coming. She should go to dinner with Kendrick. "Not tonight," she says.

His chair squeaks again as his weight drops forward. "Are you doing okay?"

"You keep asking me that."

"I'm interested," he says mildly.

"You're sweet." Behind his glasses, his eyes have dimmed. She stands. "Listen, you wouldn't happen to have a blotter roll in here, would you?"

"Printing?" He rummages in the piles of equipment that clutter his office.

"Umhm."

"New work? I'd love to see it."

She rubs her jaw. What if Ross is the same break for her work that she was for Kendrick's? She can't show the pictures. With an inward smile she summons a half-remembered African proverb: the problem is not how to steal the king's bugle but where to play it.

"I'm not ready to show it yet," she says as Kendrick pulls a blotter roll from a metal cabinet. "Thanks."

He sits again. "Please don't tell me something's wrong with the dryer."

"No. I'm just … not ready to show it." She always feels like a fool repeating a lie. Or the half-truth meant as a lie. At the door, she stops. "Maybe we could have dinner tomorrow night." She's sorry as soon as she says it. Tonight Ross will have plans, but tomorrow … "I can do a curry. Or would you rather have pasta?"

"You don't need to cook."

"Something light? Veal piccata. Chicken tarragon?" Her voice sounds dizzy. He keeps looking at her in that way that makes her feel transparent.

"Why don't we just go out?" he says.

When she reaches the photo lab, Ross is standing in the doorway with his back to her, talking to Lori and DJ, who gaze up at him so moonily she'd like to slap them both. He's spoiled with sex. Do they have to roll over and wag their tails too? Neither woman seems to notice her; she has to squeeze past them, and only then do they chorus a weak "Hi."

In the darkroom she sags against the stool. At home, in her bed, she may tell herself that she should have had this affair years ago and mean it as congratulations, but here, at school, it is clearly so miscast that the least hello in the hall is tinged with her desperation. It's degrading, everywhere she turns, to catch the word or glimpse that makes her feel as if she's spying. She should have had an affair years ago, yes, but not this one. And yet, even as she knows how foolish it is, how utterly adolescent, all she has to do is hear his name or see him disappearing around a corner to be stung with jealousy and longing.

Years ago when she thought about taking a lover, she used to think if Ted wasn't dead, then he deserved it, and if he was he wouldn't care. She just never met anyone who interested her enough. And now, of all possibilities, a student. True, she knows male faculty do it all the time, but that doesn't make her feel easier, it doesn't make it right.

At Ross's knock her hands tense on the lip of the sink, and she closes her eyes. She wants to see him, wants him to come to her until he does, and then she's irritated. He has no sense of discretion. She lets him in, lets him kiss her until her head is light, then pulls away. "Are you crazy?"

He shrugs, a reckless half-smile on his face. "About you."

"Keep your voice down," she reminds him. He steps to the sink and turns the water on, then slides a finger down her ear, so lightly the sensation is gone by the time she jerks her head. Except the sex, all their gestures seem intolerably self-conscious. She no longer has the luxury of observing him, and she misses with a renewed pang those moments when, on a platform, across a room or a dinner table laid for a dozen, some small, artless motion in Ted's body would catch her eye, filling her with a lust so vivid with tenderness that it stands in her mind as the very panorama of love. She turns away, busying herself with the blotter. "I have a meeting this afternoon."

"Skip it." His breath stirs her hair as he rubs her shoulders.

"I can't."

He drops his hands. "You had a meeting yesterday."

"And I have another one tomorrow." He picks up her print, examining it without comment. Surely he knows she's going to break it off. She has to. She just wants to sleep with him one more time before she does.

When she's laid the proof sheet and test strips in the roll, she holds out her hand, and he gives her the print. It doesn't seem to bother him a bit that she's photographed him without his consent. "Are you trying to tell me something?"

She looks at her boots. She should end it now and get it over with. "I told you already. I have a meeting. Grow up, and you'll learn about these things." But he chooses not to bristle, instead waits while she ties the blotter, then pulls her to him, his hands slipping beneath her cotton sweater to the bare flesh of her back, sending splintery little thrills down her spine as he kisses her again, deeply, and presses the length of his body against hers until desire rises inside her like sap, and she has to fight the tingling in her breasts and hollow ache between her legs to repel him. "I can't do this. Not here. Not now." Her chest heaves. For a moment they exchange baleful stares. His eyes are black with indignation. Let him think it's because the floor is filthy, or that she draws the line at school property; she wants him too badly to refrain for either reason, and that is the reason: she can't give him that much power. Doesn't he realize someone might hear them?

"I wanted to see you," he says simply.

The roll of her eyes escapes him. Men claim to be the rational sex, but it's her observation that the irrational is their genius. They have the shrewdness of the two-year-old who refuses to accept no for an answer. For a moment she sees Ted again, standing in the kitchen of the apartment in Colorado. "You got in my head," he says. But that was different. She was always going to go with Ted, from the moment she first saw him. The only power Ross has over her is sex. For which she resents him. What surprises her is how much the resentment hones desire. Her knees are weak; his presence brings all her blood to the surface of her skin and clots the air until she's short of breath. Carefully she squats to stack the trays beneath the counter. "Did I tell you I found a used rubber in the darkroom?" She straightens. "Kids crawl under the counters to screw. I hear them." She pauses to let the effect of that sink in.

"Okay," he says and steps back against the sink. Little bits of his hair stick out, mussed by his collar. She loves his hair, dark and very straight, always just slightly shaggy, as if tomorrow he will spoil it with a haircut.

"Are you going to the opening?" Ross asks.

"I'm on the faculty. I have to go." Irony pulls at her mouth, but he doesn't get it. Her voice softens. "Are you nervous?"

He shrugs. "Maybe. A little bit, I guess."

"It'll go fine," she promises. She saw his paintings yesterday, when they hung the show. He does huge canvases, female nudes whose neutered faces and big, fleshy bodies seem almost sexless for their mass and lack of detail. What is striking about them—almost shocking—is the way they contrast to the erotic, bulging curves of the furniture, the coiling table legs and obscenely overstuffed sofas and chairs. He's good—no doubt about it—though she wants to think he's latched onto a style and confused it with vision, that it will become a gimmick if he lets it. She thinks of Edward Weston's nudes, so cool and sexless in comparison to his still lifes, the voluptuous whorls of his seashells and vegetables, not merely caressed by light, but positively copulating with it, though Weston always denied the sexual intent. Vision is a mystery; all style requires is talent. There is something a little too stylized about Ross's work. Or perhaps she thinks so because she doesn't want to like it.

"There's a party afterwards," she says. "I hear Buck's got a keg of green beer."

"A keg and a bag of nose candy." Restlessly his eyes rove the small room, crusty as a fish market. A darkroom isn't meant to be seen in the glare of the overhead light. "Are you going?"

"I don't know Buck," she says flatly, toeing the wooden floor grid. "Will your parents be at the opening?"

"My parents live in New Zealand."

"Oh." She didn't know his parents lived on the other side of the world, though clearly he did not grow up there. He has an American accent, so familiar to her it's one she can't place. Not Southern, not Appalachian, not Midwestern, not New England, not New York. She should ask, but she doesn't.

"Marjean's coming."

"Good."

His neck jerks as he turns back. "I'm not ashamed to bring her here." His face is splotched. "And I don't like the way you seem to think you have to remind me to do right by her. I'm not an asshole, okay?"

But she doesn't want him to do the right thing by her, which makes her an asshole too. "I'm sorry."

"I mean it's not like I can take you, is it?"

"No," she admits. "It's not like you can take me."

He kneels to unzip her jeans, and her body quivers at the soft, warm shock of his tongue. She has to hold her hand to her mouth to keep from crying out. With her other hand she clutches the counter. The strength has gone out of her legs. When she gives in to the ecstatic shiver of her climax, he stands and wipes his mouth.

"I'll see you at the opening," he says.

Chapter 11

1960

A few days after their visit to the Beauman house and the quarry she ran into Kendrick in the university bookstore, where she was cutting mat board to fit the baskets on her bike. As she pushed her hair back from her eyes, she saw him come in. He paused at the magazine rack, and she went back to work, hoping he wouldn't come back to Art Supplies. The arm of the cutter wasn't long enough; she had to turn the board, and when she brought the blade down again, a strip of the paper finish tore across the surface. In disgust she tried to fold the ruined board and stuff it in the trash.

"Hello."

"Hello." She didn't look up.

"Mind if I show you something?" he asked after a minute. He took one of her smudged mats and at a block at the end of the counter used an X-Acto knife and T-square to trim the edge. "Eleven by fourteen? Twelve by sixteen?"

"I don't know. I guess so." She refused to look at his face.

"Eleven by fourteen it is then."

Alex pulled a wadded dollar from her pocket and stooped to scratch a mosquito bite on her ankle.

When he finished, he handed her a neat stack. "Going to mount some prints?"

"I thought I would." He lounged against the counter while she waited for the clerk. She dropped the change in her pocket, and he followed her out to her bike, taking the boards while she crouched to undo the lock. The sky was colorless. On the sidewalk his shadow looked faint.

"Ever done it before? I can show you how."

"No thank you." She divided the boards between her baskets and backed the bicycle from the rack.

"You can do it with an iron, but they'll look a lot more profession-al with a press. Have you got dry-mount tissue?"

"I don't know what that is."

He rested a hand on the handlebar as she straddled her Schwinn. "I've got some. You're welcome to use my press."

He needed a shave. If she began to pedal, she would run over his foot. "I'm going to use rubber cement."

"You'll ruin your prints."

"I'm not going to spill any."

"You won't have to. It eats through from the back. Well, it'll take a few years, but eventually." He released her bicycle. "I missed you. You don't come around any more." After a minute he stroked his jaw. "Hey, I'm growing a beard. What do you think?"

"I think it looks stupid," she said and pushed off with her foot. The breeze lifted her hair from her neck.

"Well, wait a minute," he called, but she was coasting downhill, and when she glanced back, he was out of sight.

Late that afternoon, when she returned from the pool, where she had sputtered and squealed each time Kevin threw her in, she was surprised to hear voices in the living room. She glanced out the narrow window beside the door and froze. Even through the colored glass there was no mistaking the dented front fender. Kendrick's white station wagon sat parked just beyond the grassy ditch. In the living room her mother was murmuring something about Wallace; when she paused the rising inflection of Kendrick's question filled in. As quietly as she could, Alex closed the door behind her and circled to the back.

"Alexandra?" Her mother's voice was brittle. A week ago Alex might have felt sorry for Kendrick; her mother didn't like to be interrupted while she was working. "We have company. Alexandra, did you hear me?"

Reluctantly Alex halted outside the door to her room. "My bathing suit is wet."

She changed into clean shorts and a bandana-print halter, leaving her suit in a soggy heap on the carpet. Conversation purred on in the living room, but she couldn't make out the words. Her heart thumped. He was mad at her, she didn't know why, except that she was mad at him. He was mad at her, and he would tell, he would tell about every day that she had come to his apartment, would tell about *that* day, and though she had not lied—her mother *didn't* care what she did—he would tell, and now her mother would have to be mad at her too. She had never been in trouble before. Oh, she had dripped chicken pot pie all over the oven, she had left towels wadded in the bathroom to sour, once she forgot a Redon book on the deck and it rained—but *this* kind of trouble … "I *can't*," her friends would say, "my *parents*," and their words took such cowed, mysterious twists she didn't want to hear them; she didn't want to know about the threats and groundings. Her life was different. She dawdled as long as she could, braiding and unbraiding her thick, damp hair.

"Alexandra!"

"I'm in my *room*." She dragged her feet down the hall and dropped into the farthest chair, where she slouched with her hands between her knees, staring at the long slant of light where the drapes had been left open.

They were having drinks. Hélène's sundress rippled at her calves as she flexed her foot, letting a white sandal dangle from its lattice of straps. Kendrick hadn't caught her mother working after all; he had called.

"Hi," she mumbled when her mother prompted again. Alex picked at the nubs in the upholstery. He had shaved and changed into a pale blue shirt and tie.

"Another, Steve?" Her mother rose. *Steve*. The palms of Alex's hands felt clammy. So that was it. Why not? Her mother had dated younger men before.

"Been to the pool?" Kendrick asked loudly while her mother banged a metal ice tray in the kitchen. Alex studied one of Hélène's wall hangings. A moth would starve; the thing had more holes than fabric. "Nice house—I like the open ceiling." A cathedral ceiling, her mother called it, but the wall that divided the living area from the bedroom hallway split the church in half.

"I was just telling Steve it's too bad the weather has been so sultry. We'll make a bad impression." Her mother frowned as she sat. Alex jiggled her foot. To spite her he had told, and now he would take her mother to dinner. Why else had her mother dressed up? Alex supposed they would have sex. She supposed that was what her mother did when she was out, though Alex had never bothered to speculate before. But now it occurred to her that was—wasn't it?—what adults did when they dated. She remembered the platinum hair spread across Kendrick's pillow and felt her face warm. Well, of course she had known it. It was what he meant when he said "professors who dated students ..." To spite her, or maybe—and this made her stomach sink—he wouldn't do it to spite her; maybe he would do it because he wanted to.

"Steve says you've been doing some modeling."

As Alex jerked to attention, Kendrick's chin shifted toward the fireplace. She had missed the portrait propped against the stone, glass so superimposed with reflections that she had to rise from her seat to make sure he hadn't set her out for her mother nude. But there she was framed by the spokes of her bicycle wheel, every bit as blameless as the boyish cuffed white shorts and ruffled halter top she sat in now. She had the same picture in her drawer.

"Don't you look pretty?" her mother said. Her tone was patronizing as she turned to Kendrick, and Alex realized that her mother disliked him. "Do you do any work that isn't representational?" Or perhaps she had no opinion of him but disliked the photograph. It was not the kind of thing that she would hang.

"Some," Kendrick said.

"I hope so." She turned back to Alex. "Steve's come by to take you to dinner to show you how much he's appreciated your sitting." Now her voice was impeccable, and Alex couldn't hear what he'd told. She felt a mustache of perspiration forming. She wished with her whole heart that she had been nicer to him in the bookstore.

"I have a date." Her mother raised an eyebrow. Alex supposed she had never mentioned to her mother that she dated. "Well, Jo and I promised we'd meet these guys at the movies."

"Jo," her mother said. "Jo Ann Yellen."

Alex nodded, hoping her mother wouldn't call Jo, who probably did have a date—it would be just like her, the way she stood next to Alex at their school lockers with nothing to say until she spotted one of the five hundred boys she liked, then began an animated conversation, pretending not to notice when the boy walked by. Surrounded by boys at the pool, she never stopped talking.

"Bob Yellen's daughter?"

But of course her mother wouldn't call Jo.

"What movie?"

"Whatever's playing."

Hélène frowned. Discreetly Kendrick studied the spines of the art books on the shelves. "You didn't tell me."

"Well, I would have, but you weren't home. Well, Jo had to let them *know*." She stared at a lone freckle on her knee. It wasn't fair. Her mother never asked what she did. And she really couldn't bear to whine in front of Kendrick; she never whined.

"Steve has asked you to dinner. I think you should call Jo Ann and tell her you won't be there."

"He didn't ask me. He asked *you*."

"As a matter of fact he asked both of us, but I have plans." Her mother smiled. "Now be a good girl—and change your clothes when you go in to call Jo Ann."

Alex scowled and scuffed her bare feet as loudly as she could along the hall carpet.

"Well, where are we going?" she demanded when they were in Kendrick's station wagon, his equipment bumping around the back. "Wherever, I think you're a dirty, rotten son-of-a-bitch."

He laughed. "You shouldn't ought to cuss like that, Alexandra. What would your mother say?"

"Go to hell." She adjusted the elastic at the shoulders of her flounced white dress. It was her mother's dress, but her mother never wore it, so Alex helped herself.

"Such a filthy mouth. What are our high schools coming to?"

"Ha ha ha," she said, though she was a little shocked herself. "You can let me off at the Towne Art."

"You really have a date?" He squealed around the corner.

"Hey!" She clutched the dashboard. "Yes, I do."

He looked at her sideways. "I can't tell if you're lying or not."

"What do you mean?" She raised her chin. "I want a steak. I want a T-bone steak and a baked potato with sour cream and butter, and I want a salad with bleu cheese dressing, and for dessert I want a big piece of chocolate cake with vanilla ice cream and hot fudge sauce." The early evening sun stabbed her eyes, and she lowered the visor, instantly regretting the curtained feel it gave the car. "They have good food at Bill and Thelma's. It's a family place. You have to get there early."

"You know perfectly well what I mean."

Her voice took on a nervous cadence, fast, with a rise in pitch. "It's too bad my mother couldn't come. Turn right at the next corner."

They had pulled up to a stop sign. "Friday night—I heard she was really smashing; I figured she'd have plans. Well, obviously she doesn't keep close tabs on you, but I could hardly count on her blessing. Now I'm not so sure." He shook his head. "How was I supposed to know you were telling me the truth?" As he took his foot off the brake, the car began a slow roll. "Even I know who Jo Yellen is."

"I don't know what you're talking about," Alex said, but her hands trembled in her lap.

He leaned across to open her door.

She didn't move. "*Okay*. I'm sorry I was rude in the bookstore. You hurt my feelings, and I wanted to hurt yours."

"You sure did." He turned his head toward her and tapped his chin. "Shaved the stupid beard, did you notice?" He looked her in the eye. "Are you going to use that door?"

She turned her head away.

"The Towne Art's not but two blocks." His arm brushed her skirt as he closed it. Beneath the gauzy cotton her legs went stiff. It was too hot for stockings, but she wished suddenly that she'd thought to wear a slip. "Of course, if those high heels pinch, I'll be happy to drop you." Between them on the seat his herringbone jacket smelled of Cherry Blend. "You look beautiful in white, by the way. You were wearing a white dress the night I met you, and, believe me, I had no idea you were only fifteen."

He hadn't mentioned the last time she saw him.

She closed her eyes and saw again the white-blonde hair tumbled on his pillow, heard the spinning of the fan and, beating through it, the bedlam of her heart. Of course she had known it. But she had never made herself imagine the mechanics. *Slept with, made love. Dating*, that was her word. It didn't force her to confront the staggering fact—which was nakedness, men and women looking at each other without the cloak of art, their secret places coarsened by exposure, revolting as chicken skin or public toilets. They might as well watch each other doing *that*. Maybe she had imagined kissing him, maybe, though it seemed to her she hadn't even gone so far as that. She was fifteen years old. She had a right to the softly folded clothing of confusion and vague promise.

When he pulled up to the Towne Art she said, "Jo Ann Yellen is a slut, and if she's in there I'll bet you a dollar she's breaking her back on an armrest in the balcony." It was at best an exaggeration, at worst an outright lie, and the little smart of conscience made her angry. She bit her lip. "You said we were going to dinner."

"Do you want to?"

"No."

"Because I'll take you. And then we'll say good night if that's all you want."

"It's not all I want."

"Are you sure?" He cut the engine.

"You had a *drink* with my mother."

"I'm not interested in your mother." He turned away, his voice fading as he took off his glasses to wipe them. "This isn't a game to me."

"I don't play games." Her voice was shrill.

He faced her. In the light from the marquee his eyes were the color of webbing moths. "You can't imagine how beautiful the photographs are. Except you didn't do it for the camera, you did it for me."

Behind them a car began to honk. "You …" His words were lost as the horn continued to blare. "I'm parked in a loading zone," he said hopelessly.

"So move the car," she said.

After a moment he began to laugh.

"I mean it. Move the car. Or do you want me to drive?"

"Do you even have a license?" he asked as he pulled away from the curb.

"No," she said tartly, but then her voice softened. "I love you."

He didn't answer. "Aren't you going to say you love me? I'm *scared*."

He slipped a hand from the steering wheel and found hers. "Are you sure?" In front of his house he drew her into his arms. "I'm scared too. Because yes I love you, which is not only inexcusable, it's a crime."

Chapter 12

1966-1967

Then suddenly it was 1966, the year of the new working class theory, when teachers and students joined the ranks of the oppressed, and Dogpatch moved off the Hill to a larger house near campus.

Nelson was still seeing Peggy and sometimes a small, intense Jewish girl from SDS named Leah; they turned up at the table first on alternate nights and then together, all three of them smiling sweetly at one other. Stacy had taken a job as a maid in the Wallace Union, unable to convince herself she ought to leave Matt, though she would not commit herself to him either. Alex hemmed her skirts higher and twined her fingers in the curls that had grown out to Ted's collar. The folkies were has-beens; Dylan had gone electric, the Beatles transcendental. The meadow behind the Wallace Union was always pounding with a concert or demonstration. Students were flocking to the antiwar cause now that they were in danger of being drafted. Stokely Carmichael, who had argued against letting white volunteers into Mississippi in '64, became chairman of SNCC, and as Ted had predicted the last whites were removed from the civil rights rolls. "Black power" was on everyone's lips, and across the country that summer ghettoes went up in flames.

Garth and Lizzie had a baby girl; Garth plodded back and forth to his library carrel, oblivious to the gaudy youth cult springing up around him. "It would drive me crazy," Lizzie said to Alex of the new collective or commune or whatever they had become, and Alex had to laugh, Garth and Lizzie still living in a one-bedroom house crammed with toys and soaking diapers. They had added members:

Tulip was a senior with lank brown hair who edited the new underground paper *The Grass Root*. Nearly everyone in the house wrote for it; Alex did the photography. Tulip shared her room with an orange cat that promptly had kittens and a series of transients—a girl who had broken up with her boyfriend, another whose landlord upped the rent, a runaway who later returned to her parents. The small bedroom above the stairs was let by Michael, a bearded grad student in psychology whose conversation was full of words like *nexus* and *group synthesis* that he picked up from *New Left Review.* Tulip, who considered all psychology tainted by Freud, took to calling him Penis Envy. "Pass the potatoes, PE," she said. The penis wars, Ted dubbed the ensuing debates, in which Jung, Wilhelm Reich, Herbert Marcuse, and Norman O. Brown were all summoned to join Laing, Freud, and Adler at their dinner table. "You can laugh if you want to," Leah scolded, "but there is no event more political than orgasm."

"How about the war?" Stacy said.

The big, airy front room on the second floor was her refuge with Ted. Mornings the light from the bay window turned the room golden. Coming out of sleep, still in the possession of its images but already unable to recall any but the vaguest impressions of them, she would roll against his length until the warmth of her body stirred him and he would turn to make love, so that in her memory the hazy web of dream, lucent promise of morning, and sweet, solid weight of his body were one. On the few nights when they weren't busy, they lit candles on the mantel of their sealed-up fireplace, propped themselves on pillows, and talked.

"Did you ever wonder what you'd be doing if there wasn't a war?" she asked.

"Not really," he said. "Retire to some tropical paradise and sleep in the sand all day while you fetch gin and tonics."

"Ho ho," she said. "I mean really."

"Really," he said. She felt the familiar flutter in his kiss. When she opened her eyes his fixed on hers. "This is the only really I know." But he meant all of it, not just her.

All the same, in their room the velvet darkness and constant echo of footsteps, music, telephone, and voices outside the door defined a privacy more luxurious than if they had lived by themselves in a little house like Garth and Lizzie's, for in such reminders of others its quality was enhanced. Officially only seven people lived there, although there were always at least a dozen overnight.

"I couldn't stand it," Lizzie said, and Alex just laughed. "This is my life," she said. But there was always something happening in Lizzie's life too. Garth was studying for his comps; the Co-op was thriving; Tice was talking; Lucy was crawling. Lizzie kept diving after her as she and Alex sat at the dining room table drinking tea. The afternoon sun glared through a cloudy white nimbus of dirt on the western windows.

"Ted got nine signatures from the History faculty on the petition against Dow," Alex called into the kitchen, where Lizzie had gone to brush kitty litter from Lucy's hands and wipe the baby's mouth. "I'm going to move that damn box. I don't know why Tulip can't keep it in her room." She gagged as she opened the back door to put it on the stoop. On her way back to the dining room she snatched a pot from the pegboard. "Look, Ticers, a drum."

"Hey, Liz." Nelson slung a box of pamplets on the table and helped himself to a macaroon. "What's for dinner?"

"We're going out." Alex and Ted were eating at Minelli's with his parents, who had gone with Jeannie to the football game that afternoon. "Tulip's at the *Root*. Somebody missed a deadline, and there's a hole on page 2." She glanced at the handouts for Tuesday's demonstration and gave him a sly smile. "Maybe if you're lucky she'll finish up early."

"Maybe if we're really lucky she won't." He stepped over Tice, and Alex hollered up the stairs, "If you see Ted, tell him his parents are picking us up at 6:30." The phone rang, and there was a flurry of feet in the hall. Lizzie was sniffing at Lucy's pants.

"Ooh, Luce, I thought so." Lizzie reached into her bag. "Nuts. I'm out of diapers. Have a good time with Ted's folks."

"I don't know how you stand it," Alex said, meaning the diapers, and Lizzie laughed. "I'm used to it. Besides, your own kids' poop never smells that bad."

"Poop?"

"Poo-poo and pee-pee, blankey and choo-choo. We speak another language at our house." She pried the pot from Tice's fingers. "Say bye-bye."

The football crowd had packed Minelli's, and they had to wait for a table in the bar. Ted's father returned his drink ("A *vodka* martini," he repeated), and Jeannie twirled the paper parasol from hers. "We had a ball," Justine was saying of the game that afternoon. Alex glanced at the stool where Kendrick had been sitting the night they met. She thought about him sometimes. He seemed so long ago, not just him but those nights in the Cellar that in her memory were shot in black and white, like the foreign films they had attended. The world was Technicolor now. Sometimes on her way to the *Root*, she caught sight of the Towne Art marquee and did a little double-take. She missed Kendrick sometimes—or not missed exactly, but felt, now and then, a small pang of nostalgia. The big Victorian house on Leverett Avenue was only a block from the house where he had lived on East Maple. These days toys were strewn across its yard, and once or twice she had paused on the sidewalk, spooked by the image they offered, the toddling children, she and Kendrick a young family much like Lizzie and Garth. In those moments she was almost frightened by a sense that she had lost some part of herself. It was true; there was the evidence: somewhere in this world she was bending to tie a shoe or tuck a blanket, stirring sugarplum dreams with a damp breath of goodnight kisses, all those predictable things her future had intended. She glanced at Ted. They lived by a heightened standard. She only wondered sometimes what Kendrick was doing. She hoped he'd met someone—he would have, she thought, and that's who it was, not herself but some other woman, straightening his tie and bending to brush their children's hair. And what she felt, standing on the sidewalk, staring at the toys on his old lawn, was neither jealousy nor loss but the oddly bereft kinship one feels for the stranger who occupies a place where she once lived.

The heavy smell of Italian sauce wafted in from the dining rooms. She wasn't hungry; her drink tasted off. She'd been pushing herself too hard, staying up too late.

Jeannie was talking about the paper she was writing on Virginia Woolf. Justine was listening attentively; Brad looked bored, but was more likely just impatient with the waiter. Alex couldn't get a fix on

Ted's parents. Justine had a streak of witty flamboyance that Alex suspected she'd cultivated to distract from her husband's air of inattention, though that too seemed a put-on. Mildly, she disliked them. They hadn't wanted Ted to marry her. Why did it matter so to Ted that his father couldn't respect him?

"I was so excited to see Bloomsbury." Justine touched the back of one enameled nail to her big white mum. "And then—well, I was so disappointed. Chelsea is ever so much more charming. We had a ball picking out all the literary houses, didn't we, Dad?"

"She led me around by the nose, and I held the umbrella," he said. "How's your daiquiri, Alex?"

"Fine." Guiltily Alex brought the glass to her lips.

"I can't wait," Jeannie said. She was spending six weeks in England next summer.

"Take your raincoat," Brad advised.

"We wanted to send Ted," Justine noted, but it was water over the dam, the fact that their son had preferred to go to Mississippi.

"How's the car running?" Brad asked Ted, who was pleating his napkin around his whiskey sour. Alex's muscles tensed. Justine's year-old white Impala had been a wedding present, but it felt more like a trust they had failed, for it spent most of its time in the shop.

"I loved that car." Justine scratched at a jot of caked lipstick. "I hate the Riviera—it's so hard to park. Dad says there's nothing wrong with it, but the wheel pulls to the right."

"There's nothing wrong with it," Brad said.

"Did you catch the Series?" Ted asked him.

It was unfair of Alex to think they chose sports as neutral territory. Ted *liked* to talk sports. He would have gone to the game if he hadn't been so busy with the upcoming action against Dow. It bothered her that she couldn't imagine the argument that sent Ted to New York. She could surmise the substance, but she couldn't imagine her father-in-law's raised voice.

When they were called to their table and she stood, she felt light-headed. "You okay?" Ted whispered behind her as she steadied herself between the table and heavy captain's chair, so dizzy that for a moment she was afraid she was going to black out.

"I'm fine. Just, I don't know, a little off." She hoped she wasn't getting sick. She ordered the prime rib and left it untouched.

"Are you sure you feel okay?" he asked again as they undressed. "You were awfully quiet tonight."

"I'm just tired," Alex said, hanging up her skirt. Her body felt heavy.

"It's my parents, isn't it?" he said.

"Really," she promised, "I'm just tired."

In the morning she woke with sore breasts. Her nipples wanted touching. She reached for his hand before he'd waked and tamped it against her so roughly that he started out of sleep, then laughed with pleasure. "I'm glad you feel better," he whispered.

But sautéing onions that afternoon she felt sick, and when she pushed away from the dinner table her head went funny again. She had cramps, a sluggish shadow of pain deep inside her belly. "Make love to me," she demanded, returning his hands to her breasts until the skin chafed. She had a tendency to retain water before she menstruated, and a week or two of every cycle her breasts hurt, some months more than others. "I wish my period would start," she said when she rose to go to the bathroom.

"Is it late?"

"It's always late."

He sat up. "Are you pregnant?"

It hadn't occurred to her, and she dropped to the edge of the mattress, stunned. "Well, I don't know. I've never been pregnant before." She felt stupid. "I couldn't be." After a minute she added, "If I was, wouldn't I be throwing up? I don't feel sick. Just my head's sort of weird and I don't feel like eating."

"Plus you're horny," he observed.

"That's not a symptom of pregnancy." She turned to look at him. "Is it?"

"Ask Lizzie."

She sucked her lip. With Stacy she might talk about sex; with Lizzie she might talk about pregnancy and labor, but never about sex. "I'll ask her about morning sickness," she conceded.

That's great," Lizzie cried as she leapt from the dining room chair to hug her.

"Well, I don't know," Alex said doubtfully. "I think maybe I'm just getting the flu or something. I mean—shouldn't I be throwing up?"

"They're all different. I was never sick a day with Tice. With Lucy I thought I'd bring up my socks." Lizzie opened her blouse for the baby, who made funny little gurgling and sighing sounds as she sucked, cutting her eyes flirtatiously at her mother. A thrill ran from Alex's nipples to her crotch.

"Do you want some tea?" she asked, already on her way to the kitchen.

"You don't have to play guessing games, you know," Lizzie called.

When Alex returned, Tice was tearing at Lizzie's knees. "Okay, okay," Lizzie laughed, spreading her legs to make room for him and holding out an arm. With the arm that supported Lucy, she unbuttoned her blouse the rest of the way. "He's so jealous. I swear I'm going to have jugs down to my knees before this is over." Alex had been astonished the first time she witnessed Lizzie with a baby tugging at each breast, blushing as she explained, "Well, I was still nursing him when I got pregnant. Really, it doesn't take anything from Lucy. The more they use the more your body makes." Tice clamped his mouth around the magnificent red nipple, but not before cutting his eyes at his sister.

Alex swallowed. "I don't know," she mumbled. "A test seems so conclusive."

Lizzie laughed. "Pregnancy is like that." She ruffled the back of Tice's hair and squeezed Lucy's pudgy thigh. "Conclusive."

"Alex." Tulip poked her head through the archway from the living room. "Did you take those pictures of the African art? You know, it's really hard to run a paper when people keep missing deadlines."

"The deadline's not till Friday," Alex said.

Tulip glanced at Lizzie. "I wish you'd do that somewhere else."

"Actually," Lizzie said when Tulip left, "I do need to wean Tice. I've got some news of my own."

Alex stared. "You're kidding."

"Finished, Ticers?" She set Lucy on the floor, closed her blouse, and giggled. "I swear all Garth has to do is walk through the room and I get pregnant. Whoever said you can't conceive while you're nursing ought to be strung up by the balls." Lizzie sighed. "Oh, but Alex, this is so great—they'll be the same age, you can join the Co-op."

"I don't know," Alex said again. She pictured Dr. Bagwell, the OB-GYN, bending down to pull a baby from her, white scalp gleaming through his crewcut. Years ago when she'd gone to him for the pill, he'd looked at her so sternly she was afraid he would refuse. But he'd written the prescription, admonishing her not to wait too long while his wife and five children stared disapprovingly from the picture frame turned outward on his desk. It pissed her off, especially when her delight in the little lavender wheel of fortune as she called it disintegrated into chronic nausea and dull headaches. Her stomach hurt, she felt bloated, dizzy, so weak her bones seemed soft—almost exactly like she felt now. Impossible that her symptoms could be side effects, Dr. Bagwell had scolded. She quit the pill anyway. A doctor in New York had fitted her for the diaphragm she hated and second-guessed with rhythm. In short, she had every reason to be pregnant.

Lizzie drained her teacup and stood. "Well, tell Ted I hope you are. Say hi to Stacy."

It was funny, but until the results came back, Alex thought of pregnancy entirely in terms of her own body, staring at her stomach, poking at her breasts (bigger than yesterday, bulging with blue veins), but as soon as the nurse said "positive" she began to think about the baby. At the supermarket she craned her neck toward infants in shopping carts, detoured through the babywear at Block's, peeked in strollers, couldn't keep her eyes off Lucy. It was impossible—all the books said so—but she swore she felt the embryo, a warm pinpoint of light inside her womb. She had been afraid Ted would think they were too busy for a baby, but he suddenly seemed more solidly built, straighter, taller, almost as if his bones were more sure of themselves, his blood brighter. Or maybe that was just her imagination.

"You're not kidding?" he said finally, a few days later. "Okay then. I mean … well, what should we name it?"

"I don't know," she said, reclining in the clawfoot bathtub, water drawn over her body like a blanket.

"Do you want a girl or a boy?"

"What do you want?"

"A girl," he said. "A girl just like you. And when she's old enough she'll follow a boy just like me all the way home."

Alex pursed her lips and blew out a little breath. "Why don't we have the boy just like you too, and then he can be her brother?"

"Spoilsport," he said and drew a soapy mustache across her upper lip. "I like my story better."

"Of course you do," she said. "It's about you."

"Not true," he corrected as he dunked her. "I saw you first. Remember? I asked who you were."

"Boy or girl," she said. "I don't care. I'm happy."

She bought a tiny tee shirt and embroidered a duckling on the chest; in the evening while the collective gathered to talk about campus issues—student representation, women's hours; the grievances didn't matter half so much as calling students' attention to them—she cut a bear from a quarter yard of calico and stitched the seams by hand. What did she care about representation or curfews? Her interest in a student movement, never strong, had waned. She had more important things to do. Even as she sat, she was gestating. It was impossible to waste time.

At eleven weeks she started spotting. "Don't worry about it," the doctor said, but every few minutes she locked herself in the bathroom to check her pants—it had stopped, no, it looked darker, it had stopped, no. She felt a twinge and called the doctor back. "If the flow gets heavier or the cramps become severe, come in and the doctor will check you," the nurse said. The third time she called, the nurse agreed to an appointment with an elaborate sigh. A good sign, she promised herself, but when the doctor had examined her, she dressed and waited in his office, staring at the wife and kids with a hot wall of tears behind her eyes.

"Am I going to lose the baby?" she asked him.

"The bleeding may get worse as a result of the pelvic." He made a notation in her folder. "Call me in a week if it doesn't lessen, and we'll take another look. Or in the meantime if you should hemorrhage or pass the fetus."

"Am I going to lose the baby?"

With an irritated scratch of the pen, he looked up. "I really can't say."

Walking home, she felt the light in her belly flicker out and started to cry.

The next day the cramps were worse, the blood darker. Normal, she told herself sternly, scrubbing the potatoes. The pinpoint of light had been a figment of imagination. You couldn't feel a baby until four and a half months; all the books said so. Angrily she yanked an iron skillet from the pegboard. Tears ran down her face as she sliced the onions; she didn't bother to turn on the light; the oil was smoking; the onions hissed and turned black as soon as they touched the pan.

Matt found her doubled over with cramps, blood soaking through the back of her minidress. He snatched the skillet from the burner. "Alex, what is it?"

"I'm having a miscarriage," she sobbed.

"Jeez." He crouched awkwardly beside her. She buried her head in his shoulder, and he put his arms around her.

"What's burning?" From the corner of her eye Alex saw Nelson, backing away from the kitchen doorway. He raised a hand. "Hey, it's cool, man."

"PU." There was a clatter of footsteps in the front hallway, and a girl Alex didn't know trailed Tulip into the kitchen. Tulip glanced at Alex. "What's with her?"

"I'm having a *miscarriage*." Alex sat up. Her dress was sticking to the back of her thighs.

"Well, you don't have to burn the house down." Tulip opened the refrigerator.

Nelson knelt beside Matt. "Should we call a doctor?" Alex nodded.

The front door banged, and Stacy came in, eating an apple. "Somebody firebomb us? What's going on?"

"Alex *says* she's having a miscarriage," Tulip said. "Laura, this is Stacy."

"Jesus." Stacy set the apple on the drainboard and knelt. "You poor kid. What are you guys, standing around like a bunch of clowns? Has anyone called Ted?"

"Where is he?" The men looked at each other. "We were just going to call the doctor," Matt explained.

Stacy draped an arm around Alex. "Are you in pain?" She looked up. "How the hell do I know where he is? Try Garth's. Try his sister. Try the *Root*."

"I'm okay. I have cramps is all." Alex burst into tears.

"Come on, let's get you to bed."

"Oh gross!" Tulip was staring at the floor. "She's *bleeding*."

"So why don't you get a rag and clean it up?"

"You know, you have a really abrasive personality," Tulip said.

"Yeah? Well I think you're a royal pain too." Stacy guided Alex to the stairs. "I hate that bitch," she said when she had closed the door to Alex's room. "Whose idea was it for her to move in? We don't have to be *that* democratic." She rummaged in the closet while Alex hunched and pressed her arms into the knot of pain. "Do you have any Kotex?"

"I'm pregnant," Alex sobbed. "Why would I have sanitary napkins?"

"Oh god." Stacy sat down hard on the mattress. "Allie, I'm so sorry." After a minute she stood. "All I've got is Tampax." The door creaked against its hinges as she thrust her head into the strip of light from the hall. "Tulip! Have you got any Kotex?" She disappeared into the bathroom and came out with a towel. "Come on, let's take your dress off." Alex shivered as Stacy unzipped the back and let it fall. "God, look at you. Three months pregnant, and you're skinnier than I am."

Alex bunched the towel between her legs and slid into a flannel nightgown.

"Do you want to sleep?"

Alex shook her head. "Stay." The light from the windows had dwindled to a soft gray. She closed her eyes while Stacy ran water in the tub to soak her dress. After a while Stacy picked up a pile of photographs, standing near the windows to examine them. "These are beautiful," she said. "You do good work."

Alex reached out her hand. "I like you too, Stacy."

When Matt knocked the room was dark. The hall light spun silver webs in the split ends of Stacy's hair.

"The doctor can see her tomorrow at ten." Matt's silhouette shifted slightly. "She's supposed to save the pad. If she passes the fetus she should put it in a jar and bring it with her."

"Fucker," Stacy said. "Run to the store, would you, and get some

Kotex." Matt didn't move. "Oh, for God's sake," Stacy said and stepped into the hallway.

When Ted came in Alex was asleep. She woke to a hum of voices, and then the creak of their door. "Baby," he said, and she flung herself into his arms. "It's not fair," she wept as he blew kisses through her hair. "It's not fair," he agreed. "It's not fair to you at all."

Actually, the doctor assured her the next morning, it was quite routine, the cramps, the bleeding, the D and C he would schedule for the afternoon. At least one of four pregnancies ended in a miscarriage; likely the embryos were abnormal. Hunkered on the edge of her chair not to look at the offending family photo, Alex thought bitterly of the high school English teacher who had told them that a noun could no more be "very unique" than a woman could be "a little bit pregnant." Apparently Miss Dredge had never heard Dr. Bagwell's statistics. "But why?" Alex said. "Does this mean I won't ever have children?"

He looked annoyed, or maybe bored: now that she was no longer pregnant he'd lost interest. "That's impossible to say."

She woke in the recovery room with her insides on fire, a white-hot pain piercing the thick grog of anesthesia. The nurse gave her a shot, and by dinnertime she was home, by bedtime sitting up, eating a few bites of the hamburger Ted brought upstairs. A few days of napping and solicitous inquiries from her friends, and that was that. Dr. Bagwell checked the lab report and gave her the good news while she was still on the examination table. There had been no fetal matter.

"So," he said cheerfully, "nothing to it. You didn't even lose a baby."

She sat up, clutching the paper sheet to her chest. "What do you mean?"

"There was tissue, but no fetal matter."

"What kind of tissue?" Outrage burned her throat. He had told her himself she was pregnant.

"Just think of it as a little accident of nature."

"Are you telling me I had a hysterical pregnancy?" The paper sheet rattled.

He sighed. "Conception occurred. In my opinion women worry too much about these things. Just try to relax and with a little luck next time everything will go fine."

Alex went to the library, but the most helpful book she could find had only a footnote referring to "the spontaneous abortion of a fetus, commonly called miscarriage." After twenty-two weeks the event was called "stillbirth." Juanita, her old supervisor at Vardys, had had a stillbirth. The doctor had known the baby was dead, and still Juanita had to go through the wracking thirty-six hour labor. Horrified, Alex had seized upon the detail. Yet how else was all that dead tissue and hope to be dispatched? *Tissue*. She hated the word, though she supposed she should feel lucky. A blessing in disguise, Justine called it. She meant well; so, Alex thought, did the doctor. He had no way of knowing that knowing there had never been a baby made it infinitely worse, a grief without an object. He had taken away her right to mourn what might have been.

Over and over she made Ted tell her it wasn't her fault, but she found fault with his voice—it lacked conviction, it wasn't stricken. Why should he have to tell her he didn't blame her when there was nothing she could have done? "It wasn't your fault," his voice insisted and grew thin. Instead of grief she heard frustration. "We have each other," he said. "We have the collective. We have our work, we have our friends." In the mornings she opened her eyes and rolled carefully to the outside of the bed. It reminded her of death to make love.

"I want a family," she said.

"We have a family," he said.

"You can try again," Lizzie promised, and Alex stared angrily at the ugly mound of Lizzie's stomach. Tears of sympathy stood in Lizzie's eyes. "I feel so guilty," she confessed, Tice and Lucy pulling at her skirt.

"It's not your fault," Alex said.

"It's not Ted's fault either."

"What do you know about it? I don't blame him."

"No. But he thinks you do," Lizzie said.

She didn't, but they held each other from opposite sides of their helplessness and could not speak. There was nothing else she could talk about and nothing left for him to say.

She did not cry once the first shock had passed, though she flinched at the most banal reminders—an ad for baby powder, pregnant women everywhere. And once, passing through a lounge in the

Wallace Union where three girls were watching a soap opera, she overheard a teary actress confront her lover in the weighty monotone of melodrama: "They told me it would have been a boy," she said, and a sob split Alex's throat. The three girls turned as Alex clapped her hand to her mouth, fleeing to the lavatory, where her sorrow broke in a keening so thunderous and primeval she might have been no more than its shuddering vessel. When the last howl had shaken itself from her, she sank to the floor. She felt no better, only exhausted and utterly empty.

"I cried today," she told Ted that night.

"About …" His voice trailed off into weary resignation.

"I cried and cried," she said, unable to explain that she was not the subject of her sentence but the object. She lay her hand against his cheek. "I don't want to lose you too," she promised.

Lizzie's baby—Caton, another boy—was born at the end of April. In the hospital Alex stared blindly at the newborns through the glass.

"He's cute," she said to Lizzie when she had taken a seat in the room.

Lizzie set the unopened gift aside and rose from the bed in a stiff shuffle, touching Alex's hand as Alex pressed her eyes closed on the tears. When she lifted her head, she smiled for the reach of Lizzie's kindness, and knew at last that she had come through her grief and would recover.

Chapter 13

1982

"I brought you some wine," Kendrick says, handing Alex a plastic cup that is immediately jostled from behind. She's late. The two floors of the gallery are overflowing, and the few guests who try to see the student show have to work their way along the edges of the crowd. All the motion makes her dizzy. "You look nice."

"Thanks." After the meeting she slipped home to shower, and a musk of dampness clings to her thick French braid. She's belted her favorite shirt over a skirt of print challis because wearing a dress makes her feel pretty. She scans the crowd for Ross. "Another year down," she murmurs by way of a toast, lifting the cup to her lips, although she doesn't really want it. The wine tastes acidic.

"Don't be so hasty," Kendrick advises. "We've got miles to go before we sleep. Have you seen the show?"

"I came over while it was being hung."

"Smart." She feels as if she's pitching forward in her high-heeled sandals. "It's not bad. There are a couple of printmakers and a sculptor who're pretty good." They already know the good photography students.

Alex waves at one of her advisees, who lifts his arm, showing off the red satin lining of his dramatic black cape. The Art School is out in full-dress tonight. From where she's standing she can see two vintage pillbox hats, a sequined taffeta bustier, and a feather boa from the thrift shop. One of the boys is wearing a tuxedo with a hot pink tee shirt and chartreuse Nikes.

"Did you see your student's paintings? You know, the pretty boy with the crush." She stiffens. "They're quite striking in a vulgar sort of way. That sofa's practically pornographic."

"Yeah, I thought so too," she says weakly.

A student approaches Kendrick, and Alex takes the opportunity to drift off. Damien, the new printmaking instructor, glides up, cupping her chin in his hands and warbling, "It's beautiful, but is it art?" In the next room she sets her drink on the serving table strewn with tiny foil shamrocks. Halloween is Pollak's holiday of choice. Last fall Damien came to the party as a banana and peeled. Across the room she can see a slice of Ross's canvas. The appeal of his photographs is that they are very simple and straightforward. He prefers painting, he's told her, because he's not restricted to what he sees. "Of course you are," she said.

"Hi." Two of her former students edge in toward the fruit tray. Ming Tayler has cut her hair very short to show off one long feather earring. When she was in Alex's class her trademark outfit was a ruffled calico nightgown and matching yellow knee socks. That was Alex's first semester, and a boy in the same class rode a unicycle up and down the halls until security made him park it in the bike rack. "Welcome to Ah-h-ht School," Kendrick had laughed when she told him.

"Have you seen the show?" The other girl, Kim, wears a button that says FELLATIO IS FUN. Alex has begun to wonder if everything always related to sex. The past week seems distorted with it, as if the world has no substance of itself but serves only to mirror her own warped libido. Surely it's just a problem of perspective. She was celibate by choice for so long she became celibate by habit. Now she's kicking the habit. Like any other addiction, it's left her out-of-whack.

"How does it feel to be graduating?" she asks them.

"Wonderful," Kim reports as Ming submits, "Scary." Kim helps herself to an orange slice and wipes juice from her chin. "I'm looking for a job, and—" Ming points to Kim—"she's going to Majorca for the summer, if you want to know the difference."

"What are you doing this summer?" Kim asks Alex.

"I don't know," she says. The question takes her aback. She doesn't know what she's doing right now.

"Oh, I thought you'd be going to Greece," Ming says innocently, a blunder for which Kim sneaks her a look scarcely less subtle than a stiletto heel. Then both of them mask curious glances at Alex.

All right. If they want to jump to conclusions, let them. Ross has let her know that more than a few of her students think she sleeps with Kendrick; it's his way of accusing her. She supposes it's the obvious conclusion, though it surprises her all the same. She wouldn't have thought students took that much interest in teachers' lives. Accused this past week, she's thought of it herself. Impossible, she realized at once. You can't have casual sex with someone you love. Already Ross has become so sulky she's beginning to wonder if you can have casual sex with anyone at all.

"You must be thinking of Steve Kendrick," she says sweetly, for revenge.

She assumes he's still going. Last fall they talked about going together to take pictures, but now it's out of the question. She can't leave the country with Ted in a coma. Even if she hasn't seen him in eleven years, even if she won't see him now, even though he could die any minute, and then that would be it—she would have lost the chance forever, and yes, she would be sorry.

She has no idea why she's so irked with these girls. "My husband is in the hospital," she says in a stiff voice. Instantly remorse clogs her chest. It's as if in mentioning Ted, in using him for an excuse, she has violated their last bond, one that no one else—certainly not Ross—could sever.

The gallery seems suddenly airless. "Excuse me," she says. A swirl of noises wraps her like smoke as she tries to make her way back to the entrance. Someone bumps her, spilling wine down her skirt. And then, just as she's almost reached the door, it opens, and in steps Marjean with the last person Alex wants to encounter. She shrinks back into the crowd, but it's too late; Ross has spotted her.

"It's nice to see you again," Alex says, extending her hand to Marjean even as Ross is still stumbling over his reintroduction. Her smile feels trembly, and her eyes ache with a swell of unsheddable tears.

"You too." Marjean's eyes sparkle as she takes in the scene. "I can't wait to see the show." Alex feels a twinge of guilt—she goes to too many openings. "Are all these students graduating?"

"I can't *wait* to graduate." Vehemence burns through Ross's voice. His color has deepened. Even his eyes seem scorched. He stares at Alex. "You look pretty," he says softly.

Acknowledging the compliment with a pinched nod, Alex drops her eyes to her Dior stockings and expensive apricot suede sandals and wishes she hadn't changed clothes. Marjean is wearing chunky-heeled sandals of crinkly imitation black patent and a polyester dress that hits the thick of her calves and makes them look heavy.

Ross looks as if his boots pinch. He's miserable, and if he's not careful, Marjean is going to know it and know why. "Enjoy the show," Alex says. "There's wine and cheese in the next room."

"I'm glad we saw you." Marjean's smile is so genuine that in spite of Ross Alex feels her own open. Marjean has the touching radiance of an exhausted mother who doesn't often have a sitter for the night.

"How are your children?" Alex asks.

"Oh. Well. They're fine." Marjean swallows a laugh and cuts her eyes at Ross, who apparently knows the story but gives no indication. "The reason we're so late—Karen whopped Derek—that's one of the little boys I keep—over the head with a firetruck, and we had to go to the hospital for stitches."

"Oh no."

Marjean gives a cheerful shrug. "It happens."

Unexpectedly Alex recalls the injuries Lizzie's kids used to inflict upon each other, remembers with a searing in her heart out of all proportion Tice kicking sand in Lucy's eyes and herself saying sternly, "Apologize to your sister," their two faces round with babyfat and id. Recalls the children who will pull each other's hair forever in the photographs from Crow Hill.

"I worked with children once," she says slowly, almost in a whisper. She doesn't hear Marjean's reply. Outside, in the small brick courtyard, she doesn't remember taking her leave.

A pearly twilight deepens in the trees. The sound of the party tinkles through the open windows, and a breeze fragrant with tobacco skitters through the magnolia leaves. She feels unbearably sad, in a nameless way she wants to savor, almost as if the shock and anger, even the concupiscence, of the past two weeks have worn through to something truer. A plane skims along the sky, winking lights on its way to Byrd Field, and she closes her eyes, imagining the cozy dome of light inside the cabin, the flight attendant moving down the aisle to bring a pillow, a man snoring softly as somewhere in the front a baby cries, and then she opens her eyes as if she is falling from a height, sinking into the darkness that has come, perfectly, just in that moment, to cover her like honey. When she hears Ross's step behind her, she whirls in fury. "Don't be a fool."

"Am I?" Kendrick says. She stares at him, blinking. "Are you okay?"

For several moments she can't speak. Finally she says, "I swear, if you ask me that one more time I'm going to scream." She tries to press her lips in exasperation, but instead they loosen themselves into a smile that is only half peeved. Somehow she doesn't mind his intrusion.

"Sorry." His smile is sheepish. He sniffs the air. "Nice out. Want to take a walk?"

As they leave the courtyard, the cobblestone alley snares her heels, and she stumbles, steadying herself against his shoulder. She walks in silence for a minute, concentrating on her feet. "My sandals are killing me," she admits when they reach the corner.

"Have a seat." As they sit on the low wall in front of the brownstone mansion that serves as the administration building, he dips his head to inspect them. "Why did you buy them?"

"They match my skirt."

"Good for you," he says, and inwardly she smiles. All practicality himself, he is always encouraging her to live a little, buy something, go somewhere, have a good time. His single indulgence is a vintage MG, though he drives his equipment around in a second-hand wagon with split vinyl seats.

"This always reminds me of that big stone house across from Holy Trinity in Limestone," she says. "Remember? The coffeehouse, the Cellar, was in the basement."

"That's a blast from the past."

"This is prettier though." She tips her face up to the plush, star-studded sky. "It's such a beautiful city."

"Are you telling me you want to leave?"

"No." She turns to him in surprise. She's never thought about leaving. What would she do without him? She hasn't thought about this either, but as she says it she knows it's true: "I just want to quit VCU."

"You're a good teacher," he points out.

She thinks this is true. Or was, before she started carrying on with one of her students. She likes teaching, though she wasn't certain when she started that she would. "I don't know how to explain it—it's working for the university, it makes me feel owned." Self-consciously she laughs. "I know. You're going to tell me to grow up. You're going to point out that Eugene Smith went crazy working for *Life* and remind me how I used to bitch about working at *Geographic*. Nobody's free."

"You want to go back to freelance?"

"I don't think I know what I want to do right now," she says honestly.

"Maybe it's not a good time to be making decisions."

"I just don't want to teach kids how to make routine images a little bit better than everybody else's routine images. They want to learn to be successful, to make a product, and who can blame them? Or maybe it's just that I grew up around an art department. It seems like such a small world." She doesn't add that it's such a small world she's bedded her own student. "I think I need to do something that doesn't let me hide quite so successfully from myself." She shifts on the stone seat. "Did I ever tell you I tried to teach photography to children?"

Kendrick turns his head. "And how did that go?"

"Lousy." She laughs. "I had this romantic notion that they would pick up the camera, discover the world, and be transformed. I didn't have the faintest idea how to go about it of course. I ended up taking pictures of them. So maybe I was the one who learned to see." *I didn't go to Mississippi to save the Negro, I went to save myself*, Ted had said, but she had been young enough to think he could save both. Well, she got what she deserved. She'd been so young she'd meant for him to save her too.

"The Crow Hill series."

She'd nearly forgotten she'd published them, not as a book, but a magazine spread. "Umhm." Then she blurts, "There was a woman in the gallery—one of my students brought a date—who reminded me of someone I used to know back then. Her name was Lizzie. She was such a natural person—or maybe that quality just stands out when you spend all your time around artists."

"No doubt."

"She loved kids. She had three—well, four, but I never saw the last one. They moved away." Alex pauses.

"Do you hear from her?"

"No," she says. So many lost connections. It's been a decade since she visited Nelson, soon after he got out of prison, to ask if he would contact her if he heard from Ted. A flickering TV screen illuminated the room where they ate ice cream with his mother; later he took her into the kitchen to show her his poetry, freighted with dogma that struck her as better left to prose. When she asked about Ted again, he didn't answer.

Ted. Matt and Stacy. Her mother. Her father. All the people who left and never said good-bye.

"I never would have thought we'd lose touch," she as his hand brushes her shoulder, and she realizes that she should have a jacket, she's cold. "It's hard to believe her kids would be almost grown. She was having a baby—it was something she was good at, her husband called the night the baby was born, everything seemed fine, but I guess they found out later there was something wrong with him, I never did understand exactly what, just he needed a lot of special care, and I guess she was so busy …"

For several minutes they sit in companionable silence. It's unnecessary for him to say "I'm sorry," just as it seems unnecessary for her to explain that thinking of Lizzie after so many years, she's sad, but also feels as if she's found something she had lost.

"It happened right after Ted disappeared, so I didn't find out for a long time, but if I'd been there, maybe things would have been different. I could have helped her, she would have told me what to do about Ted. She always said I needed to make a life with him." But they hadn't made a life, and it took her longer than it should have to understand he had never wanted to. "Of course, that's not to say I would have listened. After all, I've never listened to you." She offers him a sad smile, then stands, brushing the folds out of her skirt. "Anyway, it's time I let you get back to the party."

"You're not going back?"

She shakes her head. "I've put in my appearance."

"Me too." He stands. "If you don't mind, I'll walk you home." They both know she shouldn't be walking by herself in the Fan at night, but it's where she lives; she can't lock herself in every dusk. "Unless you've changed your mind about dinner."

"I'm not hungry. I don't feel good," she admits. "How about an ice cream cone?"

He falls in step beside her. "Baskin-Robbins?" They could walk to the shop on Grace Street, but he seems to understand that she doesn't want to run into anyone. "My car's just a few blocks up Floyd."

As they pass the house where Ross lives, at the corner of Harrison and Grove, a little throe of memory shakes through her. Already Ross seems a long time ago. She won't see him again; without knowing it she'd decided in the gallery. She glances at Kendrick, but he is whistling softly and hasn't noticed. As if there were anything to notice. An impetuous little roll in the hay is all. Men do it all the time and never miss a train. She's not *derailed*, for god's sake. There's been a sexual revolution. No one's looking for her scarlet *A*.

She sinks into the leather seat of the open MG as he brings her a jacket from the trunk, corduroy worn to a velvet softness that smells faintly of gasoline. Wind whips tendrils loose from her braid as he slips a tape in. Brahms' Fourth Symphony. She closes her eyes to listen.

They eat their ice cream in the car. Stars pierce the inky sky, which seems as full of promise or illusion as the hoods of the cars gleaming with neon light. It's the kind of night when teenagers fall in love. When she's finished her cone, she balls up her napkin and drops it in the pocket of his jacket. "This is nice." She faces him. "I guess I don't have to tell you that the business with Ted really knocked me for a loop. These last two weeks haven't exactly been the best, and I want you to know how very much I appreciate everything you've done, even if I haven't acted like it. Not just now. No one could have been a better friend."

"That works both ways." He is looking at her closely.

She arches her back a little, to expose her whole face to the sky. "Do you remember the time we went to Speakers Corner?"

"Of course."

What she sees when she tries to picture London, a city so vast she never untangled the map of it in her head, is the Sunday afternoon they spent in Hyde Park perhaps four years after Ted disappeared. She can't remember why Kendrick was there; she had been on her way to photograph the Isles of Scilly, and they met for lunch on a patio overlooking the lazy summer scene on the Serpentine, the rowboats and distant bathers on the Lido, a scene so rich with light that it hangs in her mind with the effulgence of a painting. Then they walked on to Speakers Corner, where the zealots were holding forth, all those communists, fascists, feminists, gays, flag-wavers, ranters, reformers, and repenters. There had not been an act among them that could touch Ted Neal, whose gift had been the beautiful attention of reason, and without his voice, his matter-of-fact voice, the words were no more than the hollow echo inside every prison of ideas. She had photographed the crowd to keep from crying: hecklers, trendy couples strolling from one soapbox to another. From the green canvas rent-a-chairs on the lawn, women in purdah tended flocks of noisy children in bright Western garb. And as she watched, an old man in an elegant topcoat delivered a grimy, olive-eyed toddler swaddled in layers of gypsy skirts into the hands of a tramp with the glittering white eyes of a lunatic. She snapped them just as gentleman and madman both bent to hear the child's solemn whisper in a way that assured her the child was not in danger. When she glanced up from the viewfinder, pleased with her luck, she caught Kendrick's smile and understood that he had hoped for such a healing.

"That was a good day," she says as he pulls into traffic. As the car picks up speed his hand loosens on the gearshift. Brahms glorifies the air that furls around them. In the neon strip of Broad Street, his profile glistens, and she wants suddenly to admit how crazy she's been. She won't see Ross again, and she wants him off her conscience. But she can't tell Kendrick. He's her chair, it would put him in an awful position.

He nudges the car into a space on West Avenue, and for a moment they sit listening to the hood tick. Light pools along the street beneath the old-fashioned lamp posts and seeps from the windows in shuttered strips. She turns toward him. "I saw your friend Jack when I went back to New York."

Stunned, she looks away. She has no reason to tell him about Jack.

"I know. He told me." Kendrick's voice is quiet.

"What?" Her indignation lasts only a second before it strikes her funny. Of course he would have told. He had seen her, and Kendrick hadn't. She gazes out her side of the car. In the pocket of his jacket she keeps rolling the little ball of her napkin. "I looked him up. I don't know why, really. I never liked him. I wanted to freelance, and I thought maybe he could help me with some contacts." She should drop the subject. "I asked about you, and he showed me your book. I hadn't known about it." Her voice is full of sludge.

Kendrick takes his glasses off and holds his head. "I'm sorry."

"I didn't mean to blame you."

"I am so sorry." His spine straightens against the seat.

"It doesn't matter. After all I posed for the pictures. It was your work. You had every right to use it."

"Not without telling you." Neither of them speaks as a couple pass on the sidewalk, voices climbing. Then slowly he says, "I didn't do it for revenge."

"I know that."

"I used to think that if I had it would be unforgivable. Now I know that would have been the only reason that could excuse me." At last he turns his face toward her. In the darkness, without his glasses, his eyes have taken on a clarity without color. "I've done three unforgivable things in my life. One was that book. Another was to think I could have any excuse at all to make love to a fifteen-year-old girl."

For a long time there is silence. She can see through his eyes to the center of the earth, where she reads all the numbers off the pennies that someone has sown in a bottomless spring for luck. She has to swallow to keep her pulse from beating at her throat. "You said there were three."

His eyes shift. "That was something I did to my wife," he says, and for a moment the words seem to hang in the air before they fall between them like distance.

Chapter 14

1960-1962

Afterwards that first night she stood on Kendrick's porch in the fragrant darkness sweetened by a drift of music from a party down the street. Beneath the wash of streetlights everything seemed to glisten. "I want to stay with you," she said as he closed his arms around her shoulders.

"I wish you could."

Her mother was still out. In her room her bathing suit lay wilted where she'd left it. Alex let the white dress fall around her feet. Dreamily she touched her clavicle, as if to confirm that there were still bones beneath her skin. The room seemed stuffy. When she lay down, something scratched her cheek. There was a note pinned to her pillow, and for a moment as she stood squinting in the light, she laughed in delight, wondering how he had managed to leave it. Only after a minute did her mother's handwriting come clear:

Call your father's wife. Nancy.

Kendrick accompanied her to L.A., where he bought her a black eyelet dress because the one she'd packed was white. She hadn't meant to be disrespectful; she'd just brought the one she liked. And staying in a hotel with him seemed more like a honeymoon than a funeral. She was sad and happy at the same time, which wasn't right. Her father had killed himself. She wanted to take everything back. Maybe if she had told him she loved him …

At the wake Nancy's dress was black, tight, and shiny. "We have to talk, we have to talk," she promised in the excited whisper of a prom queen and rushed off to accept condolences. Alex drank a pink lady too quickly and felt sick. "Aren't you on 'The Edge of Night?'" a woman asked, but was immediately corrected by her companion, who peered at Alex through harlequin bifocals and sprayed a fine mist of spit. "I remember you. You played Kathy Lang on *The Guiding Light*."

"Actually, I'm his daughter," Alex said.

"Who? Oh, *his* daughter," the woman in glasses said. "Well I'm sorry for your loss. I loved *Katie Blue*." She dug in her bag. "I wonder—would you mind signing my copy?"

"Yes, she would mind." Kendrick steered Alex away. At the table they ran up against Nancy, who surveyed Alex for a long, tragic moment. The beehive atop her head was knocked askew, and mascara had smeared beneath one eye. She was drunk and weeping. "Why did you come?" she said to Alex. "Do you think he left you money?"

"He was her *father*," Kendrick said. "She came to pay her respects."

Back in Limestone Kendrick insisted on driving her home every night. In the evening they made love, which was so thrilling and sweet it was hard to believe she'd been afraid. Afterwards his skin felt like sunglow against hers as she drifted inside a rosy parenthesis until some chance separated their heartbeats, and in the little space that opened between, she would hear the tick of the clock. No matter how hard she tried, she couldn't block it out, that dwindling inside until he drove her home to sleep in her single bed, all in case her mother should look in, which for his information she didn't. "I don't care," he said, but he didn't understand. Alex wasn't arguing, just complaining.

Only once did her mother mention her father. "I wouldn't have left that note if his wife had told me," she said. "I may have hated him, and I'm sorry I didn't want you and have never been a good mother, but I'm not a monster. It was no way to find out, and I am sorry on your account." It was the first time she could remember her mother addressing her in years, and all she could think to say back was, "It's okay," though it wasn't.

She picked a fight with Jo Yellen to account for her absence at the pool and turned Kevin down for a date, then stammered when he asked her why. It was romantic, she told herself, just like *Romeo and Juliet*, a secret love affair, though her deceptions felt more bothersome than tragic. Still, she was happy. The restlessness that had twitched inside her limbs and soured her voice was gone. What did it matter where she slept? He only grew quiet when she stormed, and if she forced him into a quarrel, she immediately collapsed in a puddle of tears because she was afraid he wouldn't love her. He was such a gentle man. He felt guilty, and it only made things worse for him to be reminded.

But he couldn't take her out to dinner. They couldn't be seen together at a movie.

School began. Alex resigned from the Arts Society and the English Club, but even so she didn't reach East Maple Street till after four, and two nights a week he taught. Committee meetings dragged out his afternoons, and as the new department member, he was invited to every party. Plus he needed some time for his own work. *Work*: she came to hate the word. She wanted to take pictures too, but for her it was just a hobby. She couldn't even join the U-School Camera Club, for fear of missing him on the afternoons when he didn't have a meeting. The Camera Club was full of creeps anyway. It made her laugh to think of what her friends would say, except she rarely saw her friends outside the cafeteria at lunchtime, where the same old prattle grated on her nerves.

For her mother fall brought the resumption of the dinners and parties exchanged around Tenure Hollow. At the end of October she held her annual cocktail buffet. Kendrick was invited.

"You don't have to go," Alex pointed out. "She'll never miss you. The whole department's invited."

"Aren't you going?"

"I have to. My mother makes me help serve." What he meant was that he'd made up his mind. She hated the way he feigned nonchalance whenever he was challenged.

"Actually, I'd like to meet your mother."

"You already did."

"Briefly," he said. "Besides, it's a school party."

But she wanted to keep her separate lives separate. “So you think if you don’t show she’s going to come to the conclusion that you must be, now let me see—well, it must be obvious, it *couldn't* be anything else—you’re screwing her daughter.”

“Don’t use that word,” he said.

They were defrosting his refrigerator. She stepped aside to let him replace the pan of hot water, then stabbed at the mound of ice inside his freezer. “Don’t you have a hairdryer?”

“Not that I’ve noticed.”

“I thought maybe your girlfriend would have left one.”

“You’re my girlfriend,” he said.

It made her mad: he wouldn’t give in, and he wouldn’t fight with her either.

She was placing an artichoke casserole on the table when she spotted him. He hadn’t seen her, and she set the burning dish on its trivet, fleeing to the kitchen for a basket of French bread. She was glad he had come after all. All day, cleaning house, she’d missed him.

“Hello, Alex.” Irene Yellen picked at the olives. “If I’d known you were going to be here, we could have brought Jo.”

“We’re not speaking,” Alex felt obliged to mutter. Drink in hand, Kendrick was talking to the department chair, Roland Tucker.

“Take a plate,” Alex told the instructor of fashion design whom she and Jo called the Mad Hatter. “My mother wants someone to start the line.”

Across the room Jaakko Haanpää leered at them. A short man with dyed black hair and a shiny mustache, he had a habit of preening on tiptoes that gave Alex and Jo Yellen fits. Wouldn’t Jo love to know that he was making eyes at the Mad Hatter?

Her mother, Hélène, whisked by, stunning in a low-cut blouse. “Alexandra, could you check to see how the ice is holding up?” Roland Tucker was still talking with Kendrick, who lifted his eyebrows and smiled ever so slightly when she passed. “I don’t deny there’s been some interesting work,” Roland said, “but you can hardly compare Steiglitz to Monet.”

Alex turned around. "Are you kidding? Monet must have painted a hundred pictures a day. Haystacks, water lilies, bam bam bam. When he got old he had his paintbrush strapped to his wrist."

"That was Renoir," her mother said. "Hello, Steve. I'm glad you could make it. Get something to eat."

Kendrick followed her mother toward the table without looking back. Was it supposed to be a crime even to know her? Alex touched her hair. She was wearing a pink angora sweater that brought out the delicate shell-pink of her cheeks. She had tried on three others before deciding. "Well, 'The Flatiron' is just as pretty as any Monet," she said to no one. What was the point of ignoring her? Her mother already knew she'd posed.

"Hey, gorgeous. Come on and eat." Dr. Yellen squeezed her shoulder. "You know, you and Jo really ought to make it up. We miss you."

Roland Tucker had rejoined her mother and Kendrick at the table. "The real question is," her mother was saying, "does it express a vision or simply record? After all, photography has gone a long way beyond making apples look like apples."

Alex sat by herself in the corner. Someone had left a cigarette butt in the pocket of a twist of stainless steel titled "Woman." When she looked up again, Kendrick was still standing near the table, chatting with a petite brunette. They were holding their plates but had set down their drinks, and the girl's free hand flew up toward her face when she laughed.

It was time for her to put out the desserts and pour the coffee. A sculptor whose name she couldn't remember held out his hand. "Where's your date, pretty? You don't want to waste your Saturday night on us fogeys."

"Don't tease her," his wife said. "Girls that age are sensitive."

As soon as she was done, Alex opened the back door and stepped onto the deck. It was a cool evening with a full, copper-colored moon just above the trees. She leaned against the railing and inhaled the smoky autumn pungence. Behind her the door clicked, and a pair of hands slipped over her eyes. "I'm not going back in there," she said. "*Why* did you have to come?" She turned around and took a step backward. "Oh."

Jaakko Haanpää smiled at her through the gap between his teeth. Then, just like that, he kissed her, his mouth sour and wet.

"Stop it." She backed from him. He was still smiling. In the light from the kitchen his eyes looked glazed. She thought of her father, who had drunk much too much but always remained perfectly handsome. Jaakko Haanpää buried his face in her neck and rubbed his hand over her breasts. "What are you doing?"

"You're so beautiful," he moaned, his breath hot in her ear. "The way you move, your eyes, your mouth, your legs, your breasts."

"Cut it out." Alex twisted as he reached under her sweater and pawed at the back of her brassiere. He had backed her into the railing, one hand jammed beneath her bra. The railing cut into her back as she raised her hand between them. "I'll scream. I'll tell my mother." His cheek scraped hers, and she wrenched free. "You filthy, filthy man," she sobbed and slammed into the house.

The crowd had dwindled, though Kendrick was still there, in a chair beside the Mad Hatter. Alex took a seat at the end of the sofa. Roland Tucker sat at the other end, swirling the whiskey in his glass. Her mother and Anja Haanpää were on the loveseat, their heads bent over a book of Japanese Ukiyo-e. Roland gave Alex an apprehensive smile. He was waiting for his wife, who was still engaged in conversation near the ruin of the table. "What are you majoring in, Alice?"

Alex started. "Excuse me?"

He fell silent as Jaakko Haanpää came in and squeezed between them. Jaakko adjusted his tie, gave Alex an oily smile, and picked up the decanter. "Anja. A glass."

"I'll get it." Her mother rose.

"No, really, we should be going," Anja said with a sharp look.

"It is that time," Nydia Tucker said, strolling back from the dining area.

"Jaakko!" Anja said, and he snapped to his feet.

Kendrick was still seated in the Barcelona chair. The hostess seemed startled as she turned back from the foyer, but she said smoothly, "Another drink, Steve?" then frowned as she noticed his untouched glass.

"No thanks."

Her mother sank to the loveseat. "I swear to God if Roland Tucker ever smiled his face would break." Alex was slumped on the sofa. "Alexandra, if you're that tired go to bed." She stood and began emptying small ashtrays into larger ones. "Jaakko looked good. He was in the hospital last summer, and he hasn't been feeling well. Did you meet him, Steve? He chairs Uralic and Altaic Studies."

Alex was staring at the empty fireplace. "He attacked me," she said in a high voice.

"I'm sure there's more coffee if you'd prefer," her mother said.

"He kissed me," Alex said, louder.

"Who?"

"Dr. Haanpää."

"Don't be ridiculous."

"He put his hand inside my bra."

"Alex, the Haanpääs have been our neighbors for years. Anja is a very attractive woman, and as far as Jaakko is concerned you're still a child."

"Well, he's a child molester then," Alex said, and as Kendrick shot her an angry glance, his first glance of the night, she curled into the corner of the sofa. All evening he had watched everyone talk to her as if she were ten years old.

"That's not funny," her mother said at the same time Kendrick said, "Stop it."

"It's not supposed to be funny," Alex said. She sat up to face Kendrick as he set his glass down. His face was tight. "He practically raped me, and you don't even care."

"Care?" he said. "Why the hell do you think I'm still here? Are you okay?"

"How do I know why you're here? I told you not to come." Alex tossed her head back. "Are you trying to put the make on my mother? Who was that girl you were talking to?"

"Are you all right? What girl?" he added as her mother gave him a long look.

"Just forget it," Alex said.

"What I'd like to know is whether your mother cares." Kendrick turned to Hélène.

"I beg your pardon."

"You heard what she said."

"Nothing happened," Alex said, sinking deeper into the sofa. "Go home. I'm sorry I mentioned it."

Her mother leaned back on the loveseat, arching her neck and observing them coolly. Alex was weeping. Kendrick crouched beside her and touched her hair. "Are you okay?"

"Alexandra, if you're going to snivel, go to your room." Her mother had taken her high heels off, and she raised one stockinged foot to scratch her big toe delicately against the other ankle. "I'm afraid my daughter likes to create scenes. And to tell you the truth I find them unpleasant. I'm sure you've become quite close friends with her in your frequent photographic sessions, but as I have no interest in knowing anything more, shall we just agree upon quite close friends and say goodnight?"

Kendrick stood and stared at her mother coldly. For a minute no one spoke. Alex had stopped crying and was watching them as they watched each other with a concentration that seemed to have thresholds that they crossed without a flicker of expression. A sickening thrill of fear ran down her spine.

"For God's sake," Kendrick said. "Don't you know where your daughter has been these past months?"

For an instant an uncurtained look of fright passed across her mother's face and was gone. "You realize I could have you fired."

"I'm sure you could have me arrested too, though if you want to have anyone prosecuted you might give a thought to your greasy next-door neighbor. I *love* your daughter."

Hélène held her hand up. "I think you've said enough." Kendrick was still lookng at her, but at last she turned away. "Personally I find these little melodramas more tedious than entertaining. What you do with my daughter is no concern of mine. But I will not be embarrassed. I will not have her hanging around you at school, and I won't have you displaying any photographs you've taken of her, which I suspect are many and lewd."

"I'm an artist, not a pornographer."

A trace of a smile curled at her mother's lips. "That can be a very fine distinction sometimes, and I think we both know that you lack judgment. Good night."

"Alex?" He leaned over the sofa.

"I'm fine," she said without raising her head.

"*Good night*, Mr. Kendrick."

"Do you not care about your daughter at all?" Alex heard the weather stripping on the front door whoosh shut and then the chime of glasses being gathered. Her mother's footsteps whispered across the carpet, and she felt a shadow fall across her back.

"Stand up." Her mother's hand cracked against her cheek, and the corner of the coffee table slammed into her shoulder. "You stupid girl." By the time she picked herself up, her mother had left the house. They never mentioned Steve Kendrick again, not even the next spring, when he hung his show in the university gallery, twenty photographs of Alex, none of them nudes.

"He didn't do anything," Alex had to promise Kendrick over and over. "Why couldn't you just go home?"

"Because I didn't like the way that greaseball was looking at you."

"Well, I don't know why," she said. There was a reason she hadn't wanted him to come. She was ashamed, and it had nothing to do with Jaakko Haanpää. She hadn't wanted Kendrick to know that until she met him she was the girl that no one had loved.

Nothing changed: she still slept on Owen Drive, but spent her afternoons and evenings at his apartment. It was at school that things were different. She could feel silence rippling away from her in waves. She and Jo passed each morning at their lockers without speaking until February, when Jo turned a pitying face toward her and asked, "Are you going to the Valentine dance?"

"No," Alex mumbled.

Jo slammed her locker door and came around Alex's. "I didn't figure you would be. Kevin asked me." Alex took her geometry book from the top shelf of her locker and raised her hand to stop a tear from forming. She didn't know why she felt like crying. "Can you believe Sue Lawrence is going with Bobby Blight? 'Scuse me, Bobby Bright."

Alex tried a smile. "So how have you been?"

"Okay. The folks are giving me the VW for my birthday if I even pass geometry." She sighed. "Not a chance. How about you?"

"Super."

"Liar. Anyway, I wasn't asking about grades." Jo drew closer. "Did you hear Tippie is p.g.?"

"Figures," Alex said.

"Diana Wells is two-timing Mike with a reeeally fine freshman at the U who's wild about her—like he sends flowers and writes her poems; her parents are *pissed*. Actually the poems are pretty gorpy if you ask me—you wouldn't believe the way she minces around when she reads them." Jo paused for breath. "The thing is, I always figured we were a cut above, you know? I mean—" she rolled her eyes—"the rest of these barfballs ... Say, you don't have to run off, do you? I mean, do you have to cook his dinner, have it waiting on the table, stuff like that?"

"He cooks," Alex said quietly. "I do the dishes."

Again Jo's look was full of pity. She lowered her voice. "Some of the girls think it's really romantic, but personally, I think you screwed up. And don't go getting huffy. Even my parents know, for Pete's sake." Alex kept her face rigid as her hand froze on her biology book. "I didn't mind that you were snotty, 'cause, well, being your best friend, a lot of guys that wouldn't ever have noticed me—I mean you were such a snob, hanging around with you, the person they got to talking to was me. Well, and we had some good times together—remember the chocolate pizza and the time we teepeed Dave Moon? But the thing is I didn't ever feel I really knew you. I mean I just didn't ever feel like you were there." Jo's brow puckered as her voice went flat.

The biology book slid onto the pile. Last night's snow had turned to slush and a bone-chilling dampness. Alex turned the collar of her coat up and closed her locker. Jo trailed her to the door, where Alex stopped, one mitten on the crash bar. "I guess I'd better get home," she said, though Kendrick had a late meeting. "Well, to Kendrick's I mean."

"That's his name?"

"Steve." For a moment Alex hesitated. She would have liked to tell Jo how she started calling him Kendrick because "Mr. Kendrick" seemed too formal and she felt awkward saying "Steve." But the alliances had shifted.

"Well," Jo said, "see you," as they both lingered, hugging their books to their chests.

"You want to go get a Coke?" Alex offered, but Jo shook her head.

"My parents'd kill me. I mean, Alex, you cost me, you know?" Jo pushed the door open.

"But why?" Alex called after her. "Why should this be different?" Jo turned around on the sidewalk. Her salt-stained flats were already sopping. "Tippie? Everybody knows Diana and Mike, and now she's got a college boy? Nobody thinks she's a leper."

Jo shifted feet. "Yeah. But the thing is you were *always* an untouchable. You were a real zero for a friend."

"Well, thanks for the honesty," Alex snapped. "I guess people who are full of shit are easy to know."

She kicked piles of slush as she walked up East Maple Street, rehearsing all the nastier, more clever retorts she might have used, but she wasn't mad exactly. At least she wasn't only mad. Or maybe she wasn't only mad at Jo. Kendrick didn't get home until seven. His committee had finished up at 5:30 and gone for a beer.

He had his own problems. He'd truly become an untouchable, that most dangerous of colleagues, a man who at any moment might be fired. But her mother refused to acknowledge his transgression, and so the issue of his turpitude could not be raised. His contract was renewed.

She didn't know where the year went. In June she turned sixteen, and Kendrick taught her to drive. He taught summer school; she took a job as a carhop at Hoot's. When he picked her up, it was too late to go back to his apartment. They kissed good night in his station wagon, and he pushed her away when she pulled at his clothes. They argued. They never saw each other. It was his fault for being busy; it was her fault for working nights. But she had to do something, and it was the only job she could find. She didn't tell him that she liked the drive-in, where the girls hauled their stools outside to sit, listening to

WLS all the way from Chicago on the car radios, chattering while the sky blackened and grew stars. Girl-talk. She hadn't known how much she missed it.

With her tips she bought a Nikon, but there was something wrong with her beautifully printed pictures—they were boring. She continued to pose, but his pictures had nothing to do with her; nor could they teach her how to fix hers. She had yet to figure out exactly what she wanted to photograph.

She went back to U-School for her junior year.

Kendrick began to meet his friends, mostly grad students, at Sammy's Ale House on occasion; he went to Wallace parties alone. He took up tennis, a game he'd played in college. She tried to play with him, but she couldn't keep her eye on the ball, and irritation clipped his voice when she missed too many easy returns or walloped the balls into the creek. She couldn't volley; she couldn't legally drink a beer. Nor could she visit Canada with him at Christmas, and though he hated to leave her he hadn't seen his parents for two years, they were getting older, they'd sent the airfare; he could hardly refuse. Her mother went to New York. Alex cooked a hot dog for Christmas dinner and felt sorry for herself. When Kendrick returned, she sobbed the old year out and the new one in on the shoulder of his Christmas sweater because she was so glad to have him back. She spent the night curled against him, but her mother returned on January 2, and once again Alex was sleeping alone on Owen Drive. They argued. She wanted to stay with him. He was sorry: he understood that she was lonely; it was his fault; he shouldn't be impatient.

She was sorry too; she was happy, truly she was, but when they quarreled she forgot. When they quarreled he felt guiltier than ever, and that was even worse. Too, she had a histrionic streak that scared her. The ferocity of her anger shocked her. Where did it come from? She had always been so self-contained; she didn't know the girl who screamed at him and threw plates.

Finally, after a particularly bitter quarrel, he said it: it might be best for them both if they broke up.

Chapter 15

1967-1968

Alex wasn't sure when the word *revolution* crept into their vocabulary. Garth used it, but he had always used it; the Russian Revolution was his career, though on his lips it never brought Bolsheviks sweeping across the dark Russian Steppes, the stutter of gunfire or splash of blood, but the dim, heavy thump of library volumes, scrape of chair legs, and squeak of the card catalogue drawer; it smelled not of death, but of dust and dissertation bond.

In the fall they were still in Limestone. Ted had too many incompletes to graduate, and their room was stacked with books for unwritten papers. He was anxious to be done, though he had another three years of law school, if he went. He was no longer sure. He toyed with running for National Office, though he complained that Students for a Democratic Society lived in a world of acronyms that no one outside it could decipher. The next day it would be union organizing, the next divinity school and a ministry for social change, and the next law school again. Or maybe he would enlist and go to Vietnam.

"Is that supposed to be some kind of joke?" Stacy asked.

Alex wasn't worried. He would never kill because it was only fair that he be killed; he would never go to to war just to prove that in opposing it he was not a coward. It surprised her that he should feel so lost, but she knew what made him say it.

Leah had brought a Viet vet into their circle. His father was a Wallace professor, and though Cal was a couple of years older, Alex remembered his picture from a U-School display case, a smiling boy with a crew cut seated at a table with the championship debate team of 1959. She was haunted by the smile, which had left no trace in the mean flick of his yellow-brown eyes or the sneer that disfigured his face like a scar. He slept indiscriminately with Leah, Tulip, and the waifs Tulip brought home, but there was no tenderness in his address, nor did they seem to expect any. They admired his anger. If he left the bathroom door open or strode into the hall without his pants, scratched his balls or farted at the table, the authority of that anger superseded any bourgeois embarrassment. He knew what the war they opposed was really like, and Ted envied him that knowledge of the real world.

"Rich white boys aren't called to service in Youngstown," Ted pointed out when he decided not to burn his draft card. "Too much poor black meat to go around."

Stacy was outraged. "So why call attention to yourself, is that it?"

"I'm a little tired of symbolic gestures," he said stiffly. He was grouchy. Jeannie had graduated that spring, and he and his father had had words.

Alex had thought, as she came out of her depression, out of her apathy and inertia, that perhaps they could try for another baby, but the war dragged on, growing despite their efforts, and Ted seemed so discouraged she was reluctant to suggest anything so selfish as a personal life. She wanted him to bring it up. In the meantime at least she was busy. She had sold her softball series from Crow Hill, and the 1966 *Photo Annual* had reprinted one, as well as a portrait of Ted, brooding, a shadow over half his face as he sat with his hand almost absently in the peace sign.

"*Photo Annual '67*," the group cheered, raising their fists for a portrait as they left for the March on the Pentagon in October. But she didn't think of the *Annual* as she crouched in Arlington to photograph the marshals moving in on the demonstrators who broke through a side door. It happened quickly, but she was lucky and got a good shot. Though she would not admit it—in the thrill of the moment she had no time to think—it bothered her, that luck of being in the right place at the right time. Not the luck itself, for there were all those days when she didn't have it, and then how she envied painters. She deserved the luck; what bothered her was something else. At the center of every art is a question of allegiance, perhaps none quite so troubling as the photographer's, for the photographer functions in the crux of her identity, watching the man on the ledge, hoping he will not jump but knowing she will get a better picture if he does.

There was a lull after the marshals led the trespassers off, and she wandered. Somewhere in the North Parking Lot Ted and the others were listening to more speeches. Garth and Nelson had already been arrested, quietly, almost decorously, for crossing a police line, which they had done in order to be arrested, for despite Jerry Rubin's prediction of wholesale disruption, the strategy of the March was the symbolic gesture. Proposed to demonstrate the entire country's willingness to resist, it had been a matter of disagreement in their own house. Alex was unwilling to commit an infraction for which she had been licensed—it was patently dishonest, she had argued, and to her surprise Stacy sided with her. Matt always went with Stacy, and Ted would do what he would do. He was impatient of the collective decision anymore. But she knew how he felt about the token gesture, and neither he nor she was into wholesale disruption. He would be listening to the speeches that were impossible to hear over the crackly PAs, listening to the speeches and bored.

When she reached the parking lot, she spent the last of the light photographing the hippies. Gotten up in greatcoats, buckskins, feathers, and beads, they were swaying to the music of the Fugs, tinkling Hindu bells and chanting, trying to levitate the Pentagon. She caught sight of Norman Mailer and Robert Lowell, then zeroed in on Dr. Spock as he demonstrated how to flush a jail toilet, his right foot extended in a karate chop at the imaginary lever on the wall. Lucky again. She was off on the excitement, the pure exhilaration of shooting that was interrupted only when she paused to change her film.

It was late afternoon, and sharpness spiked the air. More than anything else in Washington—the sight of the crowd, the speeches, the slogans, the government buildings—the weather evoked in her the continuity of déjà vu, for the demonstrations were always in the spring or early fall, the days inevitably warm and sunny, the late afternoons starred by a chill, the nights just plain cold. She had learned to dress in layers.

The light was going. She dug in her camera bag for Ted's old Pendleton and crossed the parking lot to look for him. It was not quite dusk when she found him, huddled with Matt and Stacy on the Mall. A wind had sprung up, and as Stacy passed Alex a thermos her hand was cold.

"Get some good pictures, babe?" Ted asked.

"Mmhmm," she said. "How were the speeches?"

He shrugged. "Norman Mailer was arrested."

"I saw him." She sipped the coffee. "I got a great shot of Dr. Spock. Mailer's really short," she added.

"He's an asshole," Stacy said. "You'd be short too if your head didn't reach any higher than your butt."

A line of troops guarded the entrance. Some of the protestors had thrown flowers, and petals littered the pavement. The heady pungence of marijuana thickened the air, red coals dipping and skimming like fireflies out of season. Around them small fires flared and died as students touched matches to their draft cards. Farther away broken weather fencing was piled onto a bonfire. Matt and Stacy were necking. A flashlight bobbed on the wall to their left, and Alex heard the hiss of spray paint. She began to regret that they hadn't followed Garth and Nelson. The symbolic gesture had more appeal than a vigil the newspapers would characterize by petty vandalism and the naughtiness of smoking dope beneath the federal marshals' noses. "Going to be a long night," Ted said as she tucked herself inside his arm. She was sleepy. They had ridden the bus all last night; she had taken an aisle seat to stretch her legs, and all across Pennsylvania and Maryland she had been bumped out of sleep as people tripped their way back to the john.

She had dozed off. Ted was shaking her; she was just coming awake when a shock of cold water hit her face. She wiped her eyes and, in the instant in which she looked up, had the slow-motion sensation of watching the rifle smash down. The blow caught her on the forehead. She fell flat, and her ribs exploded, she was on all fours, retching, reaching for her face, falling forward, scrambling to her knees and falling each time the soldier kicked her, again and again. She couldn't hear her own screams in the screaming all around her. "Don't hit him, don't hit him! You want him to kill you both?"—Matt—then her arm wrenched, pavement tore her cheek, and the back of her skull slammed against a wall so hard her eyes seemed to knock through the sockets. Sobbing, she crawled into the paddy wagon through a shifting of bodies and low moaning, every contraction of her lungs another assault. When she touched her head, she recoiled from the greasy mess of her blood, stinging in her eyelashes, metallic in her mouth.

"Alex?"

It was Stacy, holding her jaw and crying.

"Here." Alex put a hand out. With the other she kept trying to staunch the blood.

"Jesus Christ," Stacy said and thrust her head through the door of the wagon. "Hey, you sons of bitches! This woman needs a doctor!"

"Are you okay?" Alex asked.

"I peed my pants." Stacy shouted through the door again. "They beat the shit out of the women. The men just got busted."

"Ted?" Alex's chest had caved in; she was having difficulty speaking.

Someone slid over to make room for Stacy. "Bastards," she said. "They waited till the press went home to move in."

At the detention center they stood in line to be fingerprinted, and then Stacy was whisked off to a cell while Alex was escorted to a dispensary. The fluorescent light hurt her eyes; she was having trouble focusing. A radio on the counter was playing the Tijuana Brass, and the nurse laid out Steri-strips with a pinched dispatch of her shoulders that let them know she thought they got what they deserved. The woman who came in with Alex had lost two teeth, and the nurse packed her mouth with cotton while the doctor stitched Alex's head. "This woman belongs in a hospital. She needs an X-ray," he said when the nurse had stripped her shirts off, then shrugged and taped her ribs. He was young, no more than thirty, with a weary hitch in his gait and unkempt speckling of blue-black shadow on his chin. They were not issued prison garb, and Alex had to put her bloody shirts back on.

When the nurse jerked her arm, Alex leveled a stony gaze at her. "We had a permit," she said, staring at the nurse's barbed blue eyes. In a moment the matron appeared with another group and claimed Alex.

"Hey, my father's a lawyer," Stacy yelled at the matron as she unlocked the cell door. "What the hell? It always worked for Nancy Drew."

Several other women were already sacked out on the bunks. One sat on the toilet with diarrhea. Tears ran down the woman's face, and after every explosion she looked up and said, "I'm sorry, everybody."

On the floor a girl kept saying, "They never read us our rights."

"Stop the war," someone shouted, and they took up the chant at each pass of footsteps. "Stop the war, stop the war, stop the war in Vietnam!"

"Did you get stitches?" Stacy asked.

Alex nodded. Her hair was crusty. "My ribs are broke. How's your jaw?"

Stacy tested the underpants she had hung over the edge of her bunk to dry. "They picked you out before dark. It drives them crazy to think that gorgeous women sleep with long-haired men." She fingered her jaw. "I'm okay. There are advantages to being ugly as sin."

"You're not ugly," Alex said. Her camera bag was missing, and for a bitter moment she was more angry over the lost picture of Dr. Spock than anything.

"Yeah, I know. I got a beautiful soul."

In the morning they were charged with resisting arrest, fined twenty-five dollars, and given suspended sentences of five days in jail. They had been forbidden to return to the Pentagon, from which their bus was to leave that afternoon, and the bailiff could not tell them if the men had already been arraigned, or if they had ever been arrested.

"Tell you what," Stacy said as they stood blinking in the sunlight outside the courthouse. "I could use a bath." She rooted in her knapsack, bringing up her wallet, grinning triumphantly as she waved a Master Charge. "It's my dad's. Never go to a demonstration without it. Plastic money, your lawyer's phone number, and a dollar's worth of dimes." Alex's head was throbbing. "No kidding, I paid my fine with it."

"They stole my camera," Alex said again. Her ribs ached.

"You should have seen my face. Just to be smart I ask, 'Will you take a credit card?' and without batting an eye the cashier says, 'Bankamericard, Master Charge, or American Express?'"

"I had a great shot of Dr. Spock."

"Let's get a cab to a hotel. We can phone my dad—Matt ought to be bright enough to call him, and the guys can meet us there."

"Stacy, I am not in a good mood," Alex said.

"So who is these days? C'mon. Room service and a great big greasy cheeseburger. *Alex*. I peed my pants. I would really like to wash them."

Alex didn't feel any of the elation she'd heard you experienced the first time you were beaten. She was supposed to thrill to know she'd really done it, had the guts to put her body on the line. Her body hurt too much. She was woozy. For days she felt so fogged she was afraid her brain was damaged. She was angry. Resisting arrest—she had never been arrested, only beaten and then charged. A misdemeanor, punishable by a fine of twenty-five dollars. Five years ago she had run a stop sign half hidden by a hedge, and the cop who handed her the twenty-five-dollar ticket called her ma'am. It was a proud anger, fine. In Selma she had looked upon the face of America and thought that nothing would move it. She had moved it. It had betrayed all its discipline and shown the beast inside. She had done it; she had put her body on the line.

Three weeks after the Pentagon she and Ted stood up for Jeannie's wedding. "Since when does our government go around beating children?" Justine demanded. Dancing at the reception, Alex overheard Brad say to Justine, "He knew there was likely to be violence." Justine drew a sharp breath. "I could wring his neck," she hissed. Alex looked for Ted, dancing with his sister. What did he care? The people were on his side.

But that winter Huntley and Brinkley brought the Tet offensive into the Neals' den and exposed the president as a liar. We're winning, he'd assured the American people only days before they watched the U.S. lose in living color, and suddenly everyone agreed, if not that it was an immoral war, at least that it was hopeless. In the spring they brought him down. "I shall not seek, nor will I accept the nomination of my party for another term as your president," Johnson told them, and the collective erupted into joyous shouts. "We won!" Matt cried. "We won!" wept Leah. Horns blared outside, and music shrilled from car radios. Houses emptied themselves into the streets as rolls of toilet paper sailed into the trees, spinning a garland of white ribbons against the kohl blue sky. On the porch Ted embraced Alex. "We won," she said. "We won," he echoed, but their voices were subdued, for neither of them had much faith in the peace candidate, Gene McCarthy. Looking at Ted's face divided by the darkness, she hoped they'd won, that the war would soon be over, but already she wondered what he would do without the augmented sense of being it inspired.

"It's good news," she said. At least his father would have to admit Ted had been right.

He put his arm around her, and they stood at the rail, watching their friends cavort. Someone was shooting firecrackers. Behind them Bob Dylan growled from the stereo. "Sergeant Pepper" poured out the open windows next door. A boy on the roof across the street was flinging macaroni from a box, and Alex was amused to recognize among the revelers several members of SDS who supported the line that electoral politics were irrelevant. From nowhere Nelson appeared with a bottle of champagne. "To our side!" he exulted and the cork burst into the yard. In the street a snake dance had formed. When Nelson took a swig from the dripping bottle and poured the rest over their heads, Ted wiped his face and laughed. "What the hey," he said. "Let's join the party." They linked arms with Nelson and skipped down the steps, taking up the chant. "Hey, hey, LBJ, how many kids did you *thrill* today!"

Five days later Martin Luther King was shot to death in Memphis. Later that month Columbia University went on strike. In June Bobby Kennedy was assassinated. In August the whole world watched while the Chicago police beat them with baseball bats and inside the convention hall Johnson's right-hand man, Hubert Humphrey, announced the politics of joy.

Alex couldn't remember when they began to use the word *revolution*.

Chapter 16

1982

Only the lamp beside her bed is on when she comes up the stairs to her apartment after Kendrick drops her off. Pausing to remove her sandals, she finds her way through by the rectangle of light it casts into the hall. She doesn't own a television. Alone at night, she can't stand the sound, which reminds her of her solitude without letting her draw herself up inside it. Likewise the lights. She prefers to leave the rooms dark and read in bed.

Her bed is an ornate white iron affair, trimmed with brass and layered like a birthday cake with patchwork and pillows, bought beside an Arkansas highway seven years ago when she stopped to photograph a sign that boasted *Gas*Gro*Antiques*Workshoes*Bibles*Beauty Salon.* It was a cheap shot, but she took it anyway, and later sold it to one of those coffee table nostalgia books that make rural poverty seem like a quaint and charming national resource. That was the year Saigon fell, and she was on her way home from photographing the first Vietnamese refugees at Fort Chaffee. She drove with the bed rattling in her open trunk all the way back to Chicago, where she set it up in the barren apartment near the El tracks when it came back from the strip shop, and wondered what had possessed her. She didn't want things. Especially she didn't want an extravagant bed. Or maybe she hoped Ted would be coming home soon. Others did. Their war was over.

Now she has things instead of hope, but long after she stopped hoping, she still imagined him imagining her. It was her secret way of keeping in touch. No longer able to picture him, she pictured herself for him: propped on the baroque bed beneath a hood of yellow light, in the spell of whatever book she has laid face down beside her, on the wall, in its dusky mist of gum bichromate, Steiglitz's Flatiron evoking the sound of horses' hooves and wheels on wet pavement, in a rose-colored room he never saw.

Tonight she means to imagine him. Kendrick has counseled her to see Ted so she will finally know it's over and let go. (And then what?) Tonight she will. Better than in person: she means to see him as an act of will. It can't be that hard. She concentrates first on the room: green or beige, some hospital color, lit by a cold fluorescent glare. The chalk-white face, flesh already shrinking to the skull. Beneath the sheet the arms and legs will have atrophied. A rubber trach tube grows worm-like from his throat; beside the bed a bag drains his body's waste. She means to concentrate until he's naked and she's staring at his sunken chest and withered cock. And then she'll know what's left of the life she was once foolish enough to think they might have had together.

When she comes into her bedroom, Ross looks up. He's sitting on her bed in his sock feet, still in his dress shirt, sleeves rolled and collar loosened. He has come in through the window and knocked the plissé shade down.

The bitter taste of rage fills her mouth. Her voice, white-hot, seems to come from somewhere behind her. One of her sandals strikes him on the temple. She picks up his boot and flings it, knocking the Steiglitz cockeyed and breaking the glass. The other boot falls with a thump against the bedpost. "Get out of my bed! Get out! Get out!"

As he comes off the bed, a baffled, almost thoughtful look on his face, she seizes the lamp. Her whole body shakes; she can feel her face jerking and something deadly swollen up inside her as she brings both arms above her head. He grabs her wrists and twists sharply, until pain snaps inside her brain, she uncurls her fingers, and the lamp smashes to the floor. Without taking his eyes off hers, he gives her wrists a last, emphatic wrench and lets go.

"You'll start a fire that way," he says, almost casually, as he yanks the plug from the wall, still without taking his eyes off hers just in case she tries to bean him again, and she wonders in an odd, lucid flash if he has some special hang-up—murder is okay by him, but not arson.

"You have no right." She's panting a little.

"I took Marjean home," he explains.

Viciously she snatches his jacket and tie from the wicker rocker and slaps them to his chest. "You had no right to break into my apartment."

"Easy as pie," he says. "You're lucky it was me."

The black glass where the shade has fallen is streaked with dirt. A cool breeze comes through the open sash. Saturday outside that window a pigeon beat frenetic wings, balancing on her feeder, and while they made love she listened to the sound as if it were a fluttering in her heart.

"You had no right."

"I wanted to see you," he says, a faint whine of injury in his voice.

"It's over."

"You say." His mouth is pinched into a bloodless white line. His eyes haven't left her since she raised the first shoe.

"What do you think—you can just break in whenever you want?" He doesn't seem to understand how violated she feels.

"Not likely. I value my life." He reaches to touch her hair, but she smacks his hand away. For the first time he drops his eyes. "The window wasn't locked."

"Get out."

He doesn't move. Outside a cat yowls, its mournful human voice growing louder, then receding. When she flies at him again, he lifts a hand to deflect her, but he's not quick enough to prevent one of her fingernails from digging a long red channel in his cheek. Tentatively he touches it, then checks his finger with a bright wince in his eyes that lets her know it hurts.

"It's over," she repeats.

"It was over last week too."

"A *week*." Let him wait on someone eleven empty years and then see how much promise a week can buy. He's so young he still thinks the most interesting thing that can happen to him is sex. The way he said, in the gallery, "I can't wait to graduate"—it hadn't occurred to her until that moment that he could think they had a future. Did he really think she would ever see him in public—doesn't he realize how humiliated she would be? True, there's no shame in sleeping with a younger man, and if she didn't know it before she certainly knows now how desirable other women find him. But that's it: she would be embarrassed for anyone to know that she'd succumbed to such obvious bait, as if she has no more imagination than a fish.

But it's not *anyone* she cares about. It's Kendrick. In her mind she sees him, whistling along beside her in the dark as they pass Ross's corner. *He* would know. Thank god she'd been tired. Thank god she hadn't asked him in.

"What does it matter how long it's been?"

"It matters." She knows better, but says it anyway: "Do you know how long I was with Ted?"

But he's not interested in Ted, which was his mistake, she thinks somewhere hard and cold in the back of her mind; he listened once and thought it was done. Listening is just a strategy for him. He doesn't grasp that Ted is what there is to know about her. When someone dies you can grieve and go on, but when someone disappears some part of you is always still waiting. One way or another, you go through the rest of your life with everything qualified.

"Your husband's in the past tense," he says and with a quick cut of his eyes adds, "Leave the lamp where it is."

Vaguely she recalls noticing a hole in his sock when she came in. They are both in stocking feet, and it strikes her suddenly that you can be angry in shoes or bare feet but not in your socks. "It's all right," she says. "Ted Neal died a long time ago for me. I'm not going to kill you for it."

He touches his cheek again. "Have you got a tissue?"

"In the bathroom."

He doesn't move. "Why?" His voice is flat. Something in his eyes tells her that the passing of her anger has convinced him. But then he says, "This afternoon ..."

She shakes her head. She can't give him a list of reasons. Reasons are subject to debate.

"Were you with Steve Kendrick tonight?"

She looks down, twisting one hand inside the other. She thinks of him as unformed, he's so young, but then she remembers that Lizzie used to say babies came out of the womb with their personalities already in place, and watching Lizzie's children she had seen the truth to that. He's not unformed. She just doesn't want to know him. "Yes, I was."

"I thought so." It doesn't seem worth her while to correct him. "Bitch. Fucking whore," he says, and then he's gone.

She doesn't need to imagine Ted after all. It's over.

Chapter 17

1962

On a bright June day just before she turned seventeen, just after Kendrick said the best thing for them both might be to break up, while he looked up a book in the Wallace library, she accepted a ride on the back of a motorcycle that jumped the curb and came to a stop in front of where she sat reading on the lawn. She didn't come home for three days.

On the second day she called Kendrick to tell him she was getting married.

"Aren't you a little young?" he said.

The biker was crazy. His name was Jimmy Ray Reeves, and he wore a spangled red candy-apple helmet. She held tight to his waist while he roared down county roads to a mobile home park where he lived in a smelly eight-foot-wide pink trailer. He called her baby, and they danced into his tables and chairs and drank all day and night. "Wild," he said when they waltzed into the door and broke it. "You okay?" he asked when she slipped off the back of the motorcycle and landed on her shoulder. She was fine. She was pickled, soused, shit-faced, wasted. She was wild. She called Kendrick and had to hang onto the glass to keep from sliding down the phone booth wall. She dropped the receiver. Her quarter wouldn't fit into the nickel slot. Afterwards she thought they might as well get married. They made a good couple. She was crazy too.

She passed out in the ladies' room of the county courthouse.

While he held her up she giggled, "I do. Wackado-wackado." They drank champagne out of the bottle; when it was gone they finished a case of beer and the whiskey they had started last night. He sprayed vomit over the living room while she coughed up her guts in the sink. When she woke, he was sprawled with his head in the shower, and she kicked him to see if he'd drowned.

He came up swinging. "Jesus fuck," he said as he stumbled to a chair.

She sat on the torn couch and blinked. Through the moth-eaten drapes the light was a shrieking amber. Her head felt like a fat woman's foot stuffed inside a shoe; her stomach had ruptured and spread. There was something wrong with her shoulder. When she tried to speak, her voice curdled in her throat.

"Want a beer?" The refrigerator door smacked the tin wall, and the noise rang in her head as he dragged himself back to the table. She hadn't known her body had so many parts that could hurt. "What'd you say your name was?"

She remembered it. "Alex."

"Ain't that a boy's name?" He drank off the beer and belched. "If I was you, Alex, I'd drink a brew. Hangover this bad ain't no cure but the hair of the dog and a clean life ever after."

She shook her head. Her hair was dripping into a little pool in the lap of her shirtwaist dress. She had no idea why she was wearing a dress. Probably she hadn't done the laundry. What else was new?

"Yessir," he said as he opened another beer, "we done ourselves proud. My old lady kicked me out. What's your excuse?"

She and Kendrick had quarreled, but she couldn't remember what about. She thought she remembered calling. They had quarreled, but she thought they'd made it up. She did call. She had threatened to get married, and his tone had been positively jaunty.

"I'll tell you this, you are one crazy lady. You got an old man?"

"My father's dead."

He flashed a gold tooth, which was, she decided now that she had the opportunity to consider him in the foul light of morning, tacky. So was the serpent tattooed on his arm and the hulking show of muscle beneath his sopping black jersey. "I mean like a boyfriend or a husband."

What Kendrick had been was nonchalant. "I don't know."

"Just as well. Seein's how we got hitched yesterday—seems like I remember something like that anyway, you remember that?"

She nodded, trying not to cry.

"Some building with pillars, some prick with a Bible."

"I don't remember any Bible," Alex said.

"Yeah? Then I guess it was just some prick. Green walls. You ever notice how those places all got green walls? You go to get your driver's license, unemployment, get married, get sick, they got green in all your schools, I bet they even got green walls at the morgue." Alex wished he would get to the point. Her head hurt, and she did not want to be married. "But look here. What about the blood test? Somebody sticks me with a needle I remember that." He glanced at Alex. "You look kind of peaked. You okay, or you going to be sick?"

"Sick." She swallowed.

He kicked at the door. Outside the noon sunshine crashed into their eyes. "Yessir, baby, believe me, I know hangovers, and this one we got here's a three-day job."

She supposed she was relieved to hear it wasn't permanent.

"Well, Alex, nothing against you, but you reckon we ought to get a divorce?"

"That would be fine," she said in a wivery voice. "Except, I was thinking—how old do you have to be to get married?" You had to be eighteen, and no blood test was required. She knew because she had checked just in case Kendrick wanted to marry her. The only way she could get married was with her mother's consent. Her mother had no reason to refuse, but Kendrick wouldn't do it. They had quarreled, and he had said it might be the best thing for both of them if they broke up.

"Oh no. Don't tell me that." He gave her a black look. "You got a daddy?"

Alex returned the look coolly. "I told you, my father's dead."

He seemed relieved as he stood. "Look here. You feeling strong enough to ride? I think maybe we ought to see if we can't figure out where you live."

He had to coax her onto the bike. She dug her hands into his sides and closed her eyes against the dizzy flight of landscape.

"You like living around all these college types?" he asked when he'd pulled to a stop on East Maple Street and she hopped off the back. "Take care." He flashed his gold tooth. The motorcycle roared around the corner, and the spangled red helmet blazed out of sight.

"Well, so long, first marriage," she said to herself for the bright look it put on her face—she could be jaunty too, he'd see. But her bravado collapsed as she wobbled up the steps.

Kendrick wasn't home. She found the key in the mailbox and let herself in. She was still sitting on the mattress in her crumpled dress, cradling a mug of tea, when he dropped his tripod in the doorway. Without a word he disappeared into the kitchen. After a minute he brought a mug of cold coffee into the hallway and leaned against the refrigerator.

"You go for a walk or something? I missed you."

"I'm back," she said flatly and slammed past him into the bathroom.

"Oh no you don't." He forced the door as she tried to lock it. "You look like shit. Look at your hair." He yanked a handful stiff with vomit. "You smell like a flophouse. Look at your face." He jerked her to the mirror. One whole side of her face had been scraped open; beneath their cowls her eyes were rusty. "Where the hell have you been?"

"I told you. I got married."

He stalked from the room, then stomped back. "Congratulations. Do you mind if I ask who's the lucky groom?"

"I called you."

"You were drunk."

"I was drunk," she agreed and started to cry. "And right now you'd better stop yelling at me because my head hurts, my stomach hurts, I'm hungover."

"Turn that faucet off right now. You've been gone for three days. Where were you?"

"Ow." She wrenched her arm from his grasp and rubbed her shoulder. "I met this biker."

"That's just great. I step inside the library for five minutes, and you decide to join the Hell's Angels. Can I ask if you consummated this marriage? Never mind. Never mind that …"

"You said you wanted to break up."

"You are something." He knocked a fist into the wall. "I could kill you."

"You don't have to," she offered.

"But I want to." He kicked the bathmat.

"Go ahead," she whimpered. "Maybe it would put me out of my misery."

"Are you going to tell me why you left?"

"Because ..."

"Never mind. It's the same old story. I'll tell you why. Because you're fucked up. And you know what? I understand that. I sympathize. But I don't want to have to live with it every goddamn day." He closed the lid of the toilet and sat. "Take your clothes off. I *said* take your clothes off." She unfastened her belt, but he jerked the collar of the shirtwaist so hard the top button flew off. "Before I even talk to you, I want you to take a bath and wash your hair." He dropped the rubber stopper into the drain and turned on the water, which tumbled into the tub with a sound like laughter.

She was sunk to her neck when he returned, carrying clean towels and his own white terrycloth robe. As he picked up the shampoo and began sudsing her hair, she sat up. "I could have done that," she protested.

He pulled the plug and shoved her head beneath the faucet.

"It's cold!"

"You don't deserve hot." But the water warmed. He turned off the faucet and yanked her to her feet. "Dry off." He flung a towel.

She needed creme rinse. Meekly she stepped out of the tub. "Well, I don't think it's a *legal* marriage."

He turned his back as if the sight of her naked body was offensive. Woefully she glanced at her shoulder, colored the fierce hue of a storm sky. She wrapped a towel around her head and with the other towel stooped to dry between her toes.

"At least I came back," she said.

He turned around. The thin glaze of cornea only made his eyes look like glass ground to an impenetrable hardness. They would cut her if she said another word. He crossed the room and seized her by her sore shoulder. "Unless you have some objection, I'd like to kiss the bride."

They fucked on the bathroom floor. She closed her eyes not to see his and tried to coax some tenderness into his arched back, but he slapped her hands to her sides and rammed into her with the cold integrity of anger. Only the shudder that passed through his breath betrayed him. He dressed as soon as he'd finished. "Go sleep it off," he said, and closed the door behind him without looking back, but she saw that his shoulders were shaking.

When she woke, he was sitting on the edge of the mattress and the light through the windows was pearly. Her neck and shoulder were stiff, but she was surprised to feel hungry. She sat up. "What time is it?"

"Late. How do you feel?"

"Better."

"Did I hurt you?"

She shook her head. "I guess I deserved it."

"I was pretty mad." He turned around. "Could you eat some soup?"

He heated a can of chicken noodle. When she finished, he set the tray on the floor beside the bed. "Now what about this marriage?"

She had lied about her age; no one could make it stick. That was the first thing she wanted to establish. It was like a camera with no film, a search without a warrant, no good, inadmissable, invalid. But he was not interested in metaphors; what he wanted was the facts. He hadn't known whether to believe her or not—"I thought maybe you were just trying to make a statement"—and having to tell that she had, yes, gone down to the courthouse, yes, taken out a license, yes, said yes, stood up before a j.p. or a magistrate or *somebody* and promised to love, honor, and cherish for as long as they both should live a man whose name she couldn't at the moment recall—well, it was not the way she would have chosen to begin. Of course it had *happened*; the important thing was that, due to a technicality, it didn't count.

He couldn't say. Probably they would need a professional opinion.

The soft gray light had lost its luminescence and was deepening into shadow. He did not turn on the light, and she was grateful. She would have felt like a criminal if she had to indict herself in the glare of the overhead bulb. Maybe she would buy him a lamp for his next birthday, brass with a green shade that would give the room a cozy glow. For his last birthday she had given him a book on Man Ray. She would have felt funny picking out a shirt or tie. Those were the sort of thing you gave your father, and your mother picked them out. At least that was the way it was if you were Jo Yellen or Diana Wells.

It was *thoughtful* of Kendrick not to turn on the light. She had not said she was sorry, but she was. She loved him. Even though it wasn't until March, a good nine months away, she wished she were, right now, shopping for his birthday lamp.

But he had finished with her stupid—her childish, her spiteful, rash, inexplicable, altogether inexcusable behavior without calling it any of those things. (*Why* had she done it? She was hurt. She was mad. She didn't know.) He thought she should finish high school. College would be a good idea, but that was up to her. She couldn't see his face in the darkness, but his voice had the even distance of the carefully thought out. Another year in Limestone. Was it the apartment? They could move. Did she feel exploited by his work? She did not. If it weren't for him …

If it weren't for him … she could not imagine.

His schedule then? They hadn't had much of a life together, true.

"Maybe we could make one," he said. He tipped her chin. "I don't want to break up. I never have. But we can't keep chewing each other up like this. You know the thing that really got me? I went to see your mother—I thought you'd be there. I didn't know where else you'd go." He shook his head. "She hadn't even missed you." He paused. "I used to think if I just took you home I wouldn't feel so guilty. But you were so unhappy all the time I felt like I'd ruined your life."

Alex started to say he hadn't *ruined* her life, he shouldn't be so melodramatic; personally she thought what people did was almost always what they thought that they were doing—or at least it was the thought that counted. Because soul-searching—with its penchant for revision—always came after the fact, at leisure, and was therefore, at least to some extent, just a way to pass the time. A lot of *Sturm und Drang* designed to stretch life's little scenes into filling up its pauses. But his voice had taken on a dreamy pitch, the sound of a man talking to himself. She loved him anyway. If she wasn't capable of such reconsiderations, wasn't that her problem? She couldn't entertain herself.

"I should have let you move in a long time ago. If you want to go back, you can say so, but there isn't any other reason. The truth is—and I wouldn't say it if you didn't know—your mother was relieved when I took you off her hands. You have to finish high school. I know how the other kids treat you, I know you're smarter than that, but you've got to do it, and I'm going to make sure you study and do it right. *If* you want to live with me. I imagine that's preferable to living with your mother. Unless of course—" he allowed himself the waggish smile she guessed he owed her—"you'd prefer to live with your husband." He paused. "It won't be as different as you want, though I don't see why we can't appear together. People talk, but never as much as you think. Besides we're yesterday's news. You're bound to be disappointed: all these great times you think you've been missing are no different from the parties you've been helping your mother give for years. But if that's what you want—only not if every time you get ticked you're going to go running off to get married."

She tilted her head to look at him in the dark. "You haven't said what happens when I'm eighteen."

He propped himself against a pillow. "I've been thinking about going back to New York. I'm sick of this place." She was astonished. She'd always assumed he liked Limestone. Herself, she had never even thought about leaving. She had only hated it for a long, long time.

"You mean I'll go to New York?"

"You'll go anywhere you want to go."

It was not what she'd hoped he would say.

Chapter 18

1968

On television the police carry riot sticks and wear new helmets with flip-down face shields, but the demonstrators go quietly, save a boy no one recalls from the planning sessions. As the doors to the squad car close, he smashes his umbrella on the hood. "Police brutality!" he screams.

"He made the news today, oh boy," Alex said in disgust. In a corner of the screen she picked out Tulip, drawing her arm back to hurl an egg.

"Shh," Leah hissed. "They're going to interview Ted."

"The Wallace Reserve Officers Training Corps is using scholarship funds to recruit informers for the FBI." Ted's voice is as riveting as the first time Alex heard it. "We are not violent; we have no list of unreasonable demands. We are simply willing to be arrested to bring the university's illegal use of surveillance to public attention."

"There will be no more egg-throwing," he told them now.

"You want to throw something, throw a rock," Nelson advised from where he had stretched out on the floor.

Matt's head jerked in irritation, blond hair bouncing against his shoulders. "Oh, come on, man." Alex thought Matt might have the purest anger of any of them, because he left it unspoken.

"Frankly, I'm ready to throw rocks," Stacy said.

In June Ted and Alex went on vacation. "We want to treat you," Justine had said that weekend in Youngstown, where they had suddenly gone to make peace after Ted had declined to participate in commencement. "Jeannie misses you. Why don't I see if our old cottage at the Cape is available?" To Alex's surprise Ted accepted.

They arrived in Boston just in time to make the game at Fenway Park. "Remember when you used to go to Cleveland with Dad?" Jeannie asked, and, watching him lean forward, arms folded on the back of an empty seat, Alex felt a pang of envy for his childhood. For all his differences with his father, it was a source of sufficiency, as mysterious to her as her mother, whom she might have understood through hate or love but could not begin to comprehend through the indifference that had been offered.

They stayed in Cambridge, where Jeannie and Binks had rented a carriage house until Binks finished his M.B.A. "Got a present for you, bro." With a flourish Jeannie pinned a McCarthy button on his shirt. "Must be your influence. Seriously," she said. "I'm developing a social conscience. I hope you're going to campaign for him."

Ted was amused.

"I cried all last week about Bobby Kennedy. Ask Binks." She draped her arms around her husband. "Can you believe I married a Republican? Mom says she's going to divorce Daddy if he votes for Nixon. She was proud of you when you were on TV, by the way."

"And Dad said I needed a haircut."

Jeannie sat on the arm of his chair. "I like your hair." She wound a curl around her finger. "Isn't he gorgeous?" she said to Alex. "How can you stand to have married such a gorgeous man?"

The next day they drove to the Cape. It was too cold to swim, but they rented bicycles and took the ferry to Nantucket. At the foot of the dune in the National Seashore they made love. At night they traveled Route 28, from the sleepy Falmouth village green to the bars and head shops of Provincetown. On the beach she lay with her foot across Ted's lap and sighed with pleasure. Though Dr. Spock had been convicted for conspiracy to counsel draft resistors the day before they left, they hadn't seen a newspaper or mentioned politics since. It was the longest time they had ever spent alone together.

On the way home their car broke down. A tow truck took them to Columbus.

"Going to have to order a new transmission," the mechanic said.

They went to a Chinese restaurant and ordered eggrolls. "That goddamn car."

"At least it waited until we were on our way home," Alex said. "Do you want to hitch the rest of the way and come back?"

"I want to trade the sucker." A small vein pulsed at his temple as he set his fork down.

She poured tea, but the cup was too hot to hold. They were the only couple in the restaurant, shopping center modern, fake wood paneling with a few paper lanterns strung up for atmosphere. The waiter hovered near their table. "You ready to order?"

"No, we only want eggrolls," Ted said.

"I give you more time," the waiter said.

"I thought the visit went well," Alex said.

"My parents hate the way I live, my father thinks I'm a bum for graduating three years late and not getting into Harvard Law, and all they can say is 'Teddy, be careful.'"

"They love you." There were moments when it seemed to her an advantage to be done with her own parents.

"I love them," he said angrily. "That isn't the point."

She wasn't sure she got the point. "So let's sell the car." She laid her fork on the table. "What's wrong?"

"I've been drafted," he said.

All the circuits of her body disconnected, leaving a helpless anarchy of cells. "What? When?"

The waiter took up their plates. "You ready to order now."

Ted looked up. "Sorry, but we only wanted eggrolls."

"Moo Goo Gai Pan very good. Pork Lo Mein. Shrimp with Cashew. All good."

Alex was tearing at her chapped lip with her teeth. "Bring us an order of fried rice."

"Pork-fry?"

"I don't want any rice," Ted said.

"Pork-fry," Alex practically screamed. "And bring us the check." She watched as the waiter walked to the kitchen, watching them over his shoulder. "When?" she asked again.

"Before we left."

He hadn't told her. All the time they were at his parents', at Jeannie's, at the Cape … All that time they had been alone together he had been thinking about something else.

"I didn't want to upset you," he added by way of explanation, but his deep gray eyes were set on some private decision that spoiled the excuse.

"Have you told your parents?"

"I wanted to figure out what I was going to do first."

"But …" Her voice gave. He had been accepted at Wallace Law; he'd told her himself that rich white boys were never called in Youngstown.

"Alex, they've been reclassifying demonstrators for months. The ROTC's spying on campus, they're handing down indictments for burning draft cards, it's going to get worse."

"You haven't been reclassified—you haven't even taken the physical."

"It's scheduled. My 1-A was enclosed with the draft notice." A weak smile marred his face. "They must be trying to save postage. You know how unhappy we all are about military spending."

"It's not funny, Ted." The waiter brought the rice. "It's fucking illegal is what it is."

"It's illegal to use the IRS to harass people politically too."

For a minute they both sat brooding over the bitter, strong tea. "What are you going to do?" she asked finally, because finally it was the only question to be asked, no matter how angry she was.

"I can go to Canada. I can go underground. Or I can get my father to fix it." His eyes held steady. They were his genius, the frank gaze, the handsome face made plain and by its plainness more compelling, the even voice, though she had heard it pitched for the audience and knew he could make it resound in his body like a bell. He had the ability to look at a thing sincerely and never reveal his own substance.

"I see." He would have to ask his father. To go to Canada or underground would remove him from action, and it was out of the question that he should go. Never mind that he had flirted with enlisting. That had been a notion as out of place as the petunia in the tomato patch, sown from some crackpot of guilt and adventure that she hadn't taken seriously. *He* hadn't taken it seriously. Playing out his identity crisis as a moral drama, when it was nothing but empty threats and indiscretion. Angry tears filled her eyes. All the time they had been at the Cape, he had known he would have to ask his father. It was why they had gone. "The issue is not the issue," Garth always said.

"It's not like my dad would mind."

In her mind she saw Brad Neal sealing the envelope that contained her wedding portrait, insisting upon delivering it to the *Vindicator* himself, to make sure she appeared top center. She could see him talking to the society editor, very respectfully, the same way he might talk to a general. He liked to do things like that; he was good at them, so good that every persuasion he offered seemed quite separate from the privilege that allowed him the office. No doubt it hurt him that Ted had always made a point of not asking favors. Favors were his talent.

So now Ted would have to use his right of birth. Well, so what? she wanted to say. But it was like him to mind that even more than he minded being drafted.

The waiter was still hovering. "Want some rice?" she asked, mechanically spooning some onto her plate. Ted reached for his fortune cookie. "Don't," she said.

"Let's take the Greyhound," she suggested as they walked to the garage. He squeezed her shoulder in agreement, or perhaps to acknowledge that she had been angry with him.

"You could try to flunk your physical," she said without conviction at the bus station. She looked at him sprawled beside her in the molded plastic seat, the sturdy muscle that shaped his jeans, all the fine reason of his mind reflected in his eyes, closed now, the only hint of vulnerability in the delicate pink trace of blood inside the lids. There wasn't a draft board in the country that could find him unfit.

"Maybe I'll go," he said without opening his eyes. Across from them a drunk rocked in his seat, humming softly. The smell of urine overpowered the stale musk of sweat and cigarette smoke. "Why should some poor black die in my place?"

"Because I love you," she said, not caring whether she betrayed justice or logic. Did he think she would give him up just because love wasn't democratic? Sacrifice—as political people they were pledged to it. Or said they were. She was willing to be beaten to end the war.

She was not willing that he should die to fight it. She refused to consider whether she was willing that he should die to end it, though the question had been there ever since he'd gone to Mississippi. He'd proved his courage. She'd known from the beginning that the Movement was the most important thing in his life; she had to accept that, but that was *all* she was prepared to accept. "Why should some poor black die either?" she demanded hotly.

When they got back to Limestone he slept. It was late, but somewhere in the house someone was typing. Across the street laughter punctuated the creak of a metal glider. She listened to Ted's breath deepen and rose, fumbling for a robe in the oyster light that seeped between the curtains and splashed a narrow stripe across the floor. The bright hall light made her blink. Stacy and Matt's door was closed; from behind it she heard Matt's soft snore. Across the hall Nelson mumbled in the guttural voice of sleep. She tiptoed past the living room, averting her eyes from the figures twined on top of Leah's sleeping bag, and in the kitchen poured a glass of milk. When she came back upstairs she paused at Michael's door.

"Hey." He looked up from the typewriter. "Did you have a good time in? …"

"Cape Cod," she said. "Mmhmm. Listen, are you going to be up for a while. Would you mind if I brought Tulip's typewriter in here? Cal and Leah are asleep downstairs."

"Help yourself." He frowned at the page.

Tulip was out, but Alex took the typewriter to Michael's room anyway and set it on the floor. In the morning she offered Ted her letter.

> Gentlemen:
> I have received my induction notice. At present I am spending my full time organizing private citizens against the war, but I am pleased to be given this opportunity to expand my work by organizing troops against the war, and shall cheerfully report for duty.
>
> Sincerely,
> Bradford Seaton Neal III

"It's just an idea," she said, toying with her hairbrush, not daring to look at him. "Probably it would be more of a sure thing to ask your father." If he would only ask, his father would forgive him everything.

"Probably." His eyes settled on her for a moment. "They're going to bug the phone and nail every ass in this house to the wall," he said cheerfully as he signed it.

"So we're all honored to serve our country," Nelson said the next night while they sat around the table after dinner.

"Do you think it will work?" Matt asked.

"Of course it will work," Leah said. The evening sun spangled the haze of dirt on the dining room windows and wound itself into the smoke that purled from her cigarette toward the ceiling. "They don't want peaceniks in the army."

""You people are babies." Cal scratched at his stomach.

"I just wish people would ask before they borrow my typewriter," Tulip said.

Stacy turned her head. "Haven't you heard? Private property is bourgeois."

Ted looked amused as he scraped his chair back and held out his hand for Alex. Smiling, she rose. The bickering would go on for hours, turning corners, jumping streams, until it lost itself in the landscape of all their arguments.

Tulip's voice floated up to the landing. "She thinks she's so smart."

"Never mind," Cal said. "I'll be drilling that hole by the time your boy's on the bus."

Alex couldn't tell if Ted heard or not, but she made a point of telling Cal first when Ted flunked his physical.

"So is he going to go to law school?" Stacy asked, passing a joint and leaning back against the pillows in Alex's room. Alex sat cross-legged at the foot of the mattress. She had cramps.

"I don't know," Alex said. Stacy couldn't make up her own mind about law school. Every year she put off applying.

"Three more years in Limestone is a long time." Stacy took a sip of wine. In the bright afternoon light a delicate peppering of freckles stood out beneath the sheen of sweat on her cheeks. "I don't know—maybe you don't care as much if you're married. I'm beginning to feel like I'm just drifting."

"Why don't you and Matt get married?" Alex let the smoke out from her lungs and pulled a loose thread at the leg of her cutoffs.

"Nobody gets married anymore. Marriage is bourgeois." Stacy sighed. "I'm twenty-five years old, I have a college degree and an IQ of 140, and I work as a maid in the Wallace Union. Every other semester I get ambitious and take a grad course at night."

"You're working against the war."

"At least you take pictures. I mean, working against the war in Limestone? Who in the whole rest of the country gives a shit what anybody in Limestone thinks?"

"You could get involved with national leadership."

"What makes you think they want girls on their committees? Listen. You want to know why I didn't go to Mississippi in '64?"

"I didn't know you applied."

"I got rejected. The interviewer kept asking whether I'd have sex with a Negro and how I felt about clerical work. *She also serves who sits and types.* I mean you can bet they weren't asking the guys those questions. So here I am." Stacy sighed.

"Well, it's not New York," Alex admitted, holding her glass up to the light for the ruby shadow. The big exhaust fan in the stair landing rattled, sucking a hot wind from the open windows and tugging at the curtains looped over their rods. Stacy dug a roach clip from the pocket of her baggy olive shorts. Sunlight stretched across the floor, broken into rainbows by the beveled glass. Across the street two girls in bikinis lay on the porch roof. A white sheet painted with a peace sign was knotted to the railing. She could hear the Stones beneath the churring of the fan.

"Where's Ted?"

"Ohio. Garth had a meeting in Columbus, and Ted went to pick up the car."

"The thing about Matt …" Stacy's forehead knit.

"He's such a sweetheart." Alex took a sip of wine. She liked this, sitting around on a lazy afternoon, curing cramps.

"He is." Stacy sighed again. "It'll never work."

"Why not?"

"I hold it against him. Because I'm such a shit."

"You always say that. It's not true."

"Oh, what do you know? You like perfect men. They make me feel mean." Stacy stubbed out the roach. "You stoned?"

"A little bit."

Stacy rolled to her side and propped herself on an elbow. "Remember that black guy I brought up to Crow Hill? He was a great fuck."

"Stacy!"

"Well, he was." Stacy sat up. "I know, I'm perpetuating the myth. Do you think I'm a racist?"

"Of course not."

"Wrong," Stacy said. "We're all racists. We can't help it. Look at the way everybody in the Movement fawns over the Panthers. Half of it's out of guilt, and the other half's because secretly we believe it."

"Believe what?"

"The myth," Stacy said impatiently. "Panthers are sexy. Violence is sexy. White folks are wimps, and the Panthers are studs."

"God, Stace. Are you talking about politics, or are you talking about sex?"

"Getting hard to tell the difference these days," Stacy observed and screwed up her face in imitation of Leah. Alex snickered. "But really," Stacy insisted, "it's true."

"About the big O?"

"About white people. We let the Panthers bully us into thinking we're sissies." Stacy poured more wine and settled back, looking pensive. "Do you think the myth is true?"

"How would I know? I've only slept with two men in my life." Alex twirled her glass. "Well, three. I was married once before for a couple of days."

"You're wild, Allie." Stacy shook her head. "I keep finding out all these things about you, but they don't make any difference—you're still just as straight as I thought you were the first time I met you."

"You made me feel straight," Alex accused. "All dressed up in my prissy little work clothes, and there you were in your army jacket and boots. I thought you were a dyke."

"You thought I was a *dyke?*"

"Not that it would have mattered."

"Of course not," Stacy agreed. "We're liberated people." Their eyes met, and they sputtered with laughter. "Did it ever occur to you … I mean—" Stacy overshot the glass and poured wine on the bed. "Whoops." They laughed some more and mopped it up and tried again. "Did you ever notice how you can't say anything that isn't political anymore? I'm serious. You can't say anything about blacks, you can't say anything about lesbians, you can't say anything about the shitty racists on Crow Hill, because they're part of the working class. Even fucking's not personal, it's part of the sexual revolution."

"Well," Alex quipped, "there is no event …" but Stacy didn't laugh.

"I'm political to the bone," Stacy said. "I grew up with it, but I draw the line at my genitals." She set her glass on the windowsill. "Shit, Allie, what am I going to do? I wish I could make up my mind to leave him."

"Why?"

"I love him, I really do, but he's not smart, he's too sweet to be smart. I feel like I'm fucking the Easter bunny."

Alex had to stifle a laugh as the pupils of Stacy's small brown eyes concentrated on her anguish. For a fact Matt did look like a rabbit. "You really want to leave him?"

"I don't know. I want to do *something*." Stacy relaxed. "Anyway I'm just drunk."

There were voices downstairs. Alex got up to close the door. "You're always so hard on yourself. I think there's more to Matt than you think. He's changed a lot. It just doesn't show yet." The girls across the street had gone in. Alex stared at the sheet with the blood-red peace sign. "I wonder what will happen when the war ends," she mused.

"We'll all be a hundred years old."

"At least we won't have to worry about what to do with the rest of our lives."

"Except Nelson," Stacy said slyly. "He'll be a hundred and ten."

Later that month Alex woke to a singed smell and bad light. "There's a fire," she said, recalling dimly the sirens that had pulled her from sleep before dawn; she had stirred from a dream and gone off again. Ted stood behind her at the window, naked, watching black smoke roil across the sky. There was a heat inside the heat of the air.

"Looks big," he said. "Are you going to take pictures?"

"Can't." She pulled a beaded shift off a hanger. "I have to work."

He watched her dress. "You have the most beautiful body."

She shook her hair into place. Slinging a woven Greek bag over her shoulder, she touched his nose. "The sky is falling, Chicken Little. I'm late." They glanced out the window. The sill was covered with a fine layer of ash.

"I hope it's not the library," he said, and their eyes locked.

There had been a fire in a wastebasket in a men's room the previous week. Her heart beat in her throat. "What do you *know*?"

"Nothing. I just hope it isn't the library." He picked up his jeans. "Wait. I"ll come with you."

When they reached the library, firetrucks lined Campus Drive, and flames were shooting from the windows and the roof as a heavy black smog poured skyward. Yellow police tape cordoned off the lawn and drive, and students from the dorms streamed over the hill. In the wavy air their movements seemed disjointed. Ted said something, but Alex couldn't hear him over the whipping roar of the fire. A code of instructions crackled over the radios. At the south end of the reading room, water hissed through the shattered windows, useless. A rill washed down the sloping drive, past the Channel 4 van; newsmen moved through the crowd with heavy cameras riding on their shoulders; at the police line an officer stood chatting with students. By noon the networks had arrived, and the NBC correspondent who had interviewed Ted in May tracked him down for a comment on antiwar sentiment at Wallace. By late afternoon the south wing was a smoking ruin, and most of the spectators went home to catch a shower and watch the news.

On Huntley-Brinkley the crowd appeared to be a demonstration. "Idiots," Alex muttered as the cameras focused on a small group of cheering students. "They think they won't have to take their exams." It made her sick. For over three years she had worked in the reading room. She loved the high coffered ceiling, the carved oak tables, and iron chandeliers. To her the loss was personal, and she couldn't believe that the network chose the footage of cheering students. Standing beside her at the police line, Lizzie had wept when the first wall collapsed. Throughout the crowd there had been sobbing.

Ted's face flashed onscreen. "Antiwar sentiment across the country is very strong. I know of no evidence connecting the antiwar movement to the fire."

"What?" Stacy exploded.

"Is it true," the correspondent asks, "that you wrote a letter to the Selective Service threatening to organize American troops against the war?"

Alex turned her head. "I hope your parents are watching Walter Cronkite."

"I was drafted because I was organizing civilians against the war. I offered to continue my work in the military."

Ted turned off the TV. "Does anybody want to see the rest?" No one answered.

"The *library*," Garth said, and Alex turned her head again. She hadn't noticed he was here, seated on the floor behind her, but of course he would be. He couldn't watch the news at home; the kids made too much noise.

The phone rang. "Don't answer it," Alex said. "It's Ted's mother."

Leah raised her chin. "I think Ted should have made a stronger statement."

Matt got up to get a Coke. "Anybody hungry?" he asked on the way back. "We could order out for pizza."

"Sure," they said, and "I don't care."

"I just think Ted could have said there's no evidence connecting the Movement to the fire, but there is a lot of anger." Leah's earrings bobbed.

"You want to take credit?" Stacy asked incredulously.

"We don't burn libraries." Ted's face was grave.

"*We* don't." In the tight silence Nelson's voice had the force of a gunshot; he had faded into the dining room, and now he came forward, standing between the pocket doors that neither opened all the way nor closed. "But suppose you know someone who does?"

"Who?"

“Just suppose,” Nelson said. “Suppose you knew someone who planned to. Not likely you’re going to talk him out of it. What could you do? Unless you want to go to bed with the Shoes.” That was the name SDS had given the FBI.

“We don’t burn libraries,” Ted insisted. On the floor Alex tipped her head up to regard him, but felt Nelson’s presence behind her, in the question that no one else had dared to ask but that kept them all in the room, Ted most of all, for no matter what he said she knew he was numb with the fear that they did know someone who burned libraries. Someone had, no one they knew personally, she was sure, or hoped she was sure, but that didn’t mean he—or she—was not one of them in the larger sense.

Nelson rephrased the question: “Suppose you knew someone who was planning to burn the ROTC hut?”

“Hand ’em the matches,” Tulip said.

Nelson paused to let the implications of that sink in. “Lot of ROTC headquarters going up across the country.”

It was a sobering thought, and they were all relieved when the arsonist turned out to be a library employee who’d recently been discharged. He had a history of mental problems and no political affiliations, and none of the networks reported his arrest.

Chapter 19

1982

To the reporter it was a simple question. Was she one of them? Were they *both* with Weatherman?

It's a simple answer too. No and no. And no, Ted hadn't been in touch, she had not known where he was. It's the other question that's hard, the question she's never really answered: if he wasn't in Weather why did he run?

Honor, maybe. Conscience. He was tired, he fell apart, he panicked. He knew things. He must have known things, she thinks. "What else haven't you told me for my protection?" she had said. He loved her, he didn't love her, he loved her but ... He was lost without disciples. Or did he just do it and then it was done? With all the time she's had you'd think surely she could have got it straight in her head some way. But that's just it—as soon as it was that way, it would have been that way and no other. She can think of a hundred reasons, maybe all of them true.

So the answer depends on how she feels. It depends on who wants to know.

"I think he did it to set me free," she said just last week to Kendrick, and his foot flattened on the chair rung.

"Hero to the end," he said. "A prince through and through. Personally," he added, "I always thought he was a jerk."

"Because he left me." She was touched.

"Because you were my girl first."

The heat in his voice surprised her. "Oh that," she said. "That was a long time ago."

He looked so hurt she should have told him that it is Ted who was so long ago the why no longer matters. Maybe, she thinks now, it never did.

Still, she would like to know: did he ever regret it?

With the back of her hand she wipes her face. The Cuisinart snarls through a tube of carrots. She's making a cake. And after she's frosted it with cream cheese whipped with butter and an entire pound of confectioner's sugar, she's going to make tiropita. The phyllo is already thawing on the counter. In the refrigerator a shoulder of lamb waits stuffing. She'll have enough dinner for a party of twelve when only Kendrick is coming. So much for watching his cholesterol.

If she had bombed a building, she would regret it. (But he didn't, he wouldn't, that much she knows, that much she would stake her life on.) Crimes you repent, she thinks, but immediately takes it back. It's not the crime most criminals bewail, but getting caught. So what do people regret? Sins maybe. Accidents that were their fault. You're supposed to regret your mistakes, but she's not so sure about that. To regret a mistake you would have to recognize the error, would have to know just where it was you stumbled, where you took the first misstep. It's easy to regret something you just said or what you did yesterday, because the consequences have not yet woven themselves into your life, but to regret what you did five or twenty years ago would be to undo everything since, to unravel the whole fabric. Supposing you could reinvent yourself by wishing this or that act away, what would you see except for yourself naked on a threshold, peering blindly back at the rooms you just emptied out.

She doesn't regret him—couldn't even if she had seen this coming. She chose him, chose the life she had with him, and for a while at least, a long time really, it had been exactly what she wanted. They had had a family of sorts. And she had loved him, even if she hates him now. What she can never get straight is if he loved her.

If she hates him.

Was she one of them? She has the scars, she could pass, but no, not ever, not the way he was. He wanted to change the world. He thought it was his job, politics defined him. And because she wasn't like him, it had not been possible for her to know him, not in the way he wanted to be known.

The smell of the cake fills the kitchen, which is heating up, and she decides to start the ratatouille while the phyllo defrosts a little longer. When the phone rings, she wipes her hands. No matter what she's doing, she answers the phone. She hasn't heard from Justine in a week now, but it's just a student wanting to know if she can write a recommendation. This is one semester she'll be glad to get behind her.

What she does regret is Ross, who rarely comes to class now, and when he does he slumps in his seat and stares at his feet, mouth curled in a malevolent pout. She has no intention of docking his grade for the little bit of work he owes her, and if that's a compromise of her ethics, too bad. It's a little late to worry about the ethics now.

She feels better. For Ted's sake, she regrets that he will not recover. It doesn't matter anymore what he might have had to say. He wasn't talking when he could, and she isn't listening now, hasn't been for a long time. When school ends in a few weeks she plans to see him. She no longer has any reason not to, and it's a courtesy she owes his parents. Why, she's not sure, but for the first time in years she's begun to feel as if she has a future.

That's one truth. Because when Ted asked, "Don't you believe me?" she had said no and turned away. She will always wonder if she had said yes would he have stayed.

Chapter 20

1962-1963

In August Alex and Kendrick moved to a house on Park Street. Though in its prime the street had been far grander than East Maple—their little house was squeezed between a sagging Victorian and pillared Greek Revival—this street too had passed to the slumlords who multiplied populations by dividing houses in the neighborhoods near Wallace. Alex liked the hurly-burly of this even larger family of man, radios spilling music from open windows, students sunbathing on roofs, voices murmuring on front porches long after dark.

She was a happy *hausfrau*. At the supermarket she filled her cart with Windex, Comet, and Mr. Clean. She read *The Joy of Cooking*, painted, refinished their yard-sale furniture, and stitched Indian bedspreads into pillows and drapes. Nearly every evening Kendrick's students gathered in their living room.

Now they could do everything together. At the Towne Art Cinema she cast a glance up to the balcony, but the frat rats were making out with strangers; her friends had moved on to other teenage games. She felt truly enviable as she watched the boho girls trailing up the aisle behind their bearded dates, who didn't have the class to wait until they got outside before niggling about the amounts spend on popcorn and tickets, or the cool to discuss *leitmotiv* in private. They made her laugh, she felt so sorry for them. She and Kendrick never haggled or pontificated—they joked, laughed, wept, or—if the film was a dog—yowled together all the way across the parking lot, and afterwards, if one of them did venture an analytic insight, the other was sure to exclaim, "I was just going to say the same thing!" Poor boho girls, who gave their love for free but had to buy their own snacks and admission. They would be in their dorms by women's curfew while she snuggled beside Kendrick all night. Oh, but weren't she and he *simpatico* and lucky!

This Christmas Kendrick took her to Canada, scolding her with the small irritation of a husband when she misread the map. She was not used to such inconsequential spats; their fights of the past had been long and bitter, marked with episodes of shouting and sullen silence, with threats, tears, and elaborate, equally teary reconciliations. Despite her mother's travels, it was the first time she'd been out of the country, and though crossing the border had all the excitement of crossing into Ohio from Indiana, to his parents she was an American. They took a dim view of her (her!) foreign policy and were unimpressed with her president, the young John Kennedy, whom Alex thought dashing, quite an improvement on stodgy old Eisenhower, because he made the office seem glamorous instead of poky. She had no idea what Kennedy was up to, but felt sure she would approve, and she was shocked to hear Kendrick's parents criticize his handling of the Bay of Pigs (vaguely she remembered a debate she hadn't bothered to attend at school) and blame him for the Cuban Missile Crisis. (Could the world really have been on the brink of destruction if she hadn't known?) It made her feel a little hollow, to realize that the place where she felt so strange all week was more familiar to him, had been home to him much longer, than the one where they played house. He was twenty-nine, but had to lie about her age and sneak into her bed in the middle of the night. He even looked different now that she knew he had his mother's bones, his father's eyes, and walked just like his older brother.

When they got back to Park Street, she looked around the little house, a dollhouse really, and realized that she'd done all she could with the four rooms.

The coffeehouse opened in January, in the basement of a big greystone house up the hill from the Towne Art Cinema and across the street from Holy Trinity Episcopal Church. It was called The Cellar

Cafe, something of a misnomer since the city promptly rescinded its food license in an effort to close it down. They drank instant coffee courtesy of an urn on loan from the Episcopal Church. Father Rayle, the young minister who had instituted Sunday night folk masses and rap sessions in the fellowship hall, was among the regulars. The previous fall he had led a civil rights demonstration in front of the university auditorium while the segregationist senator from South Carolina addressed a convocation inside, and although few of the faithful had developed their politics beyond a bland love for mankind, it was perhaps out of respect for him that no one brought wine or marijuana to The Cellar Cafe, whose continued presence in a town where the Ku Klux Klan outnumbered Negro and foreign students owed largely to his support.

Alex loved the Cellar. It was like a U-School Culture Week without the dreary sanction of teachers, subversive, smoky, more intense. She took a job waiting tables; when the food license was revoked she sat with Kendrick at their table, listening to the folksingers with the friends who had drifted with them from Park Street. No longer stranded in the remote provinces where the Appalachians unrolled to the Heartland, they had taken partnership in a growing underground of happily disaffected young. Listening to Bob Dylan "Talkin' New York" on the hi-fi while she cleaned house, Alex imagined the Gaslight, the MacDougal Street coffeehouse where he performed. It would be just like the Cellar, only better. As soon as she graduated she and Kendrick were going to New York.

She never saw her mother. Since her marriage she had stopped going home. She thought of the episode with the motorcyclist last summer as her marriage, though technically it had never been one. It made her feel wildly romantic to be seventeen, living in sin with one man, already a veteran of marriage to another. *Katie Blue* had been released a year ago, and Alex felt as beautiful and bad as the heroine whose various amours made up the plot. Legally she was still under the protection of her mother, but whether her mother knew she would be leaving, Alex couldn't say. What she did know was that her mother wouldn't care.

And so she passed the last months of her life in Limestone. Her old friends were shopping for prom dresses and making college plans, but she had no interest in waltzing around a high school gym while Andy Williams crooned "Moon River," and she felt as if she had been going to college all her life. Later, she said when Kendrick pushed her to apply. She skipped the graduation ceremony. In June, a week before her eighteenth birthday, they packed the station wagon and drove north to pick up the interstate that would take them to their new life.

Their sublet was a lucky find in an apartment building on Charles Street in Greenwich Village, small but perfect, with book-lined walls and a view of a garden. Alex liked waking to the honking of taxis, the swish of the street sweeper, the shouts of the garbage men and clatter of trucks, liked the way the city's jackhammers rang in her teeth and the subway roared below her feet. Best of all she liked to sit in Washington Square Park, tilting her face up to the sun while flutists and bongo drummers gathered the parti-colored crowd into knots. She photographed the musicians and the old men playing checkers; on the Bowery she photographed bums. To her the city was a street fair, and she couldn't understand why Kendrick didn't feel compelled to record it as she did. With all there was to choose from, he still chose to photograph her. Sometimes she thought he must be after just one image that eluded him, the definitive picture, and when at last he got it he wouldn't need her any more. But that wasn't true. He would always need her. He loved her. She knew that now.

He had arranged with a friend named Jack to use the darkroom in his loft just below the Village, where industries lined the narrow streets in cast-iron buildings laced up the front with fire escapes. Papers blew through the streets that were always gray with shade, but in the loft the light was so clear it seemed made of crystal, and Kendrick often photographed her in its space. As she sat, she could hear the clacking of machines downstairs, winding thread onto spools. It seemed such a wonderfully peculiar place to live. So many people came and went she thought half the city must have had the key. To her it was like a secret city in the air, just as the subways were a secret city underneath the sidewalks. She couldn't believe how alive New York made her feel.

She did not like Jack, a painter who never seemed to paint, though the loft was littered with the appliances of art—brushes, tubes, stacks of stretchers—and hung with his canvases, bright blocks of color that seemed like last year's avant-garde. She was uncomfortable posing, for she suspected Jack thumbed through Kendrick's proof sheets and prints like a girlie magazine. He unnerved her with his winks and sidelong glances, even as his girlfriends clung to his arm. He was constantly catching her apart from the group and questioning her about Kendrick. It was not that the questions were, one by one, so odd, but that their accumulation seemed suspect. Did she love him? How long had they been together? Hot, he'd complain, taking off his shirt, and she would turn her head away from the sight of his brown chest with its triangle of prematurely white hair. He had a slow, deliberate way of stretching that seemed suggestive, and it angered her that she should give him the satisfaction of being disturbed. She didn't know if he was interested in her or mocking her for being interested in him. Which she was not. He just made it impossible for her to be unaware of him, and she couldn't understand why Kendrick didn't see what was going on, except that Jack had never actually said he was attracted to her and maybe she just imagined the electricity he tried to make crackle in the air all around him.

She was still confused when Jack came looking for Kendrick one afternoon when Kendrick wasn't in. "I can wait," Jack said. He helped himself to a beer, leaning on the doorframe to watch her as she dried the lunch dishes and put them away. After a minute he set the empty can on a bookcase. Did she want to go to bed? he asked. She did not. She was disgusted. The way he stood in the doorway, she could not get by.

She had thought he was Kendrick's friend. What made him think she played around?

He shrugged. "Just checking."

When she narrowed her eyes at him he laughed. He had thick, close-cropped gray hair and a deep tan that seemed dishonest on an artist. He was at least forty, maybe older, not especially tall, but thick, with the powerful shoulders of a wrestler or a gymnast. He moved from the doorway to let her by and plucked a book from one of the shelves, flipping through it idly. She took it from his hand and replaced it.

"The perfect hostess."

"The books don't belong to us," she said and picked up her purse.

He accompanied her down the stairs, waiting while she checked the mailbox. "Where are we going?"

She had planned to spend the afternoon at the Metropolitan Museum, but the thought of him trailing her into the subway was repellent. She turned the corner. "*I'm* going to the store."

But she passed the green grocers on Bleecker and zigzagged south. "Don't you have something better to do?" she snapped when they finally crossed into Chinatown, pushing through the crowd that buzzed like flies around the sidewalk stands of shrimp and bitter melon. Now that he had confirmed her suspicion she should feel absolved or even righteous. Instead she felt contaminated. She had hoped the long walk would shake him.

He kept in step despite the crowded street. "Does it ever bother you, being taller than your boyfriend?"

"No." She wasn't taller, and she never thought about it.

"What do you like about him?" he wanted to know.

"Everything I don't like about you."

He stopped on the sidewalk to laugh, threw his head back and let out a great roar. She resisted the impulse to ask what was so funny.

"How come you don't get married?" Turning down Mott, she paused to look at a window full of ducks hung by their pimpled necks. She didn't want to admit that Kendrick hadn't asked her. "You're a prize. He ought to tie you down before you decide you want to see the world." Jostling two Oriental women pushing strollers, he fell in step again. "I'm surprised Eileen Ford hasn't stopped you on the street."

"I don't know who that is." A lie. She and Jo used to read *Seventeen* magazine cover to cover, imagining how one day Eileen Ford would make cover girls of them.

"On second thought, you're too gorgeous. No one would look at the clothes." He smiled, trying to soften her up. Behind her someone was buying chicken feet from a vendor. "You're nice too. Nobody expects that from a beauty."

In her whole life no one had ever accused her of being nice. And, if he knew her better, which he would never, he would know how much she disliked having people talk about her looks. It was boring. "I'm not a prize, and for your information being beautiful is not an accomplishment. It's not what I do."

"What do you do?"

She paid for some bean sprouts and went into a bakery to escape the stench of fish. "I take pictures, not that it's any of your business."

"You haven't used the darkroom." She pointed, and the baker put a pastry in a bag. "Ah, I get it. Didn't want to ask. It doesn't make any difference to me, you know. I'm a painter."

The crust flaked on her chin. Good, but she didn't know what it was called; so she wouldn't be able to ask for it again. She dropped the greasy paper into her purse and licked her fingers. She hadn't wanted to ask, it was true; she hadn't wanted to owe him any favors. She'd shot a dozen rolls of film and hadn't even proofed them.

"The two of you talk? Or does he just look at you?"

"We talk." She cut back up Mulberry to Canal. She had walked twenty-five blocks just to buy a bunch of bean sprouts she didn't know how to cook. For a moment she hesitated before a white tile tank in a window. It held a turtle, like no turtle she had seen, a great brown beast with hooded eyes and a fleshy snout that flared from the black hole of its mouth in a grotesque parody of foreskin, sucking at the glass as if it were sucking after prey, but any prey this creature hunted would have disappeared from the earth sixty million years before her ancestors had scrambled to their feet and begun their headlong flight into the twentieth century. She shivered and walked on.

"What about?"

"Not about you." She gave an impatient shrug. She wasn't paying attention; she was staring at the Chinese on the street, a people nourished on claws, seaweed, ancient eggs, and prehistoric monsters. No wonder their language sounded so emphatic.

"He your first lover?" He used the word as casually as she used "boyfriend."

They crossed into Little Italy. She'd been disappointed her first time through, but now she was grateful for the stepped-up pace the drab, deserted streets permitted. "I've been married." It gave her pleasure to say it, but it bothered her that she could not remember what she and Kendrick did talk about, just things, it wasn't as if they had nothing to say to each other. They'd been together for so long they'd exhausted their life stories. It made her furious to know she would not tell Kendrick about Jack. It would be wrong of her to tell, though on the other hand it might be right. She *thought* she should not tell—Jack was Kendrick's friend; he had a good thing going with the darkroom—but already she felt her silence between them like a wedge. How dare Jack try to drive them apart? She was happy.

"Didn't work out, huh?"

"What are you getting at anyway? I've already said no."

"I heard you." After a few blocks he said, "I looked through that last batch of pictures. A dozen shots of your elbow. I'd say our friend may be a tad hung up."

The uneasiness came back. He'd seen her naked, which wouldn't matter if he would only look at the photographs the way he was supposed to, would look at them as art. She wasn't responsible for his reaction. But why did Kendrick have to leave them lying around? She flushed. "He's working on a series of textures."

"I would have picked another part."

They were Kendrick's pictures. Why didn't *he* worry about them?

"Ritzy block," Jack remarked when they came to her corner. He hadn't noticed she was no longer speaking to him. She was never going to speak to him again. "Well, so long. Enjoy your sprouts."

They looked like worms. Albino worms. She boiled them and served them with butter, and Kendrick said, "Let's not have them again."

He didn't ask her where she got them; she didn't tell him she'd walked to Chinatown. If she did he would simply assume she'd gone there to take pictures. He hadn't noticed that she hadn't printed any of the hundreds she'd already taken. What was the matter with him? She stacked his plate on top of hers and sighed. What was the matter with her? She wasn't mad at *him*.

He didn't notice the way she began to cut Jack off mid-sentence with a cool flip of shoulders and sudden business elsewhere in the loft. Of course there were always so many people: any number of them might have been not speaking to another and who would know? Whole groups fell silent as they toked up. She passed the joints that came to her. Pot never put her in the blissful, passive state it seemed to induce in all Jack's friends. When she smoked, she grew ebullient. Even more embarrassing, she got horny, had since she'd first tried it, back in Limestone, when she and Kendrick had coupled in a frenzy on the living room floor as soon as their friends went home—they could hardly wait to be alone they were so hungry for each other—and while he was pumping away—which wasn't exactly the way to put it, that dovetailing of pain and pleasure that could not be put into words without becoming crude or corny—while they were making love then, she'd opened her eyes and seen tomatoes strobing on the ceiling. The seeds turned into stars, pulsing on a field of navy blue, and then they burst, a million skyrockets shooting pastel sparks. It was great, but she thought she liked sex better without the marching band and Fourth of July show. What the drug augmented was not intimacy but a spectacle of sensation that was ultimately solitary. Like masturbation, she considered it a form of cheating.

But Jack's friends rolled number after number and got mild instead of rutty. When they did talk, they made witty remarks instead of conversation. What were she and Kendrick doing at the loft night after night? Why weren't they at Carnegie Hall or Lincoln Center or one of the Village clubs? Well, yes, she knew: they didn't have the money. And, to be fair, she had never told Kendrick that she would prefer to avoid Jack.

She *shouldn't* tell, but without telling it happened only in her head, became something she imagined, a kind of jumping in the space that went from her to Jack. She thought about him. She didn't want to, but she couldn't help what was between them. Not sex, but all the same a culpable connection. Though he'd been casual, it was impossible for her to be casual in response. Everything he said took meaning. She tried to concentrate on Kendrick, but what he said became inane in the very act of her concentration, took absurd significance, so that all day she would puzzle over "Do you want toast?" or "We're out of milk." He had a show coming up in a Village gallery—it was a big break; she knew he was nervous, she knew he was ecstatic, but all he did was fuss about the framing. The trouble with happiness, she decided, was that it was banal. Every word Jack said—stupid things; sidling up to fill her wineglass he would whisper "Hey" or "How's it going?"—was shot through with heat instead of light, full of hidden meaning. But she was sorry for him finally. Every week he had a different girl. He wasn't a happy man.

Chapter 21

1968

In August they went to Chicago. The National Democratic Convention was meeting at the Amphitheatre, though most of the scheduled actions were for the parks.

Mrs. Kitchen waved as they came into the greystone Stacy's parents owned. A dainty woman with lively blue eyes, she was assembling trays of sandwiches and cookies, telephone wedged beneath her ear. Stacy looked like her father, whose stocky build and aggressive jaw seemed as predisposed to the practice of law as a ballerina's flat chest and sinewy legs were to the dance. With bus and taxi strikes in progress, he had turned the house into an informal center for information and rides.

Mrs. Kitchen replaced the phone. "Grace Mebane. They have a crib and will be happy to put up your friends with the children."

Ted and Alex were sleeping in the guest room, and the others had brought sleeping bags. Tulip thought they might camp in Lincoln Park.

"Oh dear," Mrs. Kitchen said as Stacy picked up a knife to start spreading mayonnaise, "that wouldn't be wise. Daley's called in 25,000 troops to enforce the curfew. There are shelters, or you're welcome to spread your bedding out here."

Tulip sneezed; she had hayfever and had forgotten her antihistamine. "There's a drugstore at Belden and Clark," Stacy directed. "Turn left and you can't miss it."

"Such a waif," Mrs. Kitchen observed.

"Yeah," Stacy said, "and about as sweet as a nine-year-old pusher in Jackson Park."

Michael hadn't made the trip, Leah was staying with a friend in Hyde Park, and Nelson had already followed Peggy to the rock concert at Lincoln Park, where the Yippies were holding their Festival of Life.

"I hope they have sense enough to come back here or go to a shelter," Mrs. Kitchen said.

"I doubt it." Stacy capped the last sandwich and licked her fingers. "Peggy's turning into a hippie."

"What do you mean, turning?" Alex said. The Yippies promised a carnival; the National Mobilization to End the War promised speeches. Ted, who was speaking at the Mobe demonstration in Grant Park on Tuesday, refused to set foot in Lincoln Park. Alex thought the Yippies pretty irresponsible herself, but they also promised to be flamboyant, and she wanted to take their pictures before she dedicated herself to the Cause. It was no longer possible to pretend that she could observe and participate at the same time. She had replaced the Nikon lost at the Pentagon and wasn't eager to lose another.

Stacy went with her, listening to the music while Alex got her pictures of the clowns, Humphrey Dumpty, a topless Miss America in drag, Green Beret with a barf mat for a brain. When the light went bad they left. On television the next night they watched the Battle of Lincoln Park. At curfew the police had flushed the Yippies with tear gas, chased them down and clubbed them, the thousand beatific kids she and Stacy had observed sitting on the grass. In Grant Park Tuesday, as the crowd chanted, "Dump the Hump," Alex kept a wary eye on the sky-blue helmets of the police who watched, riot sticks at ready. "We must force the Democratic Party to be a democratic party," Ted said into the microphone. These were the police that Mayor Richard J. Daley had ordered to shoot to kill in the disturbance that followed Martin Luther King's assassination. On Monday night they had taken off their badges and nameplates and beaten seventeen reporters.

On Tuesday night they gassed four hundred clergy who had gone to Lincoln Park to join the Yippies in a nonviolent vigil. "Pigs," Matt cried. He had been deeply influenced by Ed Rayle during the years when he played guitar for the folk masses at Holy Trinity. Personally Alex thought Ed Rayle half full of shit, primarily because he would love to hear her say so. He liked irreverence; he was *relevant*. She objected to his style, but in substance he was unquestionably noble, and she was as angry as Matt. So the cops were beating priests now.

On Wednesday afternoon they charged into Grant Park. Alex caught sight of a demonstrator climbing the flagpole half a block away, and suddenly that end of the park erupted into shouts, Rennie Davis was at the bullhorn exhorting the crowd to sit down, she whipped her head around to see a line of police lowering their plexiglass face shields, Davis went down, she heard the blow amplified by the PA. The crowd was on its feet. "Walk," Ted commanded. "Running draws their attention." The hail of canisters began. She ducked and dodged, clinging to Ted's hand, blind from the teargas, choking, retching, mucus smeared across her face. People were flopping on the ground, stampeding, bleating, braying. "Don't rub your eyes," the marshals screamed. The police penned them at the bridges over the IC tracks. On the other side the National Guard held bayonets at ready. When they broke through they were halted at Michigan Avenue. They had lost the others, but miraculously she clung to Ted, vision cleared though her eyes still burned. Sirens whined in the eerie silence. "What's happening?" whispered through the crowd. "It's the Poor People's Campaign," Ted said. "They're marching to the Amphitheatre." The police parted to let the mules and wagons through. "Join them!" people began shouting, pushing forward, but the police halted them again and closed ranks. For perhaps half an hour the police held them in position. An ice of fear laid itself along her bones. To the north, behind them, another line of police blocked a retreat, and Jeeps with barbed wire shields affixed to their grills closed off the side streets. On the sidewalk onlookers were chanting, "The whole world is watching." Ted squeezed her hand, and someone passed a jar of Vaseline; up and down the ranks people were smearing the petroleum jelly on their skin and tying wet kerchiefs across their mouths and noses. Still they waited.

At last the police allowed the Poor People's wagons to cross Balbo Drive. And then they attacked.

It was as if something exploded, and the body of the crowd flew apart. The dusk shredded with screams. Police were running them down in columns, nameplates taped over, swinging clubs and roaring.

Ted went down, they were spun apart, she was weeping again from gas, choking, stumbling into the park. She tripped and raised her arm to shield her face. Someone yanked her to her feet. Blood was spurting from the mouth of a boy running along beside her; she heard a bone crack as the cop tackled him from the side and another clubbed him on the head. She ran up the steps cut into the cement balustrade, into the dead end of chainlink face above the IC tracks, and whirled, but nothing happened; she was alone on the broken asphalt pathway. As she watched, panting, crouched behind the railing, the police charged their own barricade in front of the Conrad Hilton and drove the people on the sidewalk through a plate glass window. She took off running again.

When it was over, as suddenly as it began, paddy wagons wailing off into the distance, she was sitting on the steps, dazed as the lone survivor of an air raid surveying the aftermath of carnage on the field. Twilight had congealed into darkness, illuminated by the lights along Michigan Avenue and the collapsed parachutes of clothing strewn across the park. The air reeked of Mace. Her stomach burned, and the ankle she'd twisted when she fell was swelling. She limped up Michigan Avenue, empty now, a rubble of broken glass, sweaters, handbags, shoes, to the IC station below Randolph Street, where she called the greystone.

A boy she hadn't met picked her up. "Humphrey got gassed in his hotel room," he told her. "The Democrats are finished." Indeed it seemed as if Mayor Daley, the machine boss who had elected John F. Kennedy by bringing the Cook County cemeteries out to vote, had thrown this election to Nixon even before the delegates at the Amphitheatre began their roll call. "The hell of it is this is exactly what Johnson wanted. He'd rather see Tricky Dick in office than let his flunkey Hubert have it."

"Hey, hey, LBJ," she muttered in a voice rasped by tear gas.

"Ain't that the truth," he said.

In the big second-floor bathroom of the greystone a medic was treating the injured. He washed her eyes and face and applied antiseptic to a scrape. "Better stay off that ankle," he advised. "It'll be okay in a couple of days if you don't abuse it." A wild laugh rose in her throat. She felt a little hysterical. *Hey, hey, LBJ …* She was worried about Ted.

Stacy was in the den, in a quilted robe and old pair of cat-eye glasses, drinking wine and watching the convention. "Your eyes are red," she said as Alex sat. "You get a lot of gas?"

Alex nodded. "You?"

"Yeah. I lost my contacts."

"We told you not to wear them."

"I know—it was stupid. Matt called. They broke his collarbone."

Nelson and Peggy had been arrested at Lincoln Park the night before. Leah was in jail, and Lizzie was in Stacy's bedroom, trying to settle Caton down to sleep. She had taken the kids to the Aquarium that afternoon and come over to wait for news of Garth.

"They're darling children," Mrs. Kitchen observed as she came into the den. "Are you hungry, dear?" she asked Alex. "Would you like some coffee or a drink?"

"I can't believe this shit." Stacy glared at the TV.

"Sit where you are. I'll bring you a glass of wine." Mrs. Kitchen patted Alex on the shoulder. "Don't worry about your husband. George has had the phone tied up arranging bail."

Tulip staggered in from the downstairs bathroom, wan and shaking, beads of sweat strung across her forehead. "Any word about the others?"

Stacy shook her head. "Mom, have you got any Pepto Bismol for Tulip?"

Lizzie came back, carrying a cup of coffee, and sat next to Alex on the sofa. "You okay?" Alex nodded. Lizzie glanced at the TV. "Where are they?"

"Nominations." Alex stood. "Does anybody mind if I take a shower?"

"Please," they all said together. "It's in your clothes," Stacy added. "Jeez, Mace smells like puke, but worse."

Alex wanted a bath but took a shower not to tie up the bathroom. "You missed it," Stacy said when she returned with a thick brown towel wrapped around her head. "Senator Ribicoff told Daley off, and Daley called him a Jew son-of-a-bitch."

"On *TV*?"

"You couldn't hear it, but you could read his lips," Lizzie said.

"And I missed it." Alex sat, digging her bare feet into the shag carpet.

"I feel so guilty," Lizzie said. "Me and the kids, looking at fish."

Alex squeezed her hand. "You'd feel a lot more guilty if they'd been there."

"I was scared out of my mind," Stacy admitted suddenly. Her voice was hoarse.

"You could see the Guard on the roof of Field Museum from the Aquarium. Tice threw a fit. He wanted to go see the helicopters."

"Stacy." Her father beckoned from the hallway.

Grimly Alex, Lizzie, and Tulip watched the convention. *Madame Secretary, Alabama, the Yellowhammer State, home of Paul "Bear" Bryant and the Crimson Tide, proudly casts …* The medic stuck his head in. "How's it going? Humphrey win yet?"

"Not yet." Alex unwrapped her turban. *Madame Secretary, Arkansas, home of the Razorbacks …* "Now we know what a political football means," she said.

Lizzie set her cup down. "Where are they?" Her voice rose. "He's got three kids, you know?"

"And you're the pregnant lady who wanted to go to Mississippi." Alex's ankle throbbed; the wine had given her a dull headache. She closed her eyes and saw the plate glass window in the Hilton shattering again. The cops had run inside with their clubs still thrashing. "Why did you come, Lizzie?"

"To take my kids to the museums." Lizzie's voice went flat. She was a tall woman with heavy bones, but hunched in a corner of the sofa, she looked frail. "I care a lot about this country, but I also want my kids to grow up with both their parents."

Madame Secretary, California … "Home of Richard M. Nixon and Sirhan B. Sirhan," Tulip muttered.

Lizzie and Alex glanced up anxiously as Stacy reclaimed her father's recliner. "So who's winning?"

"Ha ha," Alex said glumly.

Tulip blew her nose and dropped a Kleenex to the pile on the TV tray beside her. "If this doesn't radicalize America, I don't know what will."

"Don't be silly," Alex said. "It's going to reactionalize five times as many."

Lizzie was biting her nails. Blindly Alex turned the pages of *The*

Poky Little Puppy, which Lizzie had been reading to the children before bed. "I wish Ted would call."

Tulip wadded another Kleenex. "Tulip!" Stacy said. "Quit blowing snot all over my parents' den."

"I have *hayfever*."

Madame Secretary, Pennsylvania …

"Sorry," Stacy mumbled. "I'm just jumpy."

… the next President of the United States, Hubert H. Humphrey! A blare of horns took over the soundtrack as the band struck up "Happy Days Are Here Again."

"Well, that's it," Lizzie said.

"Turn it off." Alex was kneading the damp towel on her lap.

"Hey Mom. Hump just went over the top."

Mrs. Kitchen stood in the doorway. "Lizzie. Garth is on the phone." Alex's hands tensed on the towel, but in a few minutes Lizzie came back smiling. "They're okay." She grabbed Alex's hand, limp with the relief spangling through her. "Ted has a broken jaw, that's all. George is arranging bail."

Stacy let her breath burst. "Thank God." She drew back as Alex, Lizzie, and Tulip wept and hugged. "I didn't want to tell you. There's a rumor that one of the demonstrators was killed."

On Labor Day Alex sat with her feet in the baby pool at the Limestone City Park while Lizzie dangled Caton in the water. "Remember what I said. No adults," Lizzie called to Tice, who was brandishing a green squirt gun. Lucy darted past them with a plastic float around her waist. "Slow down and walk, Miss."

Alex turned her face toward the big pool, where a patchwork of beach towels and transistors covered the cement deck, "In-a-Gadda-Da-Vida" pounding through the squeals of the junior high girls. The scent of coconut oil wafted over, and she tipped her head back, inhaling deeply. Beyond the fence the world was on the brink of chaos, but in the sanctuary of the Limestone City Pool only the top forty and cut of the bathing suits changed. "Ticers," she said and ducked, but he got her anyway with a cold squirt in the mouth.

"You asked for that," Lizzie said. "Tice, I told you, no adults."

"Oh, let him have fun." Alex cupped her hands and poured water over her shoulders. "People shouldn't come to the pool if they don't want to get wet."

"Mom. Can I have a popsicle?"

Lizzie set Caton on the cement to play with a toy boat and fished in her bag. "One, and you split it with your sister." Tice swooped off toward the snack bar, and Lizzie leaned back. "What happened at the meeting last night?"

Alex sighed. "Talk. Are we for withdrawal or a victory by the NLF? Are we for peaceful demonstration or meeting violence with violence? Should we support the National Office in the call for a student strike? Are the blacks leading a nationalist revolution? The bit about Third World revolutions took up most of the time."

"So what are we for?"

"Who knows? It killed Ted not to be able to say anything." His jaw was wired shut.

"It makes me sick. How many years did we work to build a movement? And this new breed comes in, they haven't read anything, they don't know anything, all they want to do is pick up a gun and go tagging after Cuba." Lizzie tore the wrapper from Tice's popsicle and broke it in half.

"It's not just the new breed," Alex said. "Even Matt's saying we ought to redefine our position on violence. It really got to him, Ed Rayle's getting gassed in Lincoln Park. Nelson's been indicted for burning his draft card, we're all broke making bail, and everybody's starting to wonder if the guy sitting next to him's taking notes for the FBI. I hate it, but you can't blame people for feeling militant after Chicago." The whistle blew. "Rest period. I'll watch the kids. You go on and swim."

Lizzie stood, tugging at her suit. She wore an old-fashioned black one-piece with a skirt that didn't quite conceal the loose flesh of her stomach. "Esther Williams," she mocked, tucking her hair into a rubber cap. "I swim like the Titanic."

Alex bent over Caton. "More boat," he said.

"I don't think we have another one, sweetie."

"Mom!"

“Mommy’s in the big pool, Tice.”

He planted himself before her with a teary scowl, knees a neon pink beneath the scabs. “Lucy won’t share.”

“Where’s your popsicle? You had one.” He pointed, and near a deck chair piled with towels she spied the mound of cherry ice in a puddle crawling with ants. “Oh honey, you dropped it.” He screwed up his face and waited to see if he should cry. “Maybe we can wash it off.” Alex got up, keeping an eye on Caton as she brushed away the ants. “There.”

“I don’t want that one.” She heard her name and looked up. “Why can’t I have a new one?”

“Alex?”

She shaded her eyes. The sky seemed brighter for the clouds piling along the horizon behind her. On the other side of the pool a woman with a diaper flung over her shoulder was leaning forward. “Because. It’s the only one there is. Take it or leave it.”

“Alex, is that you?” She recognized the voice first, a faint wheezing in the vowels that recalled the banging of high school lockers, a salty burning in her tastebuds that was the Towne Art popcorn, and most of all the smell of chlorine from the pool where Lizzie’s white bathing cap now bobbed in the rhythm of the breaststroke. “Jo.”

“I thought that was you.” Jo came around the pool. Her skin was smoother; her face seemed thinner, though perhaps that was an effect of the long hair. (They should learn to flatter themselves, their home ec teacher used to say, parading them across the stage to point out the defects of their figures: Jo was hippy; Alex was flat-chested—she was not!—if they didn’t have thunder thighs, they had bony clavicles or thick ankles; they were too short, too tall, too fat, too thin. The good news was that they could hide the bad news beneath the right stripe, pleat, dart, or ruffle.) When Jo smiled, without thinking Alex said, “You got your braces off.”

“About six years ago,” Jo said, and they laughed. Alex put a hand out to keep Caton from toppling off the edge. “My mom told me she ran into you at the IGA.”

“She said you were expecting.”

Jo opened her arm. “Jennifer. Three months today.”

"She's precious." Alex extended her finger and called, "Tice! If you want to pee in the pool, pee *in* the pool. You may not pee off the side. Lucy, give that little boy his bucket back."

"Golly." Jo tickled Jennifer's foot.

"Oh, they're not mine. Their mother's getting a few laps in on the break." Jennifer was still clutching Alex's finger. Her bonnet was twisted, and she gazed placidly at Alex.

"I should be doing laps." Jo grimaced.

"You look good."

"You look great. A bikini," Jo marveled. "I would have hated your guts if you told me you had three kids."

"You always hated my guts anyway."

"Well, that's true." Jo sat.

Alex laughed. "It's good to see you, Jo." It surprised her. They'd been friends, but not like she and Lizzie or she and Stacy were. High school friends. Nothing but boredom and boys in common.

"You too." Jo bent her face to Jennifer's and crooned as Lucy waded toward them.

"Awex. Tice hitted my duck."

Jo sat up. "Mom said you're married now too."

Alex nodded, twisting her head to blow up Lucy's float as Caton crawled into her lap. Lucy stared solemnly at her brother. "Caton can't come to my birthday party. He'll poop in the birthday cake."

Alex capped the duck. "It's Tice's party, hon. Your birthday's not for six months."

"They're cute." Jo straightened the strap of Jennifer's sunsuit, and Caton wriggled off Alex's lap to go tearing after Lucy. "Mom sent me your picture from the *Register*." Alex craned her neck after Caton. "So you're really an activist?"

"Oh, the ROTC demonstration." Already it seemed a long time ago.

"I've signed a couple of petitions, but that's about it. Remember Diana Wells? She's really into the antiwar thing. You can't talk to her, it's all imperialist this and capitalist that." Jo paused to adjust Jennifer. Alex didn't know which amazed her most about children, their individuality or their similarity. At three months they couldn't sit up, but spread their wings and thought they were planes. Now Lucy was a terrible two; Tice was turning into a fearsome four. They could be awful, but nothing in her life had prepared her for how much she would love Lizzie's children. "I guess you heard about Bobby Bright."

"Your mother told me." For a minute they were silent. Bobby Bright, with the freckles and cowlicky red hair. In grade school they called him Woody Woodpecker, in high school Bobby Blight, Alex had remembered, parked beside the lettuce with Irene Yellen. She had wanted to remember something serious about him, but she'd known him since kindergarten. He was the kid who put bubblegum on the teacher's chair and barf mats on her desk, the one whose goofy face came back every time she heard a lipfart. He kissed her once under a sprig of mistletoe, and in the girls' bathroom she'd scrubbed her mouth with the gritty soap that caked in the dispensors, making a show of it, washing that kiss off. Bobby Bright, twenty-two years old and dead in Vietnam. Standing in the IGA with Irene Yellen that morning, she had tasted the gritty, alkaline soap again and wished to god she'd kissed him back.

Jo shook her head. "Did you hear Kevin's coming home? He got a leg blown off."

A chill shuddered down Alex's spine as she closed her eyes. "For nothing." And the government beat them up and threw them in jail for trying to stop it. For a moment she was so mad she wished she had a gun. Pig Daley, sending his cops into the streets to gas priests and beat reporters while the governor of Missouri told the Democrats assembled at the Amphitheatre that if they adopted the peace plank they would jeopardize the lives of the servicemen in Vietnam, and no one laughed, no one said, "Is that supposed to be a joke?" *Jeopardize their lives.*

Guiltily she opened her eyes and checked the children. Lizzie was coming through the gate, shaking her bathing cap. "Hi, baby." She knelt before Caton. "How were they?"

"Perfect." Alex introduced Jo and Lizzie.

"What's your mother doing these days, Alex?" Jo asked. "I noticed a for-sale sign at the house."

"There is?" Alex said. There was an awkward silence.

"I think your baby's getting burned," Lizzie observed.

"Oh dear." Jo snatched the diaper from her shoulder and flung it over Jennie. "It's after two. I thought …" She stood. "I need to get her home anyway for her nap."

When Jo had gone, Alex lay back, thinking about Kevin and Bobby. The water in the baby pool was tepid, and her limbs felt heavy. The shrieks of the children and warnings of the mothers rose and fell like an ancient song all around her as she listened for the pulse of the radios farther off, the churring whisper of girl secrets, punctuated by giggles and shouts, the slap of the water, the lifeguard's whistle, and, rumbling faintly in the distance, thunder. When the red quilting in the back of her eyelids darkened, she sat up. The sky had turned the color of slate, eerie in the chartreuse light that seemed to emanate from the trees before a storm. The air had stilled, pressure dropping like a sense inside the body; it smelled of ozone and warm cement. There was a soft clattering of people gathering possessions, and then a gust of wind set the leaves to clapping.

"I'm not going." Tice flung his sneaker.

"Oh yes you are," his mother said, tying Lucy's blue Keds while Alex hoisted Caton and hung swim rings from her arm. The rumble came again, and big drops began to spatter.

"Hurry up, Tice," Lizzie said. "It's going to storm."

Chapter 22

1982

Alex feels sick as she sits down to dinner. All day she's been cooking, something she normally enjoys, but the kitchen was hot, the cake stuck to the pans, the phyllo tore, and she grew cross. Her skin felt greasy. The sweet, fatty smell of the melted butter mixed with the perfume of vegetables sautéing in olive oil seemed cloying; she had a bad taste at the back of her mouth. In the middle of making the tiropita she decided the meal was too heavy. The rich food that had seemed such a joyous indulgence in the Safeway was revolting, and for a moment she considered pitching everything into the garbage.

That was when she realized, but it was too late to call the dinner off.

And if the meal is too heavy for Kendrick, he doesn't notice. Already he's loading his plate with seconds. She watches him pick up his fork and remembers, when she was fifteen, noticing the cording in his arms with an uneasy little thrilling just beneath her skin. That was desire before it had a name. Now, on the far other side of that young love, she has grown aware of him again. Something had relaxed between them since the opening of the B.F.A. show. Until this afternoon she'd felt she no longer had a secret straining her voice and skittering behind her pupils. What she should feel in his presence is comfort. Now, instead, she feels like crying.

Kendrick is asking if she'd like to go to New York for the Paris/Magnum show at the International Center of Photography this weekend. "We could take the early plane on Saturday and catch the last one back," he says. The ICP is one of their favorite museums. "Unless you want to make a weekend of it."

"Sure, I guess so, I don't know." She looks at her untouched plate, fat already congealing into little white pearls beneath the meat. She's still hot from the stove. "I should have fixed something lighter."

"Oh no you shouldn't." Kendrick takes an emphatic bite. "This is great." He pauses. "So do you want to go?"

"I don't know, I said." She pushes back from the table to get the dessert, suddenly lightheaded, so dizzy she has to grab the edge to keep her balance.

"Alex, are you okay?"

A great black spider full of dust motes darts across her vision. She sits down hard.

"Are you all right? Earth to Alex—are you okay, hello?"

"I'm fine," she says in a hollow voice.

"You look pale."

"I'm fine, I said." Her voice climbs. "Would you quit asking? Can't I have a private life?"

"I wish you would."

She shakes her head. "I've had one. Oh I've had one all right." She shakes her head again in disbelief. She's known all afternoon what's wrong with her, and it's not the heat. "I'm pregnant."

Instantly she's sorry, and her eyes fly up to his face, which works through its shock to compose itself, after what seems like several minutes, into a hard white mask. "Congratulations."

She doesn't answer. Why couldn't she have discovered this two days ago, when she could have found some excuse to uninvite him? Though sooner or later she would have had to tell him anyway, and she can't imagine that he would just say, "Oh."

"Who's the lucky father? Or was this an immaculate conception?"

She is almost out of her chair when another surge of nausea drops her, and she sits again, lowering her forehead to her hands. This is Kendrick. Did she mean to claw his eyes out the way she almost did Ross's? After a minute she hears the clatter of dishes being cleared from the table and then his footsteps returning from the kitchen.

"I'm sorry. I shouldn't have said that. It's just—you caught me by surprise. Are you joking?"

"No, I'm not joking," she says. "I'm sorry. I shouldn't have just blurted it out like that. It's just that I didn't know until this afternoon, when I was cooking." She raises her head to meet his eyes, but they are steeled on some point beyond her. She shifts her gaze. Of course she's pregnant. She was so out of her mind that week with Ross she never even thought about contraception. Her stomach clenches in a moment of pure feminist rage. Why would Ross have thought about it? Fucking's just a harmless sport to men. "Am I sure? Yes. Have I been to the doctor? No."

There is a long pause. Kendrick's face is still so closed that the neutraility in his voice seems forced. "What are you going to do?"

She's still having a hard time taking it in. Her breasts are sore, her clothes feel tight, she hasn't been hungry, and the only reason she doesn't know she's missed a period is that she's never known exactly when her periods were due. "It looks like I'm going to have a baby."

For a moment she thinks about the miscarriage she had so many years ago. She had wanted that baby so much. And after she lost it, she had hoped that she and Ted would have another.

"Do you want me to go?"

She takes a shaky breath. "You can if you want."

"That's not what I asked."

She needs for him to go but doesn't want to send him. "I'm sorry. I'm just having a hard time with this. I should have called and told you not to come."

"Do you want me to leave?"

"I don't care."

"Then you're right, you should have called. Why didn't you?"

"I don't know. Can't you just leave me alone? I don't care what you do. Go home, go to a party, go cuss me out."

"That's a pretty rotten thing to say."

"After all you've done for me, you mean?"

Before she realizes he's come around the table, he's jerking her up from her chair, his thumbs digging into her shoulders, face so angry that her hand whips to her mouth in fear.

"You're right. I'd better go." He drops his hands and crosses the room like a man who must think how to put one foot in front of another. At the door he turns. "Thanks for the dinner."

Chapter 23

1963-1964

The party on the Upper West Side had turned into such a hot, smoky bumping of elbows and slopping of drinks that Alex felt blessed by the soft August night as she and Kendrick walked down Broadway to the Ninety-sixth Street Station. Their train was at the platform, and they had to run down the steps to slip through the doors of the last car before they closed. The car jerked forward, and she grabbed a pole for balance, then walked on sea legs to the rear door, where she liked to watch the curve of darkness slide across the empty platform like a shutter as the train gathered speed and hurtled toward the next station. The lights blinked, and she caught her breath in the moment of panic that gripped her every time. When she turned around to join Kendrick, who used the subways like a native, falling into an unfocused state of wary blankness, she saw first the couple at the other end. The girl was playing with her boyfriend's ear. Then she saw the man.

He was laid across a seat, and her head snapped away so quickly that, as she watched the white talon trace up from the tip of the ear, she had the sensation of being suspended, and she had to look again to make sure he was there. She had never seen a dead man; she moved closer. His face was battered, his shirt stiff with gore. It was a blue workshirt, faded like the ones she and Kendrick favored. He was young. He wore jeans and desert boots, and his hands were folded across his stomach as if he had merely stretched out for a snooze. His nails were clean and clipped. They touched her: someone had brought him up to mind his manners and keep his person neat. As the train lurched around a curve, she clutched the handgrip to keep from toppling. Kendrick was motioning her to sit.

Now she saw the faint pulse of breath in his hands and began to worry each next beat. There was a plastic hospital bracelet snapped around one wrist. What a city. The public toilets smelled like mothballs, and the subways smelled like toilets. The buildings shot to the sky, but the people fastened their eyes to the streets, picking their way through litter, all that human refuse the noble silhouette denied: the dead, the maimed, the mad. She'd become accustomed to the winos sleeping in doorways, bare feet seeping with infections; bag ladies comparing the day's gleanings as they bedded down on the floors of the ladies' lounges in Grand Central and Penn Stations on rainy nights; the milky eyes of the blind; the glazed eyes of the crazies who came at her on the streets. She photographed them, fair game for the camera's ravening lens. But this boy with the broken face and clean brown hair that would have curled if the person who had botched his haircut would have let it—she would not have photographed him.

She sat beside Kendrick. "We have to help him."

"There are eight million stories in the Naked City."

At the other end of the car the girl had dropped her hand. Her boyfriend was still staring at the map sprayed over with black paint.

"He's been *beaten.*"

"This must be one." They were shouting at each other to be heard.

The train rocketed through a station. An express. They would have to get off at Fourteenth Street and walk. She closed her eyes not to see the forlorn faces waiting on the lighted platforms they would pass.

But she had misheard him. Kendrick was asking if they should call an ambulance.

"He's been in the hospital."

She kept her eyes closed. If she opened them, she would go to him, she would take his head in her lap and hold it until he woke up. She would ride to the end of the line, and back, all night, all day and all night, and she would never leave him.

"Our stop." Kendrick yanked her up. The couple got off; a man with a guitar case got on. She was standing in front of the boy again. "Alex."

The doors snapped.

"No."

"What's the matter with you?"

"No!" she said.

He had to pull her from the train at Chambers, and they crossed the platform to catch the uptown local that would take them back to Sheridan Square.

"New York's no place for anyone who can't ignore bums," he groused. "Keep this up and you'll be feeding your lunch to the pigeons on the Bowery. I mean it—I *worry* about you." She didn't answer. "I asked if he needed an ambulance. Does he need the police? We can call. I'm not being a son-of-a-bitch. Would you take a look around you? The truth is, even if it was *safe*, you don't have enough tears."

She couldn't answer. He was right, but if she said one word she would leave him forever and be sorry. They did not speak the whole way home. She undressed and got into bed without speaking. For the rest of the summer she looked for the boy from the subway, on the trains, in coffeeshops, at bus stops, but she never found him.

In September their sublet was up, and they moved to another on West Eighty-eighth Street. Kendrick had a card printed up; through Jack he got two classes at Pratt. Alex took a job selling ladies' accessories at Gimbels because she had not decided to do anything else. She continued to take pictures, but Kendrick used the Pratt darkroom, and she had no place to print. Maybe she should go to college. She had the grades to get into Barnard, but the tuition was an extravagance beyond salesgirls at Gimbels who didn't know what they wanted to study. Photography, but who could teach her that better than Kendrick? Besides, he was sending out applications. They couldn't live in New York indefinitely on so little money, eating off other people's dishes and reading their books. His show was a success: he should get an associate professorship. One of his prints had been purchased for the Museum of Modern Art. "How does it feel to be hanging at the Modern?" he asked her, but it was only the curve of her armpit, and it went into the archives without being hung.

In March she saw him again. She hadn't thought about the boy from the subway in months, and how she recognized him she didn't know, but she was suddenly bolting from the street into the labyrinth of corridors beneath Times Square, where she had gone after work in hope of getting tickets to *Becket*. He was taller than she'd thought, and she had to run to keep from losing him among the crowd that swelled past the vendors into the tunnels of sooty white tile. He boarded the shuttle; they had to stand, and she couldn't see him for the packages pressing her into an open *Wall Street Journal*. At Grand Central Station she spied him again, curly brown hair, sheepskin jacket worn smooth along the sleeves. "Pardon me … excuse me … sorry!" She ran. He transferred to the Lexington Avenue southbound. A shopping bag struck her knee as she leaned into the aisle to keep him in view. He was reading a paperback book, bent back so she couldn't see the title. She should be on the Seventh Avenue northbound. It was Kendrick's birthday; he was waiting to see what surprise she had planned. She had no idea where this man was taking her. How could she even be sure he was the same one? At Astor Place she followed him up the stairs. No wonder he'd been mugged; he didn't seem to notice he was being tailed. On the streets and in the subways she clutched her purse like a touchdown pass in a Bowl game. She walked head down, but without even casting her eyes back, she could tell if anyone was behind her. She was a New Yorker now. They cut up Stuyvesant to East Tenth, where he entered a red brick tenement with empty shop windows and a grill permanently locked in front of the shop door. On the landing he turned around.

His eyes were dark, and they took her measure so intently she gasped. He had lured her here. Blood throbbed in her throat and crashed in her ears. She took a step backwards, and then all at once she knew she had seen him before, not just on the subway, but a year ago in Limestone. He'd come into the Cellar Cafe with Father Rayle.

She whispered, "That night on the subway—I didn't want to leave you."

"I know," he said, and she followed him into a run-down apartment with a view of an airshaft, thinking this can't happen, it's crazy, it's absurd. He served her cold coffee in a chipped enamel cup. A sleeping bag was spread on the floor; there was no furniture, so she sat against the windowsill, still in her corduroy coat. In Limestone the daffodils would be blooming; here a raw gray wind blew from river to river; her coat had shed buttons since high school, she'd lost her gloves, and her fingers were numb. The room smelled sour with winter. "There's no heat," he said. "We've been paying the rent into escrow." His voice was riveting it was so matter-of-fact.

"Were you okay?" she asked.

He grinned to show all his teeth intact, rubbed the side of his nose where it crooked from the break. It was a handsome face, lit with energy, high boned. "It could have been worse."

It was too crazy. She stepped back from the spell he'd hexed her with that night in August. It was Kendrick's birthday. She was going to get Broadway tickets, but she'd lost her place in line. "How did you know I was there?" she asked, feeling her chin rise in the fierce suspicion she held for clairvoyance and other unnatural acts.

"You told me."

Also she did not like games. They had nothing more to say to each other. It was her mistake. One did not pursue the mysteries that occasionally cried up from the unconscious, for if the surreal had uncanny powers, the world she lived in was merely real, ordinary, and the bizarre insistence of dreams was only dull nonsense in its light. Illogically she recalled the big soft shell turtle whose image she had carried away from Chinatown just as she had carried his from the subway back into the soft August night. It was what she felt like now when she saw herself in Kendrick's photographs, a creature trapped by the sprockets of time, the expressions of a moment petrified. A museum was exactly where they belonged, between the dinosaur bones and Greek vases, lit by medieval visions that were never quite as bright as the sunshine outside. The world was a moving picture, a here, now, and meant-to-be gone. She took her empty cup to the kitchen and went to the door.

His face had the same matter-of-factness as his voice. "It's not hard to guess what night you meant."

She would have to change subways twice.

He set his cup down. "Your name is Alexandra Duchamp. You used to wait tables at a place called the Cellar near Wallace. You lived with a guy who taught photography."

She cocked her head.

"You're pretty. I asked."

"Oh." It really was as dull as that. She was still standing with her hand on the doorknob. "What are you doing in New York?"

Something like a curtain closed on his face. "Want to come to Mississippi this summer?"

She shook her head. "I ..." She opened her hands in a gesture of helplessness that meant Kendrick and the whole foolish business of her pursuit. She must have recognized him last August. That was why she'd chased him. There was no big mystery after all.

"We're going down to register black voters."

She smiled the vague little smile she had the habit of wearing when she wanted to seem pleasant. She had seen it on others at parties, sidling up to conversations that didn't make room for them. Jack's girls. Dimwits, they looked.

"I dropped out of Wallace. I was going to join the Peace Corps, but ..." He shrugged as if his reasons were too obvious to explain. "So I thought I'd go down to Mississippi with Snick."

She was still smiling inanely.

"Sorry. I'm a poor organizer." Briefly he returned the smile, which on his face was sincere. "'Never use acronyms.' The Student Nonviolent Coordinating Committee—SNCC. I got involved through Ed Rayle."

She nodded. He was one of those people whose manner makes their every word significant. She thought he could have been a weatherman reporting fair and mild, and all over TV-land his audience would have been transfixed. Why was her every gesture either superfluous or fake?

"Come with me?"

The same helpless splaying of hands. She couldn't take her eyes off his face.

"It's okay," he said.

"Thanks for the coffee." She didn't know what else to say, so she left. She took Kendrick to the Village Vanguard to hear Miles Davis. It was so crowded they almost didn't get in, but *Becket* would have been sold out anyway; she should have ordered tickets in advance.

She hadn't even thought to ask his name.

Chapter 24

1969

The boy at the back of the classroom was shouting, "We want action!" Alex turned her head. Perhaps two hundred people were jammed into this overheated space designed to hold thirty English majors required to take Milton. The ranks had swelled; she didn't know half this army wearing the imperious faces of recruits. As the boy waved his fist the long leather fringes of his vest shimmied. He was armored in peace buttons and deeply flushed. "It's time to take the revolution to the youth of America."

"'Two, three, many Vietnams,'" someone called from beneath the blackboard, and the chant took up: "Ho Ho Ho Chi Minh, NLF is gonna win."

Alex went into her meeting frame of mind, aggressive boredom.

At the table in the front of the room Ted sighed deeply. It was the same irony every time now: the call to take to the streets that kept them arguing all night in the classroom. A weary patience strained his voice. "Violence accomplishes nothing except to turn public sentiment against us."

"Bring the war home," the group around the boy yelled back.

Ted's face darkened. He was angrier than they knew, disgusted with the government, frustrated with them. Leah, Nelson, and Cal were smiling.

Someone else took up the call, and Alex glanced at Stacy, slumped inscrutably in the desk beside her, doodling peace signs on the back of a handout. She hated these more-revolutionary-than-thou shouting matches. How dare anyone imply that Ted lacked courage? Had the boy in the fringed vest been to Mississippi? Where was he when they had their heads cracked at the Pentagon?

Nelson passed Ted a note, and he read it without expression, nodding, blue hollows smudged beneath his eyes. Leah lit a cigarette. Near the front of the room the short-haired Maoists who dressed like Young Republicans and voted in the Progressive Labor Party bloc were arguing against any demonstration. The usual counter-attacks began: PLP was against North Vietnam. It regarded Ho Chi Minh as a tool of Soviet revisionism, heresy to all the Marxist-Leninists so recently converted from socialism and already, as far as she could see, on their way to Stalin. They would take up Hitler next, replace *Das Kapital* with *Mein Kampf* and never know the difference, except as they proclaimed it was the WASPs who should be marched off to the ovens. PLP was soft on racism, soft on sexism …

"What about the women's question?" a fat girl in a tie-dyed tee shirt called.

"What about it," someone sneered. The boy seated next to Alex yawned loudly. She felt like kicking him *and* the girl, her for asking, him for proving there was a question to be asked. They were divided enough without taking up that potpourri of issues that would have them yammering until dawn before they ever got back to deciding what they were going to do about the demonstration, to which the boy in the leather vest had proposed they come prepared to kill the pigs and trash the streets. It was 3 a.m. She had to be at work at 8.

Leah was on her feet. "Why the men in the Movement—who *claim* to be for justice—seem to feel the women are here just to run the mimeo and provide sexual service."

"Takes two to tango, baby," a man sang out.

"Pig, pig," the women were shouting.

Alex's eyes burned from cigarette smoke. The floor was littered with butts, sticky with spilled Coke and coffee. She'd been at the paper all day, and she was tired. Since September she'd been working in the darkroom at the *Limestone Register*. She'd applied as a photographer, but the photographers were men. (Secretly, if it wasn't so late, she would have applauded Leah's standing up; Leah was pretty, and the men ought to know it wasn't just fat girls who asked the question.) She maintained the files and processed film; she was supposed to do the printing, but the photographers were too full of themselves to let her. Just this morning Irv Stone had dashed in, snatching the film she'd hung to dry, all but pushing her out of the way as he sashayed to the enlarger, boasting, "Irvie's going to print wet today." Tall, good-looking in a smirking, self-satisfied sort of way, he was forever promising to take her on a shoot, "give you a thrill, huh, your name in the paper next to Big Irv's?" On the worst day of her life she thought she would be able to thank god that she was not Irv Stone.

"Women are victims of *class* oppression."

"Freedom is an endless meeting," Alex whispered to Stacy as she left. Years ago, on Crow Hill, that had been a joke.

In March Nelson was sentenced to two years in the federal penitentiary at Titanville for burning his draft card. Tulip took his place on the steering committee in response to the women's caucus; Leah took his room. In May Michael finished his dissertation and moved out; Cal moved in. And in June Garth and Lizzie moved to Seattle.

Alex and Ted helped load the truck; by noon the house was empty. Clad in cut-offs and a grimy T-shirt, Alex sagged against the porch rail, trying not to cry, while Garth and Ted rearranged the last boxes in the U-Haul. Garth's mother had the children.

"I'm going to miss you," Alex said.

"I'll write—when those monkeys give me a chance." Lizzie's voice strained at lightness; her eyes were puffy.

"I'm going to miss them too." Alex missed them already. She dragged a hand along the chain of rusty circles where Lizzie's coleus had summered in red and yellow coffee cans, and sniffed the honeyed air. She would never celebrate another June evening by sitting on this porch with a glass of lemonade, drunk on the heavy fragrance of the linden tree in the front yard, while the kids chased lightning bugs. The door to the house was still propped open, and when she turned she saw a slice of the bare front room. "First Nelson, then Michael, now you."

"You'll visit," Lizzie promised, but it would never be the same:

Alex wouldn't know where the spoons were; Caton would hide behind his mother and have to ask her name. At the curb, Ted and Garth had finished. "It'll be nice to have some space for the kids."

"I don't know how you managed." Alex wiped a filthy hand on her cutoffs. She had felt very little going through her mother's empty house last fall, observing the soiled traffic-patterns on the carpet while the realtor extolled the virtues of its closet space and neutral colors. All the warmth she would have expected from a mother or older sister had come to her in this little house where she'd arrived with Ted five years ago, a teenager dispossessed of everything she knew, overwhelmed by Lizzie's competence and gravid belly.

Lizzie laughed. "I never figured out how you manage in that madhouse either. I know—you like it." Her expression turned serious. "You and Ted should have kids."

"We will," Alex said, though she could no longer imagine it. Lizzie's children were her family, Lizzie, Nelson, Matt, Stacy. "I'm happy for you. I just wish Garth had found a job somewhere closer."

"So do I." Lizzie's eyes were soft. She had the kindest eyes Alex had ever seen, pale gray, with a shimmer of rainy light. She was not what anyone would call pretty, but hers was a face that anyone but a fool would trust. "Anyway you still have Stacy."

Alex shook her head. "We aren't as close as we used to be." They were not at odds, but over the spring a nearly imperceptible reserve had come between them. Matt had grown much more resolute in the past year, and Alex suspected that Stacy thought she and Ted were lagging.

"You need to build a life with Ted."

Alex smiled. "This is my life with Ted." She had never understood Lizzie's life with Garth. They had not been the sort of friends who complain of spouses, rehashing petty quarrels for solace. She and Ted rarely quarreled, though she considered that until she met him she'd had a quarrelsome nature. The way she saw it, Lizzie was loyal to Garth. Of course Lizzie loved him, but it was hard for Alex to imagine a romance between them. It wasn't a matter of being unable to imagine them having sex—it was always hard to imagine other couples having sex, unless you lived like she did and kept tripping over them. She couldn't imagine Garth's kiss, couldn't imagine Garth and

Lizzie lighting candles and sipping wine in bed, trading words that the sweetened, flickering dark turned special. But then they slept on a fold-out couch with three kids in the next room.

"It's your life in the Movement," Lizzie said.

At the curb Garth banged the rear door of the U-Haul and shook hands with Ted. Alex's chest tightened. "I hope the kids like the books."

"Oh, they'll love them." Lizzie's eyes brimmed and shifted. "I'm not going back in there. If we've left anything, we can live without it." She pulled the inside door shut and dropped the key in Alex's hand. The cement block that held the screen door scraped as Lizzie dislodged it, and the door clapped shut. "Good-bye, old house," she called softly and turned to Alex. "Well ..."

They hugged. Beneath the sweat Lizzie smelled like her children, a mixture of grape jelly, soggy Rice Krispies, and dirt. "Promise you'll visit."

Alex bit her lip and nodded. Lizzie gave her a quick, hard squeeze, and ran. At the curb Ted kissed her, Alex crossed the yard to hug Garth, he climbed into the cab, Alex and Ted lifted their arms, and the truck rolled up the street.

They stood in the yard for a long time. Ted's arm settled on her shoulder. A car slowed before the discards heaped at the curb, then sped up when the driver spotted them.

"Let's take a walk," he said. "You don't want to watch the scavengers make out."

They walked in silence, turning uphill behind the grocery. For a while after they left Crow Hill she had tried to keep up the story hour, but when the weather turned she'd had no place to hold it. She hadn't been back in a long time. "Looks like the Sanitation Department still has our proposal on advisement," she noted.

"The great liberal welfare state." A contempt he never betrayed while dealing with it hardened in Ted's eyes. He kicked the gravel. "All technicalities and no action."

At the crest of the hill they stopped in front of their old house. The yard was swampy. "I guess no one fixed the sink," she said.

Ted swept his arm out and smiled. "I want to form a collective to live up here and do community organization." His smile faded, but the tenderness it gave his face lingered for a moment, and he laid his hand along her cheek before he turned away.

"You're better than any of them. It's not your fault they won't listen."

"I did it backwards. I didn't want to take the time to build a base. And now everybody else is getting ready to throw the base away." He turned toward her. "Something very bad is coming down, and I can't stop it."

"I know."

"If we just could have made it work." He meant Crow Hill. He took her hand, and she scuffed her feet to loosen the dust that settled on her sneakers.

"I miss Nelson," she said.

Nelson wrote, but the letters didn't say much. Maybe they were censored; she couldn't decide whether his tone was careful or subdued. Depressed, Ted suggested. He'd been to Titanville, but Nelson was allowed only one visitor a week, and usually his mother drove down from Muncie. "Nelson depressed?" Alex remembered Stacy scoffing. "No way. He's in his cell right now, organizing inmates." She'd been washing dishes while Alex surveyed the refrigerator and made a grocery list, and just then Matt came in to announce that they all ought to visit every Sunday; if they couldn't see Nelson they could see other convicts, blacks, who were all political prisoners as he saw it.

Alex had stared sadly at Matt, who stared boldly back. His overgrown-kid face had matured; there was a hardness in his jaw, a lean purpose to the mouth that had always been set on sweetness. "All black rapists are not Eldridge Cleaver," she said, which wasn't exactly what she meant. He would accuse her of thinking all black prisoners were rapists.

Matt kept his level stare. "All black rapists *are* Eldridge Cleaver."

"Just because you're oppressed doesn't make you good," she tried again, waiting for Stacy to agree, but Stacy just kept piling dishes in the drainer. "Any more than it makes you bad. I feel sorry for the blind man on the square, but that doesn't mean he's not an asshole." Her voice rose. She was right, but it was a bad example, and she knew it. "Maybe he's a great guy. The point is I don't know him, I'm sorry for his *condition*."

Stacy's voice was cold. "Blacks don't need your pity, Alex."

Alex had asked for it, but still she felt betrayed. And she didn't believe for a minute that Nelson was organizing inmates; if he were Ted would have known it. Nelson was doing exactly what he said, taking a creative writing course in the prison education program that he'd set up himself eight years before.

"It's a great idea," Stacy told Matt, turning from the sink for the first time. *White bread*, Alex had written on her list with a vengeance, *Coke*. Matt's guitar was growing dustballs in a closet. She missed Matt too.

Weatherman. It created itself at 11 p.m. the Saturday after Lizzie and Garth left Limestone: after a twenty-four-hour caucus, Bernardine Dohrn mounted a stage before the fifteen hundred delegates to the convention at the Chicago Coliseum, read all those who did not agree with her principles out of the organization, and stormed from the hall. Seven hundred delegates followed, fists raised, chanting "Power to the people," off to train for armed revolutionary struggle.

In the morning Alex drove to Chicago, meeting Ted at the Museum of Science and Industry, where he filled in the details. PLP had held the floor, and so he had turned in his delegate's ID and quit. "But what are you going to do?" she asked. His identity was bound up in the Movement in a way that hers was not, for at her core she guarded a private anarchy. They formed their plurals differently: he multiplied and strung zeroes; she counted on her fingers one by one. It would take her whole life to get to a million, but that was a right she reserved, to understand all masses as a number divisible by one.

"I hate the war. It ruined everything," he said.

A group of children charged up from the stairwell and ran screaming for the displays with phones and activating buttons. For a moment she heard their shrieks distinctly; then they blended into the oceanic babble. They walked past a model gotten up in a motley of anatomy, a suit of metatarsals and phalanges on the one side, on the other a leotard of dangling nerves. The body politic, she thought. "What happened to the others?"

"They went with Weatherman."

"All of them?" She clutched his wrist. "Leah? Cal?"

"It's a free country."

She dropped her hand. "For how long?"

"You don't mean that," he said mildly.

"I do. They don't believe in freedom."

"Neither does your government."

The following week a member of the National Bureau accompanied Cal, Leah, and Tulip back from Chicago. Their house had been selected to become a Weather collective. Flanked by her comrades, Leah read the rules. Counter-revolutionary attitudes must be destroyed. Those who could not remake themselves could not hope to remake society. Personal savings would be signed over; belongings would be shared. No one was to leave the house without the decision of the entire collective or to absent him or herself from the company of at least one other member; no relationships outside the collective were to be permitted; no pets would be allowed. Heterosexuality discouraged women from developing their full strength; monogamy encouraged individual loyalties that undermined collective strength. In the new society monogamy would be smashed.

Alex kept her eyes on a crack in the living room wall. As Ted's tennis shoes squeaked on the floor Leah raised her voice. They would maintain discipline with daily karate drills and self-criticism. They were to cease consumption of corporate products, including tobacco. Marijuana and LSD were the people's drugs. From the hall Ted flung Leah a glance of contempt mixed with pity. Alex stood. She had found this house; she loved it, but any protest would only run up against a wall of dogma. Let them have their Weatherworld.

The poisoned silence followed her from the living room, almost as if the house were bugged, which was a possibility. She and Ted went to bed in silence. They would have the rest of their lives to talk, after they moved out tomorrow morning.

But in the middle of the night she woke to a sluggish pain in her stomach that grew more insistent even as she tried to will it out. By the time Ted rose she had taken her pillow into the bathroom and vomited.

"Baby?"

She looked up. A film of sweat chilled her face. "I have stomach flu."

"Poor kid." He squatted to feel her forehead. "Can I get you anything?"

She shook her head and closed her eyes. For a while she drifted off, aware only of the gritty tile against her flank and the rock inside her gut. When she came to, Leah was perched on the edge of the tub, talking. Alex vomited in the toilet. "We want you to be strong." Leah made her voice sweet. "It's hard, I know it is. It's hard for all of us."

Alex wiped her mouth and raised her head. "You people are so fucked."

"We're all fucked. We grew up on lies. Our parents lied, our teachers lied, the government lies, even our friends and lovers lie. Lies are what we know and we want to cling to them, but we have to place the Revolution above our selfish interests."

Alex had heaved her guts out, and still her stomach hurt. She sank back against the wall, pressing her hands against the slick, cold sweat on her face. Her throat burned; against her haunch the floor was nasty; she was naked and felt exposed. "And I can do that by letting you sleep with Ted."

"Don't you see? In sleeping with one another we bind ourselves to the collective." Leah had quit smoking; her hands twitched in her lap. "The collective thinks it would be a good idea if you and Tulip slept together. You need to form more solidarity with your sisters."

"Leah, I'm sick." If she weren't sick, she would laugh. All their work had come to this. She vomited again.

"Listen to yourself, Alex. *Letting*. That's the language of possession." Leah wet a cloth and bathed her face as Alex lay down again and closed her eyes. "You think your personal happiness depends on Ted, but what right do we have to be happy? The only true happiness comes from fighting the Revolution." Alex cracked an eye and saw the curve of Leah's breast and one dark nipple lit by the morning sun through her shirt. The white tiles were as blinding as an interrogator's naked light bulb. This was the new society, the relentless voice of the commissar all through the night. *Weatherpeople living in a Weatherhouse, thinking Weatherthoughts and talking Weatherwalks, doing*

Weatherdrugs and having Weathergasms. Somewhere in the house, she supposed, someone else had gone to work on Ted.

Alex woke to the vision of a dead silverfish and a net of cobwebs clinging to the tub's clawfoot. "Feeling any better?" Stacy leaned against the doorframe. The light had lengthened into afternoon.

"A little." Her limbs were stiff. She got to her feet and brushed her teeth. For a minute her hand paused on the faucet; then she threw the unrinsed toothbrush in the trash. A new life, new place to live it; she might as well start out with a new toothbrush too. She picked up her pillow, and Stacy stepped aside to follow her into the bedroom.

"I brought you a Coke."

"Thanks." She found a pair of clean bikinis, slid one of Ted's T-shirts over her head, and lay down. Stacy sat on the floor. "Are you staying?" Alex asked.

Stacy's eyes wandered, and she nodded.

Alex raised herself to sip the Coke, grateful that the house had not yet been purged of corporate products. "So who's Matt sleeping with tonight?"

"It's not just the sex." For a while Stacy didn't speak. "I don't know," she said finally.

"I can't believe you're going along with this."

"Maybe we do have to change ourselves for the Revolution."

Alex sat up straight. "Bullshit. Leah, Tulip—they can come in and give me the party line, but not you." She slid back down. Stacy's hair needed washing. In the swatch of yellow light from the window it was dull. Her face had a haggard look, and it occurred to Alex that Stacy had been up all night. They were too exhausted to maintain the distance that had been their recent habit. "You're staying because Matt wants to."

Stacy's small brown eyes shifted, but her voice was defiant. "You're leaving because Ted wants to go."

And if Ted wanted to stay? But he wouldn't. There was no reason for the sudden hollow in the air, no reason for her to wonder. How much of his character had she known that night when she first saw him and something in his image staked its claim on her, as surely as if he had driven the stake straight through her heart, how much had she known the day she stopped his hand on the door in Colorado? You *fell* in love, uninformed, without volition. But if you stayed in love you willed it, in the sense that you were willing. There were wives who stood by men who turned into child-molesters, rapists, even murderers. Did they love these men for what they were or in spite of what they were, or were there habits of love that the self maintained, that had only the most marginal relationship with any other? Her thinking felt confused. Maybe the question was whether Ted would have stayed with her, whether Matt would follow Stacy if Stacy chose to go.

"So to keep him you have to share him."

"It's only sex," Stacy said.

"The politics of sex," Alex corrected. "Jesus Christ, Stace, don't you remember how it was on Crow Hill—everything we tried to do ran up against some bureaucratic bullshit. I must have filled out a thousand forms, and Catch-22 was the fine print on every one. Every march we went on, we had to negotiate a permit, and now you're going to have to apply to a fucking *politburo* just to take a bath."

As if she'd taken a hint, Stacy sniffed her armpits. "You make it sound ridiculous."

"It *is* ridiculous." Alex sat up again.

After a minute Stacy broke their gaze. "You see trees; I see the forest. It's not just this little rule and that little rule—it's an attitude. We have to learn to think as a collective."

"Shit. I've been buying groceries for five years. I already think collective." Rice in twenty-pound sacks, peanut butter in five-pound pails, three gallons of milk at a shot. She brushed her hair back from her face. "I don't believe my values would be improved by letting a bunch of fascist sickos hold me prisoner in my own house, and I really fail to see how I could be remade by licking Tulip's twat. You're my best friend," Alex said. "You and Lizzie."

Stacy picked at a fleck of paint on her cutoffs. "That's why I wish you wouldn't go."

"And after I do you're forbidden to be my friend at all."

"Oh hell." Stacy shifted slightly, and a band of saffron light crossed her knee. "When I was in eleventh grade my father forbade me to see Mike Pinski. I told him I'd joined the jazz club, and every day after school Mike played the same Ornette Coleman record on his parent's hi-fi while we fucked on the rec room sofa." She smiled again, briefly. "I never did like Ornette Coleman. To tell you the truth, I didn't like Pinski that much either."

"How can you commit yourself to an organization whose rules you don't even intend to follow? Haven't you heard Tulip's latest: anyone who's serious about revolution ought to kill her parents first?" The ice in her Coke had melted, and Alex drained the flavored water. Maybe Tulip didn't mean it literally, but Alex didn't trust the Weathercrowd to know a metaphor from a mandate. "You're too smart for this." Unsuccessfully Alex sought her eyes again. "You really love him that much?"

Stacy shrugged. After a minute she said slowly, "We always treated him like a kid brother. Our sweet, dumb kid brother. Me as much as anybody. Maybe more."

Had they? Alex had *thought* of him as a sweet kid brother. So now he had to prove himself. How stupid. How predictable and banal.

"And things have happened."

"Chicago happened," Alex said impatiently. "I was there." It had been a turning point for all of them. Running from the cops in a rage of righteousness, they had discovered the exhilaration that violence arouses in the senses. But this was afterwards, and they had met, they had argued, they had analyzed; they had a responsibility to reason. It was the logic she finally couldn't go along with, the assumption that because one is wronged he is right, that the uncorrupted are incorruptible, that the powerless are a morally superior species. They had corrupted themselves, in the dullest way imaginable, by choosing the drab madness of a faulty syllogism. They would practice the martial arts and dose their middle-class guilt with masochism, the one guilt they didn't earn, and congratulate one another on the smug fantasy that they had transformed themselves into Supermen.

She knew the answer to her question: she would have chosen to go even if Ted stayed. And if that was so it didn't matter whether he would have stayed or gone with her.

"Come with us," she said. "We can work for peace in our own way."

Stacy flexed her fingers. "Why is it you think you and Ted make this inviolable unit? It's like you think you two make a whole and everybody else is half a person. Frankly I think it would be good for you if Ted got it on with Leah."

Alex felt her eyes harden. "Why Leah? Why not Matt?"

"Why not?" Stacy said in a voice equally cold. Her chin rose. "You live in a dream. You think the world would end if either one of you ever even thought, just the teeniest, most idly curious thought, about what it would be like to fuck someone else. Your whole world would fall apart if you ever so much as had a cross word with him."

"He doesn't make me mad."

"You don't let him make you mad."

She took a deep breath and fixed an unblinking gaze on Stacy's outthrust jaw. "*You* make me mad."

"That's what a real relationship is like."

"That's what your relationships are like. Mine are different." Her face was stiff. Why should she have to judge herself by Stacy's standards? Why should the values everyone else was raised on—love, fidelity, harmony—make a prig of Alex? She reached for her Coke, but the glass was empty, sitting in a wet ring on the scuffed hardwood floor. At least they were arguing about something personal. At least Stacy's voice was human. "You're just trying to turn things around because Matt's gone crazy."

"I'm telling you why I don't want to come sleep on your living room floor. Ted couldn't exist without disciples—he has to be the hero. Do you really think he's encouraged your photography for your sake? He loves the way you follow him around with the camera. Why should I want to be a part of that?"

"Because you shouldn't be a part of this." Period. Discussion over. Anything else they had to say would just take them in circles. Where was Ted? It must be after six o'clock. Surely by now he'd found a place for them to live. He certainly wouldn't have spent the day listening to Leah's bullshit. What did it matter why he encouraged her photography? She was an artist—she didn't want to be a leader. It was the difference between them that held them together. She sighed and reached for her empty glass again. "Have you seen Ted?"

Stacy shook her head. "Matt and I were up all night fighting, then I crashed. Think you could eat some dinner?"

Alex's stomach shriveled. "Maybe a little broth."

When Stacy was gone, Alex lay down again. She supposed she should begin packing, but she didn't have the energy. Voices from the street came up to her as if someone had just turned on a radio. She heard the rattle of the downstairs door. Ted? Or just someone going out? (Had the collective met on it? Had a vote been taken?)

Stacy came back with a teacup full of bouillon chattering on its saucer. She set it on the floor. "He's been busted. Leah took the call while you were asleep."

It was not extraordinary news, but still. "What for?"

"Parking ticket."

It was a favorite trick. The cops picked someone up for questioning and got around his right not to be held by charging him with a traffic violation. It didn't seem to matter that Movement people always paid their tickets, never jaywalked or bounced checks, precisely to avoid giving the cops an excuse to arrest them.

"Why didn't Leah tell me?"

"Lighten up. You were asleep."

She rephrased the question. "What do they want to talk to him about?"

"There was a break-in at the ROTC hut last week, remember?"

Disgusted, Alex stood. Stacy was sitting on the mattress when she came out of the closet, pulling a batik shift over her head. "He wasn't even here last week."

"You might as well drink this broth. They're not going to set bail for a parking ticket. Maybe they won't hold him."

Angrily she picked up the cup. "Yeah, and maybe they'll plant a lid." The police had found a joint the last time they'd charged in to search the house without a warrant; they'd found the joint in Stacy's room but missed the lid in Nelson's, and Ted was the one who got charged with possession. Sandy, the house lawyer, had gotten the charges dismissed—Alex doubted the police had intended them to stick. It was just more harassment. All year Ted had been the one counseling restraint. Why was he the one they always arrested?

"It's a crock," Stacy said as Alex flew downstairs to call the lawyer.

Chapter 25

1982

It's never happened before, but all week when she walks down the hall, Kendrick's office door is closed, and she's afraid to ask the secretary if he's inside. She doesn't have the nerve to phone, but she wants to tell him, now that she can be rational, how sorry she is. She would never deliberately hurt him, and she wants to tell him so. But he knows that; so there is really nothing she can say.

Once she passes Ross in the hall, and at the sight of him her whole body sickens. They no longer speak. As he disappears around the corner, no more than a flash of running shoe and cuff of baggy gray pants, she would swear that the speck inside her womb shudders.

A baby. When she tries to imagine it, she sees the baby from the king cake the year she went to New Orleans to photograph Mardi Gras, no bigger than a gumdrop, lying in her jewel box with stiff little pink rubber arms and legs sticking up. But of course it looks nothing like that. Does it even have arms and legs yet? She tries to picture the appropriate embryo from the exhibit she and Ted saw at the Museum of Science and Industry in Chicago the day after he quit SDS, but remembers only the ghastly calm of the unborn petrified on their faces. Deliberately she does not think about her miscarriage.

It doesn't seem real, though she knew in the same instant she realized she was pregnant that she would have it. By the time the nurse at the doctor's office asks, "Do you plan to continue the pregnancy," Alex has moved on to another question, and she starts as if that were the one that has been spoken aloud. "No," she blurts, then stammers, "I mean yes." Her blush deepens as the nurse, pregnant herself—there is so much fertility in the office the air seems to give off a slightly rank fecund smell—stares at her coolly for a minute before making a notation on her chart.

Is she going to tell Ross?

The thought of speaking to him, of being alone with him even long enough to say "I'm pregnant," the thought that no matter how cold, how impersonal, she made her voice, she would by the mere fact be acknowledging an ongoing connection, is repellent. And she can hardly leave it at that, because he too will want to know what she plans to do. Would he be angry? Indifferent? He could hardly be glad. Perhaps he would demand that she have an abortion. But she has no responsibility to him. He got his rocks off, shot his wad. She's under no obligation to report what she did with it. So that's that.

Or would be, but … There is the matter of the baby—or not the baby, the *child*, the *teenager*, the *adult* this micro-dot inside her is on its way to becoming. Already the cataracts and brittle bones of its old age are programmed in, unless she changes her mind. (At the thought her hand flattens protectively on her stomach. If she would change her mind—but she won't—her body would resist her.) The question is so much more complicated than "Do you plan to continue this pregnancy?" She has a right to answer that one no, no questions asked; she can just have the mote sucked out, along with its skinned knees, braces, first date, and career, its bifocals and children's children, each with a constellation of heart as marvelous and uncharted, as its own. What is so frightening is that by answering the first question yes, she gives up the right to answer the other one no just because she wants to. She can't consent for it to exist without agreeing that she will act in its best interest, even when that act is in her worst. She will never be alone in who she is again.

Can you really raise a child refusing to tell it who its father is? Give birth hoping it won't ask? (*It. It.* What an ugly sound *it* has.) What about all those letters to Ann Landers? Grown children tracking down their unsuspecting parents, only to be met with bitterness and denial. If one day twenty years from now this *whatever* means to knock on Ross's door and say "Guess what?" doesn't she have the obligation, not for his sake but for her child's, to have prepared him?

And what if Ross doesn't want to wait twenty years? He seemed comfortable with Marjean's children. What if he wants to have a hand in raising his?

But it's not a matter of how she feels. A child is owed its genetic history. It's a medical imperative. One her mother didn't feel, though she supposes things were different then. If *Katie Blue* hadn't made the best-seller list, she might never have known who her father was.

Her mother. How ashamed she'd once felt to be a girl whose own mother could not love her.

She's still too shocked to be excited, though in an odd way she thinks she's happy. Her hand keeps touching her stomach; she stands in front of the mirror naked to inspect her body for change. "Enjoy your pregnancy" had been Lizzie's advice. "To tell you the truth there's really nothing you can do that will prepare you for a baby."

All right, she is not prepared. The only thing that seems real is that Kendrick has abandoned her. For which she can't blame him, though it hurts more than she can say, because he is the person she wants to say it to.

Chapter 26

1964

The name came up to her through the intercom on West Eighty-eighth Street while she sat organizing Kendrick's file of negatives at the end of May. "Ted Neal," he announced in that voice she found so charismatic. She was standing in the open doorway by the time he reached the top of the stairs. Kendrick was at an interview in Colorado.

"I came to say goodbye," he said.

"Come out on the terrace." Theirs was a fourth-floor flat with a rooftop patio that made up for the cramped two rooms. She sent Kendrick's box of glassine sleeves under the sofa with her foot as she passed. They stood at the railing, looking down at the tree tops, a narrow parkway of backyards between Eighty-eighth and Eighty-ninth that ran all the way from Central Park West to Riverside Drive. "Nice, isn't it? You'd never know it was here. Can I get you a glass of tea?" His dark eyes were not brown as she'd thought, but slate. They made her nervous. She pointed across the green canyon to the mirror apartment on Eighty-ninth. "Our neighbors have dinner on the terrace every night. They bring a white cloth out and light candles and open wine. After dinner they make espresso in a little silver pot." Why was she telling him this? "They do the dishes together; then they take papers out of their briefcases and work. At eleven they watch the news." After the news the couple made love; it struck her sad, she didn't know why. "I could make coffee if you'd rather." She turned her face so he could kiss her. "I don't even know you," she said.

He followed her into the bedroom. He was five or six inches taller than she was, with wide shoulders, and she liked the way she felt enclosed by his arms. It was not like making love with Kendrick, slower, more deliberate, as he held her hips up to him and probed the tender maze of her nerves, until she whimpered for the pleasure. But that was, surely, because she didn't know him. One did not give the familiar such exquisite concentration. It meant nothing. There was nothing between them but this secret, that and the little thrill of guilt that accompanies betrayal.

She shouldn't have done it.

His skin was full of heat. When he released her he got dressed. "I'll call you when I get back."

"I don't know where I'll be." She sat up. "Actually I still live with him—the photographer; I should have told you. I met him when I was fifteen. Well, I suppose it was a schoolgirl crush, I threw myself at him, but he's been good to me. He took care of me, and nobody else did that, ever. So, well, what I mean is, this has been very nice, really, but I don't make a habit …"

"I'll find you."

When he was gone, she threw herself back into the pillows. Every cell of her body seemed to be dancing in disorder while she herself was suspended in a rosy calm. She was sleepy, and though her heart ticked on with the clock, time stretched and yawned. It was the loveliest feeling she knew, the way after sex the world drowsed and waited. Then she got up and defrosted the refrigerator and alphabetized her spices in a burst of energy that took her halfway through the laundry. She was sitting on the bedroom floor amid piles of colors and whites when she socked her hand to her mouth and cried. She had never done anything she felt truly guilty for before—oh, her marriage, that had been bad and she was sorry, but maybe if it hadn't been for that she and Kendrick would never have settled in so smoothly together, so in the end Kendrick really hadn't blamed her, and if he didn't blame her then she had no cause to blame herself. But *this*. Ted Neal would find her. Of that she was sure.

Kendrick came back from Colorado in high spirits. "Got the job," he promised. "They haven't said so, but I could feel it, and you're not going to believe how incredible the light is. I shot a roll of Tri-X at 200, I'm going to underdevelop, and, baby, those tones are going to knock your socks off. *They loved my work!*" She had never seen him so animated. "How about a celebration with my favorite model and best girl?"

"Okay," she agreed, but her voice sounded threadbare.

At Tout va Bien he ordered an extravagant Bordeaux, and they clinked glasses. His hair needed cutting; it was falling in his eyes. She shouldn't have let him go off to an interview like that. She should take better care of him.

He forked a piece of his *rognon* into her mouth. "I know someone who's got a birthday coming."

"Who?"

"Well, Jesus Christ, Alex." She tried to smile so she wouldn't look so glum. "Aren't you going to ask what I brought you?" He produced a small velvet box from inside his jacket and laid it beside her wine glass.

"What is it?" She had to force herself to sound interested.

"Open it." The diamond flashed in the dim restaurant light. "Like them?"

"They're very pretty." She kept her head bowed.

"Let's see how they fit." He slipped the solitaire on her finger.

"They're lovely," she repeated.

"Well, it won't be a long engagement, but I thought you might like a ring—I know you never wear jewelry, but this is 14 karat, the chemicals aren't going to hurt it, and anyway you ought to listen to me and pick up your prints with tongs. Ever wonder why you get those stains on the borders?"

Her stomach hurt.

"City Hall okay with you? I figure we're not exactly the type for St. Pat's."

She didn't answer.

"Hey," he said, his voice softer. "Look, if you're upset because you think I meant to put it off, it's nothing like that. I just thought you should have some time before we made it legal. Sometimes a change of scenery can have a bad effect on a relationship."

She stared at her dinner. The *blanquette de veaux* was as pale as macaroni in its cold, thick white sauce. “Then maybe we ought to wait till we’ve gone to Colorado.”

“You’re only going to be eighteen one more week.”

“Please,” she said to the waiter, who asked if he could take her plate. “What difference does that make?”

“I promised I’d marry you when you were eighteen.”

“I don’t remember that,” she said, though she remembered he had promised no such thing, and was afraid she might cry because either way it didn’t make any difference.

“Sure I did—maybe I didn’t say it, but you knew that’s what I meant.”

What he had promised was that she would go wherever she wanted. But she saw what he was getting at. They had both assumed she would want to go with him, always.

“I didn’t say it because it seemed only right to give you time to change your mind.” He lowered his eyes. “ Have you?”

“No.” She was going to cry.

“So what is it?”

She bit her lip.

“Afraid to rock the boat?” He sat back again. “I can understand that. But this won’t change anything.”

“Then why do it?” she said and was sorry for the wounded look that surprised his face. Why did he have to propose in a restaurant with the little tables the size of Parcheesi boards jammed together as they were everywhere in New York? She couldn’t drop her napkin without picking up her neighbor’s fork. How many times had they sat in the cheap breakfast shops pretending not to notice when, just inches beyond them, another noisy heart broke? She had never been anyplace where so many women cried in restaurants. But then she had never been anyplace.

And why did he have to buy the rings in Colorado? He couldn’t take them back.

She had not thought about getting married since that morning she had come back to him hungover and already wed. It had been so inevitable it hadn’t required thought. And maybe—yes, yes she had taken a small pleasure, maybe even pride, in the little glamor their arrangement gave, had thought they must appear terribly romantic, at least in

Limestone, where life had more confines than it did in New York. You could see anything in New York. It was nothing to the man who sat chewing *boeuf bourguignon* beside her whether she got married or not.

"I don't mean it like that," she conceded. "I love you, you know that. I just don't feel like getting married." She took off the diamond and fit it back in the box. "I'm sorry about the rings. They really are beautiful."

"I have good taste," he said and put the box back in his pocket. "Coffee? Have some dessert. There's no sense in letting the dinner be spoiled."

He was such a game companion. She watched him spoon up his mousse with an ache that was love. He considered himself weak for the very fact of their union, but she had learned how strong he could be, and he was decent. He had grown in the years since; whereas she was still a selfish, undisciplined child, in the thrall of a purposeful stranger whose purpose she didn't know. She understood herself no better than she understood the fifteen-year-old girl who got exactly what she wanted and then was so unhappy she threw plates. But surely she should have figured out who she was by now. She didn't deserve Kendrick. "I'm sorry," she said again.

He shrugged it off. "We've got a good thing, Alex. Being married or not married isn't going to change that."

He did get the job in Colorado, and they gave notice on their apartment. They would spend the summer doing the New York they hadn't done—the Empire State Building, Broadway, Radio City Music Hall. He confessed that he had always wanted to walk across the Brooklyn Bridge; she confessed that she wanted to buy something stamped Saks Fifth Avenue. Of course, he had lived in New York before, she offered, in case his zest were feigned, but that was the point, he insisted—he'd lived there, he'd never visited. Life could be a holiday, he promised, and when they moved—well, they would have Rocky Mountain National Park on their doorstep. Was there any reason they couldn't go to Aspen and learn how to ski? Mesa Verde, Pike's Peak.... He was taking so much trouble to entertain her, to *woo* her, she felt a little sick with shame.

Chapter 27

1969

The lawyer phoned her back. It was not a parking ticket but a parking lot. Ted had been charged with leaving the scene of an accident after the police produced a note from a witness who swore to having seen their white Impala sideswipe a car at Hoot's Drive-in.

At least it was a misdemeanor. "It's a good thing they didn't happen to have a fresh hit-and-run victim lying around," she said tartly. "Can I pick him up now?"

"I'll pick you up," Sandy said. "Can you come up with five hundred dollars cash?"

"Tonight?"

"Better call a bondsman then."

When the Mercedes pulled up, Tulip protested that Alex had no right to leave the house without permission.

Alex slit her eyes. "I'm not a member of this collective."

"As long as you're living in this house you are."

"Go to hell," Alex called over her shoulder.

At the station Sandy loaned her fifty dollars to pay the bondsman, and they sat on a bench to wait. Dusk had fallen by the time Ted was released. At the sight of him across the room, she drew her breath in sharply. It was as if the pressure in the air changed; even with her eyes closed, she thought that her skin would know when he was present. She kissed him, wishing she'd had time to take a bath.

"How do you feel?" he asked.

"Better. How are *you*?"

He flashed a grin. "Not guilty. Sorry I didn't have time to find us a place."

They slid into the front seat of Sandy's Mercedes. "I'd thank you for coming down, old man, but I'm beginning to think I'm paying for this boat," Ted said.

"Just the gas." Sandy smiled. He was a large man with with a florid face and a long straggle of white hair thinning at the crown. On the wheel his fingers looked powerful. She liked sitting in the car between them; there was something about their combined masculinity that made her feel safe. The rich leather smell of the seats came up to her nostrils like the return of appetite. "I'm hungry," she said.

Sandy glanced at the clock. "Where to?"

"Anywhere but Hoot's," Ted requested, and Alex felt so much better she laughed.

Sandy's breath skimmed Alex's hair. "That's an old scam. Guy needs some body work, so he goes to a parking lot, picks out a license, and gets two friends to write anonymous notes. The detective finds a worn spot on your bumper, and if he likes your looks, you just call your insurance agent; if he doesn't, you've left the scene of an accident. If you kids have any bumper stickers or peace decals on your vehicles, get 'em off. Not everyone believes in First Amendment rights these days."

Alex turned to Ted. "Stacy's joining Weatherman."

"I thought she would."

"Alex," Sandy cautioned. "Don't tell me anything."

"It's not against the *law*," Alex protested.

"The law, my dear, is ten percent statute and ninety percent interpretation."

Chastened, she stared at the lighted dial of the radio. Sandy turned the corner onto the strip of bars and headshops that stretched between the courthouse square and Wallace.

"Sammy's okay?" Sandy slowed for a parking place. Sealed inside the air-conditioned Mercedes with the horns from *The New World Symphony*, watching the kids perched on the burnished hoods of the parked cars, Alex felt as if she were inside a hermetic bubble. It took her a full minute to pick out the reflection of the flashing blue lights.

"What the hell do they want?" Sandy pulled over and reached for his wallet.

The cop thrust his face down, ignoring the license and registration Sandy proffered. "I'd like to talk to your passenger."

Sandy folded his wallet. "I'm an attorney at law, and my passenger is my client, who has just been detained for several hours."

"Get out of the car."

Ted opened the passenger door. "Don't you guys ever get tired of me?"

The officer stepped back without seeming to have heard, and Sandy opened his door. Alex scrambled after Ted. "My client is free on bond. Unless you have a warrant for his arrest on an unrelated charge, you can't legally detain him for at least twenty-four hours." The officer took Ted's elbow. As Alex opened her mouth, Sandy shook his head.

A knot of kids had gathered on the sidewalk. Inside Baskin-Robbins people were pressing their faces to the glass. Ted stared straight ahead as he was escorted to the car.

"Clear this sidewalk," the officer ordered.

"Pig!" The crowd swelled. Near the entrance to the ice cream shop, a dog was licking the pavement. The officer stared coldly at Sandy. "Tell your clients to disperse."

"My *client* is in your car. As his attorney, I demand to know what you intend to question him about."

"Move back," the officer commanded again. "Clear this sidewalk now."

Sandy inclined his head toward Alex and said quietly, "Take my car. Don't worry—this is illegal; I'll have him out in an hour." He reached into his pocket for the keys. It happened so quickly Alex missed it—there was a gasp from the crowd, and Officer Church was holding his gun.

"Take your hand out of your pocket slowly and bend over the car."

"Anything you say. *Sir*," Sandy muttered.

A rock shattered the Baskin-Robbins window, showering the sidewalk with glass and sending the crowd screaming. Yelping, the dog shot down the street. The officer spoke into his radio, and within seconds another squad car screeched around the corner. Alex stood paralyzed while the other cops pursued the fleeing crowd. By the time the squad cars drove off only Alex and the cursing manager of

Baskin-Robbins remained on the street. She bent to pick up Sandy's keys from the gutter.

At the station she was told they'd been charged with attempting to incite a riot. Bail would not be set until morning. It was after midnight when she got home, and the collective was assembled in the living room. Their voices carried up the stairs. Matt's commitment to the Revolution was weak; when the rank and file of had called for the ousting of certain members of the steering committee that spring, he had been silent; he had balked at giving up his dog. Alex had caught a glimpse of him as she came through the hall: sitting in a straight-backed chair, eyes on the floor, complexion mottled. *Tell them to fuck off*, she willed him from upstairs, but the litany droned on.

In the morning Alex called the courthouse, but the hearing wasn't scheduled until 10:30. She drove to the *Register*. At ten Irv strolled in. "Get your camera, babe. Big Irv's going to take you out today and show you how it's done. Full-page spread, 'Beating the Heat,' photographs by Irv Stone and Alex Neal. How's that grab you?"

"As a matter of fact, I was just on my way out." She picked up her bag. *"Beating the heat?"*

"So it's not *Life* magazine. Little girlo's got to start somewhere." Irv hoisted himself to the darkroom counter. "Didn't know you were working part-time these days. Opportunity only knocks once, you know."

"Look, I don't mean to be a snob, all right? Another time. I have personal business."

"Hey." He jumped from his perch to follow her through the newsroom. "Where you going?"

"To the courthouse."

In the parking lot he watched her dig in the bag for the keys and then inserted himself between her and the door of the Mercedes. "Nice car."

"It belongs to a friend." Irv whistled. "My husband's lawyer, if you have to know." Impatiently she plied the keys.

His leer curved into an insinuating grin. "You and hubby having trouble? Tell Big Irv."

She glared at him, and he moved aside, but held the door once she was settled in the car. "Look, I have to go," she said, hands on the wheel.

"I'm just trying to be a nice guy," he protested.

"Well, you have no talent for it." She sighed. "Go to the pool, Irv. Go find yourself a lemonade stand. I have to be at the courthouse."

"There's no story at the courthouse. Today's story's at the jail." She turned so sharply that she nearly bumped his head, thrust down inside the car. "Gotcha." He closed the door and backed away, but she rolled the window down. "Well, you work at a newspaper," he said lamely.

In the darkroom, by herself. *"What story?"*

He squatted beside the car. "Is your husband in jail, Alex?"

"Yes."

"Better slide over and let me drive." The smirk was gone. "Some kid in a holding cell hung himself this morning."

It wasn't Ted, she reminded herself, it couldn't be Ted. Providing, of course, that the kid had hung *himself*. Her heart was pounding. She had thought so smugly that on the worst day of her life she would be able to thank god that she was not Irv Stone; it had never occurred to her that on the worst day of her life she might have to be with Irv Stone. She slid over. Her hands were shaking, too moist to hold the wheel.

The police refused to release the identity of the suicide, pending notification of the family. Tears were collecting in the corners of her eyes; she stood digging her nails into her palms and didn't protest when Irv put a supporting arm around her shoulder. An officer coming in through the lobby glanced at the desk sergeant and said, "Give the lady a break. It ain't her husband."

Ted's arraignment had been postponed until afternoon. At 11:30 Sandy was released on five thousand dollars bond, and Alex handed him the keys to the Mercedes.

"What happened?"

"I don't know." Sandy's hair was disheveled. "The kid was in the drunk tank. We heard the commotion when they found him. If he threatened and the guard didn't keep watch, his family could sue, but I doubt they'd win. The police cover themselves pretty well in these situations, but, believe me, they don't want them to happen."

"I want Ted out of there." Alex slumped on the leather seat. "Why did they postpone his hearing?"

"Don't worry. These charges won't stick. They're hounding him. They don't care about keeping him in jail. They just want to discredit him."

"*Why*? The Weathermen are the ones who are talking about offing pigs. He's the most reasonable antiwar leader in town."

"Why?" Sandy repeated. "That's why. The government doesn't want an antiwar movement that seems in any way moderate. It wants the antiwar movement to alienate the country. They keep arresting Ted, people think he's a bum."

"But he's not that big on the national scene—I mean he's *known*, he does a lot behind the scenes, but it's not like he's the Chicago 8." She didn't really know what Ted did behind the scenes. "He's afraid he'll lose his ability to organize at the grass-root level when the war is over."

"Apparently the government believes in the importance of the grass-root level too." Sandy pulled up in front of the house on Leverett Avenue. On the porch Lizzie's plants were drooping in the heat.

Sandy rolled his sleeves. "I'm going home to shower. I'll pick you up at two, and in the meantime I want you to get your things—yours and Ted's—together. You can't stay in this house. In fact, once we get these charges dismissed and Ted's accident case is settled, I think you two ought to consider getting out of Limestone. There's nothing for you here."

"Law school," she said. Amazingly, Ted had completed his first year.

Sandy gave her a clement look. "A law degree may be useful for other things, but believe me, in this climate he doesn't stand a chance of being licensed." He put the car in gear, and Alex opened the door. "I like your husband. The war won't last forever. You should talk him into going somewhere where he can use his talents." Tapping the wheel, he added, "All of your things. Anything you can't pack by two, leave."

She filled her suitcase and three grocery sacks with their clothes, dumping her photographs in another. In the kitchen she wrapped her dishes. Matt, who had a ragged look after last night's barrage, came in to ask her what she thought she was doing. "That's collective property," he said.

"These dishes were a wedding present." At the rehearsal dinner he'd delivered a blushing toast: "I'm really happy for Ted and Alex, 'cause I love these people, man."

"In the revolution there are no personal possessions."

She set the stack of plates back on the shelf. She didn't have a box anyway.

At two Sandy helped her lug her enlarger and trays to the Mercedes. When they were finished, she asked Sandy to wait and went back into the house.

"Where's Stacy?" Alex looked from Leah to Tulip to Matt, lined up at the foot of the stairs. "What have you done—locked her in her room?" She stood directly in front of Matt. "Tell her I said good-bye." She hugged him, but he stiffened, and she let her arms drop to her sides. "Good-bye to you too, Matt," she whispered.

On the porch she knelt by Lizzie's plants. She couldn't ruin the Mercedes' carpet with a bunch of houseplants in rusting coffee cans, and they'd fry by three if she put them in the Impala. She tipped the first can and watched the dirt pour out. Then she dumped the others, exposing the frail white roots, burying the leaves beneath a mound of soil. Weatherman could have her dishes and her pots and pans, but she'd be damned if she'd let them have Lizzie's plants to wither.

Ted's bail was set at $25,000. Grimly he whispered with Sandy. With another bond outstanding, even if their friends could come up with $2500, the bondsman was unlikely to accept it. (What friends? Alex said.) The best thing would be for his father to make bail.

"The whole thing?" Alex asked.

"The whole thing," Sandy said. "Unless you feel strongly that you want him out tonight, in which case you can ask his father to wire $2500, and I can try to persuade the bondsman."

"I want him out tonight."

She phoned Brad. But the bondsman couldn't be persuaded. Brad had to pay the bond in full; and without a local address Ted would be required to spend the weeks until his trial at his parents' house in Youngstown.

When they retrieved the Impala and returned to the motel where Alex had piled their belongings, she sat beside him on the bed. "What did my folks say?"

"They love you."

"Yeah, I bet that's what my dad said."

"They were upset. What do you expect?" She took a deep breath. "Why does your father have to understand you on your terms? You've never understood him on his. Why can't you just agree to disagree?"

He stood.

"Jeannie and Binks are separating," she told him. She thought of Jeannie in Cambridge last summer, sitting on the arm of Ted's chair, winding his hair around her finger, saying, "Isn't he gorgeous?" while Binks watched sullenly from across the room.

"Poor Jeans. How're Mom and Dad taking it?" He gave a heavy sigh. "Never mind. I guess we'll see them tomorrow."

She lowered her eyes. The way Sandy had said "Get him out" she should have known that Ted objected. Sandy had advised him to plead guilty to the charge of leaving the scene of an accident in lieu of proof that he hadn't, and was sure that the riot case would never come up. In the meantime, the Limestone police would have no further chance to arrest him. Picking at the chenille spread, Alex felt a chill of remorse and wondered how long they would have to be in Youngstown.

Chapter 28

1969

July. Every night they watched the news in the Neals' den. Nixon announced the first reduction of American ground troops; American astronauts landed on the moon. And on Chappaquiddick Island a young secretary drowned in a car that plunged off a bridge into a tidal pond, and the Democratic senator from Massachusetts was charged with leaving the scene of an accident.

"That's it for Little Brother," Brad exulted. "You can kiss the Kennedys good-bye."

Justine turned a troubled face toward Ted. "You know you have our love and our support, dear."

Ted stared at the rug, profoundly embarrassed. Brad shot his wife an angry glance and snatched the *TV Guide*.

Alex was almost relieved when Leo, the basset hound, began to hump her leg.

Negotiations. What should they have for lunch, for dinner, when should they call Jeannie, should they open the windows or have the AC, how did they want their steaks? The Paris Peace Talks, Alex thought, had nothing on them. Lying in Jeannie's canopied bed at night—the one in Ted's old room was a single—she was acutely aware that even the air she breathed belonged to Ted's parents. And he was so depressed she could hardly catch his eye.

They passed a morning seated on the floor of the sweltering room over the garage, going through the wedding presents still stored there.

Ted hadn't volunteered, and she had to ask him to help her, irked that he hadn't leapt at the excuse to spend a few hours together. It wasn't his fault they had no privacy, but at least he could notice that this visit was taking its toll on her too. In Limestone there had been a lot to keep her busy, but *here* when he abandoned her like this, she felt obliterated.

He held up a pair of Hummel figurines. "Zwei guten Kinder."

"Zwei Waises hä lich klein," she corrected. "Give them to Goodwill." The cartons that contained her china and crystal were scurfy to the touch. "I'd forgotten how pretty these are," she said as she peeled newspaper from a Wedgewood plate as useless as the knickknacks and linen bridgecloths. Sweat stung her eyes. "I wish we could go home," she said.

"Haven't got one," he reminded and drew a baleful look. She wanted to make love, but any minute Justine might come charging up the stairs with a pitcher of lemonade and cheery "How's it going?" They ought to do it anyway, she thought. At least he could think of it.

He got up to see if he could raise the windows any higher, then bounced a ping-pong ball on the table, caught it and bounced it again.

"I really don't know what's in your mind," she said out loud. He glanced at her with a goofy half-smile, bounced the ball one last time, and let it roll off the table. "You're too strong to fall apart like this. I want to know what's going on."

"Nothing's going on."

"Here." Her finger tapped once, hard, against her temple. "If you don't want to tell your father what your plans are, you could at least tell me. I want to know what we're going to do when this is over."

"I don't know what we're going to do. I'm depressed is all, and I don't think I should have to say so."

"Why not?" She searched his face. He picked up the ping-pong ball, and she caught his wrist mid-bounce. "Stop it."

"What do you want me to say? It's a disaster for me to be here."

"Because your parents make you feel like a kid? All parents make their children feel like kids." Not hers, but that was different, and there were times when she was glad.

"Maybe, but in this particular case the timing's really rotten." He walked to the window. "I fucked up. There was something very good that was happening, and somehow I let it go right down the drain."

"You didn't let it. It just went." She stood behind him.

In the yard two jays were squawking and diving at Leo, who yelped and ran in circles. "Jeannie's right. That is one dumb dog." He covered her hand and turned around. "You're a good woman, Alex," he said softly. "The only thing is you have no mercy." He could as well have slapped her.

At last she said, "Have it your way then," and started to turn away, but whirled back. "Mercy is what I was offering you, goddamnit!"

"I fucked up," he said again.

"*You?* You and you alone." They stared at each other. "What makes you think the world is yours?"

"I feel responsible."

"You feel self-indulgent." When at last he looked at her again, something in his face gave. "You have time to think," she offered.

A sound like a half-laugh stuck in his throat. "That's the last thing I need right now." He walked to the ping-pong table. "I could have it out with my dad—I'm itching to—but I'm stuck here until my case comes up, whenever that is, I still owe him twenty-five thousand bucks, and doesn't he know it." Morosely he turned away. "He thinks I'm lying about the accident."

"I know."

"My own father thinks I'm a liar. A chronic fuck-up and a liar."

"Your mother doesn't."

"My mother." He sighed.

"Your wife doesn't."

"My wife," he said and came back to touch her cheek. "I didn't know it was going to turn out like this."

"Ted." It was Justine on the stairs.

"I wanted you," she said, though she hadn't known it would turn out like this either. What had she thought? That he would save the world in his spare time and then they would live happily ever after? "I love you."

"Ted!" Justine knocked. "Ted, your lawyer's on the phone."

Sandy got the riot charges dropped, and at the end of August they returned to Limestone, where Ted was convicted of leaving the scene of an accident and fined five hundred dollars. The case behind him, he seemed more cheerful, and over dinner they made plans to go to New York. He could do outreach work or leftist journalism. She wanted to look for something part-time and try to freelance. She was still chattering in the car on their way to the motel when Ted said quietly, "We're being followed."

"Are you kidding?" Her muscles tensed with irritation. "Cops?"

"I don't think it's a squad car, but I don't want to be stopped for speeding."

He drove slowly, checking the rearview mirror. Around them the landscape was dark. After a few minutes the car behind them flipped on its brights and pulled out. "Oh my God," she said. Ted rammed the accelerator as the hooded figures in the car careening along beside them turned their eyes, nothing but slits cut into their white sheets.

There was a screeching of metal, and the nose of the other car ground into their fender. For the eternal instant while the Impala rocked at the edge of a ditch, she was still frantically rolling up her window, Ted was still gripping the wheel, eyes fixed straight ahead, his face as white as bones.

They were pulled from their car, pushed into the other, and driven down a series of dirt roads. The only sounds were the shuddering of the car and spit of gravel. Alex sat in front. When she turned to find Ted, she was looking into those pitiless black slits. Her body worked with fear, but her mind had ceased to function. When the car stopped they were dragged into a dense wood where Alex caught the faint mossy smell of quarries. "You have been tried by the Knights of the Ku Klux Klan and been found guilty of treason," one of the apparitions recited. Two of them held her with their meaty, human hands while she screamed and the other three beat her husband with a baseball bat. It didn't happen, even as it happened.

Irv Stone came to the hospital to take their pictures. It was a lucky break for him; the wires picked up the story, and *Newsweek* ran his shot of Ted. "Hey. Don't cry." Tears rolled down her cheeks, but she wasn't crying; her eyes just leaked. "Big Irv's going to make you famous."

A voice splintered from her throat. "I want to see Ted." In the doorway she saw police. "Is my husband dead?" she asked.

Weatherman issued a statement to the Liberation News Service claiming the victims as martyrs, just as they would later claim Fred Hampton, the Black Panther murdered in his bed by the Chicago police, even though by then the Panthers had denounced them.

Ted was in the hospital more than a month. When Alex was discharged, she took an apartment in one of the new, boxy brick buildings in the university ghetto. She went back and forth to the hospital, back and forth to the therapist the Neals insisted upon paying, who asked her how she felt about being attacked while she stared vacantly at the diplomas on the wall and rolled lint balls on her knee. She felt nothing; she felt dead. Why should she have to describe her symptoms when the therapist could look them up in any textbook?

Talking with Lizzie long distance, Alex broke into tears at unexpected moments; at the hospital she buried her head in Ted's bedding and wept. The only place she never cried was the office of the therapist, who made her angry. "Good," the therapist said. She was supposed to feel anger in order to get rid of it. Alex thought it would be a lot more efficient not to feel it in the first place. She didn't have the energy for all those extra steps. All in all she made a disappointing victim. She didn't wake up screaming; when she closed her eyes the Halloween faces did not appear. The attack was just another thing that had happened. The doctors had said Ted would be all right.

"It was political," she said.

"It may have been politically motivated, but it was still an assault upon your person," the therapist insisted.

"I'm a political person," Alex said.

But she wasn't. She read the news and found it no longer applied to her. Ho Chi Minh had died. After a summer of running around beaches with NLF flags, the Weathermen were busy breaking into high schools, beating up teachers, and holding students captive while they bared their genitals and lectured. They had scheduled a National

Action in Chicago for October, promising to bring out ten thousand to kill the pigs and do battle in the streets, but only a few hundred showed up. In November four members of a radical collective in New York were arrested for a series of bombings, Lt. William Calley was charged with the massacre of 109 Vietnamese civilians at My Lai, and a million Americans marched against the war. The world was going on exactly as it would have if she were alive.

At the hospital she knelt beside Ted's bed. When she cried, it was because she had been so mean to him in Youngstown last summer.

Stacy called and asked to meet her at the Pizza Pub. Sucking at a Coke until the straw went flat, Alex scarcely looked up as Stacy asked after Ted. It mattered to her not at all whether Stacy was breaking the Weatherrules or working around to quitting Weatherman. Alex had nothing to say, except to refuse a slice of pizza. It was to be expected: she had no appetite. Everything was to be expected; all actions were reactions. It was what she found so tiresome about the whole business of aftermath.

Stacy worked at the strings of cheese. She was going on, condemning the police for failing to arrest the Klansmen, the police and the Klan, both agents of the state, working hand in hand to perpetuate the racist system. Alex supposed that she still believed that, but found she no longer cared. As Stacy rattled off all the old charges against the power structure, Alex glanced up once. "You've lost weight," she said.

"Oh," Stacy said in a distracted voice, "yeah." Excitement kindled in her eyes. She and Matt had been to Cuba, where they'd met with a delegation from the Provisional Revolutionary Government of Vietnam, beautiful, strong people, who gave them friendship rings forged from the salvage of American planes that had been shot down. It seemed to Alex that she had not stopped talking for a minute, although the pizza was gone. Stacy had been arrested at the Days of Rage in Chicago. She leaned across the table and in a hushed tone confided that she didn't plan to stand trial. Weatherman was disappearing into the bowels of Amerika, where they would fight the Revolution from within. Victory glittered in her eyes, and the dark metal ring scraped against the table. Alex was surprised that Stacy should be telling her so much. But as she circled back to the Klan attack again, the calculated brutality with which the state tried to eliminate them, Alex understood that Stacy had been sent. She and Ted were being given one last chance to join Weatherman, underground where the state could not touch them. In their presumed rancor, they could yet bring their politics into line. Sure enough, Stacy was talking about the way violence opened eyes.

Alex interrupted. “It wasn’t the police.”

“The police, the Klan.” Stacy waved her hand. “I thought Ted went to Mississippi.”

“It wasn’t the Klan.” Her voice was very low. She knew something, not the way you know a fact but the way you know a truth. Facts were like the infidelities a man might confess to the wife who has found a trail of lipstick on his collar. Details—true but irrelevant to the truth, which was looking into his face and knowing that he did not love her. She had no facts, but she knew what she knew.

“Who was it then?”

“You know who it was,” Alex said, looking at her steadily.

“The Boy Scouts? Casper the Friendly Ghost? I think we’ve got a basic problem with credibility here.”

“It was Weatherman,” Alex said in a level voice.

Stacy’s mouth fell open. She braced her hands against the table as if it might sail away. When she finally spoke, her voice was hoarse. “You’re crazy.”

“Am I?”

“Fucking certifiable. They ought to put you away.”

Alex raised her chin. “Deny it.”

“I do. You can’t go around saying things like that.”

“I don’t intend to tell anyone.”

“Tell what? That you’ve got some crackpot theory? What about ‘our hero’? Does he suspect Weatherman too?”

“I haven’t asked him.”

“You won’t ask because you’re afraid he’ll have you locked away in the looney bin.” Stacy’s mouth jerked as she jabbed the air. “Man, the Shoes must really love you.”

She would never ask because you cannot ask if the truth is true. “I don't talk to the FBI." She slid from the booth. "I've got more loyalty than your new comrades do."

Stacy tossed her head. "You really think he's important, don't you?"

"Someone does," Alex said and held out her hand, but Stacy didn't take it.

Chapter 29

1982

Two weeks pass before she sees Kendrick. When he knocks she is just out of the shower, standing at the mirror with water rolling down her swollen breasts and dripping off her buttocks. Almost guiltily she grabs a robe. She knows it's him before she opens the door, because she sees his silhouette through the curtain as she comes down the stairs to the vestibule. There is a stiffness in the way he holds his shoulders; his eyes are fogged with distance even in the moment when, involuntarily, he drops them to her body. Her hair has wet the apricot satin through. Embarrassed, she wraps her arms across her chest, tucking her hands flat beneath her arms to cover the cloth clinging to her nipples.

"I thought you might want to go for a ride," he says.

"I'll dry my hair." She turns, aware of the wet cloth sticking to her backside.

When she comes into the living room, in baggy painter's pants and an old shirt that neither hugs her body nor hangs so loose he might think she chose it because she is pregnant, he's leafing through an old *Aperture*. Without looking at her he stands.

"The Dean's given the go-ahead on the Kemp line," he says as they walk to his car.

"Oh." Ordinarily she might have said, "Now that everyone we interviewed has accepted another offer," but her voice lacks bite. Both of their voices are curiously flat, as if they have no interest in anything either of them might say.

He's got the MG with the top down, and as they head south,

through the parks, he slips a tape into the deck, filling the space between them with welcome sound. They cross the Nickel Bridge and wind back along Riverside Drive, turning into the Twenty-second Street parking lot for the James River Park. From the massive concrete steps that spiral down to the bank rise the laughter and shouts of a returning group. It seems to her that she and Kendrick must look strangely grim to those ascending holiday-seekers with their dogs, coolers, and chaise lounges. They stand aside as two young men in cut-offs, arms hung with inner tubes, bound past them. Last week's cold rain reawakened memories of winter, and today, the first bright, warm day in a week, the park seems unusually crowded. "Nature as we know it," she murmurs. At the bottom of the steps they turn west, crossing a footbridge, then swinging out toward deeper water, passing the sunbathers spread on the rocks until they reach less populous territory and settle on a boulder.

"I was horrible the other week," she says finally. "I never would have blurted it out like that if I wasn't so upset. Anyway I'm sorry."

"I'm sorry too. I shouldn't have made such a nasty crack. I was pretty shocked." He sits with his legs apart, elbows hooked over his knees. "Have you decided what you're going to do?"

She can't read his expression. "I didn't mean to hurt you."

"I know." He turns his head away again. "Who is the father, Alex?"

She doesn't know if she's ashamed to tell him, or if she can't because she has no right, not having told Ross.

"I know it's none of my business. But is it somebody you care about? Are you getting married? Are you going to raise this child together?"

She doesn't answer.

"Are you going to have an abortion?"

"No." To everything. *Raise this child.* Though it's what she thinks about herself, she's startled when someone else, the doctor, the nurse, Kendrick, refers to the baby as a done deal, a *fait accompli.*

"Are you going to give it up for adoption?"

Impatiently she pulls at a weed growing out of the rock. Does he think it's the '50s? As if she's a teenager who will be sent to stay with a distant relative until the shameful ordeal is over? As if somebody got her in trouble? "I used to wonder why my mother didn't give me up. But maybe she thought I would give her some power over my father. I didn't get it then, but I think she was in love with him. It's why she hated him so much."

"It's a tricky business, love." He looks her in the eye. "Why do you want to have a baby?"

"Because I'm going to have one."

"That's not a very good reason."

"It's the best one I can think of right now."

On a distant rock two girls in French-cut bathing suits listen to a boom box. The rock beat carries over the water, too faint for her to pick out the group. She doesn't know the new groups anyway. When Ross looked through her albums, mostly classical and jazz, he expressed surprise that she had no Dylan, no Beatles, no Stones, no Hendrix, Joplin, or Jefferson Airplane, no Dead. "Sixties music," he said, and she gave him a pained look. She loved that music; did he really think she could bear to listen to it again? *What'll you do when you get lonely and nobody's waitin' by your side?* Crank up the stereo every night and weep while Credence Clearwater tells her to put a candle in her window or the Stones suggest she paint it black? Once that music made her feel she was going to live forever.

"Have you considered abortion?"

She turns her head toward him again. "I always wanted to have children." Once she had thought that they would, eventually. She feels herself growing irritable again. Why does someone who's pregnant have to justify having a baby? She doesn't want to talk about this with Kendrick, who means well, but has no children himself and can't know the first thing about it. If he wants to become a father at seventy, he can, but she's nearly thirty-seven. If she doesn't have this baby, she's afraid she'll never have children. "I support Planned Parenthood and NOW, all right? I don't think I should have an abortion just to prove it."

"I wasn't talking about Planned Parenthood and NOW."

"I was so happy when I was pregnant before. But then I lost the baby." Hadn't, according to the doctor. There had been no baby to lose.

"I'm sorry."

Sometimes she sees them growing old together, like a devoted brother and sister. She doesn't want to lose him; she doesn't want anything to change between them. But of course it already has.

"Does the father know?" His whole body turns toward her, and she is aware, even in the shapeless shirt, of her full breasts. "I didn't think so." After a minute he asks, "Are you going to take a leave?"

He has a right to ask this, and somehow that makes it worse. "I know," she says weakly. "I need to let you know. There's a lot I still need to work out."

Altogether it's not a very satisfactory day. She has the feeling they are just going through the motions as they navigate the rocks back to the car. Once she slips, and though he reaches his hand automatically to catch her, she feels in the looseness of its grip a hesitation, as if he has no right to touch her. What will happen is that they will make the effort to keep up the friendship—dinner every other week perhaps, then every other month, and finally not at all. It's ironic, she thinks: now when at least technically she is not alone, precisely because she isn't she feels more alone than she ever has. She thinks of Ted, sealed forever in the isolation of his coma. He seems even more remote now that Justine's calls have tapered off. There is no reason to call: nothing changes. A fact that seems especially poignant now that she is pregnant. A pregnant woman is unable to resist the future. Day by day she is drawn into it.

But Kendrick comes back the next evening, and they go to a movie whose title she forgets as soon as the lights come up, and when she offers him coffee or a drink, he turns off the ignition and follows her upstairs. She squats before her liquor cabinet, finding only a bottle of Grand Marnier with half an inch on the bottom, some vodka but no mix, and the bottles of dry vermouth and cheap sherry she uses for cooking.

"Coffee's fine," he insists. "Will you have some?"

She lowers her lashes. "I'm supposed to avoid caffeine."

"How about some water then? A vastly underrated beverage." He follows her into the small kitchen and opens the freezer, prying a tray from its mountain of frost. The ice crackles as he runs the water. He hands her a glass. "Have you thought about getting married?"

She sets her glass on the porcelain drain board and reaches behind him to tighten the faucet. They've been through this. "I'm already married," she says.

"Divorce him."

Their sleeves are touching, but she doesn't turn around. "What for?"

"I thought you might want to marry someone else."

She turns then. "I can't marry *Ross*!" The name wrenches from her lips, and she stands trembling, waiting for the flurry of explanations that will stumble into her throat.

"I didn't mean you should marry Ross." His voice softens to a resonant whisper as he adds, "Whoever." His gaze is unblinking. "I'm asking you to marry me."

Stupidly, she picks up her glass and takes a single swallow. It seems to her that she is waiting for the earth to open, the walls to crack and ceiling fall, but instead they are just standing in her badly lit kitchen, looking at each other with unchanged faces. She breaks their gaze.

"Because of Ted?" His voice takes an edge.

"I don't know. Not really. Maybe I will divorce him. God knows I've got grounds." Briefly she touches his cheek. "You've been super, but don't you think marriage is taking friendship a little too far?" She rubs her arms. "It's 1982, duck. Haven't you heard? Pregnant ladies don't *have* to get married anymore."

"I'm not asking you because you're pregnant."

"Oh. Well." Light-headed again, a little breathless, she turns away. Something panicky flutters inside her.

"I love you. I've loved you since you were fifteen years old."

"I love you too," she says in a voice so chipper it breaks, dissolving the hot film over her eyes into tears. Behind her she hears a glass fall and break. Her elbow bangs the doorframe as she tears from the room. The next sound she is conscious of is the footstep that cuts into her sobbing. She gasps for breath and raises her face from the bed, shutting the waterworks down with a faint chuffling and wobbling of shoulders. He's holding out a box of Kleenex.

She takes a tissue and blows.

"I'm sorry," he says. He sets the box beside her. "I didn't think that would come as such a surprise."

Five minutes ago she didn't know. Now she knows that she always knew. Is it possible that both are true?

Idly Kendrick examines the top of her bureau.

"You were married," she says.

"I was married," he agrees. "I made a mistake." *That was something I did to my wife,* he said. And she had thought that what came between them was distance. He sets her hairbrush down and turns. "I thought I would get over you." Has he ever been in this room? To make a phone call maybe; she can't remember. "Are you in love with him?"

"God no."

"Your student." Distaste pulls the corners of his mouth. "Jesus Christ, Alex. The guy's phone number might as well be written on the bathroom walls. I've ridden in the elevator with girls who were talking about his dick."

Remembering the girls in the film closet, she colors, and for just a moment she is piqued with him. "So?" But then she remembers the night Ross came to his farmhouse. Maybe he thinks it was in his guest room bed that she conceived this embryo that has, no matter what he says, changed everything between them. And she can't tell him otherwise. He doesn't want details.

He lowers his eyes. "Sorry. My feelings aren't exactly neutral."

She shrugs. "I expect the students have said a few choice things about us all."

"You anyway. I'm not young and beautiful."

"You're beautiful to me."

For a minute he seems to wait. Then his face takes a wry stretch. "Close—but no cigar." At the door it takes him a few minutes to speak. "If you're not going to have an abortion, Alex, you have to tell him."

"I know." She shifts her eyes, looking at the window for a minute. For the first time it occurs to her that Ross might not believe he's the father. He's convinced she slept with Kendrick. What a joke. She looks up. "This changes everything, doesn't it?"

"Yes." He doesn't add call me if you need anything; he doesn't even say good-bye.

Chapter 30

1964

On the twenty-third day of June, a hot, sticky Tuesday that made even the beach at Coney Island seem a hemisphere away, the *New York Times* reported three civil rights workers missing in Mississippi.

The paper shook in her hands. It was as if it were the terrible confirmation of a secret she had suspected, and she realized that every morning she had been searching the *Times* for just that news, for the word *Mississippi*, though she had told herself she was reading only because she ought to be informed. Ted Neal was not among the missing, but the three men were part of the same voter registration drive. Freedom Summer he had called it; in boldface type on the front page of the *New York Times* it had become the Mississippi Campaign. The names were like a fist tightening inside her stomach. Having more than his word for it, seeing the letters spelled out in print, meant he was caught in a force that had a freedom of its own. Campaign had the sound of a war.

She tried to find his face in a dim corner of memory. The spring before she left Limestone Father Rayle had led a second civil rights demonstration; she had seen the protestors when she cut across campus to meet Kendrick. They were holding hands around the fountain. Exactly what they were protesting she wasn't sure, but they were not hurting anybody, nor were they really in anyone's way. She had been impressed by their silent dignity, and annoyed with herself once again for taking so little interest in what went on in the world. The next day a large sign that read SPONGE had been tacked across the doors of Holy Trinity. She had to ask what it meant that night in the Cellar, and even now she thought it might be a joke: Society for the Prevention of the Negro Getting Everything. It had to be a joke; the Ku Klux Klan did not deal in reprisals so mild. She searched the circle of faces again for his, as if—by placing him in the spray from that fountain on a windy March day with high clouds and a sweet, fecund scent in the air, while the students went to their classes, quietly chatting about this party and that exam—she could keep him from harm. But the faces were lost, blurred by her failure to take note. It had seemed an event of no consequence.

Two of the missing men were white. The FBI was called in. In the ladies' room at Gimbels she scrubbed at the newsprint that blackened her hands. She had begun to learn the vocabulary of Mississippi, and all day on the floor—straightening belts and folding scarves—her ears buzzed with the words. *Philadelphia. Neshoba County. CORE.* On the twenty-fourth day of June the Ford station wagon in which the three men had vanished was found burned. *Bogue Chitto Creek Swamp. McComb.* In McComb a Negro house was bombed. At the Neshoba County Courthouse the newsmen were attacked and warned to leave town. Every morning she trembled as she opened the *Times. Michael Schwerner, Andrew Goodman, James Chaney.* Three men who had ceased to exist, and in Mississippi the name for that was *murder.*

At Radio City Music Hall she sat on the edge of her seat, digging moons into her palms and grinding her teeth down to roots while the Rockettes kicked up their red, white, and blue heels. She felt sick with rage. Lyndon Johnson signed the Civil Rights Act. It was illegal for the white people of Mississippi to discriminate on the basis of color. The Yankees lost, and she and Kendrick dragged back to the D train in gloom. It was illegal to live with your boyfriend. At the Cloisters the unicorn was hunted and trapped. It was illegal to smoke marijuana; it was illegal to live in the lofts south of Houston or to play a musical instrument in Washington Square Park. The Circle Line boat ferried them around Manhattan. "On your right," the loudspeaker crackled, "you see Welfare Island … To your left you're looking at Harlem." From the Statue of Liberty she looked back. Eight million stories. It was illegal for a twenty-seven-year-old man to have sexual intercourse with a fifteen-year-old girl. Very likely, she thought, it was illegal to kill yourself. At the beginning of August the bodies were found. The white men had been shot once through the heart.

At the end of August she and Kendrick packed the station wagon. They drove over the George Washington Bridge and set out for the West. She did not drop pebbles along the highway, or was it crumbs of bread? Her face was turned resolutely toward the sunset. Even if he looked he would never find her. She was relieved. In Colorado, if he still wanted to, she would marry Kendrick. They had a good thing, like he said.

Ted Neal came to the new apartment before she could even buy dishes. The bell rang, and there he was on the threshold. She would have laughed if she hadn't been so upset.

"Well," she said. "We've got to stop meeting like this," but neither of them smiled. Her hand flew up to snatch the bandana she'd used to tie her long hair back while she scrubbed the kitchen floor. The gesture was so automatic she might have been greeting the Fuller Brush man, but then she stared at the knotted kerchief as if it were the pelt of an animal she couldn't identify. He looked tired, and his face seemed thinner. She stepped aside to let him pass.

For the nonce the living room suite was a pair of lawn chairs. She chose one. He dropped a bulky knapsack beside the bucket of dirty water in the kitchen doorway and sat in the other, crossing his legs as if he'd just happened in for a chat. She couldn't look at his boots, army surplus combat issue, suitable for manhunts and other Mississippi sports. The spattered greenish-brown leather was cracked.

"He's at school," she said, though Ted Neal hadn't asked. "Getting things ready. He got a job teaching photography. That's what he does."

"I know."

She was annoyed. "We're getting married." She hadn't removed the furnished drapes yet, big gold flowers bonded to rubber that made the light an ugly yolk-yellow. The room smelled of disinfectant and previous tenants. "We've been together over four years now, it's about time, I think we should." He was still looking at her intently, and she had to avoid looking back. "I think we'll like it here. It's a good job, it seems so *clean* after New York, and the light—maybe I didn't tell you, I'm a photographer too." She took pictures; that did not make her a photographer. It didn't make her anything. The knuckles resting on the aluminum arm of his chair were scraped, and that annoyed her too. You just can't keep out of trouble, can you? she wanted to snap. "As soon as the weather turns we're going to Aspen." He uncrossed his legs. "Do you ski?" she asked.

He leaned forward as if he were trying to figure out what she meant. "I do."

"I read about the murders," she admitted.

"They'll have to indict Rainey and Price." His words came in a rush and his breath was bitter, but she couldn't remember Rainey and Price. She had looked only for the two words of his name in the reports. "They'll be passing out indictments like fans at the Mt. Zion Church, but nobody will ever be found guilty, you can bet on that." She had nothing to say. "It's a beautiful system. The FBI paid to find the bodies; they'll pay to get the indictments, but that's where it ends. They told us at the training camp—the United States Department of Justice stood up and told us—the federal government can *investigate*; *protection* you have to get from the local police. The Deputy Sheriff of Neshoba County was one of the hitmen." He wound down. "Now you know why we went."

"No." She hadn't offered him coffee. The floor wouldn't be dry yet, and besides she did not want him to stay. "It sounds like a good place not to go if you ask me."

"That's what my parents said."

So he had parents. She had thought of him as someone completely without context, just as she considered herself without context too. Her family hadn't taken. And what she had loved about New York, what had compelled her to take picture after picture, was her notion that in every lost, hungry face she might find her own. But that was melodramatic. The faces had been too lost and hungry. She had photographed them with an excitement of horror and pity that might have belonged to any young girl. Choose one. Choose his face (which she did not dare look at now), a bloodied mess on the subway with perfectly manicured nails. Only it was her nails that were ragged and stained, her face that was perfectly composed. He shouldn't have come; she didn't want him. He would understand that and go.

Of course he had parents. She had known them the instant she first saw his hands. They were nice people. And they too had read the papers all summer searching for the same two words. Probably he had written them letters. Sent postcards. Called collect. Good. He wasn't her responsibility any more.

She meant to dismiss him. "Anyway nothing happened to you."

"More or less. I got a few traffic tickets."

So had she, before she left Limestone. Big deal. "You should drive more carefully."

"So I was told." His voice was wry, and then she remembered: three men had been arrested for speeding and were never again seen alive.

For the first time she looked directly at him. "What are you doing here?"

"I said I'd call you when I got back." Nothing she said seemed to take him off-balance. She remembered how she had trailed him from Times Square to East Tenth Street—he had known she was behind him all along; he was just waiting to see if she'd go all the way before he turned around. His face made her dizzy, floated up from Bogue Chitto Creek Swamp as if from a dream, wearing its undisturbed flesh like the miracle of consciousness regained. She looked away.

"We don't have a phone yet."

"I know." This time there was a crinkle of humor behind his frank mouth.

"Well, I don't want you here." She stood. What were they doing in lawn chairs? As if they'd pulled up together at a garden party. His hair, cut short again, was bleached to the color of caramels. Summer sun. What had they done to relax, that army of young volunteers, who had parents and rolls of stamps and coins to call the operator on pay phones? Kids—they would have laughed and had fun. She could imagine them skinny-dipping in a swimming hole rimmed with pines, the smell of Christmas in the soft auburn needles beneath their bare feet. White boys, colored boys, together; she could see the water beading on their champagne and coffee-colored skin. And girls.

Because it wouldn't have been a brotherhood only of man. Crystals of light in the wet curls of their crotches. One of them had cut his hair, would have brushed his bare shoulder to fasten the towel, tipped his head up and fallen, into the dark, steady pool of his gaze.

She didn't care.

But his face was paler than it had been. He looked like the Holy Ghost, or maybe he had just seen one, dressed up in a Grand Wizard's best Sunday white robes. From a distance his eyes seemed brown, but she had let him make love to her and knew they were slate. "I told you before, I don't do this. We had a nice time. I have other commitments."

He stood, and the room tipped, she felt faint. She was standing near the bucket where he would bend down to pick up his knapsack, so close she would feel the heat of his skin on her own.

"Do you want coffee?" she asked, because he had come a long way for so little, and she did want him to leave but not now. She wanted him; it was out of the question. She couldn't let him go.

But in the kitchen she thought better and turned around. "This is ridiculous. We don't know anything about each other. Why are you following me around?"

He didn't move.

"All right," she said. "You got in my head. I saw you lying there on the subway one night, and you stuck. Like one time when I was in Chinatown, and I saw this turtle. It was just a big soft shell turtle, but I'd never seen anything like it before. I grew up in Limestone. Actually I didn't grow up in Limestone. I grew up in the academic sector, which is smaller than small town. I never even saw a bum before I went to New York, you know what I mean?"

"I thought about you in Mississippi," he said.

She turned her back on him, rinsing the percolator with a loud splash of water. The grounds spilled across the counter. Her sleeve was wet where it had come unrolled. She jammed the plug in and faced him. "What is this supposed to be? Some kind of war you went off to all by yourself and lonely, dreaming about the girl back home? You're a handsome man—you must have had one-night stands before. Didn't anybody ever tell you they don't mean anything?"

"You got in my head," he said.

"We've got nothing in common. I mean you want to save all the colored people in Mississippi. I don't *care*. The only news I paid any attention to in my whole life was the assassination, and that—it was in all the papers, the magazines, on the radio, on TV. I could hardly miss it, could I?"

"You read about Chaney, Goodman, and Schwerner."

"I was looking to see if they were you." Her breath caught. For a minute his gray eyes held her. She turned away. "You were someone I knew, that's all." She washed one of the two cups in the sink and handed him coffee. "There's milk in the refrigerator." The box of sugar was sitting on the counter. "I'll see if I can find you a spoon."

"I take it black," he said, and she was angry all over again, as if it were a willful deprivation, though she took hers black too. "Your father wrote *Katie Blue*," he said slowly. She jerked her head. "It was a big movie."

"Did you see it?"

"No."

"It wasn't much worse than the book." She sighed. "Who told you?"

"Somebody at the Cellar—I asked who you were, remember? The daughter of the man who wrote *Katie Blue*, your mother taught at Wallace, you lived with your boyfriend, who was also on the faculty and who took pictures of nothing but you."

She flushed. "So even the saints of the civil rights movement gossip." When he had come to West Eighty-eighth Street, he would have noticed Kendrick's photographs all over the bedroom walls. When he had come to West Eighty-eighth Street ... A flutter of weakness went through her. She could feel him behind her, as near as he'd been on the terrace when she'd felt the pressure of his eyes on her hair and turned. She snatched her cup from the sink and poured coffee, drinking it so quickly she scalded her throat. Now it was time for him to go.

"It's not hard to find you. I just look for your boyfriend. I would never have thought of you again, but you really got me that day you followed me home."

He filled the room. It was as if, when he was present, nothing else could catch the light.

"I'm from Youngstown, Ohio. My father's president of the Sheet and Tube. I have a younger sister, Jeannie. She's a sophomore at Wallace—our dad's an alum. My major was history before I dropped out."

"So?"

"I'm not a saint of the civil rights movement. I'm a rich white boy who had an argument with his father and went to New York." He hesitated. "I meant to stay in Mississippi—they wanted us to, the black people who came to the Freedom Schools, they told us if we believed what we were teaching we couldn't leave."

"If you're trying to tell me you left because of me ..."

"I left because it isn't my movement." His voice was as simple as if he had told her again his apartment was unheated; it had the grave integrity she associated with people whose lives are shaped by something larger than ambition or petty romance, like the sharecroppers whose noble poverty had lent the Depression art. It shamed her. "J.E. Chaney wasn't the only black man to be lynched in Mississippi this summer. The others didn't die in the company of white men; their names didn't make the news." She tensed. "He's your saint. He died *because* he was in the company of white men, and now the whole world knows. That's why we went down there. We just didn't know it." He set his coffee cup on the counter. "We were needed, but we're not needed anymore. I left because twice I had the shit beat out of me and a shotgun shoved between my eyes. I was afraid I'd be too pissed off to remember it isn't my movement when J.E.'s heirs figure that out and get shut of my likes."

The nerves that had stitched up through her body relaxed. She had been afraid he was going to tell her the truth in gory numbers. "What were you doing on the subway that night?" Because it was *his* face that she'd seen all summer, reading the *New York Times.* His battered face and bloody blue shirt, haunting the muddy swamps of Neshoba County.

"Two guys jumped me for my wallet and I didn't have one. It had nothing to do with my politics."

"You were in the hospital," she corrected.

"I walked out. I don't have insurance."

A twinge went through her appendix. She'd never been in a hospital. She was the only nineteen-year-old with tonsils she knew. She didn't have insurance either. One more reason to marry Kendrick.

"Were they colored?"

"Who?"

"The men who mugged you."

"They were Negroes," he said.

"I guess I just don't understand you." She set her cup next to his on the counter and reached for the plug. "Do you want any more coffee?"

He shook his head and ran water over his hand. She jumped from his touch as if she'd been burned.

"You had dirt on your face."

"I was washing the floor," she explained, but her voice came apart in her throat.

"I'm going back to Limestone. This time I *want* to go to law school. It's a good place for me. They need unions. Three major electronics corporations with plants in the middle of nowhere because they don't have to run union shops. I came here first because ..." He actually looked sheepish. "I was hoping you'd come with me."

She stared. Then she laughed, a humorless little burst of sound. "You've got to be joking." She passed him and picked up his heavy knapsack. "I told you, I'm getting married."

His eyes were unflappable. She looked down.

When she spoke, the hostile edge had worn off her voice; she was tired. "I'm not the kind of person who could go off on a crusade. I'm sorry if something I did made you think otherwise." He took the knapsack. "Do you know the summer I met Kendrick I thought something was wrong with my head, I mean something physical, like a disease? I spent the whole summer in love and didn't even know it." The explanation confused her. "What I mean is I guess I'm just not a very introspective person."

He set the knapsack down.

"If you know about my father, you probably know he committed suicide. Maybe I never wanted to think too much. My mother never married him. I don't know why she didn't have an abortion or put me up for adoption."

"Maybe she liked the idea of having an illegitimate child."

Just as she'd liked the idea of living in sin, but it was an idea that had no meaning, because she had no sense of sin. The offhand truth of his remark disturbed her; it was the quality that made his eyes so matter-of-fact. He saw things for what they were.

"Maybe."

And wanted to change them. She admired him. She thought that for his efforts the Negroes of Mississippi would surely get their due rights. She was glad. It was not quite true that she did not care: she had not cared, but then he had gone to Mississippi, and three men had been murdered for remembering the document that declares *all* men to be human. Two bullets through the heart of white sympathy, and for the soul this black lesson: the human skull is a fragile house for the mind. For James Chaney had not died exactly like his inalienable white brothers. His skull had been smashed like a teacup, its fragments driven deep into his brain. Every bone shattered, every organ torn, and then, to make sure, he was shot. In a way that had nothing to do with Ted Neal, she had been seized, by that power of outraged justice that is vengeance, is wrath.

"Anyway, it doesn't matter. One day when I was in junior high I was going to follow my thoughts for an hour, just to know what I was thinking, you know? Only there was this jingle that kept going through my head, I don't know, some ad. And that's what I thought for an hour." She looked up. "I mean my head is empty."

"Maybe it's not your head." He picked up the knapsack. "Keep reading the paper. It's good for you."

She watched him cross the room from the brink of sorrow. It was the land she had always lived in, that puny sadness that had begun before she was born and annexed every disappointment of her life. It seemed a very empty place, a land wasted by its failure to nourish anything outside. And she lived there, but she did not thrive.

She wanted him.

She fit her hand over his on the doorknob.

She couldn't let him go.

Dinnertime, and for the third time Kendrick detailed the layout of the darkrooms at Colorado and his plans for a wall where students could use pushpins to put up their prints. She didn't mind. It was her own guilt that nagged her. She was leaving him; that was her right, but it was his right to know.

She couldn't find the words. There were no gaps between his. They ate standing up at the counter. She cleared it while he disappeared into the linen closet to load a roll of 120 into a tank, and met him at the bathroom sink. "I'm going back to Limestone," she said, quick, before her knees could wobble.

"I thought you hated that place." He checked his watch and gave the tank another rotation, that turn of his wrist that was to her as familiar as the earth turning on its axis. If she told him she was joking, if she took it back? He would finish the film; they would make love and more little red circles in their guidebook to Colorado. He poured out the developer. "Well, at least this time you're sober." The stop bath, the fixer. "You are sober, aren't you?"

"I'm serious," she said.

The stainless steel lid rang in the sink, and he held the reel up to the light, unwinding a short strip of film. "Hand me that bottle with the funnel, would you?" Her hair brushed his pant leg as she crouched at the dishpan full of stained plastic bottles. She bumped her head on the pipe and stood. "Who is he?"

She ran her finger over a rough spot on the doorframe, avoiding his eyes in the mirror. There was no point to denying. "How did you know?"

His glance reproached her. "Can I assume he doesn't ride a Harley?"

"I don't think so."

"Well. There's that to be thankful for. I won't have to worry about you smashing your brains out." He squatted to select the hypo-clear.

"I feel terrible." Her eyes spilled. "I do love you."

"So you've said." When he had poured the hypo-clear back, he began filling the tank with water. She had picked the right time after all, for him. He had something to do while his heart broke, he didn't have to look at her and see that hers was breaking too. "Okay, I won't be nasty. I know you do. Well, I always had to figure you might take off sometime; you weren't exactly the age of consent when you took me on." She wiped her wet cheek, waved away that old regret, and wiped her cheek again. "And when I came back from the interview I knew. The only thing that surprised me was that you'd deceive me. You can be impulsive and self-destructive, but I never figured you for a cheat."

"I only cheated once," she said, but she'd only run off and gotten married once too, and he had been the man who went with her before the judge, stood between her and one Jimmy Ray Reeves while she declared that she was sixteen years old and wanted this marriage voided. As a defense, once sounded pretty thin.

"Maybe you ought to give it a second chance. The novelty might wear off."

"I said I feel terrible."

"Yeah? Well, maybe that's not bad enough to suit me. Think about that." He dumped the tank for the last time, bathed the film in Photo-Flo, and unwound it. "Why not go for groveling awful?"

"You never would be serious when it counted."

"Now, now, no recitations. Let's do each other a favor and not list our sins."

"You don't even care if I leave you."

"Oh, I wouldn't say that."

"Bastard." She followed him to the kitchen, where he opened the freezer and began to scoop ice cream into a bowl.

"Want some?" He held out the carton.

"You son-of-a-bitch."

"Please." He held the spoon up. "All these names are going to give me a headache, and there's no point to an argument unless you might change your mind. Do you think you might change your mind? I promise to shape up, and you agree to forgive me, because all you really meant was to make me a better boy? I'd like to think better of you than that." Ice cream was melting down his wrist.

"No, I'm not going to change my mind." But it wasn't her mind that needed changing, and it wasn't her heart, and if it all came down to sex, why hadn't she and Ted Neal made love that afternoon? She bent to wipe up the ice cream that dripped to the floor. At least she could leave the place tidy.

"All right then."

Later, after they had gone to bed, turning their backs to undress, already formal as acquaintances, she couldn't sleep. The narrow space between their bodies was a zone of no trespass, and they lay rigid on either side. A pair of headlights swept the wall; a car door slammed. She wondered what he would take pictures of now. She could imagine him falling in love with a student, and it hurt, though she had given up the right. He was staring at the ceiling.

"Is it Jack?" he asked.

She reached into the space but stopped before she touched him. "No. Oh no. Of course not."

"Do you love him?"

"I don't know him very well."

"I love you so much," he said.

In the morning, when she woke, he was gone. She left the five twenty-dollar bills he had laid out on the kitchen counter, packed a suitcase, and hung her Nikon around her neck. She met Ted Neal at the breakfast place she'd named, and they walked to the highway. They did not kiss or hold hands; though they had their whole lives to exchange, neither of them had much to say. But he smiled as if to promise something, and she thought maybe it would turn out okay. Her bag banged against her shins; she slipped her fingers beneath the camera strap to ease her shoulders while he balanced the bulky knapsack and waited for her to catch up. He stuck out his thumb. In the incredible Colorado light she was leaving, so pure it was palpable, a luster crystallized of the platinum gold sun and blue memory of oceans and ice, she fixed her eyes on the face that had conscripted all her future, smiling bravely and waiting for the rest of her life to begin.

Chapter 31

1970-1971

They took a dingy two-room apartment on East Sixth Street. The neighborhood had changed since the day she'd followed him home six years ago, but that was hardly a surprise. *Time* magazine and tourists had discovered the East Village. Still an enclave of Ukrainians and Poles, whose meat markets pocketed the neighborhood, it was overrun with hippies who couldn't afford the West Village rents. For a while it had been a hippie Eden with free light shows and concerts at the Fillmore East, but crime, bad acid, and the resentment of the fiercely nationalistic, anti-communist Ukrainians had strained the atmosphere of peace and love. Though the panhandlers and purveyors of psychedelia and sex along St. Mark's Place could pass for the flower children of two years ago, up close they had a demented look, speed-pink eyes and ashy skin. Preteens in miniskirts tugged at the sleeves of old men on their way to the Polish Democratic Club; muggers patrolled in the guise of guerrilla actors; runaways and narcs alike thrust hallucinogens beneath Alex's nose while Gray Line buses disgorged vacationers who took their pictures and paid twice the going rate for the tie-dyed T-shirts and hand-tooled belts laid out at the curb. It was no paradise, but it was lively.

Ted found a job as Youth Director at a neighborhood center in Morningside Heights, through which Alex acquired an eleven-year-old Little Sister named Yvonne. On Saturdays she and Yvonne rode the subways to the city's museums; Monday through Friday mornings she opaqued negatives and burned plates at a small printing plant in Lower Broadway. She had no idea how to go about setting up a freelance business, and after more than a month's hesitation she called Kendrick's old friend Jack. She'd never liked him, but why should that have anything to do with it? She wasn't the silly teenager he'd intimidated so many years ago.

The loft looked much as she remembered, though Jack's hair had turned completely white. She sat in a frayed butterfly chair while he went through her portfolio and jotted a few names and addresses on a slip she tucked inside her wallet.

"Can you do food?" he asked.

"Well, I haven't, but ..." She fiddled with the strap of her purse. No woven Greek bag any pickpocket could reach into for New York.

"Toughest assignment there is. It wilts under the lights. You have to beat egg whites to get the bubbles in milk and blow cigar smoke through a rectal tube to make the coffee steam. And you thought only artists were creative." He returned to leafing through her pictures. "These are nice, but you're not going to make any bread shooting bums and freaks. Give Hal a call—do a good job with his vacuum cleaners, and I'll set you up with a couple more."

"I appreciate it." She was talking to his back as he laid her work out on the counter. "Do you ever hear from Kendrick?"

He glanced over his shoulder with a narrow smile. "Still carrying a torch?"

"I just wondered. I'm married now, you know."

He swiveled on his stool and held out a photograph. "Your husband?" The wheels of his stool scooted back against the counter. "Your old pal Steve gets up to the Big Apple now and then. He's hot stuff. A little too esoteric for my taste, but the art-farts eat it up. How'd your heroic hubby like his book?"

She shifted in the chair. "You've heard of Ted?"

"Heard you had a little run-in with the Royal Knights. Steverino told me—he read about it in the picture show. I'll tell him I saw you. He'll be glad to know they didn't mess up that gorgeous face."

"Is he still in Colorado?"

"Well, look." He scooped her photographs back into her portfolio. "I've got his address somewhere."

"No," she said.

He laughed as he faced her. "A woman with a guilty conscience. Aren't many of those around anymore. You're a real old-fashioned girl."

She should have known he would give her a hard time. She wanted to get her pictures and go. "What book?" she asked.

He took a long look at her. White hairs spilled over the open neck of his embroidered shirt. "It's a pity—babies always ruin the line of a woman's hips. Otherwise I'd say your husband must keep you barefoot and pregnant. You're in the business."

She shrank into the chair, feeling as naked as pork chop. "Not really. I've been pretty busy with the war and all."

"Like I say, a woman with a guilty conscience. I'm not a bird-watcher myself—too cynical if you want to know the truth. Actually I always thought you were rather like me and didn't know it. You're the only woman I ever wanted to fuck and didn't."

"What book?" she insisted. He'd known she would ask again; he was already off his stool, hunting. "It's his photographs of me, isn't it?"

His hand brushed her knee as he put it in her lap. "You must have signed a release."

"Probably. I guess I did. I must have." Her eyes watered; the cover blurred. "Thank you for showing it to me. Thank you for the leads. I don't want to look at it."

"It's only art," he said. Gently he lifted the book. "Of course, I'm not an art lover. I prefer the real thing to a picture of it."

She looked up. "You remind me of my father."

He reached for her hand.

"No," she said.

"Sure? You'd be surprised how many women confuse me with their fathers." He found a joint in an ashtray, lit it, held it out to her, and when she shook her head he laughed. "You win. Give me a call about the vacuum cleaners. Don't worry. I won't come on to you again."

He meant it. But of course she never called him.

She didn't know if it was the neighborhood or their isolation that made their life seem so inert. They had never lived by themselves, and the small apartment felt almost too big. They rarely spoke; once

New York had made her feel so alive, but now neither of them seemed to have anything to say. Ted volunteered at a crisis center; they joined a group bringing pressure on the city to crack down on slumlords and enforce building codes. They did not cease protesting the war by design, but after the moratorium of November, which promised to reassemble in Washington every month until the war was over, there were no more national demonstrations. Instead, on a sunny day in April proclaimed Earth Day they mingled with the gentle crowd in Central Park that danced in rainbow costumes, munched granola, stretched out on the grass in a haze of marijuana smoke, and sweetly vowed to pollute no more.

"Disneyland," Ted pronounced disdainfully.

Weatherman had gone underground, and across the country radical collectives were issuing communiqués claiming credit for bombings. Nixon invaded Cambodia, and the Ohio National Guard fired into a crowd of demonstrators at Kent State University, killing four white students. Alex and Ted went to Washington after all, and Ted spoke on the steps of the Capitol, though even as his voice pealed the words sounded wan.

They were still recovering. She had only the scar where her ruptured spleen had been repaired, but felt the weather in her reknit bones like an old woman. Ted still limped; he had trouble with his vision, and the vitality that had lit his face was gone. He stared into space, rubbed his lip, jiggled his foot, put the water on for coffee, then abruptly took it off, all his energy turned nervous. He was bored with Harmony House, bored with talking glassy-eyed kids through freak acid trips at the Switchboard. At night they clutched each other, but there was a dead place inside her. While he mourned the disintegration of the Movement, she mourned the loss of friends. And as long as she couldn't heal herself she couldn't heal him.

Lizzie was pregnant again. "I must be crazy," she said and laughed happily into the phone. Alex wondered if they might have a baby. Surely that would snap them out of their depression, but she was afraid to bring it up. They didn't have insurance. Ted's parents had paid the hospital bills last fall, a debt that, like everything else, they were careful not to mention. No doubt his father blamed him for what happened. He wouldn't even have to say so; Ted would simply know it. Just as he would know, if he thought about it at all, that it wouldn't have been the Klan who attacked them, then drove them back to town where they'd be found. She hoped he didn't think about it.

Almost from the moment they arrived in New York the FBI had tailed them. On New Year's Day the ROTC hut at Wallace had been leveled by a bomb, and perhaps a week later they had received their first visit. Alex came up the stairs with a bag of groceries and found two agents waiting outside the apartment door. She had to set the bag down to find her keys, and they pressed their cards into her hand. Standing in the dim hallway while her ice cream melted, she promised to give the cards to Ted. When they left she called a lawyer.

Neither of them were under suspicion, the lawyer reported; at least he didn't think they were. The FBI only wanted to talk to them about some people they had lived with. "No," Ted said firmly. From then on the feds had dogged their footsteps. Alex would come home from work to find their gold Plymouth parked on East Sixth; Ted would spot it idling outside Harmony House; every night he tore the apartment apart for bugging devices, though their conversations were so inconsequential she didn't know why he bothered. The agents popped up behind the canned goods at the grocery and trailed her to work. Mutt and Jeff, she called them.

Once at the laundromat she startled Mutt behind his *New York Times* and jerked a thumb at her washer. "I'm going to the drugstore. Put my clothes in the dryer when they're finished, would you?" He might as well prevent a theft if he was such a dedicated lawman.

At the Museum of Natural History with her little sister, Alex spotted the familiar face of Jeff across the room. Catching her eye, he dipped his head in a half-nod.

"We have to go," she said to Yvonne.

"I want to see the dinosaurs," Yvonne protested.

"We'll see them another time," Alex promised, walking briskly toward the exit.

Yvonne's shoes squeaked. She had long, thin legs and a knock-kneed walk, and in the boys' white tennies with red laces perpetually undone her feet looked like pontoons. "You be weird," she said.

On Central Park West she skipped along beside Alex, mollified by a blueberry Sno-Cone that glistened on her lips. Alex didn't dare look over her shoulder, but she thought that the agent had not followed. She wondered what her old collective was suspected of. Surely the FBI would not tail them so persistently for one lousy ROTC hut. Though she had not softened her attitude toward Weatherman, she found it impossible to regret that the hut had been blown up. Of course, once you blew up an ROTC hut, you could blow up anything. The bomb that had gone off accidentally on West Eleventh Street was studded with roofing nails intended to kill people. She thought Weatherman's saving grace was that it was incompetent, but that didn't mean that a few more deaths wouldn't happen along the way. Three of their own were dead already.

Yvonne scuffed her tennies against the low stone wall and turned her head to follow a woman strutting past in tight white vinyl knee boots and satin shorts. "Did they have hot pants when you was young?" she asked.

"I am young," Alex said.

Yvonne stopped skipping and examined Alex's face, wrinkling her nose with a wide grin. "Nah."

Alex pressed her lips together wryly. "Contrary to what you may think, Miss Age-of-Aquarius, we even had cars and electric lights."

"You have the Temptations?"

"We had Elvis Presley."

"Huh," Yvonne said. She slurped the last of her Sno-Cone and dropped the wet paper funnel on the pavement. Alex picked it up. "You have hot pants?"

"We called them shorts. Don't litter, please." Alex cast around for a trash basket, noting that the FBI was not in sight. "It may sound backward, but we didn't wear our shorts with boots and pantyhose. We did the bunny hop. We had hula hoops and Davy Crockett."

Yvonne was unimpressed. "Hot pants be so *bad*. Delphine got some with rhinestones, and they *tight*. Mama said she kill her if she wear them."

Alex perched against the wall. "So I guess she doesn't get to wear them then."

Yvonne broke into a happy grin. "Delphine say she don't care if she be dead long as she look pretty." Alex laughed. "You just too old to wear hot pants," Yvonne said matter-of-factly.

Alex squeezed her shoulder. "I'm not too old to wear them, baby. I'm just too old to die for them."

Yvonne shrugged her arm off. "Aw, nobody kill Delphine. Mama just mad 'cause she don't like Raymond."

"Who's he?"

Yvonne's face flattened itself into an expression of impatient disbelief. "Raymond Precious daddy." Precious was her niece. Yvonne was unfailingly literal; she was sweet. She was also very pretty. Coming home nights, catching sight of the runaways in the shadows of the East Village stoops, Alex thought of Vonnie and shuddered. If an eleven-year-old black girl was unlikely to end up selling herself on St. Mark's Place, she was all too likely to follow in her sister's footsteps. Delphine was fifteen, and already her daughter Precious was one. Yvonne was too hasty to grow up, and too fatalistic. When her brother graduated from high school and Alex asked what he planned to do, Yvonne had given her that same disbelieving look.

"He do what everybody do," she'd said. "He get drafted and get killed."

Alex had nearly wept as she asked, "Doesn't that upset you?"

"Yeah, it upset me. When it happen." Alex had drawn her close even as Yvonne added without rancor, "You husband just get his leg busted. He white." Alex had come full circle since the days on Crow Hill when she believed in working against poverty but doubted her ability to connect with the individual poor all around her. She and Yvonne connected, but there was nothing Alex could do to change her life.

Now Alex said, "I didn't know Raymond still came around."

Yvonne scuffed her tennies. "Not when Mama be there. Mama *mean*."

"She sounds okay to me." Alex stood.

Yvonne took her hand as they walked to the IND. "You be just like my mama," she confided. "You don't want me to have no hot pants either."

At dinner Alex complained to Ted. "I can take them watching the apartment and going through my dirty underwear at the laundry, but when they start tailing me with Vonnie it's too much. I had to make her leave before we'd seen the dinosaurs, and what can I tell her? Sorry, but the FBI's after your big sister? Her mother's got no truck with a revolution—all she wants is to feed her kids and keep them out of trouble. What am I supposed to tell her when the Shoes start double-parking on 123rd Street and following her to work?"

Ted pushed his plate aside. "What did you tell Vonnie?"

"Nothing. She forgot about it." Alex folded her arms on the table. "I want it to stop. I want to talk to them." Ted shook his head. "Why not? Why can't we just explain that we don't know anything? Just tell them we don't have contact. Maybe they'd leave us alone."

"They're not going to leave us alone. They're watching to see if any of our old friends try to get in touch."

"At least we could try." Alex stacked the plates, and abruptly Ted rose to stand in front of the window, looking down at the airshaft piled two stories high with trash. Alex had done what she could to make the two rooms cozy, but the plaster was crumbling, the light was bad, and she couldn't get rid of the bugs. It was a joke between them that when Homework succeeded in enforcing the building codes they'd be on the street.

"No," he said.

"Why?"

"Because it's not true. We do have contact." He turned around. "I saw Leah."

Her knees buckled, and she had to sit. "When?"

"A month ago."

Nausea churned in her throat. Was it a month ago that she thought she'd seen Tulip? On the D train her eye had lingered on a slightly built woman whose Supphose and gray hair didn't seem to fit her orphan's face. Under her gaze the woman had shifted and raised her newspaper, chapped nostrils jerking like a rabbit's. Alex had not mentioned it to Ted.

"What are you telling me?"

"Nothing. She was waiting for me at the IRT station after work. Pretty risky with all the Shoes around, but they're desperate." His face betrayed nothing.

"What did she want?" she asked dully. Why Leah? A needle of fear ran through her veins. Why, she wanted to ask, did Leah come to see *you*?

"Money. I gave her twenty dollars."

The mugger's fee. One did not travel the streets or subways without twenty dollars for the mugger. He should know. "*Why*?"

"She needed it."

"That's not an answer." She banged the table. "Did you sleep with her?" She meant ever. It was the question she had promised herself never to ask him.

He looked surprised. "No." She stared at the dirty plates. "Don't you believe me?"

"No," she said, although she did, and turned away.

For a while neither of them spoke.

"They're our people, Alex."

"They are not our people!"

"We disagree with them, but they are our people. It's not so easy for them underground."

"That's not my fault."

He pushed his chair back. "I don't understand you. Twenty dollars is nothing. You begrudge them twenty dollars?"

"It's not the money," she said. "*Yes*. I'd begrudge them fifty cents. The amount is not the point. How could you do it? If you gave them anything you're involved. The FBI is following my little sister."

"Why are you so *rigid*?" He paused beside the doorway to the closet kitchen. "You don't know they bombed anything."

"I know they would."

"You're being unreasonable about this. The feds are not our people," he said. "And they're not following your little sister; they're following you."

"I'm sick of sides." *Never trust anyone over thirty. If you're not with us you're against us.* "I'm not on Weatherman's side *or* J. Edgar Hoover's."

"Then don't tell me you want to talk to the government."

Blazing up from the table, she jerked the cloth, and the dishes shattered on the floor. For a minute they both stared at the pot roast gravy soaking into the ribbed cotton, pieces of carrot and potato lying among the shards.

"What was I supposed to do? What would you have done if it had been Stacy who turned up asking you for money?"

She knelt to pick up the pieces. "At least I would have told you." She looked up. She had sworn in front of Stacy that she would never ask Ted if he knew that it was Weatherman who had attacked them, and she was honor-bound not to ask him now.

"I didn't tell you," he said patiently, "for your own protection."

Fair enough. If the agents asked, she knew nothing. She gathered the broken crockery in the tablecloth and stuffed the cloth into the garbage. "What else haven't you told me for my own protection?"

"Look, I didn't invite her to meet me. She showed up, she needed money, I gave her what I had. We didn't exactly exchange addresses and promise to keep in touch."

She had sworn. Because she couldn't let him think what happened to them was his fault. She picked up a rag. "Forget it," she said. "I'm just tired."

That was August. All fall they were careful with each other. For weeks at a time the agents left them alone; then she would read of some new bombing and go out for bagels to find the gold Plymouth parked across the street.

Yvonne turned twelve. "I wish my big sister always be my best friend," she said as she blew out her candles. "You make good cake." But Ted was out and missed the party.

Lizzie called. Alex had almost forgotten she was pregnant.

"Do you still want to have kids?" she asked as she and Ted sat in Tompkins Square.

"Do you?"

"I asked you first."

"I don't know," he admitted. "To tell the truth I haven't been thinking about it." She touched his knee, and after a minute he let his arm settle on her shoulder. "I suppose it would be good for you to have something to look forward to."

"But what about you?"

"I told you."

"I miss it all too, you know," she said.

Christmas came. She bought a scrawny, overpriced tree and dragged it up the three flights to their apartment. Alex and Yvonne baked cookies; they strung popcorn and cranberries; they went ice-skating at Rockefeller Center. On Christmas Eve she and Ted joined the tourists strolling on Fifth Avenue. Across the street people were lining up for St. Patrick's midnight mass. On the corners women in Salvation Army bonnets rang their bells, and a car cruised down the avenue broadcasting carols from the loudspeaker on the roof. The crisp air bit Alex's cheeks and brought water to her eyes. She tucked her hand inside Ted's pocket. "It'll be okay," she promised.

At home they made love by the light of the Christmas tree. "Sure," he said. "Okay, if you want. I owe you that much."

On January 4 the FBI came back. After a series of holiday bombings, they wanted to talk to Ted. "I'll give him your message," Alex promised, leaving the chain between them on the door.

"He can talk to us now or he can talk to the court when he's subpoenaed. You tell him that."

On Thursday the lawyer called her back. He was a Movement lawyer, recommended by Mary Muñoz, a Puerto Rican woman from Homework whom Ted and Alex sometimes met for dinner with her boyfriend Joe. "There's been a major investigation. There are going to be indictments. He'll be called to testify."

"What if he doesn't?"

"He could be charged with contempt of court. They can put him away for that."

"I guess it could be worse," she said.

She went to the lobby to check the mail. The gold Plymouth was parked outside.

On Saturday she was followed as she walked to Canal Street to shop. Back at East Sixth she peeled the shrimp and chopped vegetables for a gumbo, singing along with the radio as she stirred the roux. The sounds of an argument rose through the pipes, shouting, a slammed door, the tinkle of glass. After she set the pot to simmer, filling the apartment with its rich, smoky aroma, she went downstairs. The agents were parked half a block up the street.

"Go away," she whispered.

She took a bath. A cloud of steam followed her into the bedroom; she left wet footprints on the floor. Standing at the stove in Ted's flannel robe, she stirred the gumbo. The radio was playing Dylan's country album; the whine of the hair dryer drowned him out, and for a second when she unplugged it she couldn't place his voice, panicky as if someone had crept into the apartment. She started to pull her jeans back on, but changed her mind and found a striped peasant skirt in the closet, pausing before the mirror to check her body. Her breasts hurt, but she didn't think that she was pregnant. They hadn't been trying long enough for her to know. Her leather boots clomped on the tile floor of the lobby. Still there.

"Leave us alone," she whispered.

She called Mary Muñoz. "Hi. It's Alex. Have you seen Ted?"

"Not since yesterday." Mary had a low, melodious voice with a trilling accent. "He picked up a stack of Homework posters at the office."

Alex looped the cord around her arm. The simmering pot had steamed the window. "I know, he went out this morning to put them up. The FBI's here. He's being subpoenaed. It's a relief, in a way. Maybe after he testifies they'll get off our case."

"Will he testify?"

"He doesn't have anything to hide." She wanted a baby. He would testify. "I don't know why they make me so nervous. I ought to be used to them by now."

"They make everybody nervous," Mary said. "It's their job. Take a hot bath. Relax. Did you have a good Christmas?"

"Umhm. You?"

"We went to Joe's parents." There was a crackling on the line.

"Listen," Alex said. "Why don't you and Joe come down for dinner tomorrow? I'm making a cauldron of gumbo. It's always better the second night."

When Mary had hung up, Alex listened to the rush of air before she replaced the receiver. When she went down to the lobby again, the car was gone. The light in the street was deepening to a blue twilight.

Upstairs she snapped the lights on and washed the lettuce, spraying herself as she twirled the metal basket. A yellowish light came through the windows. She put the rice on. In the bedroom she studied herself in the mirror again and tied a scarf around her hair. Her boots clicked through the apartment. On the radio Eric Clapton was wailing "Layla." *What'll you do when you get lonely and nobody's waitin' by your side?* It was stupid, she told herself, the bad feeling she'd had all day. He'd lost his money and was walking home from Harlem. It had happened before. She set the table. He'd be cold after the long walk. The gumbo would hold, but she didn't want to miss him by going out for wine. *You've got me on my knees. Layla.* On her knees she searched the cupboard for the sherry. Nearly half full. More than enough to warm him. Ted hadn't said a word when she told him he was being subpoenaed. She turned the gas off beneath the rice and waited, but he never came home.

Chapter 32

1982

A phone rings with the shrillness of a summons, but may be a wrong number after all. Alex takes the call in her bedroom, where she's watching the weather on the TV she bought last week—why she doesn't know, except that Kendrick used to complain from time to time about living out beyond the cable, but that's pretty stupid, because Kendrick is no one she sees, save at school in passing, anymore. And as of next week school is out. She already has her ticket to Youngstown, where Ted has been moved to a nursing home. As she picks up the receiver she punches the remote, and the picture disappears with a small click of static. "What time?" is the first question she asks when Justine tells her Ted has passed. That's the word she uses, *passed.* As if he hadn't passed beyond them long ago.

There is a calendar on her bedside table open to the date. Monday, May 10, 1982. Five p.m. She would have just left the Pollak Building. Traffic on the bridges would have begun snarling, and men in three-piece suits would have been dashing in front of cars in their rush to the bar at The Tobacco Company in historic Shockoe Slip, where at this moment they are draining their second Michelob drafts and dispersing for dinner.

"When is the funeral?" she asks. Outside the sky is drained of color. The sparrows on the feeder have scattered hulls across the windowsill.

"Friday. That should give people time to make arrangements."

"I'll get a flight." That is what people do when people die; they make arrangements.

"Oh." There is a pause. Justine's voice is cool. "You're planning to come then."

Of course she's planning to come. "Justine …" The phone presses against her jaw. Her hand is wrapped so tightly around the receiver the knuckles are white. "Will it be possible for me to see him? I'll get the first flight I can. Please—you haven't …" In the ragged space of her breath she hears muffled voices at the other end of the phone and realizes that Justine is conferring with someone. "I want to see him."

Finally there is the little rustling of Justine's return. "I don't think that's a good idea."

"I know you think I should have come before, and you're right, I'm sorry, but …" Alex's voice has dropped to a keening whisper. "You haven't …?" She can't say the word. "I need to see him."

"He'll be buried Friday morning, if that's what you mean," Justine says coldly. "There will be a private viewing for the family, but …" Her voice too trails off for a moment. "Dad and I both feel it would be better if you didn't come."

"Please." Desperation chokes her voice. "He's my husband." She's crying, hot, salty tears turning the phone slippery and leaking off her chin.

"*Was*. He got married again. He has another wife." Justine's voice is as strict as a knife splitting a melon into two clean halves. It dries Alex's tears cold. "They have two children." Her tone softens. "We have grandchildren, Alex. I can't tell you—well, it's made a world of difference between me and Dad."

There is a dull ringing in the back of Alex's head, as if she has been struck a heavy blow.

"Legally it's a bit of a mess, but we have grandchildren," Justine echoes. "You can't imagine what that means now that we've lost him. We'll settle something on you, of course, but …"

Alex is pressing the base of her skull into the metal post of her bed. "What are you talking about? What do you mean, settle? Money, is that what you're talking about?" Her voice climbs hysterically. "Are you talking about what you're going to *leave* me? What he's leaving me? You think I care about that?"

"He had children, Alex. A boy and a girl. Legally, I don't know—

we're still talking to the lawyers. But it's more than just a matter of wanting to provide for them."

"He left me—that's what he left me."

"To tell you the truth, it would be a great help if you would agree to have the marriage annulled."

Like it never happened. Like a three-day marriage to a biker so drunk he can't recall her name. "It's what I lived on for eleven years. Why do you think I wouldn't see him? Why do you think I haven't come? You think it was because he didn't matter? You think I didn't *care*?" Her hand goes to her stomach. "I didn't come to see him because I couldn't bury him until he was dead."

"I realize it's a shock. But you have to understand. He had another life. You know how he always wanted to help society—he worked at a free clinic in Kansas City. His wife had no idea who he was. She was afraid to come forward, but there are children involved. You can't just think of yourself."

Her voice is dead. "I understand what you want, Justine. I can't even say I blame you." There is a stone in her chest that will never dissolve. "You don't have to settle anything on me. I'm not going to sue, I'll sign any papers you need, but I will not have my marriage annulled, and if that makes his kids bastards, I'm sorry. They'll survive. I did."

"He was married to her too."

Her hand tightens on her stomach. "I kept faith with him." It was Kendrick she hadn't kept faith with, and she knows now that he's the reason she kept faith with Ted.

Justine's voice is rigid. "I'm not having my son's funeral turned into a sideshow."

"I'm coming, Justine," she says. "You can't stop me."

The spacious lobby of the funeral home is furnished with reproduction antiques and noiseless gray carpet. Discreetly Alex stares out the front window, at the immaculate expanse of pale green lawn and dark clumps of shrubbery lining the long curve of driveway. The air feels sanitized.

Behind her, in the hall, there is quick, heated flurry of whispers. Justine and Brad can't agree on the etiquette: if a man has two wives and each gets a private viewing, what is the appropriate order? In the wingback chair in the corner Jeannie, whose Sikh name Alex can't remember, sits straight as a plumb-line in her narrow pants, tunic, and tall white turban. Her face has the scrubbed look of a nun's. Inner peace has tuned the voice once sly with humor; she speaks in the vapid, sweet monotone of those who cannot be reached by the sorrows of this world, though a faint husk at the back of her throat and catch in her gaze hint of an energy not focused by her regimen of meditation and exercise.

All of them speak, Alex thinks, as if their voices have no connection with their bodies but rise from polite, fleshless recesses of their clothes. Ted's other wife sits on the striped sofa, flanked by his children. Grace Dimoff. The daughter, Zöe, is six. She sits solemnly in her voile dress and big white hair bow, holding a child's plastic pocketbook stiffly on her lap. Her slate-colored eyes are Ted's; she is destined for Jeannie's sleek long-legged prettiness. "Quit," she says when her three-year-old brother, Eben, reaches around his mother to pinch her arm. At the pointed shake of his mother's head he withdraws his hand and tumbles forward. Grace bends to pull up his knee socks and tie his shoes. He looks like his mother, though there may be some of Ted in his dimples and chin.

Carl Dimoff. The name means nothing to Alex; she can't get used to it. She hates the sound, hates the harsh, consonant taste of the syllable in her mouth. Alex sweeps Grace Dimoff with a glance. She is small, almost blonde, pretty, with teeth that overlap in the middle and light-colored eyes that flit nervously about the room. Beyond that Alex hasn't noticed. It's not a face she wants fixed in her memory. If you could choose your own name, what would it be? But he wouldn't have chosen it; he would have found it in an obituary and sent off for a birth certificate. After that it would have been no trouble to get a driver's license, social security number, credit cards. That was how it was done. Did he like the name? Get used to it? Or did he ever long for someone who would call him Ted as he and Grace Dimoff whispered sweet nothings? Alex had never known who he was apart from the Movement. The woman on the sofa, the two prettily dressed children that flank her, at least one of whom visibly bears his features, are proof. It doesn't matter whether he regretted it or not. It doesn't matter whether Grace Dimoff ever felt that peculiar quiver in his kiss or that it would have been her light-colored eyes he gazed into when he shivered inside her. The only thing that matters is whatever faith he must have lost in Carl Dimoff that caused him to abandon them. And that is something none of them will ever know.

Grace Dimoff's voice cracks the silence that has fallen since Justine and Brad have concluded their disagreement and gone into the viewing parlor. "He was a wonderful father. He brought the kids bubblegum and took them to the park everyday." Alex drops the heavy swag drape that, like everything else in the room, is a tasteful no-color color. Grace lowers her eyes. The air-conditioning fills the room with a faint drone of sound that is supposed to muffle voices but instead distorts them, amplifies them and turns the least remark unbearable. "Behave," she whispers to Eben, who is scrunched up on the sofa, rocking, and aims a soft slap at his calf. His sister stares straight ahead. "I want to *go*," Eben whines.

Ted's widowed aunt edges close to Alex. She and the other aunt and uncle who stand quietly near the door have already been into the parlor. Brad and Justine have orchestrated the viewing in stages to make sure, Alex realizes, that she and Grace Dimoff are at no time left alone in the lobby together, though it wouldn't have mattered. Alex can't imagine that she or Grace Dimoff could bear to speak to each other. She knows too much as is: the year Saigon fell, the year she photographed the refugees at Fort Chaffee and bought her elaborate bed, the year the Weathermen began to come home, would have been the year that he and Grace Dimoff conceived their daughter, Zöe.

Justine seems to have relaxed a little now that they've been introduced, now that it's evident they won't cause a scene, won't get together to compare notes or squabble over the corpse. They have been introduced to Ted's relatives as his first and second wives. The widowed aunt, whose name is Kate, fingers her necklace. "Aunt Kates are like the measles—sooner or later everyone gets one," Alex remembers her saying at their wedding.

First wives first, second wives second.

When it is her turn, Brad glides up behind her, surprising her with an uncharacteristic little squeeze of her hand that she supposes he means as sympathy. Or perhaps it's gratitude for her conduct; after all she is here over the family's objection. Brad's face is drawn. Like Justine's, it seems strange to her, aged by what proportions of time and pain she can't say. Justine's lipstick has bled into a delicate web of new lines; her once dark hair is blonde.

Alex opens the door to the parlor, averting her eyes from the raised half-lid of the casket spotlighted against the far wall, making a little tour of the room, skirting the coffin as she inspects this table and that childhood picture, until she is back at the door again, and then—because this is what she has come for—squaring her shoulders, she strides forward, close enough for her face to reflect the burnished aura of heavenly light.

He is dressed in a gray suit and deep red tie that seems to bring out the color of his cheeks. A nerve in the back of her hand begins pulsing as her fingertips press against her mouth. She has imagined this moment, but failed to imagine him, lying in a bier of shirred white satin, flesh so expertly tinted that he might be flushed with a dreaming sleep were it not for the authority death has conferred upon him. His hands are folded across his stomach, and as she fixes on his manicured nails, the stone from her chest lodges in her throat, and she swallows. There have been times when she could have imagined herself weeping, the word *why* tearing from her throat, flinging herself upon him, screaming, cursing, even kissing his cold lips, but all she does is look. The mortician has returned him to youth; his face is stranger for its familiarity after the long stay in memory's soft haze. Here above his lips is the indentation where she lay the tip of her finger a thousand times; there are the lines that deepened into dimples when he grinned, the crook in his nose, the blunt bones and exquisitely hinged jaw. The mortician has done a good job. He looks peaceful, and here, in the ethereal glow of a well arranged wake, she understands the point of the funeral industry and all its clichés.

It really is him. And he really is dead.

There is a film of moisture in her eyes, but she does not cry. She lays a hand against the cheek stiff with the secrets of the business and rigor mortis. It's as cold as she expects, and when she takes the hand away she warms it against the folds of her taupe skirt that yield to the soft curve of her belly.

In the lobby she waits with the family and his children, who are too young to go in, while Grace Dimoff bids a final farewell to her husband Carl.

In the cemetery the young minister is winding up the prayers. Down the row Alex hears a shifting in the folding metal chairs and Grace Dimoff's whisper, "Soon." The grave gives off a fertile smell, redolent of the rich, loamy earth of Limestone warming with spring. It's a beautiful day; heaven looks nearly gaudy, embellished with a puff of luminous white clouds. The casket is on winches. The minister releases his handful of dirt, sifted to make sure that the sound as it strikes the coffin is of dust to dust and not the hollow echo of clots, reminding as they do what a long, lonely place is a grave. It's a pretty coffin, color of a silver-blue Mercedes, with pewter handles and a lavish spray of cream and yellow flowers. She stared at it all through the eulogy, but she can no more imagine him inside than can Zöe, who whispered to her mother as they filed into the tent, "You said we were going to say goodbye." "We are," her mother promised. "Then why isn't Daddy here?" Zöe demanded, staring dubiously at the casket.

Perhaps, Alex thinks, it's only at weddings that things go wrong. Like everything else—the viewing, their solicitous murmurs, the weather—the eulogy has been politic and flawlessly accomplished. Listening, she felt a wave of sympathy for Grace Dimoff, who has come to her husband's funeral only to hear a stranger eulogized. At least the man they claim to bury is the man Alex thought she knew. For his parents and for her, a long ordeal is over. She had been surprised to spot Garth as the family waited in the limousines for the crowd and ministers to assemble. It hadn't occurred to her that their old friends would come, but then she'd spotted Nelson, Larry Veaux, whom she recognized from pictures, Bob Phelps—so many leaders and acquaintances from the New Left. Marc Forman, a former anti-war activist who ran for the Ohio state legislature and finally made it on his third try, has delivered the eulogy at Brad and Justine's request. The particular circumstances of the shooting made it possible for him to speak of victims on both sides and the healing long overdue. According to him Ted Neal was a man of vision and rare courage. She believed that once, believed it even after he stopped believing it himself, and for an instant of pure grief she wishes she could tell him so. If he were alive she could tell him what she knows now, what they would have learned on Crow Hill if they hadn't been so young that they believed rare courage was a thing you could bless yourself with, and that is how ordinary and therefore more precious is the courage it takes to go on living in a world you discover you haven't been granted the power to change.

It's almost over. Earth to earth, ashes to ashes.

She pushes her chair back. The mourners are offering their condolences to the family, congratulating Grace on the children's behavior, embracing, and shaking hands. Alex pumps a dry palm, murmuring, "Thank you," and turns to squint at the crowd breaking into groups, chatting. Garth is standing off to one side with his face slanted downward, reading the inscription on a marker.

She crosses the lawn, taking her sunglasses from her purse. "Hello, Garth. Thank you for coming."

He smells of wintergreen as he hugs her. "I'm sorry, Alex." He's aged well, save a sadness that has clouded in the eyes behind his horn-rimmed glasses.

"Is Lizzie here? How are the kids?" she asks.

Across the broad yard Eben and Zöe are jumping over the flat markers, chasing each other and running, the melody of their play carried on the breeze like a tinkling of bells. Eben's shirt has pulled out of his shorts, and one of his knee socks is drooping. A little apart, their mother stands with her back to the crowd, her shoulders heaving.

"Fine." Garth drops a hand into his suit pocket, and for a moment Alex hopes he will bring out pictures. "Tice starts at Berkeley in the fall."

"Unbelievable." Near the road Nelson is talking with Stacy, whom Alex somehow missed while she sat watching the mourners arrive through the tinted glass of the limo. Alex hasn't seen her since they parted at the Pizza Pub in 1970; when Stacy surfaced after the charges for the Days of Rage were dropped, she refused to meet. "You know I can't tell you anything," she said when Alex reached her on her parents' telephone, and later, more curtly, in a letter, "My attorney has advised me not to meet with you." Tulip came up at the end of 1980, Leah last year. Matt is one of the few Weathermen still missing.

"What about Lucy and Caton?" She should ask about the baby, whose name she doesn't remember, who is not a baby anymore. Caton will always be the baby to her.

"Teenagers," Garth says with a little grimace. "You know Lizzie and I divorced? I'm remarried. My wife's a psychologist. I have two step-daughters. It's a full house when all the kids are there."

"Congratulations," she says, feeling empty.

Stacy is looking straight at her as she leans to say something to Nelson.

"What do you do these days?" he asks.

Garth has written a book on the organization of the New Left, and another on the rise of conservatism in American politics, but she hasn't read them. She looks at him blankly for a minute. It occurs to her that he may never have noticed she took pictures. "I'm a photographer. I teach at a university in Richmond, Virginia." From the corner of her eye she sees Nelson and Stacy moving toward her.

"Alex." Stacy stands a few feet away. "I'm sorry about Ted."

"Thanks." Stacy too wears sunglasses, and for what seems like minutes they stand looking at each other a little warily through their dark lenses. Stacy feels, Alex knows, the same self-consciousness she does for not hugging. Stacy's hair has been cut like a Roman emperor's, a style that seems to suit her, though it doesn't flatter. "I'm glad you came."

"Hey, Garth. How are you?"

"Stacy." Garth extends his hand. "Nelson."

Stacy's eyes roam the crowd for a moment. "He really brought out the faithful, didn't he?" Marc Forman is circulating, shaking hands, running for office, Alex thinks a little contemptuously, at the same time she thinks that's what Ted should have done—what a shame he never thought to turn to electoral politics once the barricades exploded. He could have finally made his father proud. "Forman did a good job. He can't speak like Ted could though."

For a moment there is silence. "The boy had a gift," Garth and Nelson agree.

"Remember that civil rights rally where he spoke after he came back from Mississippi?" Nelson asks. "They didn't expect to be moved by the white boy. Afterwards Jeff Miller went around saying, 'If that boy'd been black, he could have been King.'"

Everyone smiles with the memory for a moment, and then their smiles fade, perhaps each of them thinking about what happened to King, what happened to Ted; perhaps, Alex thinks, they are thinking about what happened to them. Don't they remember it was a joke? She can still see them gathered in the College Club, Matt, ears reddening as he asks, "What have you got against nonviolence," Ted blushing and lowering his head.

"Who's the swami?" Stacy asks.

"Oh." Alex's mouth curves into a half-smile as she turns. "That's Ted's sister."

"You're kidding. Sorority Sue?" Stacy's eyes follow Jeannie, who is performing some kind of exercise on the grass.

"She married a Sikh."

"She's married?" Stacy gives Jeannie a last, definitive look. "What do they do, chant all night?"

Alex laughs as Garth looks away. "What are you doing these days, Stacy?"

"I work with a citizen's advocacy group in Chicago—still chipping away at the state, you know me." The corners of Stacy's mouth flatten. She looks at them, one to another, a deep line pleating her brow. "We accomplished a lot—all of us," she says with sudden vigor. "I don't know why we're supposed to be ashamed. We ended segregation in the South. Who knows how long the war would have gone on if it hadn't been for us? Women's rights, the environment."

Her voice trails off as Nelson says "Amen," and this is true, Alex knows; they changed a nation's concept of what it could ask of its government. She doesn't add that, through the complicated chain of things, she believes they also elected the regressive administration they've got now. Give it a few years, and see how many of their accomplishments are left. It boggles her mind, the complicated chain of things. Garth writes books about it, in retrospect. Even for him the future is never more than a hope and blind theory.

Eben's high giggle ripples the air, and Stacy turns her head. "So he got married again and had kids," she says softly, almost to herself. She turns back to Alex. "What about you? Still taking pictures?"

"Some. I teach at a college in Virginia."

"Oh." Stacy's voice is noncommittal, but Alex no longer feels the need to apologize for what she does. The politician speaks to the greater good, the artist of the recalcitrant imagination. The millions and the one. In the complicated chain of things, they are essential to each other.

"You're married," she says to Stacy when Stacy lifts her hand.

Stacy polishes her sunglasses against the hem of her tan jacket. "My husband's a lawyer—he used to clerk with my dad. We do a lot of citizens' group cases. My dad died last year."

"I'm sorry."

Stacy lifts a finger to point at the back of Nelson's gray head. "Can you believe this guy? He's an old man." Her voice is rich with affection. "Nelson." He turns back to them from Garth. Without the sharp contrast of ebony hair, his skin seems less pallid. The pockets of purple beneath his eyes have been there for as long as Alex can remember. "Did you ever finish school?"

He draws his mouth into his old smile. "Indeed I did. I got my B.A. from Penitentiary State U."

"Hah. They wouldn't let him drop out," Stacy whoops as she puts her arm around him. "Nelson's rehabilitated. He doesn't even write letters to the editor. Did you hear that Rennie Davis became a disciple of the Maharaj-Ji? Jesus. What they did to us." She drops her arm, and her hands clench at her sides as she casts her masked eyes toward the coffin waiting on its winches in the tent. "To Ted. They killed him."

"Stace," Nelson cautions.

"It's okay," Alex says. After all, it's not as if the government had nothing to do with it. The bright clots of people scattered over the lawn are beginning to break up. In the distance Grace Dimoff is on her knees, tying Eben's shoe while Zöe takes a last two-legged hop across a bronze vase filled with silk flowers, and then slowly she stands and walks with her children toward the limousines waiting with open doors.

"It's been a long time," Stacy says. "Did you remarry?"

The breeze, rustling through a stand of trees off to their side, lifts the loose hairs at her neck. In the distance she sees the idling truck of the grounds crew. There is another fresh grave near them, a straight line of sod stripped back in place beneath the drooping flowers.

"No." Instinctively her hand brushes her stomach. She looks back at the navy blue tent, with its slab of shade and expensive coffin, which the grounds crew will lower after they leave, after the crew packs up the Baggies and apple cores from lunch. Beyond it is another stand of trees, maples maybe, or oaks, but what she sees is the line of tall pines that mark the horizon the other side of Kendrick's pond, and she knows when she comes in from the airport this afternoon that is where she's going. For a minute she considers telling Stacy about him, but then recalls with a start that Stacy wouldn't even know who he was.

"I love you guys," Stacy says as they too begin to move off. "Remember Tulip's cats?"

"They used to shit in my sandals," Nelson says. "How could I forget?"

"Is that why your feet smelled?"

Kendrick will be in the driveway working on the MG as her car crunches in the gravel; she can see the streak of grease along his cheek as he slams the hood and looks up. By the time she is out of the car, he will be wiping his glasses on his sleeve, and for just a moment she will see his moth-colored eyes unguarded.

"Excuse me," she says to Stacy, who has asked her something else.

"Do you still like to cook? I swear I have dreams about your gumbo."

"Ted died," she will say, but perhaps he will have heard. "You were right. I've been so angry I didn't want to let that go." As they walk toward the pond she will tell him about Grace Dimoff and the children. "Pretty weird scene, huh? Two wives in the funeral tent. You just can't figure a guy like that."

Nelson is laughing about something else they have remembered as the children seat themselves inside the limo.

"It was good to see everyone," Garth says. "Too bad it's not a happier occasion."

But that's all wrong. She needs to tell him the moment she arrives why she's come—not because she needs him, but because she loves him. She always has, though if she hadn't left him all those years ago she wouldn't have been able to grow up, wouldn't know what she wants now.

"Alex?" Stacy asks.

Or maybe it won't happen that way at all. For all she knows he won't even be home.

Alex nods. "I remember," she says softly as they walk toward the line of cars sparkling in the sunlight.

BIRTHS

The Richmond Times Dispatch

MCV, December 15, 1982
Mr. and Mrs. Stephen Kendrick, a boy

MCV, November 2, 1984
Mr. and Mrs. Stephen Kendrick, a girl

MCV, October 29, 1986
Mr. and Mrs. Stephen Kendrick, a girl

Acknowledgments

This is a work of fiction. Some of its events are matters of public record, but Alex's experience of them is her own. I have borrowed Marc Foreman from public service for Ted Neal's eulogy, but Ted, Alex, and all of the other major characters are entirely products of my imagination. Alex's understanding of what happened in Mississippi in the summer of 1964 is based on information that would have been available to her at the time, though I have chosen not to confuse the reader with the misspelling of James Chaney's name in the initial news reports.

I am grateful to the many authors who have published their experiences, analyses, and/or impressions of the American New Left for providing my cast of fictional characters with a social and political context, especially Jane Alpert, Bill Ayers, Sally Belfrage, Kathy Boudin, Taylor Branch, Seth Cagin, Philip Caputo, John Castelucci, Peter Collier, Philip Dray, Charles E. Fager, Todd Gitlin, Tom Hayden, David Horowitz, Mary King, Norman Mailer, Florence Mars, Allen J. Matusow, Doug McAdam, James L. Miller, Kirkpatrick Sale, Susan Stern, Tracy Sugarman, Elizabeth Sutherland, Irwin Unger, Cathy Wilkerson, and Milton Viorst. Lawrence Lipking's study, *Abandoned Women and Poetic Tradition*, helped clarify for me the historical role of abandoned women in literature. The late Henry Holmes Smith first taught me the wordless art of light and shadow, a gift that has sustained me through days when I seemed mute. My thanks to the North Carolina Arts Council for a grant that bought precious time, to the Blumenthal Foundation and Wildacres Retreat, to friends who read parts or all of much earlier drafts and offered suggestions: Steve Christy, the late Marcy Thompson Diamond, Charles Tisdale, the late Robert Watson, and my husband, Michael Gaspeny. A salute to Rebecca Friedman for her ideas on restructuring. A heartfelt thank you to Luanne Smith for recommending me to Kim Davis at Madville Publishing, to Kim and Jacqui Davis, and to Caitlin Hamilton Summie once again for her caring expertise in publicity and marketing. And to my family, Michael, Al, and Max, eternal gratitude for your love and your support. You are the real world I inhabit.

About the Author

LEE ZACHARIAS is the author of three previous novels, *Lessons*, *At Random*, and *Across the Great Lake*, a 2019 Notable Michigan Book, as well as a collection of stories, *Helping Muriel Make It Through the Night*, and a collection of essays, *The Only Sounds We Make*. She has received two silver medals from the Independent Book Publisher Awards, won North Carolina's Sir Walter Raleigh Award, and the Philip H. McGath Book Award, and held fellowships from the National Endowment for the Arts and the North Carolina Arts Council. Her work has been reprinted and frequently cited in the annual volumes of *The Best American Essays*. You can read more about her at www.leezacharias.com.

www.ingramcontent.com/pod-product-compliance
Lightning Source LLC
Chambersburg PA
CBHW030623310726
48979CB00003B/851
* 9 7 8 1 9 5 6 4 4 0 2 1 8 *